MEAN CITY

Also by Ron McKay

The Catalyst
The Prophet

MEAN CITY

Ron McKay

Hodder & Stoughton

First published in Great Britain in 1995
by Hodder and Stoughton
A division of Hodder Headline PLC

A CIP catalogue record is available from the British Library

ISBN 0 340 61742 X

Typeset by Phoenix Typesetting, Ilkley, West Yorkshire.

Printed and Bound in Great Britain by
Mackays of Chatham PLC., Chatham, Kent

Hodder and Stoughton
A division of Hodder Headline PLC
338 Euston Road
London NW1 3BH

For Rosa

Author's Note

Mean City traces crime in Glasgow from the 1930s when the city was notorious for razor gangs, drunken brawling and crude extortions, to the present day, where the bullet has all but replaced the blade and the currency of crime is drugs. Glasgow, according to the World Health Organisation, has the highest per capita incidence of injecting drug users in the world. Deaths by overdose are rising all the time and crime – particularly violent crime – has spiralled as junkies desperately attempt to feed their habits. The flow of drugs is controlled by a few major criminals well-known to the police, but largely untouchable. Even the most famous, Arthur Thomson, succumbed to a heart attack rather than the due process of law (although he did survive several attempts on his life by rivals, his heir to empire, Young Arthur, was shot dead in the street outside the family stronghold). The last few years have seen a series of assassinations and botched attempts as the major families battle for territories, casual assaults are on the increase, so much so that the city council has introduced a curfew on clubs and surveillance cameras in the city centre streets.

This book looks at crime in the city and abroad (because the drugs trade is international) through one family who, needless to say, bear no resemblance to anyone living or dead, although one or two of the incidents may bring a smile of recognition.

I am grateful to several people on opposing sides in the war who provided insights and who, naturally, do not want to be identified. I intend to be around to write the sequel.

Ron McKay, July 1995

Prologue

He always remembered it the same way.

'I was standing there with God, and this bloke was lying on a mattress on the floor with his head hanging off the edge. He had been beaten with a hammer which was lying on a soiled pillow. And then he'd been strangled with a length of clothes line. Whoever had killed him had taken a painted wooden fingerbowl and put it under his head to protect the carpet from the drips. It was the first carpet I had ever seen. I don't know if it was the first body, just the first one I remember. He had obviously been there for several days. All the windows were closed and it was one of those occasional, very hot summers . . . well, that's how I remember it.

'There really is nothing as repulsive and unforgettable as a rotting human corpse. I suppose I must have known he was a Jew even then. He would have been East European, probably from Russia. I had gone round to ask if I could light his Sabbath candles because these Orthodox Jews hired weans to do that for them. I wanted to ask him if he was a Jew and if I could do that because we needed the money. Now, I don't know whether he was a collector or whether he had stolen them, but one wall was covered with Russian Orthodox icons. There's a particular order in hanging them, the most precious and valuable is bottom left, I think, and they go along and up in descending order. Descending to heaven. I don't know if he had them arranged like that. And, of course, at the time I didn't think anything about it, that it was unusual for a Jew to have all these Christian artefacts. But everywhere I looked on the wall God was there, with me, just looking at me, impossible to gauge the eyes but, I knew, judging my reaction, waiting for me to start bawlin' maybe, or praying for forgiveness. But I just stared back, not flinching, until I had satisfied myself that I had faced him down.

'And I remember, too, that there was an open Bible on the dresser. I know that it probably must have been the Talmud, but *then*, for me, it was the Bible. I mind thinking, I wish I could read, so that I could find out what it was he had been looking at, considering, whether there was any message there about what it meant when he was killed.

'I think he had been a moneylender. And someone had killed him either for cash or to rub out the record of what they owed. They never did find the jotter he kept his tally in. And I don't think they ever found who killed him. Who would care anyway? Just an old Jew that no one would miss, probably didn't even speak the language, except the numbers.

'Just me and God and the rotting corpse of the old moneylender and the memory of someone who cared more about the carpet than that life.

'I wanted to keep it all secret, so that I could keep going back there. But they must have found him later that day – maybe I left the door open or something. You would have thought that people might have noticed the smell. But not really. There was always the smell of filth and decay and rotting, so that your nose got used to it. The toilets were constantly blocking up and overflowing, pouring down the stairs. It wasn't unusual. You'd have eight families, sometimes fifty people or more, sharing the one toilet on the half-landing and drains would block and pipes break and the factor never did anything about it, probably because most folk were in arrears. So there was that smell of shite and putrescence all the time, rubbish out the back in the ash lands, from the fires, overflowing drains, rats . . . I'm not talking it up. That's just exactly the way it was. And with the sun cooking it all, that summer anyway, you wouldn't be surprised that the decaying corpse of an old Jew wasn't detected. I'm just surprised the rats didn't get to him before me.'

That was how he remembered it.

Then he had taken a small, circular icon from the wall, the Madonna and child. She, olive-skinned and with a long red shawl edged in gold covering her hair, the child against her cheek, head uncovered, wearing a fading yellow robe, both their haloes flat, upright and intersecting. What had attracted him was the way they both looked. Disappointed, slightly ashamed, eyes looking

10

down but also some way off, into the future they both knew
would not be any better. There was a sense of shame in the
picture.

He pushed a scuffed wooden chair against the wall, scrambled up and carefully unpicked the icon, which was surprisingly
weighty, painted on some old hard wood, but no more than three
inches tall. The distemper was flaking from the wall and as he
took the picture from its nail, small particles, like snow in the
hot room, fluttered down. The area behind the icon was clean
and bright and detectable but even at that age – what had he
been, four or five? – he knew that if it was noticed the theft
would be blamed on the one who had been there before. He
had no thought to its value, he didn't intend to try to sell it.
All that he could think was that he wanted it for himself, something of his own. It wouldn't really be his, of course, because
even at that age he realised that it could never be owned, that
it passed through history with occasional custodians and protec-
tors. But he wanted that, to guard it, to pass it on eventually.
Everything he had, the little he had, was also handed on and
had been worn and lived in before. These were public things,
but this picture was private. He needed to find a place to hide
it. Later, when he looked back on what he had done, he wondered if this had been the closest he had ever come to a religious
experience.

For days afterwards, of course, he heard talk about the murder,
but no mention of the pictures, his picture. The talk was of the
old Jew, Kilbronskie the moneylender. 'He was from the Baltic,'
Sammy McArdle said. 'Lithuania.' McArdle had been a sailor
before and after the Great War and knew those things. 'Aye,'
he went on, while the other men gathered round the mouth of
the close nodded, deferring to his knowledge, 'they used to take
their money off them, the shippers, tell them that right enough
they were going to the New World. They'd drop them at Leith,
say to them that they were just outside New York and if they
walked west they'd come to California and more riches than they
could ever have dreamed of. These old Jews like Kilbronskie would
start walking, clutching their purses, coats buttoned up against the
snell wind, not speaking the language or nothing, meet up with

others on the way and end up here. Jesus. He probably died still thinking he wis in California.'

The taxi lurched as it slewed round a corner.

'Christ,' she said, 'you've ripped ma stocking.'

'Ah'll buy you silk ones,' he said, running his hand once more up the cold flesh of the inside of her leg and nuzzling into the side of her neck, scenting the perfume like dew on the grass.

'He's looking,' she whispered, 'in the mirror.'

'He better no' be,' removing his hand, detaching the fingers from under the rim of elastic in her pants. 'Driver,' he shouted, sitting round in his seat, 'are your eyes on the road?'

'Absolutely, pal, where else?'

The male passenger in the back was in his thirties, round of face, slightly pasty and running to seed. 'Good man. Careful and attentive driving gets its reward, you know. Like a tenner or two.' He slid back into his clinch. 'There you are,' he said softly into the naked hollow at the base of her neck, beginning to lick it and to taste the astringency of the cologne, taking the flesh in his teeth and noticing her quiver as a shiver ran through her. His left hand was inside her coat and unpicking the last fixed button, then it slid inside the cotton, ran around her naked nipple then cupped her breast and began to play with it. In the restaurant he had told her to take off her brassiere and she had smiled conspiratorially, gone to the toilet and come back with the three top buttons of her blouse undone then leaned over to give him a better look, at the same time slipping her foot out of her shoe, bringing her leg up and letting her toes play with his groin. Now her hand was moving to his crutch, the heel of it rubbing around, before she found the zip and began to pull it down.

'I should have made you take these off back there.' He heard her words float softly past his ear and felt her fingers search for an opening. 'At least you haven't got Y-fronts on,' and he could hear the amusement in her voice.

'The first one'll be quick,' he said. 'It's been a long time.'

His cock was straining against fabric and then he felt it break free and she slowly began to pull at him. 'This can't be why they call you Junior,' she whispered and began to giggle and masturbate him more fiercely.

'Not here,' he said, laughing too, grabbing her hand. 'We're almost there. I don't want ma da to see me with a flagpole in my trousers.'

'I'm not screwing your da too.' Her face loomed close into his and her tongue began to lick at the socket of his right eye. 'Unless, of course, he's particularly attractive.' She moved away and began to button her blouse. 'A boy your age doesn't still live at home, surely?'

'Yeah – but did yir man no' tell you?'

'All he said was, "A special friend wants to take you out for a night you'll never forget."'

'Him? Never.'

'All right, it wasn't quite in those words.'

'No? What did he say?'

'He said he'd seen you in the shower and you were hung like an orang-utan, wi' a wallet made out of an entire cow hide, so voluminous was it.'

'That doesn't sound much him either.' He lifted her hand away after she had zipped him up. 'Had you heard of me?'

'Of course.' She leaned into the side of his face, gently licked the inside of his right ear and then whispered, 'And he said you'd have some good stuff too.'

'I've got the good stuff, certainly, no problem.' The taxi began to slow down and the street outside came slowly back into focus. 'Anywhere now, driver,' he said.

She was beginnning to sing, in a husky voice: 'Oh Johnnie, oh Johnnie, how he could love—'

You certainly get what you pay for, he thought.

'—heavens above, oh Johnnie, oh Johnnie, Ohhh!'

He took the icon from its place on the wall, noticed that there was no bright shadow on the wallpaper behind, then kissed it gently. It was ridiculous, he was only religious in the most perfunctory way, but he knew that the lustred picture held special powers. It had protected him; it had done more than that, it had guided him, brought him everything. He had tried to find out more about it over the years, with no great success. He wanted to know the family it had belonged to, what had become of them, what had made them give it up. Somehow he just knew that the old Jew had not been its real owner. He was a dealer, a trader, a moneylender. And the wrong religion. A few years back, after the collapse of Communism, he had taken it to an art dealer, a specialist in religious artefacts, and asked him what he could tell him about it. For insurance purposes, naturally. The man had looked at it, put in an eyepiece, shrugged a lot. 'Twelfth or thirteenth century, I should say. The thing is that, even now, we don't know a lot about these icons. There was no register, no systematic logging of them under Communism, obviously. Many of them were looted from churches under Stalin, others were taken down by the Orthodox priests and devout families and kept in protective custody. Others, of course, were family heirlooms, passed down through the generations. I don't want to be too optimistic but it just may be a Rublov. If you left it with me I'm sure I could find out more, have it—'

But he had taken it from his hands, shaking his head. There was no way he could let it out of his possession. It was too – sacred?

He walked with it towards the kitchen, intending to find a clean cotton cloth to brush off the dust gently. Frances had gone to bed, Owen was upstairs watching TV or playing video games; he could hear a dull electronic burr somewhere far off. Almost without thinking, as he did dozens of times a day, he stopped in the hall at the bank of television monitors and scanned them. He saw the taxi drawing up a few doors down and stood, gently playing with the picture in his hands, until the passenger door opened to the pavement and he made out, in the flat and grainy black and white screen, that it was his son. Then a woman came out after him, someone he did not recognise. But then, why should he? He smiled, peering at the screen, wondering if the boy would come along and say goodnight. He chuckled. Some hope.

He pulled out a wad of notes, peeled four tens off and stuffed them into the cabbie's hand.

'Cheers, pal,' the driver said. 'No need to say enjoy yirsel.'

Laura had her arm round his waist and was playing with the roll of flesh at his waistband and whispering, 'I'll soon get that off you.'

'Ah'll look forward to that. Ah certainly will,' he said, pulling the girl towards him and stumbling with her away from the kerb as the taxi slowly pulled away. He stopped, turned away slightly and gave a wave over his head, knowing the old man would be watching.

'You're mad,' she said, 'there's no one there.'

'Let's go,' he said, planting a wet kiss on her lips.

'Hot lips,' she said. 'Probably the vindaloo.'

The father began to turn away and then stopped.

The son began to turn away from her, hearing the running footsteps behind, and stopped.

The running shape appearing in the frame had transfixed him.

He felt a tug as Laura pulled from him and then the rattling flinty roll of steel heels running away.

There was no sound inside the house, just the small running shape on the screen becoming larger.

The boy, befuddled, slightly drunk, deadened to panic, realised that the man was running towards him, that there seemed to be someone behind him. He was alone on the street and he knew now what was happening.

Inside the house the father was also alone and he, too, knew what was happening. He began to shout and move towards the door.

Stumbling into a run now, looking back over his shoulder, seeing the gun in the hand at last, then a small flash, a tiny sparkle as the hand holding it came up, and although he could not see the face, it was shrouded in darkness or masked, he knew who it was. The ring, he thought, as the first bullet tore a fiery track into his back and the pain seemed to flare and roar through all of his body as he tumbled to his knees.

The old man dropped the icon as he fumbled with the complex lock. All he could see now was the bomb-proof door but, in his mind he could see through it to what was happening, what would always be with him, as he threw the locks in too much haste so that the tumblers jarred and refused.

He had stumbled on to his feet and was moving forward, his failing legs trying to keep up with the impetus of his falling trunk. He felt nothing now, even as the other bullets hit him, some residual nervous impulses providing the locomotion.

The old man got the door open at last. He would always remember the colour of the night, like mustard gas in the mix of lights, yellow from the street lamps, harsh white from the security beams as the boy's falling body set them off. He put his arms round him and tried to lift his son as blood tore free from his gullet and spurted over his chest. He could feel it warm, hear the spatter of it hitting the white shirt, the bright stain of gore seeming black in the monochrome. His two arms under his lad's and around his chest, feeling the head loll against his cheek, warm blood running down into the hollow of his neck. 'It's all right,' he kept shouting as other hands joined his and pulled the boy into the lobby.

The cameras had recorded everything.

Hours later, when only the tidying up mattered, he would wipe the tapes.

Chapter One

'He's his son all right, yir brother's.' They were the first words he could recall his mother saying to him, or about him. Perhaps, because she had said it so often and vehemently, it had just seemed that way. He hadn't understood the edge to it until later, the implication. His father, when he was there, would bite down on his teeth, stifling curses if he hadn't been drinking. If he had he would start across the room at her, drawing back his hand, but always stopping, whatever his state, just short of where she stood with her burning cheeks taunting him. Then he would shrug, take a few deep breaths, jiggle his hands in his pockets to see if he had the price of another round and, whatever the sound, leave the house. Peter Stark was always leaving the house.

It wasn't a house but they were all called houses, regardless of the size of them, and however high off the ground they were. Theirs was two up, one room, a single-end, for the three of them, but uncrowded for the close. Most of the other houses had six or more weans, grandparents, assorted relatives and other chancers. No one took any notice of the metal plates screwed to the outside detailing how many could live behind each door, except when the sanny man was on his rounds and then a rippling warning would flow through the streets, faster than the man's legs could fly up the stairs, and by the time he arrived, panting at the door, the surplus weans would be out in the street, great clots of them at the corners, gathering round the smoky entrances to the pubs and the bread shops for warmth.

Their house was dry – the family above, the McNultys, took all the penetration from the leaking roof – with a cold water tap at the back window, a black-lead grate constantly alight, a press with their few household things, including the hand-embroidered linen tablecloth which his father claimed to have won somewhere (although everyone knew it had been stolen by his brother) which

17

was kept for the special celebration which never came, and the items of food high up on the shelf. Bread, potatoes, oatmeal for the porridge, a bit of tripe or mutton out of the back door of the Duke Street abattoir for the weekend, all wrapped up in newspaper, always the *Bulletin*. 'So they can't be got at,' his mother said as she wrapped, meaning, but not saying, by the mice and rats which scuttered in the floorboards and left their traces, gouges and deposits around the sink and grate. And still, on him.

The scarred patch under Johnnie's left eye distorted his face, but it became less livid as he grew. He couldn't remember it happening at all, he hadn't been more than a few months old and sleeping in the bottom drawer of the dresser still. A rat had bitten and torn at his face in the night and his mother and father had woken to the mixed screams, him and the relishing moan of the rat with the taste of blood in its mouth, and to see the yellow eyes turn to them and stare before almost contemptuously shuddering away. His father went after it but couldn't catch it. His mother wiped at the blood with the hem of her nightgown sleeve, then boiled water on the range and scrubbed at it over again. They couldn't afford to call out a doctor. His dad had found some iodine and poured that on his wound.

Apparently he had cried for hours while they shushed him and waited for the fever to come. Waiting for the plague. The Black Death. It had been shut up in the medical books and the histories with the plates of Hogarthian revels and gin biddies since the Middle Ages, eradicated, according to the same books, in fire and efficient sewerage and carbolic, buried with the 68,000 who died in London. But after almost 250 years, less than thirty years before, in 1900, the year his father had been born, it returned to these streets, raging down Rose Street and Thistle Street, into Oxford Street, back again to Thistle Street, and around and around. There was no tolling bell in the street, no cries of 'Bring out your dead,' but thirty-eight people had died and more than a hundred others were badly stricken. The Corporation had burned down the affected tenements too, as the fire had consumed the first plague houses. But just because it hadn't returned in almost thirty years, after it had lain dormant like a volcano for getting on for 300 years, didn't mean it wouldn't erupt again.

His mother and father watched as the blood fever developed. His father Peter thought of the viral chain, of the fleas infesting the bodies of sick rats which jump to new hosts as the rats die, to lice, to ants, to ticks and to humans. He was a well-read man, having studied at night to take on his father-in-law in arguments about politics. But he had cared then. Books, politics, had been the ruin of him, he considered, and his mouth, which couldn't be hushed. Still, he couldn't bear to get rid of them and they lay in dusty piles and pyramids round the walls.

Now when he looked down at his son, beyond fretting, hanging on the lip of death, he felt only shame. He could sense too, his wife Isobel hating him. And he understood. He stood up, unable to stay, not man enough to remain in the shame. He touched his lips to his fingers and then to the wee lad's brow, dry and raging, the boy carrying his brother's name and his mark now, chiselled bloodily into his cheek. Isobel would always blame him for the child's name. For his brother, Johnnie Stark. And staring down into their bed, at the child bundled up in the torn bedclothes in the alcove, he saw his brother lying on the cobbles, the livid white scars on his face still cutting through the mud where he had been kicked, and the crusting of blood around his eyes and nose. Then he crossed himself, because he didn't know what else to do, and he went out.

His wife did not say a word. Neither did she when he returned eighteen hours later, with the young boy sleeping peacefully now, the fever broken.

'I'll do something,' he said.

She nodded. She had wanted him to *be* something.

And the boy. Now, when she looked down she saw the brother.

It had not changed much. For over 200 years it had been a leper colony and it was still occupied by the wretched, the dispossessed and vanquished, the disenfranchised. It had become the most populated area in the country, more than 600 people to the acre according to the official figures, but probably considerably higher. The huts and cottages with mud and heather roofs had gone and in their places were the rows of three- and four-storey tenements, built out of the sandstone blocks cut from the Giffnock quarries, shaped by teams of masons into honey-coloured stones, now blackened by half a century of coal fumes and polluting chemical gases. The tenements were built in a grid system, in long redoubts, with wide streets, seventy feet across, so there would be no impediment to tanks and the militia, local legend had it. They were privately built and owned and had been put up to house the workers who fired the industrial revolution, who produced the iron and the steam locomotives, the ships and machine tools, the bridges, the woven cloth, the beavering men in caps who loaded and unloaded the huge merchant ships which clogged the port, carrying tobacco, sugar, cotton and dyestuffs, the same kind of men who, with their picks and swung hammers, built the railways which made it all possible. And as they poured in, the small houses were divided further so that still more could cram in.

From the straths and glens of the Highlands came the clanspeople cleared from the land for the Cheviot sheep, those who couldn't afford the fare westwards to America or Canada. From Ireland they came eastwards, those who hadn't the price of the ship to the New World, whose families and lands had been scoured by the potato famines. They travelled like the slaves taken to America, herded below decks, locked up and battened down in the bowels of a flotilla of small boats, few of them over 500 tons. The *Londonderry*, just 277 tons, brought 3,383 Irish to Glasgow in ten days in 1847, 175 steerage passengers at a time packed into a hold measuring twenty-three feet by eighteen. The dead they dumped overboard on the way. In those same ten days one observer counted 11,749 arrive from Ireland on just four boats. The Jews, the Lithuanians, the Poles came too, seeking a life away from pogroms and persecution.

This outland created for uncounted lepers had grown from a smattering of houses along five streets immediately south of the river, to a smoky, raucous, dense barracks. As the first lepers had been pushed over the one bridge south at the points of sticks and guns and bayonets it was known as Bridgend. Then as the townland, or *gorbaile* in the Gaelic of the first wave of immigrants. The law, such as it was, was harsh and unforgiving. Thieves were branded on the face – Johnnie, if he had known about it, would have sympathised – and scourged through the streets and banished. Women escaped the fiery brand but were still thrown out of the Gorbaile, now called the Gorbals by the Lowland tongue. But few knew the history of the place and even fewer cared. It was a place without a past or, for most, a future. Escape was in the head, or in the glass, more like. There had been famous sons. Lipton from Crown Street who became a grocery millionaire, Allan Pinkerton, born on the site of the old leper hospital, who sailed off to America, guarded Abraham Lincoln – 'No doubt he'd be in the foyer bar when Wilkes came callin',' said Peter Stark – and then had gone on to form the world's biggest private detective agency. Others too, like John Buchan, the novelist. And hundreds of unknown ones who died in the mud and the treachery of Flanders, Ypres, Passchendaele and the Somme with the Highland Light Infantry, the HLI, the Ladies from Hell.

Now the place was restocking itself. There were around 50,000 people in the 200 acres of tenements. 'The size of a small farm,' Stark would say to his wife as he pulled off his boots after a fruitless day looking for work, 'and they wouldn't be allowed to keep a tenth of the number of beasts on it.' What was unusual – poverty and dank overcrowding were matter-of-factly endemic in the city – was the composition of the population. Unlike the rest of Glasgow, and particularly the neighbouring district of Bridgeton, *Brigton*, this was a Catholic enclave with over three-quarters of the people Papes, Fenians and 'left-fitters' to the wider citizenry of Glasgow.

There were 5,000 Jews there too, Malkovichs and Rabinovichs and Goldsteins and Finkelsteins, with their beards and strange hats, all or most from Eastern Europe, adapters, survivors, who kept to their own. The Prods did too. They didn't parade their religion behind flutes and drums and black bowlers and sashes and past chapels and statues on the Twelfth of July. Or if they did, it was outside the area. Their biggest gang, the Billy Boys from Brigton, named after the man on the white horse, King William, who were led by a Billy, Billy Fullerton, went into battle screaming, 'God save the King,' like some regiment of eighteenth-century dragoons, but they had been smashed by the police. The Norman Conks, the Fenian boys from the Gorbals and its airts, were on the wane too, probably for lack of a cause of belligerence. But there were memories, and marks, of the pitched battles with bottles and pit staves and knives and the flashing bright razors. And most of all, of Johnnie Stark, the Razor King, carving out a bloody course through the centre of the savagery.

The police were now led by a man from Sheffield, Percy Sillitoe, who later collected the obligatory knighthood for busting the Glasgow Neds, who introduced fingerprinting and forensic science and added police boxes, seemingly on every corner, so the force could keep in touch and on top. Sillitoe, who also went on to head MI5, the security service, tried to put an end to corruption, attempting to crack down on the illegal bookmakers and shebeens, the bribes to the beat men and the officers, but it was like resisting the wind, crime would always find a way round.

Peter Stark was walking towards the river, which started as a tiny trickle in Leadhills before it twisted and turned through Lanarkshire, then bisected the city, picking up filth and sewerage as it did so, chemical waste and toxins, gathering strength, widening and hitting the sheds and docks and jetties of the yards like John Brown's, Fairfield and Lithgow's, taking away their steel ships, the liners and tankers and warships, to every part of the world. It was dark, or should have been. Behind him was the perpetual sunset of Dixon's Blazes, the huge furnace fires of the steelworks which cast a sodden red light over the streets and blew more smoky yellow dragon's breath into the laden night air. He had skirted the lanes and tracks where the spilled molten metal had turned the cobbles to silver and he was backlit by the furnace light as he made his way down Crown Street in a bloody aura. He seemed to be muttering to himself and occasionally he would kick out at some object only he could identify, the tackets on his work boots sending sparks skittering off the pavement. Now and then people would nod to him, wish him well, but he rarely acknowledged. His cap was pulled down tight over his eyes, the lapels of his jacket up against the smirr of rain and his hands were thrust deep inside the pockets. His fingers were playing with his brother's only legacy, the two cut-throats with the mother-of-pearl handles and the honed steel forged in Sillitoe's own home town.

That last time Peter had fought at his brother's side until they had been separated in the mêlée of rage, but he had seen Johnnie going down surrounded by men hacking and kicking at him, and when he had finally got to him it was clear, in the lost eyes and lolling head, that he would not last long. They took him to hospital, him and two others, dragged between them, lying around their shoulders in a sloppy embrace, until they commandeered a taxi. Peter had removed Johnnie's razors before they got there. He remembered being surprised that they were still with him, in his pockets too, after the battering he had taken. Now, thinking back, he imagined someone, one of the battalion, had picked them up and slipped them into the jacket.

No crossed swords for John Stark or bloody shield to be borne away on, just the damp blades and a stuttering old Hackney with a terrified and cowering driver.

Peter was almost at the river now. He had wanted to walk off the impotent rage he felt in himself, the sense of worthlessness, but he knew that he had neither the time nor the stamina. He had searched Marx and MacLean, his heart too, and although he could cite reasons he could not find answers. When he finally stopped walking, feeling the rain heavier, trickling down his neck and sticking his shirt to his skin and searching for a close mouth to shelter in, he was outside McBrearty's. Could there ever have been a clearer providential sign? he asked himself, searching his trouser pockets for change.

The light from inside the pub filtered through the green and yellow whorled glass over the doorway and coloured the wet paving stones a dull, dun gold. Turn again, he thought. Then he looked across the street at the pawnbroker's sign hanging outside Goldberg's and smiled quickly to himself. As he turned back and pulled at the swing doors the vacuum it created sucked at the thick air of tobacco smoke and curled strands of it around him. The conjuror's entrance, he told himself. If I just had the power to turn the few scraps of base metal in my pockets into gold, preferably Bell's, a fuckin' caseload.

He pushed through the crowd to the bar and ordered a half and a half, drained the whisky in one gulp and sucked on the half pint. He hadn't eaten and his stomach heaved as the mix hit it, then gently subsided. Looking around he couldn't see anyone he knew but he could detect, in the eyes that either avoided his or sought to engage them, that several people knew who he was. It felt good. Fear or respect, the difference wasn't worth a damn.

He moved across to the wall of the pub opposite the bar, known as the Celtic end because it was entirely covered with photographs of successive Celtic sides. McBrearty's was on Gerard Street, in no-man's land between the Gorbals and Infideldom, and Stark hadn't drunk in there very often. He heard loud laughter coming from behind his shoulder from a cubicle off the main room, glanced briefly round the varnished wood corner, recognised no one and went back to draining his half pint. When he had finished he put the glass beside the empty whisky one on the shelf, the gold all gone from it, the coins in his pocket insufficient for another, and eased himself off the wall and on to the balls of his feet.

'Stark, isn't it?' stopped him and he turned to look at a small fat man, out of place here in a stiff collar and tie, sweat beading on his bald head and sparkling in his long dark moustache. 'I knew your brother.'

'Everyone did,' he said. 'Or thought they did.'

'A drink, man? Let me buy you one.' The fat face was attempting a smile but Stark could see the scuttle of fear in the eyes. 'A large one!' He was motioning to the bar, two fingers up, then pointing to Peter.

'It's a rich man gets personal service here,' Stark said. The other man was fumbling inside the hound's-tooth cloth of the jacket. Out came a wallet, flicked open to show a wedge of notes. But still Stark could sense the edge of fear in the man who pulled out a pound note and semaphored it to the bar, then took Peter by the arm and pulled him towards the cubicle. 'In here. It's Peter, isn't it? Aye, son, your brother was some man.'

Peter allowed himself to be led into the rectangular room, to the cushioned seats against the wall which surrounded two wooden tables. He nodded to the other men, took off his cap which he stuffed into the right-hand pocket of his jacket, his fingers inadvertently brushing one of the razors. As he sat down and turned, one of the barmen, dutifully timely, pushed a large whisky and a pint in front of him. He was a big lad with a tattooed tricolour on his bare, right forearm. Stark nodded thanks.

'Get it down,' said the fat man, pushing into the seat beside him and wheezing as he did so. 'You don't remember me, do you?'

Stark lifted his glass, letting the peaty smell play with his nose before he took a gulp. He shook his head.

'You'll have seen me around maybe? Devanney.' He stuck out a fleshy hand which felt soft and damp to the touch. 'Mick Devanney.'

'The bookie.'

'That's me.' He picked up his glass and made a toast in the air. 'To your brother. Feared no one—'

24

'And knew no better,' Stark cut in, not wanting anyone to stake something on his brother. 'What is it you want, Devanney?'

'Mick. I'm Mick.' He tried that fearful smile again. 'Just to buy you a drink. For your brother's sake.'

Stark rubbed his nose with the back of his unoccupied hand. 'You and he had business, then?' he said, worrying at the glass with his fingers and looking straight into Devanney's face, seeing the twitch of a lie begin to form in those eyes.

'Nothing to speak of, no. Well, occasionally. Sometimes.' Devanney was trying a very watery smile.

'You owed him money. A pay-out. And you're trying to find out whether I know about it or—' he picked up the pint, took a long swallow and let the silence grow '—whether he took it to the grave with him? I'm right, am I not, Mick?' He said the man's name very carefully, letting his lips draw back across his teeth over it. Deliberately he was not looking at him but at the dying bubbles on top of his pint of heavy.

Looking up, he noticed Devanney's fingers, weighty with rings, were scrabbling at his starched collar. 'Pay up,' he said softly.

'I was going to come—'

'Of course you were,' Stark said, holding out his hand.

– next of kin, I thought—'

'You thought you'd welsh on the bet.'

'Not at all. No. When I saw—' He was tugging at the rough material of his jacket now.

'You thought you'd allow the money to mourn for a bit but when you saw me come in you thought – you thought I'd come to claim you.'

'No, no! Honestly. It was a friendly gesture – I, I was—'

'And as there wisnae a widow you thought you were just going to keep it to yourself.'

Devanney's fingers were fluttering over his wallet. 'No, I heard that times were hard and—'

Stark's right hand shot out and grabbed Devanney by the tie and pulled his sweating face across the table, his flailing arms spilling the drinks, the glasses rolling and slowly falling to the floor and exploding in dull crumps in the wet sawdust. 'These are hard times all over, Devanney, savage. Anything can happen to a man.'

The bookie dropped his wallet on the table, choking and scrabbling at Peter's clenched fist as he wound his tie round it. Finally Stark loosened his grip and Devanney jerked back into the boards on the wall behind him, his big damp head chiming off the wood. Stark opened the wallet, carefully took out the notes, fanned them in his hand and then put them down on the puddled table. He glanced around him and noticed that no one had moved to stop him, the men around just staring, not talking, waiting to see what would happen. He looked back at the money, now sodden in front of him. There seemed to be at least a hundred pounds in ones, fives and twenties, blotting the beer and whisky. Near enough two years' buroo.

'I'll take this' – Stark peeled off about half of the fan of notes, crumpled them in his hand and pushed them into his right jacket pocket – 'for the debt and the rest – for trying to welsh and fur trying to make a mug of me. And this' – he pulled up the remaining notes with his other hand and slipped those into his left pocket – 'for what's owing in the future.'

'What?' Devanney was starting to lean forward, emboldened by the loss of his money. 'For what?'

'Comfort,' Stark said, leaning back in his seat, both hands contentedly in his pockets, a man at his ease. 'From these hard times.'

'The polis – I pay—' he stammered and took a deep red breath. 'I don't need any protec—' the last word slurred as the blade of the open razor, brought upwards in a fast, silvery arc backhanded, cut him from the bottom of the jaw to the top of the ear, the flesh opening white before the blood tumbled out and spattered and drenched his white collar, pumped through the fingers of the two hands which sought to hold his cheek together as he slumped away and began to curl and whimper on the bench. The men around pushed back their chairs, stumbling up and out of it.

'Wrong,' said Stark, carefully wiping the blade of the razor on the grey and black and now red-speckled hound's-tooth, before closing it and putting it away and standing up. 'That's two wrongs, Devanney. But that' – he patted his pockets – 'makes it right.'

Myth and memory. They had become indistinguishable for Johnnie. His father coming and going, trailing with him a changing cast and a clutch of stories and anecdotes which swelled and reformed with their retelling on the street, his mother apparently docilely accepting it all. Only in the clench of her shoulders, the occasional unguardedly fiery glance, did she make clear her disapproval. He was too young to pick it up, but he knew that in his memory it became true. Gradually she seemed to become almost deformed by it all, permanently hunched, angrily tense about what her life had become, but most of all what her husband had turned into.

'John' – she always called him John, never Johnnie, trying vainly to distinguish him from his surroundings and heritage – 'when your father comes in don't get him angry, son. Just go ben the room. There's a good boy.'

He would hang under her skirts when he did arrive, scared of the man who had never hurt him, picking up the atmosphere of his mother's hatred, so that if his dad reached out a hand he would cringe into the rough tweed folds and blot out his presence. Later he realised that this had been exactly what his mother intended, using him against her husband until his comings and goings became fewer and his notice of Johnnie seemed to be no more than a quick pained glance. And until the sole purpose of her life became a hatred.

He remembered one sneering aside of hers, shouted after his father as he left. 'I'll tell them what it's like living with a legend, don't you forget it.' And then a cruel laughter and tears as she pulled him up to her and hugged him to her wet face so that he could taste the bitter salt in his mouth.

The place smelled starchy, of damp raincoats, drying tweed and beer slops, of strong tobacco and sweat. It was Saturday lunchtime, those who were working were throwing down a few quick halfs before going on to the game at Parkhead. Some had retrieved their green and white scarves from their dun raincoats, or boiler suits underneath, and were winding them round their necks between gulps. Outside the door a crowd of kids were trying to sell bread and hot pies, clutching at each man who left. Peter Stark had pushed his way past them as he had come in. Now, sitting at the heavily varnished table next to the flap in the bar where the staff came and went, he was stabbing a finger into the whorls and rings of drink on the surface.

'So what has the Gorbals got more of than any other part of the town?' Stark was asking, picking up his glass with the other hand

and swirling the whisky around so that it coated the entire inside.

'Rats?' McKenna came in. He was wearing a grubby white scarf knotted like a cravat which he considered jaunty and which he fidgeted with so that damp finger spots of beer now dotted it.

'Rickets,' offered McSwegan.

'And Tims,' added Tennant, the only Protestant in the company, putting on a superior smile.

'All true,' Stark said, getting up from the table and taking a couple of steps to the bar. 'But I'm talking about opportunities.' He broke off as he got a round of Bell's in, paying ostentatiously with a new pound note, pocketing the change and carrying the four glasses in two hands back to the table. 'Go on,' he said, putting them down and skittering the glasses towards the others with the fingers of his hand.

'Certainly not opportunities, Peter? Eh?' McSwegan asked. 'What is it in that glass that's put you in this mood?'

'For an ignoramus, Pat,' Stark said, leaning across the table and slapping his cheeks with both hands, 'you sometimes have these flashes of penetrating insight.' Then he held up his fresh glass, staring at the melted amber whisky. 'So, who's getting rich these days?' He nodded towards the bar. 'Who's prospering in aw this poverty? Hmmm? Publicans . . . and bookies.'

The three other men waited for him to go on.

'D'you know how many pubs there are in the Gorbals alone? No? One hundred and eighteen. One hundred and eighteen. That's one for every 400 men, women and children. And as the weans and the women don't count in this it's probably nearer to one to a hundred. There's fourteen alone in Crown Street. And every one of them's prospering. Does that tell you something?'

'The licensing board's bent,' said McKenna, sipping at his whisky. He was a big lad, bigger than the rest, with startlingly blue eyes and a stunning right cross. He had started out training in the ring at St Denis's but although he didn't lack the stomach for it he was vain enough to treasure his straight nose and its central location between those dazzling eyes, so he had given up ringcraft for his main sport, chasing women. But in this, while he had the steps, the guard and the shadow play, he lacked the main weapon, the direct finesse to inflict damage.

'The licensing board's always been bent,' Stark said.

'So never mind the Depression and the bent licensing board and the polis in their new checkered hats and old habits, like gettin' pissed for free in the back room,' Tennant came in, 'Sharp's and Beacom's and Hanlon's and McNab's and the Glue Pot and the Splash and the Boreen and the hundred-odd other pubs are still raking it in . . .' He ran out of steam and looked towards Peter to round off his thoughts.

'Exactly. It's a biblical lesson. In the midst of poverty, plenty,' Stark said, putting down his glass. 'I mean, by now you'd have thought the government would have come up with a scheme to pay the buroo direct to the publicans without the intervening inconvenience of it having to pass through thousands of men's bowels. But it can be very unscientific, capitalism, fortunately for us.'

'Peter?' queried McKenna, who had gone to school with Stark and knew him as well as anyone, which was almost not at all. 'Could you just spell it out for us. We all agree we've never heard of a poor publican. And—'

'So, it's a risk-free profession, isn't it? I mean, even a bookie can occasionally lose his shirt on a gimpy horse—'

'Whereas folk here would still get to the pub on hands on knees, ower broken glass and wi' both legs in stookies.'

'A risk-free profession, as I said. But imagine if an element of risk were to enter into it, all of those profits could evacuate. And I don't mean pissed up against a wall either.'

'Go on,' said McSwegan, unwilling to admit that he didn't know what Stark was getting at.

'Think of it as like insurance. You can't take out an insurance against an inevitability, can you? Like the sun going down. Or not being made redundant.' He looked about for contradiction. 'Now, someone burns down a pub, or nicks the stock and the publican's laughing, because he's got a fat insurance policy to give him more than he lost. But what if no one came to his pub—'

'About as likely as a Fenian getting a gold watch at the Harland and Wolff,' said McSwegan.

'Never happen. It's simply against the laws of nature,' Tam Tennant agreed.

'This is slow going, lads. Think – you know,' said Stark, motioning around with his hand to his head, 'what if a natural disaster happened? On a regular basis. Here. You're having a quiet pint in your good clothes, on your way to the jiggin', and the windaes come in . . . or someone deposits a ton and a half of horse shite between you and the bar . . . or, I don't know, bottles keep exploding mysteriously behind the gantry, fights keep breakin' out all over the place – naw, forget that, you'd be breakin' the doors doon tae get in. But you see my point. Most people don't want to be drinking in a place cursed with misfortune, it's just too much trouble when there's thirteen other pubs in the street they can go into. Savvy?'

'Ah'm with you, Peter,' McKenna said, grinning widely. 'I think.'

'A good publican would need to take out insurance against any alteration in the natural laws, wouldn't he?' Stark said. 'Regular insurance. To help restore the natural order.' He grinned and downed his whisky.

'Can I cast the first thunderbolt, Peter?' Tennant said, getting up and searching in his pocket for money for the next round.

'Sit down, Tam.' Stark leaned back in his seat, beaming. 'It's time to engage the concept. Wattie,' he shouted across at the bar 'four half gills here and a word in your ear.'

The big, raw westerlies beat in for most of the year, laden with ice, snow and chilling rain, straight off the Atlantic and up the river, battering off the skeletons of the big ships, the gantries and cranes, the scaffolding and rickety platforms. And the men, the Lilliputians in blue overalls swarming all over the rusty plates, tiny dots to the eye one hundred or more feet up, illuminated by the flares of the cutting torches, ignoring the driving rains, fireflies and tiny shooting stars seemingly buzzing around them which were actually white-hot rivets that rattled, scuttered and fizzled in the puddles, cooling from yellow sunrise to sunset red, before they were hammered home. The rivets – and they came in different sizes and shapes for the different joints they were to seal and had to be delivered, always, in the correct sequence – were heated in a charcoal fire blown by bellows to exactly the right temperature by the rivet boy, usually a man in his fifties or older whose strength had ebbed, then hurled by tongs, sometimes to a height of three storeys. They landed on the staging where the catch boy, or the pitter-in as everyone knew him, picked them up with another pair of tongs. In American yards they managed it, as they normally do, with more razzamatazz and ceremony, catching the fuming rivet, baseball-fashion, in a leathern pouch. When the rivets clattered on to the staging the pitter-in then pushed them home and they were smashed tight by a hauder-oan wielding a sixteen-pound hammer.

The hauder-oan and pitter-in worked on the inside, out of the direct force of the weather, and when their bolts were driven into the precisely drilled pores of the ship the men on the outside, the elite, who were working on piecework and in all weathers, used their mallets to turn the shanks of the rivets into round dull heads which, like a row of immaculate metal stitching, sealed plate to plate and kept the huge vessel watertight and afloat. These were the riveters, one left-handed, one right-handed in each squad for maximum efficiency, alternate blows, with around twenty-five squads to the bigger ships. This was the Clyde and these men and their compatriots in other yards on both banks of the dark river had made one out of every five of the metal boats which sailed all seven seas and uncountable rivers, tributaries, lakes – man-made and natural – lochs and farflung lagoons.

Razzle Dundas had been a riveter. He was now a full-time trade union official for the engineers, his wage paid for by John Brown's to organise against them, as he put it. He had been a party member, now he called himself agnostic. But whatever else, he was still a dancer. He had kept that faith. His real name was Carl – his mother had pleaded with his father, whatever his principles, not to register the boy with that Germanic K – but his dance-hall career had led to a nickname superseding his own. Razzle Dazzle Dundas became Razzle, or Raz. And no one would have dared to tell him that hard men don't dance, or wear pomade. His bulging right arm, the riveter's legacy, could still deliver a massive force, with absolute precision, to any point within reach and he could get to the point of maximum opportunity with that immaculate footwork.

Razzle had never been quite good enough to become a featured dancer, to turn professional, but there was 'only a ba' herr in it' as he had often been told in competitions. He was a regular at the Kingston Palais, universally known as the Tripe, a small dance hall in Gloucester Street, a short walk from where he lived in Eglinton Street, which during the day was a shanty restaurant with trestle tables and a basic menu (hence the nickname) but which, after the dishes and the chairs were cleared away, became as near a palace of dreams as the area could muster: mirrors you could pass through, subdued gas lights casting a yellowing flickering glow, perfumes now overlaying the cooking smells, young people swept up in each other as the muted tenor sax, piano and drums took them, in dipping turns, to Broadway and 42nd Street, anywhere other than here.

The Tripe was for real dancers, men and women with aplomb and insouciance who carved and birled their way with mastery through the densest crowd in perfect syncopation. It was for contenders, not for champions, but it was an important venue on the way. And it was, too, for the others, the simple lovers of the dance and the lovers, those who couldn't achieve the mastery but admired it none the less, those who came to gawp and grope.

But while you certainly didn't go there for a lumber, if you were that good, and Razzle was, you didn't go without. He had escorted a number of comely women away but when Hazel Hope looked at him through the smoke and the slow motion he wanted to stay with her for ever. Just like that. No doubts. First the giddying rush, the plummet inside, then certainty rushing in to fill the vacuum.

She was slim, taller than him, with unfashionably long hair tied back in an elaborate coil and he would have proposed to her with his first words if he hadn't known it was doolally to do so, suicidal. Instead he asked her to dance, knowing she couldn't refuse or she would be thrown out, and when it was over, when the trio had raggedly fizzled out and the Salvation Army band and chorus through the wall in all their Christian fervour were declaiming the friend they had in Jesus, he offered her his clean white handkerchief to dab at her brow. It was instinctive, he didn't know why he did it because it was so personal, but she smiled and took it and gently touched it around her face and when she returned it, and when he sniffed at it later, it seemed to him to smell of dewy roses, although he had never smelled a rose. Perhaps the thought had been implanted there by some movie, or book, although generally he would not read fiction because he didn't consider it aided betterment. Or maybe it had been Burns, some distant passage dinned into him by the dominie, but there it was, a quite uncharacteristically romantic seam revealed. Gently he touched the white Irish lawn to his lips and then, becoming embarrassed, quickly tucked it away.

He had been nineteen then, just coming to the end of his apprenticeship, and Hazel two years younger. Now, as he walked along the slip under the half-built liner, he was amazed how far he had come. At twenty-one the youngest convener in the yard, on the Clyde. Now, four years on, he saw himself as a veteran of the class war; the men sought him out for advice and leadership, the management was grudgingly respectful. He could and had pulled his men out several times as a demonstration of strength – at a threatened attack on piecework rates, safety, even over tea breaks – and he knew that he had within him the eloquence, the fiery persuasion, to set men's hearts arage. But he was superstitious and, although he would never have said it, he dated the birth of this power to move men to the handkerchief and Hazel – something mystical anyway in the kiss of a laden lawn hankie. 'Christ, Dundas,' he chided himself, 'what a big lassie's blouse you've become.'

Going out with Hazel had changed him immeasurably. He would do anything to please her. Small presents, of course, but grander endowments, giving himself completely to try to become the ideal he felt she sought. Night school, as much overtime as he could get, saving, cutting out drink, developing ambition. When he touched her, his big rough fleshy hands moving over her skin, callouses often catching on the cotton of her blouse or underwear, causing runs in her nylons, he was ashamed of what he was. Hazel, however familiar they became, seemed always just tantalisingly out of reach, a part of her emotions in reserve that he knew he could never touch.

Even when she came, which she did easily and uncomplicatedly, he did not feel a part of it although he had brought her to it, but perhaps there was even a speck of uncertainty about that too. She laughed at him when he tried to discuss it, accused him of wanting to own her soul, and he never did so again.

That first night at the Tripe when he walked her to the bus he caught her smiling to herself again and again, as she had continued to do since. In anyone else he would have put it down to some simpleness. He had never been able to find out what it was within her that amused her or pleased her. But it was not him or what he said, he knew that. Nevertheless, it was almost enough that she was with him.

Because he could never be sure that she would remain he pushed himself on and for a young riveter with such molten oratory there was only one way to the top, the union movement. Convener, then convener of the shipyards' committee too, and now branch treasurer thrown in. Making his capacity for work, the cause, seem limitless. Soon there would be a full-time job outside coming up with the union, it was only a matter of time, and there was nowhere he felt he couldn't ascend to in the movement, to general secretary or even parliament. He could see it. With Hazel.

Devanney the bookie was back at his pitch in Florence Street within a week of the slashing. He was scared to go back but more scared that someone else would take the pitch and his livelihood. He turned up with his stitched angry red and black wound and his runners. The beat policemen nodded at him before they pocketed their ten bob notes and when the sergeant turned up for his weekly pound he stared at the bookie's face, then asked him, 'Well, Mick? Everyone knows it was Stark. What are you going to do?'

There were only two options (confirming the assault to the police wasn't one of them) and they both involved money: paying up or paying for revenge. And since he was an outsider, since he was vulnerable and depended on the streets, there really wasn't a choice. Besides, it was a mistake to mix business with the personal, a mistake, he thought, fingering his face, painfully learned. 'Me, Sergeant?' he replied. 'Nothing.'

The sergeant, a big Highlander from Eriskay with a Kitchener moustache, turned, shook his head and began to walk off, saying back over his shoulder, 'Turning the other cheek, eh Mick? Christian, right enough, but risky,' and he chuckled to himself as he walked off through the weans playing peever on the pavement.

Before the end of the day one of Stark's lieutenants had turned up, a big lad with mad eyes whom he knew as McKenna and told him that protection would cost five pounds a week. He nodded assent. McKenna held out his hand. 'In advance.' He nodded again and rummaged in his waistcoat for the money.

When McKenna left, his runners began to filter back, leaving the lines with old Terry Phelan in the ground-floor right of number 21, handing them in through the open window and later, if there were winnings, picking up cash. Devanney never handled any of the lines, he was the banker, clean of incrimination, using Phelan and the runners as the risk, picking up the profit, a slimmer one now, on the horses and dogs which kept him open from noon to nightfall.

As he leaned against the sandstone at the mouth of the close, watching the kids, and the boys on the corner smoking and arguing, he thought again of Stark and his brother before him. Pure evil, he said to himself. But the younger one's got a head on him, mair's the pity. He cursed him and his own foolishness in not realising it before.

There was a certain elegance about the idea, Stark had to admit. It appealed to both his bravado and his intelligence. It was so obvious and yet it had never been done before. Tam Tennant was drawing the plan on a table in the Moy, dipping his finger into a pint of heavy, then sketching out the contours and the obstructions on the wooden grain. 'The gate's here,' he said, licking his finger clean then plunging it back into the beer. 'And here are the offices, away from the men, overlooking a courtyard here, where the lorry deliveries come in here, and backin' on to the river, where the boats tie up. The cashier's office is two floors up. The only security is a pathetic wee wire mesh gate that a sixteen-pound hammer would be through in one swing. There'll be, easy, 2,000 pounds on pay day. Probably mair. It's beggin' fur it.'

Tennant had worked in Brown's as a labourer until he was finally – and this was the difficult bit – sacked for persistent lateness and drinking. He had a grudge against the yard, but that was no reason to ignore the proposition. 'Would anyone recognise you?' Stark asked.

'You're jokin',' said Tennant, 'ah wis never there.'

Peter and Kevin McKenna grinned. 'Nevertheless,' Stark said, 'we cannae risk it. You'll need to handle the getaway.'

Tennant drew up a more complete plan on draughtsman's paper and armed with this Peter went to the Mitchell Library where detailed plans of all the yards as well as blueprints for every boat built were lodged in a collection. He studied the plans, drawings and photographs of Brown's until it seemed that every runnel and cobble was emblazoned on his mind. Then he took the bus to Clydebank and scouted the outside and hung around until the noon hooter sounded and the men came out, a great blue tide of them gushing tobacco smoke and banter. He mingled with some in a nearby pub and half an hour later walked back in the group to the gates.

On the Tuesday before the raid, scheduled for Fair Friday when the yard would close for the fortnight and the men would be expecting triple pay, they did a dry run. Dressed in blue dungarees and caps like the hundreds of other men making their way to the huge iron gates Stark, McKenna and McSwegan walked into the yard, filing through the clocking-in box without marking a time card and then out into the huge, raw riverside. 'Just look busy,' Tennant had warned them. They found a dunny, a craftily constructed burrow in the middle of a steel stockyard used for playing cards, where they hid out until the tea break and then they emerged into the mêlée of men and fires and dying noise and scouted the offices and the approaches. No one asked them who they were or what they were doing. They simply merged into the blue battalions who moved purposefully and about their own business, interested only in making the piecework rate, or the tea, or the impression that they were busy.

Isobel Stark wakened with a sense of relief. She felt unaccustomedly relaxed and it took her a few moments to realise that she was alone except for John, who was burbling quietly in the greater space of the bed. She sagged into the hollow in the middle and pulled the child to her. There was no sound in the house but she could hear the flinty clopping of horses' hooves outside, the scuffle of voices and the children's calling that opened the day. She lay there, hugging John, tickling him under the cut-down shirt, occasionally squinting at the scar still vivid and birthmark red, feeling a wash of guilt and then pleasure at their togetherness. 'Your da's gone, son. Isn't it nice now? Just us.'

She turned over, rolling the boy off her stomach. Across the kitchen she could now see the damp gauze light from the window. It was early, not much after six. Fair Friday. She remembered, with a rush of bitterness, that she and John were not going anywhere.

She wanted to take him to the sea, watch him in the sand, splash salt water over his wee legs. 'Look at us, son,' she said at John, a tremor in her voice, 'just look at us.'

Her best memories were of Rothesay. She could remember the building expectation as the holiday approached, the train ride to Wemyss Bay, the guddle of people and prams and cases as they pushed and scurried in a heaving maul down the sloping planked causeway under the glass roof and ornate ironwork and towards the steamer. Then, grabbing a place on the varnished slatted benches while the steamer – the *Jeannie Deans* was her favourite – pawed at the water, its great paddles foaming the surface until it pulled thudding away, with the left-behind waving on the pier and the far finger of land, Toward Point, to aim at and then, as that passed to the right (she giggled when she said starboard to herself) the arc of boarding houses and hotels that would become Rothesay.

She pulled John towards her and smothered him again. 'You'll take yir mammy away, when you're a big lad . . . now won't you now.' And she began to cry into the hollow in the cold pillow where her husband had been.

At quarter to eight on the Fair Friday morning the three joined up again and blended into the procession moving towards the gates. They were all carrying tool bags, inside of which each had stowed scarves, jute sacks, six-pound hammers and weapons. McKenna had a pickaxe handle cut back to fit the long bag, as did McSwegan. Both also had knives with six-inch blades, honed keen. The contents of Peter Stark's bag varied only in that he had several lengths of three-foot rope and four cork floats.

At tea break the yard was already winding down in expectation of the final noon hooter for a blessed fortnight, hanselled by a long afternoon in the pub. The half-bottles were already coming out and being shared into the tea cans around the dozens of charcoal fires, like besieging camps round the high nameless ship whose keel and sectional innards stretched all the way down the slip to the black waters of the river. They walked through the knots of men swinging their bags, ignoring the shapes hunkering down who were just as intent on ignoring them.

'Gettin' loused early, boys?' someone shouted after them.

'Nah,' Peter shouted back. 'Just getting into our sprintin' gear fur the pistol.'

'Well, get the haufs in,' another voice cried back.

'Excuse me, pal,' McSwegan asked a man flushed in sweat and dirt, crouched down beside a charcoal pan, a sixteen-pound hammer lying beside him. 'Can ah borrow this for a tick? Ah'm having a wee bit trouble wae the neck of ma screwtap.'

'Be my guest,' the man waved back, wiping his mouth with his hand. 'Mind an' spit oot the splinters.'

McSwegan picked up the hammer and smiled. 'Ta.'

'Chuck it in the Clyde if ye want. Mind you, it's been around me so long, so attached, it would probably crawl up the beach at Rossie efter me.'

Razzle Dundas was thinking of the holiday. In four hours he was picking up Hazel at Boots' Corner, he had ordered a taxi for her so she had help with the luggage, and then they would walk the few yards to the Central, him hefting the big cases, and the Ardrossan train. He felt excited about it, childishly so. It was the first real holiday he had been on, with Hazel or anyone else, and it would be like a belated honeymoon. He had picked Arran because it was just a cut above the Clyde resorts, he wouldn't bump into any of the men there, and he had visions of quiet strolls, sunsets, rowing boats and rolling hills, just the two of them, tea and scones and paper doilies, older folk covertly remarking on how well suited the two of them seemed . . . he shook his head and smiled. 'Romance,' he chided himself under his breath.

He was walking towards his bothy where he would have a cup of tea with a splash of whisky – well, it was the Fair – and then a final stroll round the yard, checking if anyone had anything for him to take up, fat chance on Fair Friday, and by the time he had done the slow circuit it would be about time for the hooter and off.

As he came round the corner of a shed 200 yards from the bothy he almost collided with three men carrying tool bags and one, and this jarred oddly with him, slinging a sixteen-pound hammer. He almost said something then checked, thinking, 'So, what . . . fuckin' off early on the Fair. Who's checking?' Then he stopped, watching the three striding away, and began playing with his bottom lip. There was something about one of them, something that he certainly recognised.

He shook his head. So what was odd about that? But there was something . . . what, displaced? And that troubled him. He put it down to the first symptoms of Fair fever and began to walk again towards his bothy.

The three ran up the metal stairs, Stark leading, McKenna and McSwegan almost abreast behind, boots tattooing like hammers on the grilled metal. Hard and fast, Stark had said as they walked. Hard and fast, remember! Surprise. Maximum impact. Right through any resistance. They'll be too shocked to react. They'll be licking the wage packets and dreaming of bevvy. Keep shouting and swinging. Scare the shite out of them. No one is going to be a hero for the boss's wage.

They hit the balcony and burst through the door into a small lobby with a shiny wooden payment counter, a tombstone hole cut into the woven metal for the packets to be pushed through, and a padlocked, metal-framed mesh door leading into the back room where they knew the safe was. Stark could feel the roar of blood in his ears, his breathing coming hard into the white scarf he had bound over his mouth. 'Right,' he shouted, and stood aside. McSwegan swung the heavy hammer at the lock which buckled, then shattered at the second blow, the wire mesh sagging as they piled into it, McKenna whirling back round to face the stairs, in case anyone came behind.

Stark took in the two men in the room. Clerks, in striped shirts, cuffs rolled up, waistcoats, frozen in half stance. And a woman, young and chubby, mouth open, silently screaming. Pay packets all over the table, neat piles of notes, safe open. 'Down,' he roared, smacking his pit-staff club off the table, which sent up a flurry of notes like chaff.

The woman was gibbering as he pushed her against the wall. One of the two men moved too slowly and McSwegan felled him with the club he had pulled out of his belt, the big hammer discarded on the floor. The blow sounded like an axe biting into damp wood and the man sagged down untidily. They began pulling the sacks out from inside their boiler suits and stuffing the money and sealed-up pay packets inside. When the first sack was full Stark tied it off with the length of rope attached to a cork floater, then did the same with the second. 'Move, move, move,' he kept screeching.

A third bag was full now and as McSwegan continued stuffing, Stark bent down, picked up the heavy hauder's hammer, swung it and released it, like a Highland hammer-thrower, at the window looking out over the river, which exploded as the head and then staff turned through it, churning glass and wooden struts. Stark grabbed the two roped sacks and pitched them out of the window even before, it seemed, the last fragments of powdery glass had fallen to the floor.

One of the men on the floor was moaning, he could hear it quite clearly now, but whether it was the injured one or the terrified one he couldn't tell. 'Finished?' he screeched at the top of his voice. Then, 'Go.' The two pushed McKenna towards the twisted door and started to leave, holding the two remaining filled sacks. Stark was last to leave, looking back, checking, then turning when he heard a rumbling noise, followed by a grunt. McKenna was swinging his axe handle at someone. He couldn't see the face, just a bent shape trying to avoid the blow, then he saw a flash of light in his eye, like sun catching glass, and they were away and down the stairs, pushing past a falling shape, blood raging, feeding on the energy, feeling purely indestructible and running for the dock.

Peter was cackling to himself as he ran, hitting the wooden dock planks, feeling better than he had ever felt, not even considering the possibility that Tennant hadn't shown.

But the boat was there, Tennant was holding it with a boathook against the quay and Stark, before he chucked down the two sacks, checked that the first ones had been retrieved. They lay damply on the deck, still attached to their white cork floats. He aimed the two that he carried and they bounced off the deck and skittered under a wooden bench. He began to clamber down the metal ladder, wet still, hung with green algae and slime and joined the others.

McSwegan had ripped off his scarf and was hopping around screaming, 'Ya fuckin' beauty,' as the boat bumped into gear, clattered off the concrete dock then shuddered and stuck fast, the engine whining.

'You've grounded it,' Stark shouted. 'Stick it in reverse for fuck's sake.'

The boat bucked backwards, the engine howled alarmingly, but they remained unmoving, the black river churned to foam behind.

'Get on the ladder.' Stark pushed his way to the control panel. 'All of you. Quick.' The three men stumbled towards the ladder and climbed, all hanging untidily together, a prize crop, while Peter prayed silently under his breath, slipped the gear into reverse and gently moved the boat off the mud bank, scraping and tugging, then sliding free. 'Now jump,' he called over his shoulder, spinning the wheel round and engaging first gear. He heard a long crude roll of thumps and shouts behind as he gunned the boat forward across the river and when he looked back the quay was still deserted, but now someone had set off the cawing yard klaxon, which ships moored on the river, perhaps believing it was a signal for the start of the holiday, were deep-throatedly returning.

Chapter Two

The little bouncing ball tapped in time on top of the words as the song moved along. Belfast, thought Denny McEntee, probably the most stupid song ever written. Up on the small stage, no more than a half-step off the floor and about the size of a tablecloth, three girls were howling into the microphone. The one in the middle, who fancied herself as a bit of a chanter, spilled out of a leather waistcoat and tight pants, her pink, rubbery flesh oozing down under her armpits. Her hair was severely cut and crimped, brushed off her forehead so that little pimples of perspiration were beginning to form under the bright lights. She was taking it seriously, peering at the words and grinding at the same time, whereas her mates could barely stifle giggles as they clung on to her and hollered over her shoulders at the mike.

McEntee ran the blade of a knife across the surface of the Guinness, pulled the glass out from under the tap and planked it on the Formica bar top. 'Right,' he said, almost absent-mindedly clutching the handful of change he was offered, quickly counting it as he twirled to the cash register and slapped it into the drawers. 'Next,' he said, turning back to the few faces at the bar. No one moved or caught his eye. He sighed and began wiping down the bar. Thursday nights were quiet, he wouldn't begin to make any real money until after closing time when the doors were shut and the regulars got out the cards and the expensive drinking habits.

He finished mopping the bar and threw the cloth at the small sink, then heard the door creak and he looked up to see the patch of dying daylight outside and, in front, coming into the bar, Sean Harris with a girl clutching him. Another girl. 'Sean?' he said, nodding as the two reached the bar.

'Usual, Denny,' the man said, cuddling the girl with his left arm, hooking her into him like a trophy. 'Anne-Marie?'

43

'Rum and black.' She looked about nineteen, McEntee thought, maybe younger, sinfully so. She was tall, at least five eight, but that could be heels because McEntee could not see her feet. She had a big red mouth and deep, dark eyes which seemed calm and pensive. Gorgeous, he thought, fame always hooks them.

Harris was fishing into his pocket with his spare arm. McEntee could see this in the mirrored gantry as he jammed the two glasses under the spirits, and when he had turned back Harris was whispering something into the girl's ear and she was giggling dutifully, hopping from foot to foot. The barman took the Coke and the blackcurrant from beneath the bar, opened the can and poured some of it into the whisky and with his other hand fired a long sluice from the other bottle with the neck like a stork's into the girl's drink. 'All right, Sean?' he asked.

'Aye,' the man said, handing him a five-pound note. Harris was in his mid-twenties but looked younger, with a cherubic face and sober dress which gave him the appearance of a harmless building society clerk, apart, that was, from the long scar on his left cheek. 'Anyone looking for me?' he said, sipping his drink and casting his eyes round the bar. The giggling girls had given up on the karaoke and were now sprawled around a table in the corner, smoking feverishly, limbs splayed out at angles, malformed by the drink.

'No one's been in yet, Sean,' he said, ringing up the prices and handing back the change. 'Early.'

'Aye,' Harris said and the girl gave a yelp and squirmed, where he had probably nipped her. 'Anne-Marie's slumming it, mixing wae the low-life, aren't you, hen?' He pulled her to him again and she giggled. McEntee could see now that she looked stoned, that kind of vacant pleasantness in her eyes, her mouth in a slack smile. 'She's a student. You know what they say about students.'

'Naw,' he said, wiping his hand on a dishtowel. 'Nurses. Ah know what they say about nurses.'

'Well, she's a student nurse,' he said, winking.

'No, I'm not,' the girl said, snapping back from wherever she had been. 'Politics,' she said.

'Ah certainly know whit they say about politicians, mind,' McEntee offered.

'Shitebags. Here, have one on me, Denny,' he said, 'and that's what they call word association.'

'In that case,' said McEntee, 'I'll have a double,' and he took another fiver from Harris and rammed the figures into the cash register, 'and a chaser,' he added, punching in a few more prices. 'That's alcohol association.'

The Bon Accord was just off the Shettleston Road, a single-storey building which had previously had a tenement above, but that had been whipped off years ago like the top of an egg. Slum clearance was the claim, but the Corporation, as in hundreds of other similar cases throughout the city, did not have the money compulsorily to purchase and compensate businesses like pubs, so there they remained all over the city, exactly like the Bon Accord, topless, and usually in the middle of a gaunt wilderness. The families above the bar had been moved out to perimeter estates but they still filtered back to where they knew, to drink and often to live in even more inferior accommodation than they had been moved from. Trade had not even been particularly badly affected through this massive human movement, although this was hearsay as far as McEntee was concerned because he was too young to remember, and now there were sprinklings of new housing, private as against public, which were growing up in the clearance areas, the gap sites and barren lands where formerly there had been factories, schools and swing parks.

Inside, the pub was really just one large room, with a thicket of bamboo partitioning to form a lounge, little used, where prices were two or three pence dearer than in the main public bar. The bar was functionally decorated, diarrhoeic shades of gloss melding into the one dull nicotine colour, with signed pictures of teams and football players and minor celebrities now yellowing with age. The ceiling had been painted black and a large red fan, never called into use, was mounted in what had once been an elaborate rose in the centre.

Harris and the girl had made their way with the drinks to a table in the middle of the floor. The karaoke machine screen was still periodically bursting with colours and snatches of clips and words and bouncing balls. The three girls, McEntee noticed, were now clustered around one of the two one-armed bandits, jostling to feed its maw. They'd be off to the Barrowland soon he thought, or one of the clubs.

When his eyes turned away he noticed Harris signalling him, so he flipped up the hatch and walked across to the table. 'Sean?' he said.

'I forgot,' Harris said, his hand moving around inside his right-hand jacket pocket. 'For you.' He pulled out a small, brown package smaller than a cigarette packet, taped around, which he slid across the table.

'Brilliant,' McEntee said, palming it.

'The best blow,' Harris smiled, and leaned back in his chair.

'I'll square you later.'

'Whenever,' said Harris, smiling and taking the girl's hand evidently hoping, McEntee noticed, that his largesse would impress her, which it evidently had, from the way she began nuzzling into his right ear. I bet if he fuckin' shot someone she'd come on the spot, he thought. McEntee smiled back, put the package in his trouser pocket and went back to the bar.

The room began to fill over the next half-hour. Jinty, the bar help, arrived and the two were busy serving the small knot of drinkers so that no one paid much attention when the door opened, a man in a navy blue donkey jacket came in, quickly looked around and then went back out again. A few seconds later McEntee looked up from pulling a pint as a small indistinct shape trailing a green tail soared past his eyes, bounced off the wall above the karaoke player and then fell, fizzing dense lurid smoke in the corner. Instinctively he looked towards the door which was now open and he noticed the outline of a man holding something up in his right hand, as if offering it for inspection, which he then carefully rolled underarm in a long bowling motion across the floor. McEntee watched as it skittered across the tiled floor, disappeared between pairs of legs at the bar below his sight, then the groups break apart as Jocky Doyle screamed, 'It's a fuckin' haun grenade!'

McEntee felt his legs wobble, he stumbled away to the far end of the bar where he tucked down in the corner, squirming into the wall, hands over his ears, knees up, eyes tightly shut, waiting for the ripping explosion.

How long did it take? How many seconds? He cowered there, listening to the shrieks and the sounds of panic, trying to pray, his heart reverberating. Time was moving impossibly slowly. He opened his right eye slightly and saw that his face was pressed up against a stained and webbed wall. He waited. There was no sound now. He tried to force himself to count. He got to five and forgot and started again. Then from somewhere above he heard: 'You can come out now, folks. The gemme's a bogey.'

When he eased out of his crabbed crouch and painfully and tentatively put his head above the level of the bar Sean Harris was leaning on it, surrounded by wreaths of green smoke like some released genie, the grenade in front of him next to an ashtray and a small spill of beer and several upturned glasses, like an exotic bar snack. 'Notice' – he pointed – 'the pin's still in.' McEntee rubbed at his trousers, knocking off the sawdust, feeling embarrassed and humiliated. 'So,' Harris continued, 'either the demon bowler didnae see any John Wayne films as a lad, or this wisnae meant to go off.'

Out of the corner of his eye McEntee caught sight of Anne-Marie stumbling for the doorway. 'Outside,' he choked, pointing to the door, gagging on the smoke and his fear. The two men crunched and stumbled across the broken glass on the floor and through the knocked-about furniture out into the evening air, the green smoke billowing after them, Harris carrying the grenade with him, occasionally tossing it and catching it like a cricket ball. A hoarse sound, of retching, made them both turn. Along the outside wall of the pub they saw where Anne-Marie was huddled, throwing up.

'God,' said McEntee, his legs beginning to buckle, so that he had to brace himself with the wall behind him, the circumstances of his escape now rushing in on him.

'And I thought she was a lady,' Harris said, shaking his head disapprovingly.

McEntee looked round at him. 'You're actually enjoying this.'

'Well, it was a bit of a pointless gesture, wasn't it?' He was playing with the bomb with both hands now, running his fingers over its corrugations, toying with the pin. 'A total waste of kit. Second World War, it looks like. Pretty unstable anyway.' He flashed a mean smile. 'Mind you, this will play havoc with your trade, Denny, because you're about its only victim.'

'Fuckin' hell,' McEntee said, trying to push himself off the wall, his legs rolling under him. 'Second World War. It's probably rusted to fuck and ready to pop!'

Harris smiled again. 'Only kiddin'. Russian or East German, probably. Harmless. As stable as' – he grinned – 'a Russian republic.' He tossed it up again and caught it. 'Anyway, isn't it a total waste when you could be sticking it up someone's arse like a suppository and pulling the pin?' He looked along at the girl. The rain had started to fall lightly.

'Why? I mean, what do you think about it, a warning?'

'Dramatic, eh? Aye, I suppose so. The message seems pretty clear, by the way. Stop watering your whisky or the karaoke machine gets atomised.'

Anne-Marie had stopped throwing up and was now shivering and crying gently a few paces away. But it barely registered on Harris. McEntee had pushed himself off the wall and was feeling faintly and sympathetically sick. 'Come on,' he said, 'you know who!'

'Who else could it be?' Harris said, putting the grenade in his jacket pocket and moving to comfort Anne-Marie who shook off his touch and continued crying into her hands.

Now McEntee could hear the high, far-off sound of a siren. 'Polis,' he said. 'What am I gonnae tell them?'

'High spirits. Someone let off a smoke bomb.'

'But that?' he said, motioning at Harris's jacket.

'What? That never happened. A smoke bomb, remember. Maybe a rival publican, who can tell? Anyway, must be going,' and this time he gripped Anne-Marie firmly by the elbow and moved her away from the pub on stumbling legs.

They heard it before they saw it, a hee-hawing siren and a final belch of sound as it swung round the corner and grunted to a stop at the kerb opposite, between two badly vandalised, partially burned-out cars. It was red and yellow with huge puce writing all over, a feverish scrawl which could not be read through the weeping condensation of the car windows. The rain blew in, huge gusted lumps of water, movie-set torrential, as if blown along by a wind machine and a director's whim. The car smelled of wet bodies and machine oil, there were three men inside, two in the back, the driver rubbing at the glass to make a porthole in the mist and condensation. He could see the ice-cream van across the street, children and bent grown-ups, with jackets, newspapers and scarves over their heads, skipping towards it over the puddles and sticky mud, two wet dogs barking and running behind.

'See they dugs,' the driver said, looking out, mouth twisted to talk behind him. 'This film ah seen, it wis a robbery, and they all gave themselves different names, 'know, to protect their identities?'

'Right' the voice from immediately behind, 'you can be Mr Whippy.'

The other man laughed.

'Naw, I wis thinkin'—'

'Don't. Just sit there.'

'You can call me Pokey Hat,' the other voice said. Then: 'What's that dish called? That ice-cream thing you put in the oven.'

'Baked Alaska,' the other man said and the two in the back began laughing. The driver shrugged his shoulders and continued to look out at the van. 'What's funny?' he said.

'You'll see,' a voice said.

After the laughing stopped he heard two doors slam and he watched the two figures, huddled up in their dark jackets, heads bent against the rain, meet in front of the car and then trot across the street. Baked Alaska? he thought to himself. What the fuck was that all about?

The two reached the van and one, the taller, joined the end of the queue. The driver lost sight of the other man as he disappeared round the front of the van.

The queue was about ten long, but the last man didn't bother counting it exactly as he picked up the rear. His hand was inside his jacket, the glass warm in his hand. He could feel the rain running down the back of his neck and he shivered as the droplets slid under his collar and down his backbone. Come on, he thought, hurry up. The young lad serving the ice-cream and fags was alone, which was good. No sense in involving others. He took a couple of steps forward as the queue shuffled. The ice cream guy was in his early twenties, long dark hair flicked back off a bony face; he was handing over a bottle of lemonade and then his hand went under the level of the counter and pulled out what looked like a small packet which he palmed across the counter.

The inside of the van was lit, the glass was dotted with decals of Disney characters, and as he shuffled nearer the glass window the last person looked up and noticed that on top of the van there was a large polystyrene replica of an ice-cream cone.

He felt a touch on his sleeve and he looked round. 'Okay?' he said.

'All done. Nae problem.'

They both shuffled a couple of steps nearer the van. 'Him' – he nodded towards the van – 'we'll call him Harry.'

Another couple of steps. 'Harry?'

'Aye.' He grinned and turned to his colleague. 'Houdini.'

'What?' A pause for a few seconds. 'Aw, right' – a guffaw – 'ah get yi.'

There was only one customer in front of them now, a boy of about eight who handed over a piece of paper and what looked like a five pound note. The lad inside the van scanned it briefly, pulled an empty wafer box from the side counter, slipped a sheet of white tissue inside and began delving into the ice-cream tub with a scoop. The two men stood, occasionally looking at each other, as the order was filled. After two or three minutes the man handed down the box to the lad. 'Hold on, son,' he said and then dropped a handful of change into the jumble of inverted cones and cellophaned packets. Then: 'Yes, gents?'

'Oysters,' he said. 'Do you have any oysters?'

'Sure. How many?'

'Three,' he said. And he noticed, as the ice-cream man began to pull out the wafer cups, that he had the love and hate tattoos on the knuckles of heavily nicotined fingers. Maybe he would forget the ices. He turned. 'Okay?'

'Absolutely.'

'Tickety-boo is it?' A nod. Then: 'Now would be a good time.'

The other man quickly unzipped his jacket and pulled out the gun, a sawn-off shotgun; the ice-cream man, intent on smearing ice-cream into an oyster, did not look up.

'Ahem,' he said loudly and now he did look up, blinked, and then stumbled back, dropping the ice-cream scoop.

'What?' he said, his mouth sagging open.

The first man, the one who had queued, looked away from him, conscious of movement behind him, and saw an old woman wearing dark stockings, torn slippers, hunched inside a bulky cardigan moving slowly towards the van. Her head was down, picking out the puddles to avoid.

'Hey, Grannie,' he shouted. She stopped and looked up. 'Fuck off out of here before I confiscate your pension.' She took a half step forward, saw the two men, the gun, and wheeled on her heels and staggered off, ignoring her feet splashing into the muddy puddles.

When Pokey Hat looked back to the van the ice-cream man, ludicrously, had both hands up like in a bad B picture. He shook his head and smiled. 'Heap big trouble for the covered wagon,' he said, pulling out the bottle from inside his jacket. The other man was holding the gun in one hand, resting the foreshorted muzzle on the counter, aimed at the ice-cream man's groin.

'Listen,' the man said, visibly shaking, 'I huvnae goat much. Twenty quid maybe.'

The first man shook his head and placed his bottle on the counter. 'Firewater', he said. It was a whisky bottle, three-quarters full of a bluish liquid. Then, 'Excuse me for a second.' He walked round to the driver's door, pulled out a lighter and flicked the flame alight. He held it to the lock for several seconds, just in case the Superglue had not properly hardened, then walked round the front to the other door, where he repeated the procedure.

'Right,' he said, back at the serving window 'on your knees, eyes covered, arse in the air.' The man disappeared from sight. He picked up the bottle, pulled the small plastic bag from his pocket, opened it and stuck the soaked wick in the neck. He transferred the bottle to his left hand, pulled out the lighter again, fired it and nodded to his colleague. They both took a couple of steps back, and then the second man fired both barrels into the van, glass, lemonade, shredded paper and shattered wafers and cones blowing out of the back window opposite.

The wick was flickering brightly as he hurled the Molotov cocktail inside, towards the cab of the vehicle where it shattered in a blazing fire-storm. The two men took several more steps back as the blue flames took hold, the second man fumbling in a trouser pocket before ramming two more shells into the gun.

They heard screaming from below sight level and then a flaming hand appeared, as if appealing for attention, and slowly the man himself, clothes on fire, hair burning and crackling, flesh beginning to blacken and flake, although perhaps that was wishful thinking. He tried to pull himself out over the counter, stumbled and fell back, then slowly, losing energy, managed to throw himself across the counter where he slowly and untidily tumbled down on to the pavement.

As they stood a few paces away they could hear moans from the burning mass on the ground which, with one last summoning of energy and hope, recomposed into a human shape, got on to its feet and then tottered forward a few steps before pitching face down again. The flames were quieter as the fragments of clothing burned off.

'Well,' the first one said, glancing at the blue burning body, then at the gunman. He took a few steps towards the fire, rummaged in an inside pocket and produced a silver flask from which he took a swig, then poured a thin stream on to the smoking shape so that the fire roared back into life. He corked the flask, put it back inside his jacket and smiled, rubbing his hands and holding them out to the heat. 'Much better,' he said. 'That takes the edge off a chilly evening.'

In the car the driver had been feeling much better about himself and the world. The nervousness had gone and a warm wellbeing was spreading through him, pleasing pulses of reassurance. He smiled at his reflection in the oblong rearview mirror and ran both hands through his short hair, which sent tiny shivers of electricity through his face and head, helping to cut through the drowsiness which was beginning to rise. The small blue fire in the corner of his eye caused him to turn round to look at the van, the blurry colours and kaleidoscopic shapes through the droplets of water on the window. He took in two slow shapes moving towards him, big and lowering, then the muffled drum raps of doors closing, the car shifting and settling.

'Move!'

The driver reached for the ignition key but it slipped out of his damp grasp. He groped for it but somehow he could not make a pincer movement with his right hand, which caused him to smile again.

'He's fuckin' out of it.'

'Jesus, where did ye get him?'

'Let's just get the fuck out of here.'

The gunman jumped out of the back seat of the Mondeo and pulled open the front door, pushing the driver over into the passenger seat. He slammed the door behind him, turned on the car's ignition and leaned across the sprawled shape to the other door.

'No, not yet,' the voice from behind said.

The car slewed off in a wheel spin, clipped the edge of the pavement as it took the corner then corrected and tore away.

'Hand it over,' the fire-raiser said. 'The gun.'

The new driver rummaged in his inside pocket with his right hand as he steered the car with his left and then passed the sawn-off over his right shoulder. 'Fuckin' junkie,' he said, as his eyes came past the man in the passenger seat. 'Are ye gaunnie dae it here?' he said, his voice rising.

''Course not.' The car had almost reached the Round Toll. The man with the gun, who was dark-haired, slightly chubby and looked to be in his late twenties, put his hand on the shoulder of the man driving. 'Slow it. Don't attract attention. Do a right here. Up the Garscube Road.' The Mondeo made its way towards Maryhill Road, passing the end of the road leading to Firhill, where the floodlights were on. 'Towards the canal.'

'Fuckin' junkie,' the driver said again, lashing out at the other man with his left hand.

When the car reached the abandoned lock system on the hill it bumped across the rail tracks and broken glass, over the wet mattresses, pushing the old supermarket trollies and rusted tins and pram skeletons out of the way. The two men got out. The air smelled singed with the tang of recently extinguished fires and the rain was heavier again now. 'Fuckin' junkie,' the new driver said for the third time, 'now we're gaunnie huv tae walk.'

'Ah'll treat you to a taxi,' the one with the gun said. He sighed and opened the driver's door again. The third man was still in a spill against the other door. 'Next time I'll bring a short,' he said, leaned into the car so that both knees were resting on the driver's seat, put the roughly cut barrels against the recumbent man's backside so that the metal was lost in the folds of his trousers and pulled the trigger. 'Didnae want brains all over the hair gel,' he said over his shoulder. Then he walked round to the boot of the car, unlocked it and pulled out a petrol can. He splashed the petrol in a circle round the car then emptied the remainder over the front seat and the body, then pitched in the empty container. Standing back, he checked that he had none of the petrol on his clothes or shoes, then took another step back, pulled out the lighter and lit the petrol on the ground.

The two men began to walk smartly, but not too conspicuously although there was no one to see, towards Maryhill Road. They could hear the crackling of flames behind them but neither so much as looked back even when, about a quarter of a mile further on, they heard the dull crump of the petrol tank exploding.

'I could murder a pint,' the man with the gun said.

McQuade gazed through the fronds of plastic palms which separated the news room from the classified advertising department. There was always a changing and usually pleasing cast of young women; the ruthlessness with which those deemed failures were dispensed with intrigued him but also provided him with continuing prospects of his own to be picked. Today, however, he could not see anything tempting, although the jagged headache, distorting vision and vague queasy feeling in his stomach were certainly a pretty powerful sexual appetite suppressant.

He had loosened his tie and tucked his crumpled white shirt into some shape in his trousers and his jacket was slung over the back of his chair. He rubbed his face wearily and looked at his dark reflection in the computer screen, ruffling his unruly hair into rough order, then he drained the last of his coffee and punched into the system, calling up the wire services and began to sift through the city's and the world's woes.

The running story was the ice-cream van fire but he could not see anything advancing what he already knew on the screen, just disappearing lines of colour, interviews with eye-witnesses – myopic to a man and dog – and tearful gushings from relatives. He yawned. Then he punched his way out of the wires and, putting in his own password Wragg, called up his personal screens and directories. He went first to the police section and found the name he was looking for, confirming the number which was nagging around in his head. First he dialled the direct line at Strathclyde police, his man wasn't there, then the home number. The phone purred in his ear as he waited.

'Mmhmm?' a voice said eventually.

'Harry?'

'Mmmm.'

'I woke you.'

He heard sounds of moving, a slight cough and then the voice, more alert now, said, 'Who is this?'

'McQuade,' he said, beginning to yawn himself now.

'Fuck!' Then, 'What do you want, as if I didn't know?'

'Words, Sergeant. Theories. Speculations. Whatever you have.'

'Listen, it's the middle of the fucking night for me, you bastard.'

'Crime never sleeps, you should know that, Harry,' he said, grimacing into the mouthpiece, trying to visualise the bemused anger at the other end of the line.

'It'll cost you.'

'Absolutely.'

'Give me an hour. And make it the Aragon.'

'See ya,' said McQuade, hanging up.

He looked at his watch. Almost two. Then stood up and unhooked his jacket from the back of the chair and put it on, the heavy right pocket bumping his hip bone. Reporter's sidearms, he said to himself. Not that he was going to need either the tape-recorder or notebook, this would be a conversation which never took place but which, none the less, would certainly be tangible when he claimed expenses for it.

He cast another glance over the plastic vegetation and walked towards the door, muttering to the back bench as he passed. 'Chasing up the fire,' he said. 'I'll call,' tapping the inside pocket where the phone should have been, but wasn't. That was another thing he would have to do today, construct a plausible excuse for its loss. He could try ringing the number, he thought, as he pulled open the door into the lobby, to see if anyone answered. But then again, why bother?

He sat at the usual table and arranged the drinks in front of him in the usual disposition. He was on his second beer, a cold Pils, which was beginning to take the hard angles off his hangover. The newspaper, the early *Times*, lay on the banquette seat beside him. The story hadn't advanced a jot. Big pictures of the burned-out van and then, a few pages in, another picture of a fired-out car, copy about an unidentified body in that one, but no link between the two. Even in this city, he considered, two pyres in two cars in the one night was unusual and demanded more than being separated by acres of intervening garbage about cleaning the Clyde or trading standards seizing counterfeit videos in the Barras.

He took another pull on the bottle of beer. Something vaguely country was playing on the juke box. He tried not to let it seep in. Why did everyone here want to ride off into the sunset, he said to himself, or have it come to them chemically induced? Well, the answer wasn't in the last chorus. Probably it was all to do with that stuff they put in the water? Or because they didn't, he wasn't well up on the fluoridation debate. He looked up, becoming aware of a presence.

'Ah,' he said, 'lawman. Sit down.' He waved his hand and then pointed at the table. 'Firewater. Heaps. You choose.'

He had bought two double whiskies and a glass of mineral water. Ricketts sat down on the chair opposite and selected the water. 'You sound like Wee Plum. And I never drink in my sleep,' he said. 'What is this cowboy crap anyway, McQuade?'

The music had changed to something fast and jangly now. 'Just musing,' he said. 'Have you noticed how everyone here is playing a part—'

'You and me especially,' Ricketts cut in.

'It's probably the water, or Connolly, so much to live up to.'

'Are you drunk, McQuade?' Ricketts looked over his glass at him. 'Are you ever anything but?'

'No. This is the firs – only the second of the day. Sorry, Sergeant. I'll shape up. You can depend on me. I won't – sorry, slipping into another part there.'

'Drama queen,' Ricketts said, putting down his glass. He was dark-haired, cut in a close crop, with a narrow face and what seemed like a permanent sneer – he liked to credit the laughter lines – to his mouth. He wore a faded blue denim jacket over a baggy green crew neck and battered jeans and trainers. He was twenty-eight years old and had known McQuade for most of them.

'I'm doing a pilot for a TV show for cable. It's a sort of low-rent version of those real-life American cop shows. You know, drugs, bodies, prostitution—'

'You'll be at home.'

'—and, of course, a profound moral message.'

'Oh, obviously.'

'It's going to be sponsored by an alarm company.'

'Not the Church of Scotland then?'

'I said profound, not po-faced. And, of course, when they thought—'

'Moral,' Ricketts came in, 'they immediately thought of you. Look, this is all very interesting but if you got me out of bed to boast about a burgeoning TV career I can probably do you for something like wasting police time.'

'Do me in the cell.'

'That, of course, is *de rigueur*. No extra charge, unless of course you defend yourself. Then it's police assault.' He drained the glass and leaned across the table. 'Enough of the badinage. What the fuck do you want, McQuade?' he said very slowly but with great emphasis, then held up his hand, palm forward. 'And nothing, please, about life or love or the pursuit of happiness.'

'Grumpy,' said McQuade. 'Talk about getting out of bed on the wrong side. Well, I'll start by drinking these,' and he drained the first whisky. 'The ice-cream fire. The two fires. Tell me it all.'

Ricketts shook his head and smiled. 'Don't you have any other contacts?'

'I've always gone for the best, Harry. Why waste time with the rest?'

'Doesn't everyone know?'

'Evidently not.'

'There's nothing you can print.'

'I have a large space waiting, Harry, with your fingerprints all over it. Go on.'

Ricketts shivered, shook his head, and then beat McQuade's hand to the second whisky. 'Well, that was a short night,' he said. 'We know everything, almost everything. And there's nothing we can do, no corroboration.' He took a sip of the whisky, then shuddered slightly. 'Cooking,' he said, looking at the glass. 'Here's the sketch, fill in your own characters. Once we've studied the teeth and dug over the charred bones we'll be able to put in the faces. But it goes something like this. The ice-cream van was a cover. They were selling heroin, jellies—'

'Who?'

'One side or the other. Stark or the Blackhill Team. Once we've done the dentures we'll know more. Anyway, assume for the moment it was Stark's van. The other lot roll up. One of them sneaks round the back and Superglues the locks while the punters are queuing for the pokey hats and then bang, whoosh, off you go, torch, ya bass, the fiery furnace! Then it's back into the car and off for a bevvy.'

'Just like that?' McQuade nodded. 'But there was another car and a body?'

'Ah,' he said, 'that one. Stolen. Maybe it was the motor the lads used to take them to the bonfire. If it was, no one is saying, naturally. But it's likely. It fits. And that,' he said, picking up his glass and draining it, 'is that.' He nodded with his head towards the bar.

'Yes, right,' McQuade stood up. 'And?'

'And what? Who cares? Victimless killings. Bad guys topping each other. I could drink to that, if I had a glass.'

When McQuade came back with two glasses of malt Ricketts sniffed and then smiled. 'Better. So?'

'So, it's a range war. It's pleasing to know the polis are doing fuck all about it.'

'Back to the moral message, is it?' He leaned forward. 'I didn't say we were doing nothing about it, I said we couldn't do much about it. By tonight we will probably know exactly who did what to whom and why but we won't be able to do much about it, Scots law being so unreasonable as to demand corroboration. So unless we get some numpty with a death wish who witnessed it to come forward I don't suppose we'll be making very many arrests very quickly. It's the times we live in, you know.'

'What exactly is happening then?'

'The usual suspects routine, roust a few, try and spook and cook them, visibly trail them, try and rustle up some decent rewards for touts, write reports, dash around in circles, etcetera.'

McQuade's demeanour was much improved now, with the fumes of Laphroaig and the scent of a story in his nose. 'My line is that this is part of the drugs war—'

'The polis are pursuing several important lines of enquiry.'

'Naturally. Two Glasgow gangs battling for control of the lucrative drugs trade.'

'Strangely perceptive.'

'Ice-cream vans have been the cover to vend the stuff to the young people in the schemes?'

'Didn't come from me of course.'

'What about the supply, where's it coming from?'

Ricketts laughed and tossed back the drink. 'Where not? From America we're the first easterly point of sale for crack and coke. From the south we're the last, coming in through Spain, through the ferries, transporters or the tunnel. Who's checking? It starts in Colombia, Burma, Afghanistan or wherever, or in thefts from chemists. Supply is most certainly not a problem. And the quality is good. When there is competition the junk is very pure, classic capitalism, hence the record number of ODs, the blissed-out kiss-offs.'

'You've sold me,' McQuade said, sitting back on the bench. 'Where do I get some?'

'*You* need to ask *me*?'

'Look,' said McQuade, gazing round the bar and finding it lacking, 'do you fancy going somewhere else, maybe getting something to eat? On me, of course.'

'I'm tired, McQuade.'

'Me too. A leisurely meal, a few drinks, maybe a sauna – a strictly old-fashioned kind of place, I wouldn't want you to be compromised naturally – and I'll send you home in a taxi.'

Ricketts shrugged and shook his head. 'Aren't you meant to be working?'

'I am,' McQuade answered. 'Do you think I would eat and drink with you if I wasn't?'

'Well, at least we understand each other.'

'Christ, McQuade,' Sandy Bell the news editor shouted at him as he belched past, 'it's less than an hour to deadline. Where the fuck have you been?'

He checked and turned. 'Good one, Sandy.'

Bell looked up at him from the desk from behind his large screen, waiting. He was bald, although he was still in his mid-thirties, running to fat, his belly straining at the limits of the striped shirts he habitually wore. 'Good one, as it's a fair cop, boss, or as in story? Well?' he said. 'Elucidate.'

'That ice-cream van in Barmulloch. It was running drugs, supplying heroin and temazepam and anything generally injectable along with the fags and ginger. It's been happening all over the schemes, apparently. Someone took exception.'

'Vigilantes?' said Bell, leaning back in his swivel chair, smiling and clasping his hands behind his head.

'Hardly. There are two gangs in competition for the trade . . .this was, you might say, part of a rather provocative dissuasion policy. One lot torched the other. One poor bastard got the Indian exit, the petrol and the twigs. Or maybe it was Twix?'

'Lovely. Who did who?'

'Whom. I'll know by the final edition, not that we'll be able to run the names. But the Starks are involved, and a breakaway outfit called the Blackhill Team. They,' he said, switching to a portentous, mid-Atlantic accent, 'are killing each other out there.'

'Excellent,' said Bell, lurching back to his screen. 'We'll call this one the Ice-Cream Wars.' He slapped both hands together and began rubbing them. 'Get to it, maestro. And remember, heavy on the fear and sense of public outrage.'

McQuade saluted with his hand as he began walking towards his desk. As he passed the secretary's desk he stopped and leaned over. 'Marjorie, love, could you get me all the cuts on the Stark family from the library, please. It's a bit urgent.'

He ignored her oath and the two-fingered gesture and slumped in his seat, pushing away the slurry of cups and papers so that he could reach the keyboard. Then he took off his jacket, turned and draped it over the back of his seat and logged on. He thought for a minute or two and then began typing.

Chapter Three

Hazel Dundas was waiting impatiently under the clock at Boots' Corner where she had been dumped, the two big suitcases immovably beside her. She could see across the road to the railway bridge running over the Hielanman's Umbrella and to the billows of dark smoke which hung over it as every few minutes another holiday special rollicked away. The city was on the move. There was an air of happy purpose, people weren't meandering, except for the drunks doggedly clutching their brown paper pokes filled with whisky, screwtops and Eldorado. Two men in their early twenties weaved past, one – presumably the less drunk partner – the custodian of the carry-out, the other wearing a woman's floral headscarf.

'If you've got the tickets ah've goat the time,' the one in the headscarf shouted at her as they stumbled on. His mate two-handedly cuddled the carry-out even more tightly. She smiled thinly after them and thought, If he didn't have such rotten colour sense I'd be tempted.

A couple of minutes later Carl arrived panting beside her. She had seen him dodging and juking through the crowds towards her, waving, but she pretended she hadn't. He was nearly half an hour late.

'Sorry, hen,' he said, trying to grab and kiss her but she scolded him away.

'You know that we've missed—'

But he put his fingers over her lips and said. 'Hazel, listen. You'll have to go on ahead – no, listen, I'll get a later train. There's something I've got to do.' He looked wild and distracted and she wondered if he had been drinking but there was no odour about him. She started to protest again but he wheeshed her. 'I cannae explain now. I'll be down later. There's just someone I have to see.'

63

He had his hands on the cases now. She started to say, 'But I can't possibly go alone,' but he wasn't listening and he had hefted the two large bags and was making towards the Central in big, waddling steps.

'We'll put these in the left luggage and I'll collect them later,' he called to her. She scurried after him trying to say, 'What is this all about?' dodging the people coming the other way, bumping, apologising, but he wasn't replying. When they got into the station concourse with the big polished shells and mines from the Great War gleaming, and round which winching couples and the deserted gathered, he stopped and put down the cases. His breath came in rasps as he took her by the shoulders and looked up into her face.

'You are so beautiful—' he began to say but she shook off his hands and said, 'Don't try to flannel me, Carl. What is going on? I cannae just go off on my own.'

His head was shaking wildly and he was laughing. 'Look,' he said, digging into his pockets, 'take it,' pulling out a sheaf of notes from his trousers. 'There'll be plenty more, now – from now on,' he said and then hugged her. 'Just trust me.'

'What's happened?' she said. A few feet away a Sally Army band was beginning to break raggedly into 'Onward Christian Soldiers'. 'Where are you going?' she asked him.

'I have to see someone. To make an arrangement. To fix up our future. When I get to Brodick I'll buy you a new dress, dinner at the best restaurant – I don't know.' He stumbled out of promises. 'Maybe we can even buy a house for ourselves when we get back.'

Have you been—'

'No, honest, not a drop.' He laughed again. 'And, no, ah've not been hit by a fa'ing rivet or anything. Something's happened. I'll explain it later. Promise.' He kissed her quickly on the lips, although she tried to turn her face away. 'Now', he lifted the cases again – 'the left luggage.' The two of them moved off to join the queue, her reluctantly, past the gaggle of competing paper-sellers with the billboards and headlined evening papers, not even seeing the splattered news of the raid, or hearing the barkers calling, 'Here-ah-final *Cit-ee-zen*. Read all aboot-ah Pirates Sink

John Broons . . .' 'Polis launch hunt on yard raiders,' came in the man from the *Times*. 'Clyde wage raid – latest! Cashier fights for life,' screamed the *Bulletin*.

Razzle Dundas was thinking, as he shuffled forward in the queue, This evening I will either be sailing doon the Clyde, wae a lifebelt of money, or floatin' face doon in it.

Even in the raucous smoky haar, through the knots of men laughing and shouting at each other in a release fever, their celebration was conspicuous. McKenna and McSwegan had burst in first, grabbed each other and started to waltz through the throng, kicking up tiny billows of sawdust, while Stark and Tennant organised the drink. Malts and pints.

'And after,' McKenna was saying, now a little breathless.

'What, after the high-steppin' horses and the fallen women?' Tennant was motioning for another order even before the first one had been downed.

'After the painted ladies . . .' He paused and chewed on the large glass in his hand, then looked up. 'Naw. Along with the painted ladies and the suits for every day of the week and the silver cigarette case, I'm going to buy a seat in the directors' box at Parkheid.'

'A box? You could buy every brick and stick and Tim and blade of fuckin' grass at Parkheid.' McSwegan slapped him on the arm, spilling half of the drink on to the discarded copy of the *Evening Times* on the table, the large blow-up of John Brown's on the front page slowly turning to sepia in the damp. He touched Stark's arm, leaned forward and, in a stage whisper, 'How much is there anyway, Peter? Exactly.'

Stark sat down with an exasperated sigh and leaned back in the booth ignoring the question, the mottled, stained glass in the partition behind him framing his head. He was smiling distractedly, still coming down, feasting on the feeling, the roaring in the ears of raw adrenalin, the sheer omnipotence.

'And cigars,' McKenna was going on, waving a new glass in his right hand. 'A foreign holiday. England!'

Stark leaned forward and picked up his new glass.

'A distillery,' Tennant chipped in.

'I've always wanted to taste champagne. I wonder where ye get it.'

'About a thousand miles from around here.' Stark smiled and put down his glass untouched then glanced, a finger to his lips.

'I'll collect it personally,' McSwegan was bouncing around his seat. 'How d'ye go about getting a passport, d'ye think?'

'It's easy, just enlist.' Stark waited until the laughter was failing then held up his right hand. 'Calm it down. Or the rest of this Fair and the next few to come'll be spent hunkered down over chanties at the Bar-L.'

'How much does a car cost, Peter?'

Stark drained his glass and slammed it down. Then again. 'Why don't we just all get up on the fuckin' bar and take a big bow? Eh? "You've just read all about it in the papers . . . and now before your very eyes and hot from their last appearance in the cashier's cage at John Brown's . . ." Eh? Or maybe we could get our own wanted bills printed and paste them up all over Crown Street? But then again, why go to all that trouble? Just flashing a few fivers around is advertising enough, isn't it?' No one said anything, waiting for him to go on. 'Christ, none of us is working and here we are talking about a buying binge. Do none of you think?'

The other three looked grimly embarrassed, none of them taking even a sip from their glasses.

'Before you've spent everything,' he said at last, 'don't you think we better consider maybe holding on to a bit, putting it somewhere, investing for the future?'

McKenna looked at the other two then winked. 'I understand. Brilliant, Peter. A bank! I love it. So, is it guns, chibs or dynamite?'

Stark waited for the uneasy laughter to die. He looked around at them. 'I hate to be the one to introduce reality to the proceedings . . .'

'Jesus, Peter, reality's the hangover in the morning.'

'I'm serious, by the way. We are not going to start flashing cash around. It's staying hid. With me. In just a wee while the polis will be all over here and four unemployed lads who have suddenly come into good fortune are going to be just a bit suspicious. No?' No answer. Sullen looks. 'You'll get a bit week by week—'

'Just like the buroo,' said McSwegan, unable to take Stark's eyes. 'So, is there going to be a means test or what?'

'—and the rest will be invested. Simple. Any objections?' He looked around the table seeing none, only resentment in the eyes. He thought of the blades in his pocket, hoping they wouldn't be necessary. Not here, anyway. Not today. Not in public. He tried to reach all of their eyes in turn, to face them down, but they were avoiding him. There was no mood for challenge. 'No?'

He sat back. This was triumph. He thought that all he wanted was just quietly to let it all sink in, taste what it was like after the leaping excitement settled away. Just relish it. The silence grew. Strange, when he considered it, none of this had really been to do with the money. He hadn't even thought about how much there must be, hadn't begun to count it. The joy was in the execution, that mixture of fear and blurring movement and anticipation and trepidation, exhilarated release, like an explosion of emotion too quick and complicated to understand. Like orgasm with your eyes open, he thought, and grinned to himself, while the others looked across at him now, reading relish in that fleeting smile.

'Invested? In what?' McKenna asked eventually.

'I'm glad you asked that, Kevin.' Stark was coming back now, looking around, checking no one was close, then waving towards the bar for more drink. He waited till four doubles had arrived, carried carefully on a tin tray by Nipper, then he tossed a pound note on to the surface where the golden rings still glistened, and recklessly waved away the change. 'There's more than one way to rob a bank.' He touched the new glass to his lips, breathed in the peaty scent, then tossed it back. 'To the people's bank,' he said, as the hot hail went off in his gut.

'The what?' McSwegan said, the first to break the pause. 'I don't understand.'

'Banks. They lend money. Yes?'

'Not to the likes of us.'

'Exactly. That is the point. Where we come in. We will. To the likes of us.'

'You're talking about moneylending?' Tennant asked 'You want to stake a loan shark business?'

'Better the shark you know.'

'What about the competition?' McSwegan was fumbling in a jacket pocket for cigarettes.

'You mean McGinty, Aldo Wright and them? Are you serious? We'll just explain the benefits of merger – in an exemplary kind of way, if you follow. Maybe I could send round Devanney to sketch in our business plan, eh?' He could almost feel the razors in his pockets thrum with life. 'Then we'll buy up their books, at a reasonable rate.'

'Peter,' McKenna said, grinning 'you're' – stumbling for the word – 'infamous.'

'Thank you, Kevin,' he said. 'I'll take that as a compliment. Partner.' He smiled and leaned back, stretching his arms out. 'Junior partner.'

It's only a matter of time, Razzle thought as he cut his way through the clamour of slower-moving pedestrians, occasionally nodding to a greeting from someone. A process of elimination. I know how these people think.

He had lost count of the number of bars he had been into, the red-faced, stumbling, clutching, sprawling, spewing drunks he had seen on his way. In the morning the kids would be playing hopscotch around the vomit patches. Three weeks' wages, he said to himself, it's like an annual bequest. More money in one pay packet than they'll see in a year, until the next Fair comes round.

The city was spinning down now (and so were many of the people) like a huge turbine; the factories had closed in a cacophonous stramash of hooters and whistles and jeers and those who could afford it were beginning the evacuation to Ayr and Rothesay, Dunoon and Millport. And Arran, of course. He thought guiltily about Hazel, imagined her standing in a crowded corridor as the train swayed and stuttered for Ardrossan, then dismissed that, realising some young lad would have certainly given up his seat for her, was probably even now hanging over her ear, chaffing away, which brought out an aching roll of his gut.

He pushed open the door to Herraty's, screwed up his eyes against the boiling smoke, and edged into the bar, beginning to move around the circumference, shuffling through gaps in the pack, glancing over at the tables for the face. *Stark*. He remembered him well now. From the Tripe, and in the street so many times but, memorably, inextricably linked with his older brother Johnnie who liked to call himself the Razor King.

He snorted to himself and stopped, considering what he was doing. It was foolhardy, crazy, but although he could feel pangs of anxiety there was, too, a reckless abandonment in him. Zeal. It was almost religious. The next few hours would alter his life, perhaps end it, he reminded himself cautionarily, but he was irresistibly drawn forward. What this was, he told himself, was fate.

Now his mouth was dry as he looked across at the bar, at the stirring mass of men's bodies in dark jackets, boiler suits, bunnets, and he began to push himself towards a pint. When he had at last got it in his hand, the glass clammy with the overflow, he turned back to the room, put his right boot on the foot-rail and, taking a deep gulp of the creamy cold beer, scanned the faces around him. He recognised some of them, although those he did seemed to avoid his eyes. Maybe they had some sense of what he was about? That was stupid. It was probably just that he stood out, better dressed, in a suit, that they wanted nothing to do with reminders of work and hierarchy now that they were on their own lasting time.

Stark was sitting in a corner booth. His face came swimming out of the fug as he turned to call for an order from the bar, oblivious to anything but his own necessities, Razzle thought. That would shortly and utterly change. Dundas smiled across the bar at him, which wasn't seen, and raised his glass to that forthcoming fate of his.

He sipped on the beer and waited, the roar around him having died to a buzz in his ears. It didn't take too long. He had not even got halfway through his glass when he saw Stark get up and saunter through the groups of drinkers to the toilet. Saunter? More of a self-satisfied swagger, Razzle thought, throwing back the rest of the beer, wiping his mouth with the back of his hand and pushing off across the floor.

Through the noise of talking and arguing he could hear the rattle of faint music and he paused, wondering at it, before he realised that it sounded like accordions, brass, the heartbeat of a big drum, and with the jangling percussive intrusions of badly syncopated tambourines. The Band of Hope or the Salvation Army, touring the pubs to pick up the guilt gelt from the turned-out drunks, the men walking back to their houses or onwards to the shebeens. Jesus wants me for a sunbeam, he thought, not knowing where it came from, some kind of crazy word or event association; then, what he had been thinking suddenly dawning: – Oh Christ, I hope not, begging your pardon, Lord.

'Peter,' he said as Stark came out, the odour of urine wafting after him.

'Aye?' He could tell that Stark did not immediately recognise him but knew him from somewhere not yet placed.

'Twice in the one day. Imagine that.'

'What?' Stark was narrowing his eyes, getting him into focus, flicking over his face, trying to put a context to his form.

'Seeing you. Twice in the one day. What a coincidence, eh?'

'Is it?'

'Not really.' He was smiling, standing his ground, blocking Stark's way back to his table, no way round without physically removing him. He tried to maintain the smile, keep his hands in vision, not look threatening.

'What is this?' Stark's right hand was moving down towards his right hip. Just like Tom Mix, Razzle registered, knowing what was there. 'Who are ye?'

'It isn't coincidence. Not really. More like double good fortune, Peter.' He was aware of the battered religious accompaniment getting fainter, the ragged band moving off. 'I've come to add to your blessings.' And he folded his arms in front of him.

Stark's hand had stopped. It hovered. For the moment he was unsure of himself. 'It's Fair Friday, pal, no' Good Friday. Are you a priest or something?'

'No.' Razzle shook his head. 'I'm not a priest. Far from it.'

'The second time today you said, right?' Razzle nodded. 'So where was the first? When?'

'I don't live too far from here. I've seen you about – well, you're well known – you, your brother. And at the jiggin'. The Tripe.'

'Look,' Stark said, moving towards him, putting out his right hand to push him aside, looking past him, 'I'm in company.'

'That's right.' Razzle nodded, refusing to budge. 'The same company as before, earlier.'

Stark stopped, his hand on Razzle's shoulder, his face coming slowly and reluctantly back to look at him. Eventually he looked into his face (don't show fear, Razzle told himself and, when he thought about it, he realised there was none), then slowly dropped his hand.

'You're not the polis either, are you?'

'That's right. I'm not.'

'You're not the polis. And you're not a priest. You pray though? You had better, pal.'

'No, pal' – he echoed and emphasised the last word challengingly – 'it's the other way round. He died you know. The lad that tried to stop you. He was only an apprentice, Hughie Devine. Maybe he thought he'd get a bonus from the yard or something.' He let it sink in. 'That's the rope, Peter.' He let his right hand move fleetingly to his throat. 'You see, I was thinking that what I could be – I could be your saviour here. Your only chance actually. Because I'd say that without me you are facing – what? – eternity. Without remission. Mind you—' he let the words hang in the smoky air '—I don't expect you to go down on your knees or anything.'

He could see the hesitation in Stark, the uncertainty about whether to strike out or to listen. He had banked on him not being too drunk, or stupid, having the sense of self-preservation to hear him out, and it looked like he had been right. Just. 'I've got a sizeable drouth on me. In fact' – he grinned and put out his right hand, palm up, offering it – 'it feels like 2,000 years since I had a decent drink. Come on, I'm on the bell.'

He left his hand out. Stark glanced at it, whether searching for stigmata or in contempt of the gesture he couldn't be sure. 'You better be good,' Stark said, pushing past him. 'You better be better than good. You better be the fuckin' best.'

So far, thought Razzle, I am.

The train had stopped somewhere in Ayrshire, Hazel couldn't be sure where exactly, but there were green fields and cows passing judgment and she imagined that she could hear birds sing through the thick glass of the carriage, which all added up to Ayrshire for her. A young lad had given up his seat, chivvied by his mates. He had been drinking, his mouth looked wet and slovenly, and he hung on a strap leering biliously at her every now and then. She kept drawing him black, shrivelling looks but he would simply raise his eyebrows, shrug his shoulders and swing on his hook.

She felt very conspicuous, a woman alone, one without luggage. My baggage is still at home somewhere, she thought, still boiling inside. She could feel everyone in the jammed carriage looking at her, although they almost certainly were not. That couple over there with the child with the scabby knees, the men in the grey and blue rough Sunday best suits, the scarves and caps, holding holiday fags, not the normal Woodbines, the air blue and grey whorls. She felt the smell of tobacco on her and wondered what the landlady would think when she turned up alone, unencumbered, reeking of sweat and smoke and embarrassment.

She flinched and fiddled with the clasp on her handbag, her right hand going inside to grasp around for the paper she had bought at Central. She pulled it out, it was concertinaed by folds and it slowly uncurled as she dropped it in her lap. Her skirt was tweed and the lining had ridden up on her left leg so that the starchy fabric scratched at her bare flesh above her stocking, causing her to rub and itch at it.

'Christ!' she said, looking down, taking in the headlines on the *Bulletin*, hearing a guffaw up above her. She ran her finger along the column of type, as if she had to press down the words to make them real, so that she could believe.

'Got away with thousands,' she heard, and it was the boy on the strap, swinging around again, grinning, nodding at what she had been reading. 'Nae holidays for the lads at Broons,' he said around his gormless grin.

But it wasn't that. She clenched her lips, knowing somehow that Carl was involved and she felt a rush of excitement which was almost sexual.

'Outside,' Stark said, pushing at Razzle's elbow. 'Quieter.'

'I don't think so.' Dundas was still watching for the hands going to the pockets as they moved through the drinkers together in a watchful stand-off.

'Who are you?' Stark leaned into Razzle's ear.

'What do I want?'

'That's obvious.'

'Dundas, Razzle Dundas. Half and a half okay?' They were at the bar now and Dundas was glancing away. 'You and your chinas over there, you visited me today. Where I work. You didn't see me right enough, but I recognised you, placed you eventually. And' – he fired a brief smile – 'traced you eventually. Although that wasn't too difficult.'

'This is too public,' Stark said, glancing around.

'I like that.'

'The others will be wondering where I've got to.'

'You'll be able to reassure them. Say you bumped into an old friend.

'Some friend.'

'I can be.' Dundas had caught the sleeve of one of the barmen. 'Two Bell's and two heavies. It's up to you. Or the other.'

'I don't know why I'm even listening to you. I know what you're after.'

'No,' Dundas said, shepherding the drinks across the wet walnut bar, 'you think you do but you're not sure and you're right to be – unsure.'

Stark was swirling the whisky in the glass, reluctant to accept the relationship, or perhaps it was that what he was considering was sticking it and grinding it into Razzle's face. 'Look,' he said, mind apparently made up, and downed the whisky, 'what's your price? If I was paying, like.'

Dundas moved in so that their bodies were almost touching. He was slightly taller than Stark and his mouth almost brushed the smaller man's left ear. Stark noticed that he smelled of shaving soap and he wondered again why he was wasn't opening these smooth cheeks, bloodying that three-piece suit and starched white collar. But he knew, as his brother never did, that there would always be time for that.

'I'm convener there,' Dundas said in his ear.

'That's nice. And so young.'

'Engineering. And branch treasurer.' He stood off a little, so that he could look into Stark's face. 'Have you any idea how many engineers there are on the Clyde?'

'Is this a union quiz or is there some point you're trying to make?'

'I'd like to live in a nice place . . .'

'Won't your sort have all the best places, brother, come the revolution?'

Dundas swayed back, as if buffeted by the words and Stark could see the whiteness round his mouth as he spoke. Tense. 'Decent area, you know . . .'

'Wally close. Nothin's too good for the workers.'

'Maybe even a wee garden.'

'Of course. Roses, a strippit lawn, bowlin' green nearby, churches of all persuasions around, dog-shiteless parks. What,' he said, putting down his glass, 'has any of that got to do with me?'

'You're' – he moved in close again and whispered – 'the way.'

'I know, the truth and the life.' Stark pushed him in the chest and back against the bar, jarring the arm of an adjoining drinker, splashing beer down to the sawdust.

'I recognise lots of men from the yard in here,' Dundas said, ignoring the protest from beside him. 'They'd be really pleased to know who it is that's delayed their holidays for them, held up their wages.' He saw Stark's hands move somewhat hesitantly towards his pockets and he saw him mouth at him, You are a dead man.

'Thousands of engineers, I said, all looking forward to their annual break. All paying into the holiday fund as well as paying their union dues week by week, all of that money flowing like – well, like the Clyde. Inexorably. And through *my* hands.' He held up both hands and slowly opened all of his fingers.

Stark looked at Dundas without blinking, against the pageant of noise and then brought up his two hands, both men beginning to smile, then engulfed Dundas's with his own. The purpose had become apparent and appealing. When he had finished, he said, 'Not a working man's hands.'

'Not any more. A banker's more like, wouldn't you say?'

Dundas began to shake with laughter.

That sweet and sour taste of kisses. He always associated kissing with that, the layered, souring smell of the old backing the newer, brighter taste of the biddy. He hadn't known what it was until, like everything else, he learned it in the street. Tam McPhail, from up the next stair, three years older and even at that age, which would be about ten or so, he seemed to be muscled and hard. Tufts of vicious black hair where it wasn't cropped into the skull, a wide bobbed nose, shirt sleeves rolled up past the elbow whatever the weather, which was always wet and dreich in his memory. Johnnie had seen his mother come and go to the corner, the constant jug, and hadn't thought anything about it. Hadn't even begun to wonder about the discolouration of her teeth, that laden closeness.

'Heh, Stark,' McPhail shouted across at him from his perch on the kerb where he was close in to the pitch and toss school. 'She's away again.' He looked blank. 'Yir mammy's off for her tea.' He heard a ripple of reluctant laughter from the huddled group on the pavement and from the tinge of embarrassment he knew that in some way they were laughing at him.

'Does she pee the bed? Ah'll bet she does.' McPhail was walking towards him now, emboldened by the laughter. 'Eh?' McPhail pushed him in the chest, sending him scuttering back against the dull sandstone wall. He felt his eyes begin to prickle. 'She does, doesn't she? Eh, what about you, you too? Wee pee the bed. Ah'll bet yir hoose mings, doesn't it? Biddy and peed sheets.'

Johnnie's mouth was open but there was nothing he knew to say, none of the words had been learned, only the tears which pricked in his eyes. He looked around for escape but McPhail pushed him hard against the wall, jerking his head back, cracking it against the rough stone. And in spite of himself the tears came.

'Pees like blood, does she? Aw that wine.'

'Don't—' he started to say.

'Dis she gie ye a swallie now and then?' Johnnie tried to move off the wall but was pushed hard back again. He was looking around desperately either for escape or assistance but McPhail blocked the way. 'Naebody to help yi now. Nae big brother, uncle or auld man. Nae wonder he's never around. Who'd want to be around that?' He jerked his head away towards the close, or the corner but for just a moment, in the movement, he was diverted. The sneering lack of attention combined with the opportunity, Johnnie drove his head into the side of his mouth and began flailing at him with his hands, the hot hatred driving out the shame of the tears. McPhail

75

staggered back and Johnnie noticed, even through the blurred, wild
and staggering close-ups, that he was bleeding from the mouth. And
he felt roaring joy, even as McPhail recovered, drove at him, sending
hard, heavily senior punches into his face, knocking him scrambling
back off his feet on to his hunkers then birling away as the feet came
at him, big black scuffed boots adorned with tackets which got larger
and louder until they faded slowly away.

The pitch and toss school must have broken it up. He came back
looking up at large concerned faces looking down at him, hands
pulling him to his feet, a babble of voices out of which he could
only make out the one line over and again: 'He's only a wean.'

A hand was running though his hair, another fussing with his
face, brushing at his mouth and eyes. 'You're never gonnae be a
movie star, son, except maybe Lon Chaney. But the bits are more
or less where they should be.' He recognised the face peering into
his but couldn't put a name to it. Somehow it fitted that he worked
in one of the yards, he knew that, perhaps just from talk he had heard
or it could have been the memory awakened by the smoky, metallic
odour of his overalls. 'You're gemme, son, no doubt about it. But
next time pick on someone your own size.' The man smiled, pulled
out a grimy rag from his pocket, licked a patch of it and rubbed at
his right eye. 'You're gonnae have some keeker there, pal.'

He tried to smile, join the conspiracy but the pain hit him and
he winced. With his tongue he could feel that he had lost a front
tooth and his mouth felt thick and harsh. He spat out a gob of
spittle which spun away bright red. As he looked around he could
see McPhail a few paces away, two men beside him, grinning back
at him. He felt giddy and sick and ashamed as he got up but he
tried not to show anything as he wiped at his eyes with both hands
and then brushed away the man's arm. 'I'm all right.'

He could feel his right eye throbbing now and as he touched it it
felt huge and foreign and as the swelling grew it hooded the vision
so that the earth seemed diminished and tilted.

'Put a cold cloth on that, son. Tell your maw, now.'

He nodded his head, bit down on his lip and began moving
unsteadily towards the close. The pains made him stop on the
first landing, his ribs ached as he walked and he had to breathe
back the sickness which threatened to erupt. The walls of the close

shimmered as he sat down on the step to wait for the nausea to pass. His hands cradled his head and when the sickness began to shift he slowly climbed the stairs and gingerly reached the door which opened on the turn and he shuffled in, head turned to the outside, hoping that his mother wasn't in, or was lost in inattention or, as he now realised, in drink.

There was no slurred call from her and when he looked around the small room was empty. But he knew exactly what he was going to do although to his surprise he began to sob uncontrollably.

The tears which seemed inexhaustible scalded his sore face but finally stopped and when they were over he splashed his eyes and washed away the salty traces and the blood, compressed his bad eye with a dish rag and after a few minutes, when the water ran clean and his eye felt numb, his hand scrambled for the cupboard drawer.

He had to wait for the rest of the day, until after the lamp lighter's round and until the fiery constant sunset of Dixon's Blazes lit the night sky. Johnnie was shivering, he still wore the same blood-flecked torn pullover hanging over the baggy dark shorts. His hands were inside the pockets of the trousers and he was huddled in on himself in the close mouth, hunched against the cold and crouching over his aching ribs. The street began to fill again as the weans came out after their teas and raucously renewed the pandemonium. The rain fell like dark spots of treacle so that the pavement seemed to smoulder and swim in the lamplight. Men were also beginning to emerge from the closes, tying scarves at their necks or puffing on cut-off fags lit in cupped hand as they paused briefly before sauntering away towards the pub or the dance hall, the gambling school, the night class or some furtive assignation.

Johnnie's eye was shut to a slit and it throbbed with a regular steady pulse but it seemed that it had stopped swelling. His bladder too was aching, his chapped knees he could feel throb with every shuffle he made, which was better than the state of his feet, which he couldn't feel at all. He just wanted to curl up in bed and sleep. His nose ran but it hurt to wipe it with the back of his hand. And then he saw McPhail swinging under the street light, talking to two boys of about his own age, what he was saying lost in the thrum of the street. Johnnie eased himself off the wall and out on to the pavement, hands still in his pockets, bending over as he walked, trying not to wince with the pain.

When he looked up McPhail had stopped and was staring at him, a sneering smile wide on him, hands on hips. 'Back for more, Stark?'

Johnnie noted the dried blood on his lips and the blueing of a bruise on his cheek. He wanted to smile but he shook his head and kept his eyes down.

'What then?'

Instead he shrugged and pulled up a couple of paces before McPhail.

'Your maw's passed out and ye want a hand, eh? Drag her intae bed?' That laugh in the voice again, joined by titters. Johnnie shook his head. 'What then?'

'I've got something for you.'

'Yeah?' McPhail's head was going from side to side, to his companions, checking out that his superiority was being adequately noted. 'What's that then?'

'Fags,' Johnnie said, looking down at the wet pavement, feeling the rain prickling on his bare neck.

'Well, hand them over.' The bigger boy was sneering at him again, right hand outstretched. 'Well?' he said again.

'Right,' Johnnie said, sighing a little. Then his hand came out of his right trouser pocket as fast and as hard as he could manage, which was sufficient, a dull arc in the thrown gas light seemed like a shiver of gold foil. McPhail's hand remained where it was for several seconds, demanding, even after the second frenzied swipe of the knife sliced through the wrist arteries and blood fountained high over him. As he instinctively grasped at it with his other hand the blade began arcing and worrying towards his undefended, bending and screaming face.

He felt very calm after it, in a bubble of silence while everything around him canted crazily. First he turned away from McPhail then walked slowly to the corner, no one even moving to stop him, and then, around it, he started to run, still clutching the bloody kitchen knife like a spear, the blood pounding in his ears, criminal energy surging through him, his lips curled back in laughter.

When he stopped, breathless, he realised that he had to get rid of the knife. Somewhere near the river, the night now dark and comforting around him, he put it down a stank, not a very original disposal, but then he was not really expecting to get away, just complicate the detection. He felt that he had somehow swelled and grown and as he began to walk more calmly, surprised that he no longer registered the pain in his body, the recent adrenalin of violence having anaesthetised the old, not even starting to consider that there was no remorse in him. McPhail had deserved it. It wouldn't have happened if he hadn't attacked his ma like that. He had brought it on himself.

Outside a pub he stopped and sat on the bottom step leading up to it. In the leery light from the door he could see that his right hand was sticky with blood. He rubbed it on his jersey and then wiped his running nose with the back of it, thinking about what he would do now. Later, he would want to remember this as his first mature decision.

It took three hours to find Peter Stark. He was eventually traced to a shebeen in Caledonian Road with McSwegan and McKenna and a gaggle of women, all blurred with drink. The man who eventually came over to Peter was familiar. Peter recognised him as Albert – the name had gone – Someone from the next close. He was holding his cap and was worrying at the skip of it with both hands, like he was going through the rosary.

'Well,' Stark said. The girl, Jinty, was saying something in his ear; it slurred and it annoyed him. He pushed her away and she slumped disjointedly on the bursting sofa.

'I'm sorry, Peter,' Albert Someone said, 'it's your lad. Well' – he caught his sentence – 'John.' Peter noted the proper, grown-up name and realised that something serious followed. 'He's in a bit of trouble.'

Stark unwound to his feet. 'He's hurt?' In the edges of his vision he could see McKenna and McSwegan bunching up from their entanglements expecting trouble but he made a waving motion with his left hand, sending them off duty again.

'No. No.' Albert had cut himself shaving, Stark could see, and it was a recent cut, still wet and Peter wondered if the hurried shave had been for him. 'It's the other way round. He's hurted Gus McPhail's boy – you better come.' He felt a tentative touch on his arm.

'How? I mean, what happened?'

'I don't know. A chib, I think. You'd better come and find out exactly.'

'Polis?'

They were moving out of the door, the smell of the tobacco air changing to the cold dank touch of the close. 'No,' Albert was saying into the side of his face, hand still on his arm, and for once Stark bore the intrusive closeness of it, 'at least, not yet. McPhail's taken some talking out of it. The boy's pretty bad,' he added in case Stark should be concerned, but he made no indication of it, just shook his head to himself and bit on his cheek, flexing the facial muscles. 'They had to take him to the Vicky with his ma and there's no knowing what she'll be saying to the doctors and nurses.'

Not even a childhood, Peter Stark was saying to himself. But there were, too, the warming flickers of pride.

When Johnnie eventually went home the streets were deserted. The rain seemed to smell of soot and burned wood. He climbed the steps with a wearying sense of inevitability. At first he felt, then could actually see, the yellow square of light in the thick glass pane over the door. He took a deep breath and then knocked as firmly as he could. As he waited he heard the high sounds of hysteria being silenced with deep barks of command. His father. It energised him, he felt defiant now, taking deep regular breaths to enforce it. The door swung open, he looked up at his father, a halo of light from the mantle illuminating his head and casting dense shadows over his face so that the boy could not read his mood. As if he needed to. His dad did not speak, merely moved over to allow him to come into the hall. He noticed his mother, hair in tangles and spirals, face wet and bloated, holding her hands to her stomach, sitting slumped against the table, a dark red glass at her reach, head shaking in incomprehension, sobs escaping and Johnnie felt nothing now but contempt. If he only had himself, hate would sustain him and be a needful constant.

When he turned he could see his father. He was wearing a striped, collar-less shirt, dark serge trousers, heavily belted and buckled. He waited for him to undo it but all he did was thrust his hands into his pockets. It was evidently more serious than a beating.

'Well?' Peter Stark said.

He shrugged, wanting to look hopelessly at the floor, but he kept returning the stare, determined that he wouldn't cry.

'He nearly died, you know. You cut an artery. If that nurse in 23, Jean—?' He looked at his wife for the name but she just shook her head and sobbed. 'She put a tourniquet on his arm. His face, Christ, what a mess. He's in the hospital. Tell me, son, why? Son, why?'

He knew he could say anything to his father and he would believe it but he remained silent, not even when his dad drew back his hand, then stopped and instead took him under the chin and said, peering at his face. 'Did he do that to you, son?' Not even then.

Chapter Four

He was known as Fat Boy, but never to his face. He picked up the paper and began to chuckle. His breakfast was still on the tray; he briefly glanced at the newspaper again, smiled, folded it carefully and put it down beside the metal tray. Then he slid the plate of bacon, eggs and black pudding off it and the chunky brown mug of tea and cutlery.

'Seen it, Kenny?' he said, sitting down at the metal table. 'The news.'

The man opposite, in his mid-twenties with dark, lank hair and a deep red scar down his left cheek, looked up, chewing. He gulped and then nodded. 'Pure mayhem. Never know the minute, eh?'

Fat Boy speared the yolk of his fried egg and moved the point of his knife around in the spilling yellow, torturing it. 'Aye. Mean streets. Makes you fear for your life.'

Kenny put down his knife and fork and dragged the newspaper across the table, scanning the front page. Then he looked up and smiled. 'If I were you I'd pack my asbestos underwear before you go.'

'Or I could just pass on the ice-cream.'

'That'd dae it.'

Fat Boy was about the same age as the man across the table, but taller and he was running to fat which made him look older. His nose had been broken some time in the recent past and he too had a scar, a white crescent over his right eye, the end of which cut through his eyebrow and across his eyelid, making it appear as if he were permanently mid-wink. It gave him a cocky look, arrogant. He liked it. It had come from a bottle, smashed hard into his face, but he had just managed to duck sufficiently and throw up a blocking arm so that the cut, while it passed a lot of blood, hadn't been too deep, only requiring about thirty stitches. It had been unexpected, there had not been the usual gradations of tension, and he had been almost caught out. But, although his instinct had let him down, his reactions had saved him. Fortunately there had been no follow-up – well, that wasn't quite the case, no further blow, but as he reeled away clutching the torn flesh and blinking as the blood blinded him, he heard a grunt, like a body punch being landed, a groan and then the slow roll and scatter of glasses, plopping explosions and the reverberations from bouncing furniture. When he looked back through the blood the guy, he couldn't remember his name even now, was on his knees, hands holding the handle of the long knife which protruded from just under his diaphragm. His mouth was trying to say something. And then he slid sideways, his right hand coming out to steady himself but it crumbled under his weight and failing strength and he collapsed on to his face.

'Thanks, lads,' he had said, before going into a jacket pocket, his other hand holding the edges of the wound together, pulling out his own chib and cutting through the carotid artery below the right ear of the fallen body.

'Love a black pudding,' he said, grinning at Kenny. 'Aw that blood and guts.'

'A curry, that's what I could murder. Chicken vindaloo, Bombay tottie . . .'

'A gallon of lager.'

'Goes wi'out saying. Nan breed, pappadums.'

'Pakora.'

'Don't, you're killing me.' He put down his knife and fork. 'Have wan fur me, eh? Saturday night. Let me dream and drool about it.'

'Strange thing to wank over,' said Fat Boy.

'The Shish mebbe. About ten on Saturday, eh? So's ah can think about it while you're diggin' in.'

'Ah'll save you a doggie bag.'

'Aye. Post it. But on Saturday night wae a bit of luck and the wind in the right direction ah'll catch the fumes.'

'Yi want me to fart as well?'

He picked up his knife and fork and sighed. 'Lucky bastard, by the way,' he said, chopping into a sausage.

'Ah'll treat you, shortly.'

'Maybe you could bring the menu. I could tape it up on the cell wall as a keepsake.'

'You mean you want to plaster the Rogan Josh all over Samantha Fox's tits?'

'Aw, don't,' Kenny said, between chews, 'you're getting to me.' He swallowed. 'I wis thinking more of the cucumber raita fur Sam. And lickin' it off, like.'

Fat Boy leaned over his plate and chucked his partner under the chin. 'If it means that much to you, my son, I'm sure I could slot in a Ruby on Saturday. I'll gie you a bell when I'm there, describe it chew by chew.'

'Brilliant.'

'Masochist,' said the other man, sawing into his egg.

After they had chewed for a few minutes, saying nothing, Kenny pushed his plate away, went into a pocket and came out with a packet of cigarettes. He broke open the packet, took one, leaving the opened packet facing the grinning man on the other side of the table, then took out a lighter, flicking it into flame. He stared at it for a few seconds, then shivered. 'What a way to go,' he said, lighting his cigarette, drawing, shaking his head and displacing the blue air.

'Think of it positively,' said Fat Boy, his mouth full, beginning to splutter. 'It's a perfect preparation for what's to come in the place they're gaun tae.' Both men gurgled across the table at each other in the hazy smoke.

He came to through strands of sleep like filaments of seaweed, shaking his head and coughing. The phone was ringing. He swiped at it and pulled it to him. The bedside alarm clock showed 4 a.m.

'Jesus Christ,' he said, 'it's the middle of the night.'

'For you, maybe.'

He recognised the voice immediately. 'You're getting your own back, Ricketts.'

'Absolutely.' McQuade could hear the chatter of voices in the distance.

'So, is that it?' His eyes were raw and his mouth felt parched.

'Some information.'

'Well?' he said. 'Don't spin it out. You're loving this, aren't you?'

'You might want to check with the Scottish prison service about the likely whereabouts this coming weekend of everyone's most wanted, Stark Junior.'

'How do you mean?' He was having difficulty placing the pieces his memory was dredging up into any coherent pattern. 'He's still in, isn't he? He's got – I don't know – a couple of years still to do?'

'Yes? Just ask the Scottish Office prison spokesman where he's going to be this weekend.'

He ran his free hand through his tangled hair. 'Christ, Ricketts, don't be coy. Anyway, the fuckin' Scottish Office is less talkative than a closed monastic order. All you get is the ritual crap about never commenting on individual cases. Just tell me.'

'Have you heard about the training for freedom programme, or whatever they call it?'

McQuade thought, pictured some dense type in the mist, then shook his head. 'Vaguely. Isn't it some sort of job skills thing?'

'Hardly. Stark's got all the skills he'll ever need for his particular job. No, you get time out, chances to spend weekends at home, socialisation, reintroduction to the outside world again, all of that psycho-babble bollocks.'

'That's crazy.' The wonder of it had wakened him totally. 'So he gets to go out to the pictures, for a shag, a bit of blow, blow the heid off someone . . . ?'

'Enlightened, isn't it?'

'A chance to look at the books, set up a few more deals.'

'Nah, he does that on the mobile.'

McQuade pulled the phone back from his ear, looked at it as if to confirm to himself that he hadn't heard wrongly, wasn't dreaming. 'You're not serious?'

'Almost entirely. Of course, he isn't allowed a mobile phone inside. That would be completely wrong, an insult to the taxpayer, wouldn't it? He actually uses the prison telephone box and a supply of phone cards. He's on it for hours at a time.'

'I don't believe this.'

'How do you think he keeps the drugs running? Checks the prices, seals the deals, arranges the ambushes?'

'Hold on a sec.' He took a couple of pulls from the glass of water beside the bed, sluicing his mouth. 'You're saying he arranged the ice-cream killings?'

'Certainly. Can't prove it, of course.' The noises behind Ricketts had become louder. 'Listen, I'll have to go shortly.'

'Don't you tap the fuckin' phone?' McQuade said animatedly, feeling his astonishment rise.

'What do you think? You don't think they speak openly, for Christ's sake?'

'Naw, don't tell me.' McQuade was shaking his head. 'Not code? For God's sake this is pond life we're talking about, they can barely blow bubbles to each other.'

'Wrong,' said Ricketts. 'Don't underestimate them. Look, I have to go. Anyway, I'm nearly out of units.'

'You're in a call box?'

'I would hardly call from my desk, would I? That would be clever. So that the man who looks at the print-out of the call numbers checks against the list of well-known deviants and dissidents, like yourself, and immediately leaps to the correct conclusion in this case.'

'It's a police state, Harry,' McQuade said, smiling. 'Welcome.'

'Just check out Stark. Follow him, track him from the gates. Buy him a pint. Doorstep him at home. Ask him if he's torched any ice-cream vans lately, that kind of thing.'

'Ricketts, do I tell you where to shillelagh your suspects? Just leave the award-winning journalism to me.'

'That's another one you owe me.'

'Bye,' said McQuade. 'You know, sometimes your selfless esteem for the truth amazes even me.' He hung up and began reaching for the water again when he felt something slither along his thigh. 'Christ!' he screamed and jumped out of bed, slapping at his naked leg and stood shivering on the carpet peering back in the dark at where he had come from.

'Talk about playing hard to get,' a muffled voice said from the vague tangle of his bed.

His heart was going like a Buddy Rich drum roll, he took a deep breath, tried to sort through the blurred recent memories in his head and said slowly, 'I could have had a heart attack.' And then: 'I must know you?' For some reason, either embarrassment or self-protection, he had both hands cupped over his groin, like a footballer in a defensive wall awaiting the free kick.

'Biblically? Well, almost,' she said. 'I think the languors, or the lagers got you, just before the parting of the Red Sea.'

Just my luck, he thought, pulling a comedian. 'Sorry,' he said. There was a dull ache at the base of his spine and he was beginning to shiver. 'Is it all right if I get back in?'

He heard the rustling of material and took this to be a yes. He inched towards the bed still, for some reason, holding himself. I would switch on the light, he thought, but I think I would rather not know for certain the depths I have plumbed.

As he slipped under the duvet he could feel the heat of her and it began to arouse him.

'You really don't remember, do you?' There was amusement in her voice he could tell. He shook his head in the dark, turning towards her now, beginning to run his hands over her body, which felt pleasing and slim – although undulant in the right places – to the touch. She put her arms round his neck and pulled his head down next to hers, so that he could just see the milky outline of her face on the pillow as he slowly moved his hand downwards from her stomach. 'But I'm still holding you to the promise. You know, to help. With the operation. Tangiers.' His right hand froze as his fingers touched the edge of her pubic hair. She giggled and he moved his hand again slowly, and safely, southwards.

'Was that an alarm call?' she said after a few seconds.

'I suppose,' he said, 'that it was really.'

Jean McRobbie was completely unaware of the moment when she slowly moved from being a person to a statistic and then a record. The day had opened in the familiar cramps, the blurry awakening on the mattress in the small and dirty back room in the seventeenth-floor flat in Springburn. She felt sick and sore, fumbling for her soiled clothes, ignoring the smell and the slick, dirty linoleum as she walked barefoot to the kitchen, ran the tap and fumbled for the container. One tablet left. She bit on the Valium and craned her head under the tap, turning her mouth to take the jet of water, swallowing the bitter crumbs of the drug. She was naked, her clothes bunched under her left arm as she drank, shivering as she did so. Above her a bass note was pounding on the floorboards, or the concrete membrane separating her from the couple above. When she had finished drinking she did not bother to wash, stumbling into the grey white pants she had been wearing all week, then the skimpy denim skirt and the torn tee-shirt, followed by the holed jumper. She tried to remember where she had left her jacket, wondered briefly if she had sold it, chastised herself for being stupid, the jacket was worthless, and finally decided to forget about it. Her shoes were in the completely empty living room with the screwed-shut windows and the soaring views over the city to the south. She stubbed her feet into them and then tried to remember where she had left her bag. She found it after a quick search in the bathroom, the contents strewn around the pan. Why had she tipped it out here? She could not remember. Perhaps someone else had? She shrugged, stuffing the items back in, checking her purse. Twenty pounds. Just enough. When she stood up with the bag, a khaki Second World War haversack, she glanced briefly in the mirror but failed to recognise the wild passing reflection. Her limbs were aching horribly, she shivered so much that her vision seemed blurred but she managed to stumble back to the kitchen, collect up her works and stuff them into the bag. For a moment there was a flare of panic, that she had lost her keys, but she saw them on the greasy surface next to the caked cooker, the one pan where she had cooked the stuff still on it. Trembling, she stuffed the keys in her pocket, bounced back along the corridor and out, pulling the door behind her, making for the stairs, knowing that the lift would not be working.

She caught a taxi in Gourlay Street, gave the driver the destination. He shook his head but said nothing and booted the cab. Stoneyhurst Street looked like it had been the epicentre of a major confrontation. Derelict, boarded-up buildings, blocks of grey-stone tenements partially demolished, children picking over the rubble, a few slow-moving pedestrians shuffling up the hill. She asked the driver to wait, paused as she opened the door, asking him if he wanted a quick one for the price of the fare but he shook his head in even greater disgust, pulled out his *Daily Record* to read, after first checking that all the locks were on. She found it hard getting up the six steps to the close mouth, the pains were worsening, so she stopped on the third one hoping that it would abate slightly, but it did not. She would need to buy more Valium. Then she climbed the remaining steps, pushed past the two look-outs at the mouth of the close and made her way painfully to the boarded-up, first-floor landing, to the steel-reinforced door which she hammered on until she heard a shout behind and the grinding sound of bolts being removed. She had her purse out now, the money trembled in her right hand, two fivers and a ten pound note, nothing left to pay the driver. No problem. The lad who opened the door had gelled, short-cut straight black hair, a baggy top, two gold earrings, but she took nothing in about him. Neither did she notice the man behind who held the sawn-off shotgun. She passed over the money. He smiled. 'Yir lucky,' he said, 'we've got a new batch of really good gear. Dead pure. Magic.' She thought, shut the fuck up and give me it, but she gave only a brief, cold smile and nodded, agreeing. 'Yir lucky day.' Again, she thought, shivering.

He flicked the money out of her fingers and stuffed the greaseproof paper bag in her open hand. 'Enjoy,' he said, slamming the door in her face. She sagged against the wall, suffused with exhilaration, then opened her bag and pushed the packet inside. Then, after a long sigh, she hoisted herself off the wall and walked unsteadily back down the stairs to the cab. The sky was a deep washed grey and the rain had started but she did not notice. She was entirely focused. 'St Enoch Centre,' she said as she got back inside.

'Yi goat the money?' he asked.

'Aye,' she said, looking down at her bag as the car stuttered quickly away and towards the city centre. Only when they got there did she tell him she had lied. She knew that all the doors were locked and she could not get away but she had a proposition. 'Ah'll get you a leather jaiket; ah know where to get one easy. Ah'll be back in fifteen minutes.'

'Nae chance,' he said, 'ah'm getting the polis.' She shrugged, knowing that he would not, that he would make a counter-proposition. 'You could do a favour for a pal' he said. 'It's his birthday.'

Only then did she remember that it was hers too, that today she was seventeen. 'Aye,' she said and the car kicked into motion again and began heading for Clyde Street.

It pulled up along from the High Court, in the taxi garage. The driver got out leaving the engine running, locking the doors, then after a few minutes came back with another man. The doors opened and the second man, who was bulky and bald and looked to be in his fifties, got in the back beside her. The cab lurched, made a tight circle, the guy beside her said nothing until it pulled up again, when he said, 'Down,' pushing her on to her knees, the rubber nodules on the floor digging into her already sore knees. He was unfastening his trousers and pulling out his cock and as she slid it into her mouth she heard what sounded like rain above drumming on the metal, not realising or caring, that the taxi was in the car wash. Now he had his hands over her ears and although she could hear very little she knew from the rapid motions and his squirming that he was about to come. She tried to pull her head away but he held her firm and her throat flooded with semen and then almost immediately he pushed her roughly back so that she sprawled on the floor. The rain had stopped. 'Should have washed her,' she heard a voice say above her and then a laugh. The cab was moving backwards, for just a few yards, then it pulled up again, it canted slightly and then the door opened and someone else came in, she couldn't tell who. She was aching worse now, her bones trembling, and she was trying to crawl into a defensive ball. Hands grabbed her and roughly pulled her up, turning her and forcing her head down on to the rexine of the back seat. Her legs were lifted from behind, pulled apart and she felt a tug at her waistband and then a rip as her pants came away. A hand was rubbing something wet and slippery over her arse – only later in the toilet would she discover it was engine oil – then a finger roughly entered her anus, then a second. Then she heard a sigh, felt a heave as his cock went in. He seemed to take forever, one hand on her head holding her face in the plastic, the other occasionally adjusting his aim, then he gave a shudder and pulled himself away. 'Anyone else?' she heard him say as she lay there, waiting, but no one else came.

She was thrown out, falling on to the wet gravel, her face grazing along it. Painfully she got up and began to hobble away, making for the shopping centre. With a bit of luck she might be able to grab some jewellery, a CD or two. Her imagination soared as she counted the possibilities of what she might steal, the money she might make, the stuff it could buy. But she was dirty and soaking, aching and shivering, and first of all she had to shoot up.

The escalator took her to the first floor and she stumbled the few steps to the big, perfumed, bright and clean toilets, to the cubicle, where she locked the door, took out her lighter and the little flat tin spoon which said Greetings From Rothesay on the crest, which had been – she didn't know what you called it exactly, but the thing you put a tea strainer in. The drug looked like a small discoloured snowdrift, as if covered in a sodium light. She tipped some into the tiny pan, took some water from the toilet, rummaged for her lighter and began the cooking.

When she had the works ready she paused for a moment in anticipation, then she pulled up her skirt and plunged the needle into the abused vein in her naked groin, smoothly pushed the plunger of the syringe, the chemical rush hitting her before she could even sit down, but some remembered movement took her back on to the seat. He wis right, she thought as she slid into unconsciousness, it is ma lucky day. The warm purity was glorious.

Six hours later, when they started to lock up the centre, two female security guards pounded on the door, then looked under the partition, saw the shape which had now collapsed in a ragged foetal position, immediately realised what had happened and, with less than a dozen kicks, broke the lock off the door and dragged out the girl. The late-night news bulletin described her simply as an unknown woman, believed to be in her twenties, a suspected drugs victim, the one-hundredth of the year, a record, with two months still to go. She then made less than a dozen posthumous paragraphs in all of the morning newspapers (although nothing at all in the English-based nationals) and would have made more space if there had not been sixty-six days of the year left and the probability of around twenty more deaths to come.

One of the papers, *The Scotsman*, extrapolated the Glasgow deaths, pointing out that if the equivalent had happened in London, around 900 fatal overdoses, there would have been a national outcry, an emergency debate, millions poured into preventive measures, none of which, of course, would have worked. By the following day her brief, posthumous period of fame was over.

Chapter Five

The cut-glass globe hanging from the ceiling, spinning slowly in the light, fired bright chips of light down at the dancers, strafing the dark, smoky hall, catching the eyes and the shiny hair-clips of the entwined couples, the jewellery, the glossy patent shoes and bags, the occasional bright military buttons on jackets. Peter, who had his hair swept straight back and heavily greased, lightly ran his hand up the rigid lapels of his new suit, touched the diamond tie-pin, rolling the head between thumb and index finger of his right hand, watching its icy-blue flare as the sparks of light caught it. He was looking out across the spinning people, slouched against a colonnade, hoping that he was being noticed, sure in himself that he was, watching for the flickers of interest or of fear. He hadn't been at the Plaza before, it had always seemed beyond his reach. Now, nothing was.

'All right, big man?' someone said. He nodded slowly, to himself, hardly acknowledging the greeting. He took a deep breath, slipped his hand inside the Forsyth's jacket, tapped his fingers on the top of the flask and considered going to the toilet for another nip when he felt a light touch on his shoulder which made him snap off the column and spin round, his hands, free now, bunching and coming up.

'Peter?' A woman, little more than a girl really, stumbling back away from him, a brief grimace of alarm before she caught her heel on the carpet and sat down heavily on her bottom, her legs split so that he could see a tiny patch of white cotton, quickly covered. 'Shite,' she said, looking up at him, hair tumbling over her face, just the bright red mouth visible drawn back in pain and the cool lustre of her teeth.

He started to laugh then held out his hand which she took and pulled herself to him. As he pulled her, so that she came out of a crouch too hard and clattered into his chest, her following knee buried into his groin, making him buckle at the waist and snap his head forward, catching her on the cheek with his forehead, producing a dull smack. As she stumbled away and massaged her cheek and he tried not to clutch his groin he managed to say, through clenched teeth, 'What can I do for you?'

'Hazel,' she said, left hand rubbing her cheekbone, the right fiddling with her hair.

'Oh,' he said, unable to see her face between her busying hands, so he looked down, at the slight swelling of her belly in the tight skirt, to the larger one above in the tailored jacket and at the flesh of her throat in the creamy silk blouse.

'You could be more pleased to see me,' she said and now her hands had dropped from her face and she was glancing at his groin, mouth in a sarcastic smile, a loose curl hanging down to her nose which she then set fluttering with a fierce upward blow from her pursed lips.

'I could,' he said, smiling painfully, now beginning to massage himself gently with both hands, looking for her reaction.

She looked at his hands and smiled. 'That's taking it too far,' she said looking around quickly, her long hair swinging like a switch, then back. 'It was an accident,' she said.

'No need to apologise.'

'I wasn't. Actually' – she smiled again – 'it wasn't so much an accident as instinctive. Are you all right?'

'No. But I won't hold it against you.'

'Good idea, better not.' She began to laugh and throw back her head so that Peter felt like biting her neck and did not know why. This quick and intimate familiarity with each other unsettled him. 'I am sorry. Really. Carl pointed you out – he's gone to get some drinks – and told me to introduce myself. Not like that, right enough. I've heard a lot about you over the last few months.'

'Nothing good, obviously.'

She had her hand held out to him and she seemed very much in control, toying with the situation, amused. He looked at his own hand self-consciously then shook hers. And he knew right then that he wanted her and that she knew it and somehow that, too, was amusing.

'Would you like to dance?' he asked stupidly, because he did not know what else to say.

'Are you up to it?' Her hand ran up to her cheek again.

'No.' He moved on the balls of his feet softly. 'I don't think I am.'

'We could sit.' She pointed across the floor. 'Over there, there's a table.'

'He won't be able to see you.'

'He'll find me,' she said, leading the way, moving on to the floor, not bothering to walk round the edge, dodging in and out of dancers and he was sure that he caught, as he followed her, a note of exasperation in her voice.

When Peter caught up with her she was sitting at a gilt, filigreed table looking out at the moving bodies on the floor. He pulled up the cushioned chair at the other side of the table and tried to catch her eye but she seemed to be looking past him, over his shoulder, perhaps bored, and he felt a gnawing of anxiety that was new to him, a feeling of insecurity. It made him angry.

'What is it that you do, Mr Stark? Carl is a bit vague,' she said to his shoulder and instinctively his hand went up to it, to brush away lint or dandruff, until he caught himself and stopped.

'Peter!' he said, still angry at his awkwardness. 'What does your husband say I do?'

She said nothing, just stared past him. Then: 'Do you have something to hide – Peter?' She was looking directly at him now. 'He says just that you're a businessman, that you're working on some project together. He won't tell me. But' – she smiled without warmth, her eyes dark, an unknowable colour in the gloom – 'I don't know what it could possibly be because you don't seem to have very much in common. He normally hates businessmen. But whatever it is you're doing together it seems to be making him happy. Which is good. Isn't it?'

'Of course.' He noted the amused look on her face. 'But let's just stop this – I don't know, this game, or whatever it is.'

'I trust my instincts about men. First impressions,' she said. 'And I think that you are a very dangerous one. Are you much like your brother?'

He shook his head. 'No, not much.'

'That's not what I heard.'

'Well, don't believe what you hear in the steamie . . .' Her face froze in mid-smile. 'Sorry,' he continued, 'just an expression.' He found himself looking down at her hands, which were smooth, the fingers long and slim. He chased away the thought of their touch.

She leaned across the table, the same fixed smile, and held out both her hands, palms down, then turned them over. He caught a sparkle of a diamond as she did so. 'Go on. Touch them.' He stretched out his hands, conscious of their slabby roughness, the chaps and lesions. Hers were soft and cool to the touch. He continued to hold them in some sort of ceremony he did not quite understand. 'Washerwoman's hands, d'you think?'

'I did apologise,' he said, still holding her hands, squeezing gently.

'And never will be,' she continued, allowing him the touch but not returning it. Then her smile came alive again and she withdrew her hands. 'He always wants the best for me. And that is good.'

Peter looked away to the dance floor for any sign of Dundas, but all he could see was the moving, spinning shapes in the hot, fuggy air. He didn't recognise the dance, or the music. He thought that it might be some kind of rag, the dancers birling, slapping hands on the backbeat, the music, trumpet-led, hot and thick. This was beyond him. He could just about hobble round without incapacitating a partner, but that had everything to do with intimacy, the arousing closeness, whereas the intricacies of fast dance steps demanded a kind of facility and innate rhythm and command of the limbs he would never master. But he continued to look through the rearranging shapes for any sign of Dundas, without success.

He turned back to Hazel. 'He's not a jealous man, then?'

'Why should he be?'

'No reason. Most are, that's all.'

'Like you?'

He looked at her for several moments without talking, fixing on her dark eyes. 'I could be,' he said.

She returned the gaze for a few moments of her own before she said. 'But you're married . . .' Then, still holding his eyes, 'Tell me, just what is this project?'

'I can't say.'

'Men's talk, eh?'

'No. It's up to Razzle to tell you what he wants to tell you.
Me . . .'

'You keep your own counsel.'

'Something like that. My business is my own.'

'Maybe you aren't like your brother,' she said, sitting back in
the chair, 'but I still think you're dangerous.' And she seemed
to be looking at him in what he felt was a confused expression
of apprehension and longing.

So, smiling at her, more sure of himself now, he leaned across to
touch the small lump on her cheek. 'Only when caught unaware.'

'It's simple,' Stark was telling Dundas as he splashed some of the
whisky from his flask into their two pints of beer. 'We won't
get any decent odds on him here, too much local money behind him skewing it. But in Manchester we'll get at least three
to one, maybe better, particularly if we spread it around a few
bookies.' Hazel had discreetly withdrawn, to the toilet she said,
and Stark thought, I wouldn't let that woman alone, as prey
(or is it predator?) anywhere.

'He can lose,' Dundas was saying into the head of his glass, 'but
winning within seven, that's not possible.'

'It's more than possible. I know him and I have the edge, some
privileged information. Rock solid. What we do in Glasgow is
to hedge the bet. We'll get better than evens on Brown winning, maybe even six to four. So, on the night, between here
and there, we ought to be able to double our money. Easily.
And prudently. It's a risk-free investment.'

'I don't know. Gambling's never that.' Dundas wiped away the
tiny ring of bubbles from his lips. He was wearing a stiff white collar
with a pin through it, and his face seemed to be broiling in the heat.

'Suit yourself.' Stark looked away in the direction Hazel had taken
a few minutes before. 'But think of it, all that cash. How you'll feel
when Benny takes him out. What you've missed, hmmm?' He made
a clawing motion in the air. 'Maybe something for Hazel? Jewellery,
necklace, clothes, you could take her away somewhere. And not
just at the Fair. Abroad. A car maybe, she'd like that, into the
countryside at the weekend.'

'Satan,' Dundas said, 'don't. It's too risky.'

'He's up there in the ring, think about it, he's carrying your future – that feeling, that edge, oh, that pure intoxicant. He takes a couple of hard ones and your gut is wincing like you've actually been hit, your head is dizzy but the blood's roaring, you're screaming at him not to go down, to fight back, he does, back off the ropes, he's crowding on top now, slamming in punches with both hands, Brown is looking groggy' – he put his right hand up in the air in a stopping motion – 'the only limit is your own imagination.' Casually he looked at Dundas.'And wallet, of course.'

Dundas picked up the beer and threw most of it back, Stark watching his Adam's apple bob as it went, and then he slammed it down in conviction, like an auctioneer's hammer. 'Fuck caution,' he said breathlessly. 'Explain it to me once more.'

Benny Lynch was from Florence Street. He looked like a scrawny waif, pudding-basin haircut bristling at the temples. He was polite and deferential in the street, with a wide smile and just a slight thickening of the nose betraying his profession, but in the ring he came on like a hurricane, with fast, two-fisted, perpetual punches, indefatigable. He was less than eight stones, just twenty-two, winner of thirty-nine straight flyweight fights and in less than four years had gone from a ten pound a night miller to leading contender for the world title, dropping on the way, and after only eleven months, the young wife he had married and in her place picked up a retinue of pugs, hangers-on, flatterers and guzzlers who fed on the reputation. And in turn they had introduced him to whisky. But he was young enough and fit enough, yet, to take its best and still be up in the morning with a· clear head .and muscles ravening for a run and a harsh session in the gym.

Stark had watched him develop, from early days as the gamest battler in the LMS club, through the amateurs, the boxing booth bouts with older, heavier men, to his mounting professional career, and he had always been better than anything asked of him. He also knew Sammy Wilson, Benny's manager, and he knew that in the non-title fight with Jackie Brown, who had been the undisputed flyweight champion of the world for more than three years now, Benny had carried the champion, easing up in his flurries of punches when they began to damage, pacing the fight. The result, a draw which hugely favoured the champion and insulted Lynch, meant that Benny had not closed off his chance of a crack at the title by beating the older man when it did not count.

Peter Stark had recced Belle Vue, the fight venue, and the pubs and parts around and had come up with the names and locations of the street bookies and their limits. He had organised buses for local people, rock-bottom rates, all or most of whom knew Benny, and 500 from Glasgow were expected to follow the wee man. McSwegan, Tennant and McKenna had hand-picked the punters to place the bets and Stark was to be the banker.

Razzle took the day off work, although he wasn't going with them. He watched the buses loading up the crates of screwtops, the home-made banners being carefully folded and stowed, the women kissing their men (or others' men) goodbye, the roaring banter of swearing and ebullience and the raucous departing. There was even a piper to play a pibroch, or perhaps it was a reel, Dundas could not tell, before diving on to the step of the last bus as it wheezed off and up Caledonia Road in a snaking plume of blue smoke.

Razzle smelled the air, soiled and greasy to the throat and tongue, not at all the taste of hope, he thought. A hundred pounds of his money was going south with the caravan, now just a dying sound of fading horns. It was a madness, he told himself, almost forgetting that it was not exactly his money riding on the wee man from Florence Street, that it had come from branch funds entrusted to him. But even as he thought that, the excitement of profit, of risk and enjoyment engulfed any sense of shame, although he was beginning to make accommodation and provision for the worst. There would be many other ways to make it back, to replace the money, he told himself. He was trusted, the books were only casually audited, and never regularly, certainly never by a real accountant, and anyway he would put it back with interest.

When he caught sight of himself in the glass door of the Moy he saw that he was smiling and when he went in he realised that what he felt was like sexual joy. Better, he said to himself as he walked silently across the sawdust floor of the quiet bar, leaving a neat trail of footprints.

*   *   *

99

There was no reason not to be at work or, as he saw it, no reason to be. The day was bright and after he had a couple of wee ones in the Moy he went for a walk, ignoring the red and black trams clattering past. He walked up Crown Street towards Dixon's Blazes and then further, making vaguely for Queen's Park Rec, Cathkin Park and Hampden. He was wearing a heavy grey suit, the one he had been married in, for luck, and as the sun came out he took off the jacket, opened his collar and walked on, one thumb tucked into a pocket in his waistcoat, the other arm clutching his jacket under the armpit. He considered how he was feeling, which was very calm, and he wondered why that should be with not even a tiny worry of guilt. In the months since the robbery he believed he had come to know Stark, certainly to know how to manage him. At first he had been surprised how bright he was, well read, a self-improver – he chuckled at that – and how he had confounded expectations of what a criminal should be. He hadn't expected criminals to be . . . ? To be like him, really! There was no shame in being a criminal in this society anyway, he told himself, and then felt the first tinge of worry at his betrayal, because it was betrayal, of his men. But he was going to put it all back, wasn't he? All he had done was to borrow a little to advance his own opportunities. It wasn't like a normal bet on a fighter. One of our own, he said to himself. It's not a nag or a dug, it's wee Benny fae Florence Street. Fighting for all of us. All of us sharing in him. 'God,' he said out loud, smiling, 'it's a saint I am.'

He had reached Cathkin Park now, home of Third Lanark, formed out of Third Lanark Rifles, the team that couldn't shoot straight, and now not even the third best side in Glasgow. Ahead of him was the hill of tenements which he knew shielded Hampden Park. He was beginning to feel hungry. There was a pie shop he remembered in Mount Florida and he wondered whether his feet had sent him in this direction because the area was dry, a subconscious caution not to drink too much before the evening, to savour the outcome sober or passably so. He hadn't wanted to go to Belle Vue, hadn't wanted to spend the night away from Hazel, so he told himself. Or perhaps it was just caution, avoiding being seen with Stark among so many – what? Witnesses? Partly it was that. But also, too, he wanted to be alone, to experience what was, he felt, some sort of rite of passage. It had been one thing not to inform on Stark; he could say to himself that was a crime of omission, but this was certainly one of commission, joining the conspiracy. Nothing illegal – well, betting was illegal, but so what – but this marked his enlistment, there was no going back from here.

He bought a pie and the noon *Record* and sat on one of the steps up to a tenement in Hampden Terrace, looking back at the city, the smoke from the Blazes through which he could just about make out the hilly horizon of the Campsies beyond. Biting into the crust of the pie the hot meat burned his tongue and grease spurted out and down on to the right leg of his trousers. Hazel would undoubtedly notice, he said to himself, realising once again that whenever he thought of her, through the pleasure was always a vein of unease.

There was no conversation, only the tinkle of glass against the crackle and buzz and frenzy from the big wooden radio on the gantry. Orders were whispered, or motioned; there was a reverence about and not because this was the Bible Class, as Thomson's was known after the religious outpourings of the owner. Lynch was in the ring. The background noise of the pipes which led him in had faded and the chanting had died. Jackie Brown was in there too, and the competitive babble had faded to a threnody of anxiety as both sides joined in muttered considerations of the men as their gowns came off and the referee briefed them. Dundas looked at the large glass of whisky on the walnut bar, the pint chaser beside it exactly like an offertory, he thought, the sacrament. Strange thoughts for a Marxist. Nevertheless he would touch neither until the outcome, whatever it was. Or if Lynch lost, perhaps not? His stomach was already heaving at the prospect.

The sound of the bell set off a rage of excitement and animation in the bar, men jiggling about, downing drinks, punching the air and then a huge roar, almost before it had begun, followed by waves of them, screeching hysteria from the wireless, glasses rattling and shaking on the wooden shelves against the engraved glass wall, leaving Dundas, on his own, bewildered, blinking around for enlightenment. 'He's down.' A yell from somewhere, then again, and again.

Brown was hitting the canvas with every punch that got through, Benny was on top of him and over him and had to be held back from almost falling on him to end it. Dundas was trying to imagine it. And then a lull, no sound of the bell penetrating the dense frenzy of noise, but 250 miles away the wee men must have heard it because expectancy settled in again, although in the faces around all he could read was joy. He pulled out his pocket watch and as the roaring took up again he watched the juddering second hand mark off the most important time of his life. A minute, a minute thirty, then forty and finally an amplified gasp of exultation, the staccato chiming of a bell far off and just a pocket of clarity in there when he heard ' . . .of the world, Benny Lynch'. Then someone grabbed him and hugged him, his drinks spun and spilled and he saw what seemed like a meteor soar across the bar but was only a bunnet skimmed in joy. And he felt quietly calm and certain about himself, utterly confident for the first time in his life.

Johnnie Stark stood alone, in his own little ring of space, no one wanting to brush up against his contamination. Banners had been slung across the street, from second-floor window to second-floor window on tied-together clothes-lines, banners made out of old grey sheets splashed with bright paint. The biggest and most carefully lettered read: *Welcome back from 'Chester town, Sammy and Benny with the flyweight crown*, but Johnnie did not ask anyone to read it to him, not wanting to risk either angry refusal or ignoral. There was bunting too, little hastily sewn flags made from whatever material had been contributed and it was draped from window to window along the faces of the tenements. Almost all the windows were open, filled by men and women 'hingers', people hanging out to take in what was happening. Above his head Johnnie could hear snatches of shouted, competing conversations, the occasional word or phrase and the air smelled of sulphur and ash – someone had pinched a large brazier and a small crowd around it were trying to roast some scraps of chicken. The doors to Knotts restaurant were open and a steady stream of people churned in and out for pies and bridies, stovies, plates of broth and stew. Johnnie could see garish hand-lettered posters in the two windows, but even if he had been able to read, they were too far away to decipher. On the corner an accordion player, one-legged, leaning against a close mouth, was playing, his fingers fluttering up and down the keys but nothing could be heard above the cacophony and his cap, on the dusty pavement in front of him, held only a scattering of pennies in the greasy tweed.

Johnnie was getting used to being ignored, used to the hostile glances in the street. He didn't care any more, indeed it marked him out as being different, special. Even his mother was barely talking to him, shoving his food in front of him, bundling him down the stairs, always with a hurt and resentful look. He wiped his running nose and sat on the kerb waiting for what everyone else was waiting for, whatever that was. Anyway, it was more interesting than isolation.

He could remember the police arriving, a big sergeant with razor burns, smelling of tobacco and peppermint, and a younger one with a golden moustache. He saw them when he answered the door but his father immediately jumped in and wouldn't let them in to talk to him. Something his da had said had prevented them trying, and no one else in the street would talk either, including the McPhails. His father had squared it with them somehow, either by threats or with money, might even have arranged with the factor to get them a new house because, within three weeks, they were out of the area. A carter came for them one morning and within three hours all their furniture was loaded and was trundling noisily away borne by the large, spoked, metal-rimmed wheels. He had not seen his da since. His mother, when he saw her, was usually weeping into a jar of biddy.

One night, in front of the dying fire in the grate, her teeth stained dark with the wine, she slapped him without saying a word and shook him but he refused to cry and then she had started to snivel again. 'You Starks are all bastards,' she shouted between racking gulps of air. 'It's in the blood. What made me think Peter would be any different? And you, too!' She started crying again while he looked down at her and then she held out her arms to him but he shook his head and stood his ground, determined not to break.

Cheering broke out. He scrambled to his feet as a large black car drew up, kids dancing on the running board, chasing in its exhaust. The door opened, a man in a dark overcoat with velvet collar got out, beaming, holding the door open for the other, younger man, little more than a boy, huge smile, hair damp and freshly centre-parted, skinny in trousers and shirt, not even bothering with a jacket, but clutching his hands above his head, slightly bowing to the roars of welcome and the dozens of hands reaching for him, slapping at his back.

'Here, son,' the older man said, beckoning to him, 'shake hands with the champion of the world.' Johnnie moved forward, the younger man bent down, ruffled his hair and then howked him into the air and put him on his shoulders from where, two hands holding on to the unmarked head of Benny Lynch, he could see everything below him, the envious upturned faces, and above, the bright blowing banners and bunting.

'There's something else.'

'Y'mean, what school did I go to?'

Dundas smiled and shook his head. They were standing outside his wooden howff, the air was bright with the smattering of dozens of heavy hammers on metal and the smoke from the fires was standing straight up so that it seemed almost, he imagined, like one of those Indian encampments in the films. He looked across at the partly covered skeleton of the boat, a cargo ship for Blue Cross's American run, and he thought that he had been nowhere, not even to Blackpool or Morecambe, far less on a 20,000-ton ship heading for New York.

'You were saying?' The man looking at him was in his mid-thirties, with a fierce down of dark hair through which white scars were still visible, and the first stirrings of a new moustache. He had said that he was recently out of the army but Dundas knew that his term had been spent in Barlinnie.

'Aye. There's an extra ten bob due on top of the union subs for the first two months,' he said, still looking at the shell of the boat and the tiny figures on gantries and runnels all over it. 'Special levy. For the fighting fund.'

'We're going out?' the labourer said, a knot of anxiety to his mouth.

'No. Not yet awhile.' The man, Sullivan, would be sleeping in a model, the Great Eastern probably, among the winos and dossers and the idea of a strike meant the end of the notion of a new place for himself, the modest new clothes, a delay on the fresh start. Dundas looked at him and pointed his right index finger. 'And mind, nae trouble, not when you're here. Or your arse'll hit the buroo faster than Eric Liddell. Understand?'

'Aye, sure.' Sullivan was turning away, probably wishing he had a bob or two in his pouch for a bevvy, Dundas imagined, to celebrate the start. 'Ten bob, you said.' He was a couple of paces towards the gate. 'Does everyone have to pay?'

'Sullivan' – Dundas was turning away, back to his cabin – 'you just worry about yourself. I'll worry about the others. You have to pay, that's all you need to know.' And he went inside.

The corruption of capitalism was what he enjoyed. Before, he had known it academically but nothing prepared you for the resonances of the reality, the sheer perverse pleasure money and manipulation could bring. It all seemed like some limitless exercise, how far could you go, how far could you push people, make them bend and scrape, what constructs could you put together out of fancy and avarice and imagination and actually make them happen? It was all a fable, he knew that, but he was living it. And it worked. He would be rich before he was thirty. That meant nothing, he believed that. He was just taking the opportunity and creating it for others, their network. The legitimate side of it probably employed over a hundred people now. They were doing their bit to dig the country out of the Depression.

Yes, he and Stark made a good team, the strategist and the man of action, ice and fire, the attraction of opposites. Although they were not too different. Stark could talk about politics and world affairs, not just football, women and bevvy. They worked well together. Although Hazel, when she talked of them in that way, disdainfully called them the Marx Brothers, trying to put a cruel, dual play on it, smiling in that remote way of hers: well, she could laugh, but she didn't turn down the dresses, the charge account at Coplands, the meals at Ferraris or the new car. She was learning to drive, she had given up work and where did that all come from? She knew as well as he did, although it was unspoken. She preferred not to know about the source, as long as the well-spring continued to flow.

He took a sip of his beer and wiped the suds of foam from his moustache. The Marx Brothers indeed. What was the name of the third one, the one who saw everything and never spoke? That was her role in the partnership.

He downed the whisky and fiddled with his waistcoat pocket

for his watch. She was late again. What did she find to do with her time and lose so much of it?

She walked down the steps of the art gallery, heels clicking on the stone slabs, pulling her coat around her. A watery sun was edging out from behind a cloud and she could feel the touch of it on her; it felt discreet, slightly risky. Spring was coming, crocuses and daffodils were spiking through the damp brown earth of the gardens around the elaborately turreted building which everyone said was built the wrong way round, facing the hill and the university. But she knew that was not true. She had reached Argyle Street, the rattle of trams beside her, and she headed towards town, quickening her stride over the puddled pavement.

It took her about five minutes to reach St Vincent Crescent, a curving strand of tenements, and she was slightly out of breath, but not only from the exertion. She slowed down as she walked along the street, taking in the dull fluted ornamental pillars, the faintly Greek style, until she reached number 25. The sun was brighter now, it glowed in the brass key plate and sparkled from the key as she put it in the lock. The mortice turned and she stepped into the hall of the ground-floor main-door flat and shut the door behind her. There was a smell of polish or pollen; it was dark; she picked out heavy rolled wallpaper in brown and greens, varnished doors, a thick brown carpet with quills of lighter brown, but a fuzzy square of light fell from the window above the door on to the carpet ahead of her and she thought that it seemed like a trapdoor. She stepped carefully over it and went through the heavy door at the end of the passageway ahead.

He was standing in the centre of the large room. This was like entering into another life, bright and spacious and comfortable. And deliciously dangerous. She could hear her breath loud in her ears, feel the twist in her stomach, the rustle of the carpet as she moved across it. He had his hands deep in his pockets, she took in that his jacket was thrown over one of the huge brocaded chairs which nevertheless looked lost in the formally arranged room, and the cuffs of his collarless shirt were rolled up. He continued his silence as she came up and stopped within touching distance. His look seemed to be challenging, eyebrows slightly arched, a tight, bent smile. She pulled up her skirt, not even unbuttoning her coat, and dropped on to both knees in front of him. She had been thinking of this all morning in the high halls of the gallery, among the glistening oils on the walls, the centuries of religious adoration, the armoured figures and the huge cases of wild, bare-toothed animals, the interplay of light and reflections occasionally showing her moving through them. Quickly she unbuttoned his trousers and pulled them down to his ankles, his underpants with them. He became hard in her mouth and as she moved slowly on him his hands clutched her neck, then her hair and her ears and she heard him say something above, but it was indistinct and muffled and all that she caught was her name like a cry.

'This wasn't what I meant when I said you were dangerous.' She was dressing in the bedroom as he lay looking at her.
'But you did realise.'
'What? That you fancied me?' She was smoothing round her stockings, looking back at him over her shoulder as she spoke. 'Yes. But not this.'
'You thought you could handle it – me. But now it's all turned round?'
'I don't know. It doesn't matter now.'
'Does the guilt make it sweeter?'
'I don't feel guilt.'
He laughed. 'We have that in common.'
She was standing facing him now, trying to smooth out the creases in her blouse. 'You won't tell Carl, will you?
'Not unless I have to.' He began to smile.
'It would kill him.'
'People say that. It means nothing.'
'Being unfaithful means nothing?'
'That too. But I meant – you know what I mean.'
'I thought you were friends, partners at least.' She sat on the bed beside him, dropped her blouse on the floor and began massaging her bare arms.
'Nothing lasts,' he said.
'I'm cold. Please, hold me.' He pulled her down to him. 'Does it just go on like this?'

'For now.'

'Because nothing lasts?' Lying on his chest she could feel the gurgle of laughter. 'Is that funny?'

'It's not that. It's because for now I need your husband.'

'And not me?' He did not reply. 'Is that amusing?'

'Different needs,' he said in a whisper. 'What is funny is that him finding out wouldn't kill him, but me. That's all.'

'What do you mean?' She tried to sit up to look at his face but he held her head to him.

'He hasn't said anything? He seems like the kind of man who would tell his wife everything.'

'What? What is everything?'

'Come on.' He ruffled her hair and chuckled. 'Dangerous I may be, to myself, doing this, but not stupid.' He laughed again. 'Actually, stupid too.'

'So it just goes on.'

'Not just. But on, yes.'

She turned over on the bed so that her chin was in his diaphragm. 'You and Carl? Is what you're doing legal?'

'Most of it, extremely.'

She could see his mouth now. 'That sounds boring. Is that Carl's side?' He smiled. She knew she was right. 'Tell me about the interesting bit.'

He sat up so that her face slipped into his groin again. She shook her head and sat up, watching as he folded his arms behind his head. 'Sorry,' he said.

'Tell me about the dull bit, then.'

He looked at her for a few seconds and then said, 'Okay.'

She looked puzzled at first, not expecting that. 'Why would you do that? Why take the risk?' He shrugged. 'It couldn't be that you want to whet my appetite, involve me, embroil me for some reason? Or drive a wedge between me and Carl?'

'It couldn't just be that I trust you?'

After a short, bleak look at each other, both burst out laughing.

He saw her coming from the mouth of the pub. She was walking quickly, some private smile on her lips as if about some closed knowledge, head half bowed, one hand holding the collar of her coat closed, the other deep in the coat pocket. She never seemed to carry anything with her, no handbag, or umbrella; it was as if she were continually moving between one provisioned base and another. She did not even have a purse, just kept her money stuffed into the pockets of her various garments so that when she was short in one outfit she rummaged through some previously discarded jacket or suit and invariably came up with a crumpled note or two. It annoyed him intensely.

She was almost on top of him but she still hadn't looked up. The high sun had warmed the pavements and the rainwater was evaporating in steamy wisps so that as she moved through it seemed as if she were emerging from a stage mist. Or the underworld, he thought. And silently chastised himself.

'Oh,' she said, almost bumping into him, her head snapping up.

'You're late,' he said quickly, without thinking, when actually he felt relieved to see her.

She gave him a half smile but did not explain and he, not wanting to make it worse, did not pursue it. 'We've missed the start.' He leaned forward and lightly kissed her cheek.

'It doesn't matter. I don't feel like sitting in the dark anyway. I've seen enough pictures for the day.' He looked puzzled, she touched his brow and then took his arm. 'The art gallery. All those chubby naked bodies' – she snuggled into him – 'made me all hot and—'

'Don't,' he cut in.

'Cherubim, seraphim, don't you love it when I talk dirty?'

'Hazel. Don't.'

She shook her head and detached her arm. 'You're such a Calvinist. Don't you want to fuck me?' She smiled and shook her head again. 'You look so disapproving. It's all right for you to say fuck—'

'Please' he said.

'But never in front of a woman, eh?' She turned and began walking away.

'Hazel!' he called after her. But she ignored him and kept walking through the mist around her ankles and, just as she reached the corner, he started after her.

The Rose wasn't much of a place, but it might have been. Every time

109

he walked past it, which was about three times a day, Stark thought that and cursed the missed opportunity. It was in family hands. Wattie Thomson was the latest in the long and undistinguished line to hold it and not mould and make use of it. What it had was a perfect situation in Cumberland Street, spacious premises on three floors turned over to some glorified dance school. Now, standing outside it and gazing at the peeling paint on the windows, the fading red sign with the lettering under the main legend which said, 'where dance careers bloom,' Stark spat on the pavement and then ground the saliva with his right boot, imagining Thomson's face. It was an affront, this, he told himself and then the remedy occurred to him. He immediately spun on his foot and walked away.

His son had seen him from the corner but had made no move to approach his father. He had barely seen him in months. If he came home after Johnnie was in bed then he was away before he got up. Occasionally he had heard heated voices from behind the curtain, but that could just have been dream imaginings. There was no sign of his father at home apart from the occasional piece of clothing or in the parcels of meat and vegetables that kept being delivered or, presumably, in the price of the wine his ma kept buying. He looked down. In his clothes, too. He had new jerseys, trousers and boots, even a dark serge coat which he wouldn't wear because it had a half belt and ridiculous buttons and having it on would inevitably mean some passing comment he would have to retaliate for.

He shoved his hands into his pockets, which were full of bookie's lines. All the men in the streets knew him as one of Devlin's runners. He spent the day moving around, his eye continually caught by a punter, then he would take the scribbled line, move on until the next gesture, collect that, move on, keeping an eye open for the truant man, bag more bets until his two trouser pockets were full, then trot over to Devlin's pitch in Ballater Street and hand them over. And back again.

After they were off it became a bit more frenzied, he was on his toes most of the time, shuttling between the damned, occasionally trotting back with his pocket full of notes – but only very occasionally. He had been caught twice by the truant officer, but never with any lines; he had palmed them and dumped them as he struggled and now the man was so well known that he was always tipped off by the punters when he was around and told where he was. The polis, of course, didn't bother. They were all getting their whack from Devlin, his da, somebody anyway, so he was invisible to them. Except when some polis wanted a bet, then it was all smiles and kindness, a caramel and a ruffle of the hair.

Devlin treated him fairly, couldn't afford not to, of course, but there seemed more to it than that. He paid him ten bob a day, a quid when he had a really good day, took him for meals and over the weeks and in the lulls had taught him to count, to compute odds, and now he was starting to teach him to read too, if only the arcane names of horses and dugs, drawing the letters of the alphabet in chalk on the pavement, questioning him about his remembrance every time he came back with his full pockets. 'You're a quick laddie,' Devlin would say every lunchtime, shoving a plate of stew at him. 'Yir maw must be very proud. You pick up everything in nae time.' Johnnie never replied, just picked up the spoon and got buried in the stew.

Devlin was very old, even too old for the war, they said, but, as he walked with a limp, what they said might not be gospel. He never seemed to bother with his hair after he slicked it down in the morning; it was long and grey and when it dried out flapped around his ears and neck so that he looked like some maniacal street preacher, especially when the wind whipped it up and he was tic-tacking to his men. He always wore a grey and white striped suit which nipped at his body and bulged over his rolls of belly fat and the index finger of his left hand was missing – 'A crocodile, son, in the Amazon,' then he would wink – but he recalled his da saying it was the consequence of short-changing a punter: 'If he does that again he'll be holdin' his soup spoon wae his toes,' his da had laughed.

It was on one of his trips that he heard about Kilbronskie, from one of the men lounging in the close. Kilbronskie didn't bet, didn't seem to speak English well enough to read the form, although when he was out, the dark cap clenched on the back of his white head, his nose was always in a book and he seemed to mumble to himself as he went. He would nod to Johnnie, give him a tired smile or sometimes a sweet and then shuffle away. It was probably just talk about where he was going, by the men in the close mouth; to the synagogue one said. That brought up the idea of taking care of him at Shabbat when he couldn't cook for himself, maybe to light the mantles or the fire for him.

That was what he was thinking later, going up the stairs, pushing open the door into the sticky smell of blood and the shining wall of icons.

He still had not told anyone about the little picture. It was the first thing he had really owned of his own and, despite the circumstances of getting it, he felt sure that Kilbronskie would not grudge him it. What had happened to the rest of the pictures he did not know. The old man didn't seem to have had a family, not one that anyone knew about anyway. Perhaps the little pictures were all just thrown away – that seemed to make his all the more valuable when he thought about it – but that wasn't very likely. They were probably valuable to someone. It stood to reason. Kilbronskie was rich, near enough, rich enough to be killed anyway and all of those pictures, if they meant so much to him, must have had some value. Perhaps some of the other Jews had taken them, split them up, taken them to the synagogue. He didn't know. It didn't matter. He had his, wrapped in greased paper and cloth and hidden. At first he had slipped it under the mattress, knowing that was one place it would not be found because his mother had neither the strength not the inclination even to wash the filthy sheets, far less turn the mattress. But, in his mind, he could feel it there, vulnerable to damage and he knew that he had to move it. It should be displayed, but that was impossible. One day, he thought. Then, when he had mulled about it for months without a solution, having considered and rejected various hiding places, like behind the cistern in the toilet, or buried somewhere, like in the chapel maybe, it had come to him. Devlin would look after it for him until he was ready. Ready to have a place of his own to hang it.

The old bookie chuckled at first then, when he saw that he was being serious, his long, old face changed. 'Sure, son. No problem.'

'I don't want to tell you what's in there.' He had wrapped the package in brown paper and fixed the joins in red sealing wax which he had stolen from Ma Liberty's wee shop and melted, painfully, into large gooey dollops on the range and then smeared with a knife over the brown paper.

'That's fine. I'll take it home and lock it in the safe.' Devlin lived in Dennistoun, a place, Johnnie believed, somewhere across the river.

'Ye'll need to give me a line for it.'

'Sure,' the old man said and began to write on the back of a betting slip with a stubby brown pencil. Then handed it to Johnnie.

'What does it say?' Johnnie gazed at the rising and falling pencil marks, the dots and whirls.

'It says . . .' Devlin took back the paper. 'It says, "Received from Master John Stark one package, wrapped in brown paper and sealed, about six inches by four, the contents of which are unknown, delivered into the safekeeping of Ernest Devlin."' He pointed to the bottom line. 'And this here. That's today's date.'

Johnnie stared at the paper and the pencil lines. 'Teach me the words, Mr Devlin,' he said at last, 'teach me them all, please.'

The old Austin drew up outside the Rose. Stark watched the girl get out the passenger side, ducking back inside to pull a heavy sheaf of papers out after her. He eased himself off the wall and moved towards the car on the other side of which, in the street, the man was fumbling with the lock. As he reached the door he could feel the heat blowing back from the engine. 'Here,' he said, putting on a wide smile to the girl, 'let me.' He pointed towards the papers.

'It's all right,' she was starting to say, but he had tugged the thick file away from her.

'No problem.' The girl was, he thought as he looked her over, about twenty. Gawky, slightly protruding teeth, spectacles, but tall and even elegant, with a way of holding herself. 'Stark,' he said looking past her at the grey-haired, stooping elderly man in the homburg and dark overcoat, 'Peter Stark.' He smiled again. 'Wattie,' he said.

'Leave us alone,' Thomson said, averting his eyes, seeming to slump into his collar as if, Peter thought, his backbone were crumbling.

'You don't know why I'm here,' he said pleasantly.

'Father . . .' The girl was looking puzzled.

'I'll be up in a minute, Jennifer, just go ahead.'

She paused for a few seconds, in fluttering indecision, until Thomson said, 'Go on,' once more and Peter turned on his bright banishing smile.

'What can you possibly want with me?' Thomson said, barely audibly against the staccato of his daughter's heel taps as she went. 'I don't have anything.'

Peter looked down and flicked through what he now saw were music scores. He gave a deep exaggerated sigh, looked back over his shoulder at the Rose and then again at Thomson. 'The bloom's a little blighted on the bough,' he said to the man on the pavement in front of the burnished old car, 'but not so's it can't be nourished and restored. Come on' – he waved the music papers at Thomson – 'we'll talk inside. Your daughter, Jennifer?' he said, beckoning with his finger as he turned. 'She's the pianist, is she? I noticed her fingers. Long, elegant. I bet they look lovely in long black lacy gloves. Mine,' he said, looking at his right hand, knowing that Thomson was watching, 'the only thing they would look good in is splints.' And he laughed, turned back and winked at Thomson.

He had never been inside the place before. It had a large marbled reception and two staircases with walnut balustrades going up on each side of a fountain long since dried up and the floral bowl with large red floral motifs was now dulled and stained with encrusted dirt. Stark smiled to himself, taking in the dark, grease-sheened carpeting on the stairs and the dun-coloured walls riven with cracks. The stairs ached as he walked up them, the smell of stale dust pricked his nostrils and he fancied he could detect the scent of pomade and face powder in it. The main dance area, when he walked up and into it, surprised him by its spacious, airy feel. He walked through an archway on to floorboards which shone in the streaming light from the high windows and, grasping the musical file to his stomach with his right hand, he raised his other and began a slow two-step across the wide surface towards the piano, where Jennifer stood, and then, when he had almost reached her, he did a dipping turn to face back towards Thomson who was standing, still in his hat, looking across the distance to him.

'Never could master the proper steps,' he said. 'I'm always treading on other people's toes.'

He turned back towards Jennifer and held out the file to her which, after a hesitation while she seemed to be looking past him to her father, she moved on to the floor on tiptoes and took. 'But I can carry a tune, all right, Wattie.' He looked around him. 'Why

was I never here before? It has a . . . a rather welcoming feel to
it.' He shrugged. 'Ah well.' He paused and looked from the man
to his daughter and back. 'You'll have somewhere private, I expect,
where we can cosy down and have a wee chat.' There was no trace
of a question in his voice and the steps he took across the bright
floor squeaked as he moved.

The office was hung in discoloured pictures of dancers, former
pupils, champions and, in the facial lines not hidden by age, a
younger Thomson perhaps, but Stark did not know nor care.
There were diplomas, framed yellowing newspaper cuttings, boxed
files, spilling papers on an old bureau and a cracking leather chair
which sagged on its springs as Stark sat in it and swivelled to look
at Thomson in the doorway. He stood there, as if awaiting sentence,
his big grey hat still pulled down to the ears.

'Christ, Thomson. Take off your coat and hat and we'll talk.'

Thomson shook his head and remained framed by the door.
From downstairs, filtering up through the ceiling, the sounds of
a piano. Stark did not know the tune or the dance it would go
to, but it sounded like brave music, defiant, something to march
or fall to. He could imagine Jennifer screwing up her head to
look at the floor between them, hammering at the keys of the
big old upright. Perhaps there was some message in the music to
her father but it didn't matter.

'I'll get straight down to it. This place' – he motioned around him
– 'it's a bit of museum, a historical relic. It needs to be brought up
to date.' Thomson remained silent. 'It's obvious from the look of
it that you don't have the cash to do it.'

'It's the way I like it,' the other man said, not looking at him.

'But it's not' – he searched for the word – 'progressive. Modern.
It's a waste of potential.'

Thomson continued to look at him dolefully and eventually his
eyes darted away again. 'I'm not looking for potential . . . the police,
maybe.'

Stark laughed and scattered the papers on the desk. 'What for?
Threatening you with the twentieth century?'

'I can't pay you.'

Stark laughed again. 'It's obvious from the look of the place you
cannae pay anybody.'

'What is it you want?'

Stark got up and took two paces across the floor so that Thomson shrank once more into his coat. 'Never try to threaten me, Thomson. Go to the polis? That's pathetic. If you were worth it I might even get angry. But I'm here to help you. And Jennifer, of course. You want her to have a future, hmm?' He reached out towards Thomson, who cringed, expecting a slap or a punch but, instead, Stark took the curly brim of the hat and pulled it off then spun it towards the paper-strewn desk of the bureau. He took the frail man by the shoulders and pulled him towards the desk and then gently pushed him in the chest so that he sagged into the seat.

'Now,' he said looking down, 'let's get this over with.' The music, he noticed, had stopped and he considered that Jennifer might be listening in the shadowed hall but, again, he didn't care. He put his hand into his inside pocket and brought out a handful of papers. 'I own you, Thomson. You and this mildewed rose of yours. I've bought your bills, your past and future. So don't get superior with me. What was it that did it? Horses? Dogs? Young women? Or was it pawned, all just to keep up appearances, put your daughter to the right school, that kind of thing? The lessons at the Athenaeum?' Thomson said nothing. 'Not that it matters. It's lucky for you in a way because I had decided anyway that I had to get into the dance business and this way it all happens without any of the nastiness.'

He let it sink in. 'Dream world, Wattie. That's where you've been these years. Wake up. If it hadn't been me it would have been someone else.' He threw the papers into Thomson's lap. 'There's always someone else.' The music downstairs had started again, jangling, strident, like a polka or an arabesque. 'But at least I can carry a tune, Wattie.'

The older man looked down at the scraps of paper on his dark coat and on the floor and then both of his hands went to his face and began to rub at his eyes.

'Come on,' Stark said, taking him by the arm, 'let's go downstairs. Tell Jennifer of the big plans.'

She was sitting at the piano, hands on the keys staring into space, as they came into the room, Stark guiding Thomson by the arm. 'What do you think, Jennifer? We're going to be seeing a lot more of each other.'

She looked round and he could see in her eyes that there was no fear, only hatred. She said nothing, just watched as he pushed her father in front of him up to the piano.

'Wonderful thing, to be able to play the piano, I wish I could.'

'It takes training and dedication,' she said, 'application and talent. More than that, a soul.' She began to play again, something dramatic and menacing it seemed like and then he caught on. It was the kind of tune, strident and rolling and full of dark tension, which played in the cinema to the arrival of the villain. And she was smiling mockingly at him as she played.

Stark took a half-pace forward and in quick movement flicked down the lid of the piano, catching her fingers and in the same move sat down heavily on the lid. Even above the discords he could hear the bones and cartilage snap while he continued to sit there, smiling down into her screaming and writhing face and when, eventually, her father moved towards her he pushed him away with the sole of his foot so that he stumbled and slipped backwards, sprawling down on the polished floor, where he started to cry.

Stark stood up just as the girl, her eyes rolling back and colour draining from her, slipped unconscious off the piano stool.

Chapter Six

Ricketts looked at the spread of bursting manila folders in front of him, the spilling paper, the stapled sheets, the blue report forms, the grainy photographs and thought, Where do you start? Where did this all start? All this paper, all this work, the man hours, the investigations, the psychological profiles, the tips, the suspicions, the interviews, the hypotheses, the crime sheets, the concealed frustration and anger, all on the one family. It's a testament, he thought, to the failure of detection, evolution, redemption, the welfare state, society, whatever you like – the fucking hopelessness of hope.

'Why don't we,' he said across the desk to Alice Blantyre, who was sitting opposite him, yawning slightly, working through the jet-lag that had accompanied her co-option to the squad from the NYPD, 'cull them at birth, a discreet pillow or a vitamin overdose . . . or, cheaper, just fit them up.' He motioned towards the desk. 'Actually, that's been tried, according to the young lad.'

'I don't understand.'

'Me neither. But what, in particular?'

'Fit up?' She was about thirty, maybe younger, Ricketts reckoned, like one of these TV cops you only see on TV, long curled hair tied back severely behind her head, which only accentuated her fine features, wide dark eyes like .38 entry wounds, a loose frame, evidently athletic. 'Like, plant stuff?'

'I bet you,' he said, 'that you've got a degree as well.'

'Of course. As well as what?' she said, looking fairly amused.

Everything, he thought, everything! 'I'll tell you when I put you on the plane.' He motioned at the files. 'The boy Stark, the young innocent, reckons we planted him with dope and coke.' He stretched back in the seat and clasped his hands behind his head. 'That's what he claimed in court. Never mind that we found enough marching powder in his car to render *hors de combat* an entire infantry division, never mind the stuff he was shovelling out the car window in the' – he made as if he was consulting a file – 'eight-mile chase at speeds touching 105 mph.'

'He was driving with one hand and ditching stuff with the other?'

'Nah, there were two of them. Anyway, fingerprints all over the packet, a shooter in his pocket—'

'Which he claimed you had planted.'

'Naturally. Never mind that it had his dabs, DNA, semen and soup stains all over it – well, his prints anyway.'

'And he's getting out for the weekend.'

Ricketts leaned forward and cupped his head in his hands, elbows on the desk. 'Do they do it this way in your place?'

She touched her right hand to her mouth, suppressing another yawn. 'Not any more. Recreation is off the syllabus. Unless you count rolling the ball or skipping the chain.' She was wearing what Ricketts was sure was a designer suit, grey with faint chalk marks. How did he know it was designer? It had the same kind of crumpled, dress-me-down elegance you didn't see in Marks, which you caught mainly in the style pages or in the newspapers on the back of some Rangers player, normally shortly before he came up on an assault or drink charge, often both.

'Ours not to, etcetera,' he said, sitting back up. 'Tell me, did you get to bring your gun with you?'

She shook her head and smiled.

'And expenses? Dollars or sterling?'

'Sterling, I'm afraid. I claim here.'

'Shite. So it's soggy chips and splitting a bottle of ginger.'

'Ginger?'

'The patois. Lemonade.'

'I don't suppose I'd get a sensible answer if I asked why?'

'Why what? Christ, woman,' he said, pushing one of the files in her direction, 'there are no sensible answers in this city.'

She looked at him for a moment and shrugged her shoulders. 'Are you trying to impress me?' she said eventually.

'Am I?'

She shook her head. 'Not so far. But give it another go. Give me a résumé of the story thus far and I'll take these back' – she motioned her hand over the files – 'for some bedtime reading. And' – she put the palm of her hand up – 'before you ask, no, I don't have anything better to do. And yes, I do enjoy my own company. And yes, too, perhaps I am a dyke.'

'I'm sorry. I didn't mean to – well . . .' The sentence trailed off.

'Come on?' She shook her head and gave a wan, familiar smile. 'Sure you did, you just didn't expect me to mind. Look, no offence.' She threw another bleak smile. 'I didn't come 3,000 miles to flash my eyelashes and become the talk of the locker room. I came to work.'

'Again, sorry.'

'No problem.'

'But forgive me because I still don't quite understand . . . you know, why you came here to work, as you put it?'

She threw her head back, rubbed her eyes wearily with both hands, and let out a long sigh. 'Look, don't take this up with me. If your superiors don't trust you enough to brief you properly, well, you complain to them, don't try and weasel it out of me. Clear? Now, can we get on?'

Ricketts closed his eyes and took a couple of deep breaths. 'Yeah. Excuse me, I obviously got it wrong. You do it different over there, clearly. Here it's us and them, colleagues together against the rest, that word you used, *trust*, interdependence, watching out for each other—'

'Please, Sergeant, the story. Spare me the homilies and the self-pity. Go get yourself an analyst, or a dog, whatever works for you but for chrissakes just get started! Please.'

'Okay,' he said, slumping back in the chair and throwing his right leg over the corner of the desk. 'What you have to understand first of all is that all these coves know each other, they've come out of the same sewers, the same streets, avoided going to the same schools, they use the same pubs and clubs and women, they have the same pitiful dreams and ambitions, all of which involve money, and when thwarted, or even mildly inconvenienced, their route one response is extreme violence. And' – he held up his right hand cutting off any intervention – 'I am not trying to explain that the criminal mind here is any different to the varieties you grow back home; what I am saying is that this is like a civil war in a small town. This is not 8 million people or even 800,000, but what you have is international crime contained in a comparatively small space, without the distance or the normal operating procedures.

'As I said, these guys all know each other, they shop in the same places, support the same football teams and what keeps them from brawling in these same venues, most of the time anyway, is fear of the consequences. Because, as I said, this is a small place and not only do they know each other, drink in the same places, etcetera, but we know them all, we drink in the same places, etcetera – so all the players know each other intimately. Which means that malevolent manoeuvrings have to be very resourceful or, and this is where the wild card enters, powerfully and graphically violent, so hideously out of scale and character for this familiar place that any innocent bystander witnessing would immediately divine the message.'

He pointed at the heap of files. 'This all started really, the out-of-character stuff, within the last three or four years. Before then crime creaked along in its traditional manner. Protection rackets, prostitution, bank robbery, computer crime, the whole gamut, but nothing outward to cause fear and alarm in the citizenry. Now, I'll skip back a further few years. You'll see in the files that the name of John Stark is omnipresent. At your leisure you can read *Stark: The Early Years*, it's all in the old files, but to sum up, he's usually been at the heart of all the clever stuff that has gone on here for the last three or four decades. Moneylending, girls, soft drugs in the sixties and seventies – he did well, we rarely got near him. He made a lot of money, brokered it through several legitimate businesses. We called him' – he smiled at Blantyre – 'the Godfaither. Sorry, that's the patois again. He'll be over sixty now, and it had been put about that he was in retiral, that his young brood, with John Junior, were now running things. Now, well, who knows. But I'll come back to that.' He stood up. 'I'm thirsty. How do you take your coffee?'

'As it comes,' she said. Ricketts, who was using the DCI's office for this briefing session, walked over to the Cona machine and poured two black coffees into two paper cups, turned and deposited both in the no-man's land in the middle of the desk. Blantyre took hers, cupped it in her hands, and began blowing on the surface.

'Don't ask me why,' he went on, 'or the psychological or social deficiencies which lead to it, but this has always been a city which likes to get off its face on whatever happens to be the most efficacious

– and, of course, cheapest – brew, potion, libation, inhalation or, lately, injection around.' He picked up the remaining coffee and swirled the liquid in the cup so that the steam twisted and spiralled. 'The heroin started to come in around the start of the eighties. Maybe it's the macho, hard man culture; sociologists will tell you that it's the loss of hope, but, whatever, kids started taking to the needle. In Edinburgh they snort it or stick it digitally up their tight arses, here they inject it. This is the world's injecting capital. I tell you, if they marketed milk in capsules and ampoules we'd have the healthiest kids in Christendom, they'd be grinding it, cooking it, sticking it into their veins and bulging muscles. Instead, it's heroin, or temazepam, diazepam – eggs, jellies in the argot – or both, or all, or basically anything they can shovel into an arm or leg or unblocked track that induces the big doolally.' He took a sip of his coffee. 'It's gone from the swallie to the doolally in a generation.' He smiled to himself. 'Sorry, that just occurred to me. I'll translate. Gaun fur a swallie, is going for a drink, a swallow. Doolally is madness, a term often affectionately applied.'

She put down her cup. 'Really? Whoever it was said about us being divided by a common language clearly was not Scotch.'

He took another sip of the coffee. 'Scots. So, at the risk of repeating myself, this is a small place but it's a busy thriving market, and it's a gateway too, all of which is very attractive to a monopoly supplier. Which brings us back to Stark. As I said, the word was that the old lad had retired. And maybe he even had. Certainly Junior was the one cutting the deals, until he made the mistake of getting caught.' Another sip. 'Actually, could be that *we* made the mistake catching him. After that it got really bad. With Junior and his first lieutenant and passenger Kenny Ward absent, some of the younger and more ambitious footsoldiers got ideas and desires above their station. There was a split, comings and goings, mergings and general confusion but a young guy called Sean Harris, very cold, very dangerous and without the trace of a scruple to discard, led off the rivals. And then it became very bloody and personal. Is this clear?'

'Sure,' she said. 'It has a depressing familiarity to it. Go on.'

'That is about all we know for certain. This next bit is extrapolation. So, with Junior inside and the struggle going on outside, even although he is keeping in touch by telephone, such is the penal society we have here, it's reasonable to suppose that Daddy steps back in. Which certainly might help to explain the two unfortunate accidents which then occur involving him. First, John Senior checks himself into a private hospital ward saying that he's had an unfortunate accident while involved in some DIY.'

'DIY?'

'Do-it-yourself. What do you call it? Home improvement?' She nodded, which he took as a sign to continue. 'According to him he's drilling something, possibly someone's kneecaps, when the bit breaks and miraculously impales him in the groin. The surgeon looks at the small, neat wound, does a bit of probing and discovers metal. Not, however, a broken-off bit but a .22 bullet.'

'An easy mistake to make.'

'Exactly. The hospital tells us about Stark's confusion over the accident, but the man himself, as you might expect, has absolutely no recall whatever of any violent incident directed at him. Why should he? He's a reputable businessman, as he keeps telling the world. Maybe, he says, the surgeon got his retrievals mixed up? We all know the long hours these doctors work. So, probably, hc goes on, a puzzled shooting victim can't understand why he keeps receiving get well cards and offers of compensation from Black and Decker.'

The coffee was cool now, so Ricketts, taking a big gulp, went on. 'Then a few months later, something similar. Stark is out taking an evening constitutional – staggering back from the pub more like – when a car mounts the pavement and knocks him through some railings into a front garden. Then comes back and runs over him again, but either the railings he had become entangled with somehow saved him from more serious damage, cushioning the impact, or he was extremely lucky, or, more likely, something scared off his assailants. No one, of course, in the immediate vicinity saw anything but a couple of people a few blocks away report hearing a car backfire several times, perhaps three times. A beat polis, rather uniformed officer, a quarter of a mile away saw a dark-coloured car, possibly a Sierra, speeding along the main road nearby just afterwards. Later that evening a dark blue Sierra was found in flames on some waste ground three miles away. Either the fire hadn't been set properly, perhaps the occupants were anxious to get off their marks, or the heavy rain and winds tamed it. Anyway, when the fire brigade got there they put it out and managed to save some of the evidence. Well, not really evidence as such, but they did discover what might have evaded us all if all that had been left was a smoking piece of burned and twisted metal: three neat holes in the bodywork and one .38 calibre, snub-nosed and very compacted bullet on the floor pan. Consider!'

'So,' Blantyre said, putting down her now empty cup, 'Stark or someone else—'

'A minder perhaps.'

'Put a few shots into the car.'

'Thereby scaring off the potential assassins. It's a fair presumption. Three cartridge cases were also found a few yards from the earlier scene, so that's a wrap. Anyway, the grapevine and a bit of astute guesswork – well actually the trail of droplets of blood – led directly to Stark's door. Our lads followed and woke the household. But either Stark was not in, as his wife said, or more likely he's hiding in the back, but anyway they did not manage to talk to him. There was a murmur about getting a search warrant but the advice was that this would be knocked back.'

'Where's the probable cause?'

'It certainly is a bit unconventional to roust the victim, I'll grant you. So we didn't get to talk to him. Next day he checks himself into another hospital with multiple fractures to one leg and more contusions on the body than you could count, and claims he fell down the stairs, or off the roof or something equally unlikely.'

Blantyre got up from her seat and turned her back on Ricketts and began to stretch and Ricketts, thinking that this was exactly what she would expect from him, followed the shiver of her body from the nape of her neck to the slim ankles accentuated by the heavy shoes, not forgetting to linger longingly on the curves of her buttocks. When she turned to look at him he could see in her knowing look that she knew – without peradventure, she'd probably testify – where his eyes had been prying.

'He's a tough old sonofabitch' – her mouth had the faintest of sneering smiles – 'but even so, he must have had someone to help him away, act as a crutch, because he sure as hell didn't hop very far. How far away does he live?'

'Half a mile.'

'Coupled with that you said the cartridges were found a few feet away. Indicating that whoever he was with either jumps out of the way of the car, or is nudged but not seriously, and then pulls out the gun while the car is revving and reversing over Stark and looses off, not fatally, but enough to scare off the driver. Then helps up the old man and takes him home.'

'That's exactly how I work it out.'

'And you figure, Sean Harris did it?'

'Check. Or associates, more like.'

'The question is, if the old man isn't back in the play, why would anyone want to take him out of it? Pull the final curtain?' She smiled, the first time she had since they had met.

Ricketts leaned back in his chair and folded his arms. 'Absolutely.'

McQuade was drinking beer. He did not know what it was other than that it was not designer, he had insisted on that, and it was flat and lukewarm so it was probably local, or had acclimatised well. He was upstairs in King Tut's, waiting for the band to go back on. His ears were still humming and the lines of coke were still racing around his veins, or wherever they went, short-circuiting the synapses, or whatever they did, and his mouth felt dry and metallic.

'It's exactly like sucking lead pencils,' he said, to no one in particular, 'the taste.' There were a few people around him he vaguely knew, from the same pubs and clubs they all went to, the circuit. 'Don't you think?' he added. 'Remember at school, sucking lead pencils, it's exactly that taste.' He took another swig of the lukewarm beer from the bottle it was too dark to identify by the label, then passed the back of his hand across his nose. 'And a nose like Lassie, that's another thing. Why does your nose always run? I suppose,' he went on, 'you could recycle the hankies. Like an anaesthetic dressing, slap them on your sore parts.'

He was aware that although the phosphorescent faces in the dark occasionally looked at him, no one was listening. Which was hardly surprising, he had to accept, given the volume of the pumped music which reverberated around the room. The air, he thought, such as it was and through the snotty rivulets in his nose, smelled of burned blotting paper and hair lacquer, or perhaps that was another side effect.

'Excuse me,' he said to a girl with a low-cut bodice pushing past him to the bar, who looked at him, cocked her head like a budgie as she checked and gave a faint smile, clearly unable to hear him. 'Never mind,' he shook his head at her, then dipped his eyes at her neckline. 'Wonderbra?' he mouthed slowly.

She stopped, tossed her head, and took a couple of paces back towards him, stood on her toes and screamed in his right ear, 'Naw, hormones.'

'It's true, they do. You've noticed. All the time. About the fake orgasms but especially, *especially* whingeing about the price,' he shouted back. 'Fortunately I'm rich.'

He lip-read her 'Fuck off', shrugged his shoulders, watched her back disappear in the crush. Big arse, he said to himself, took another swig and then out loud to the inattentive company 'I'm bored. That's another side effect they don't tell you about drugs.'

The piercing music tailed off and McQuade turned back to the stage, noticing that the musicians were meandering back, picking up instruments, adjusting their bobble hats and trying to look ineffably cool.

'Dermot McQuade?' He spun back, searching for the voice, until he felt a touch on his arm.

'I don't know you, do I?' he said, looking at the girl who seemed to be as tall as him. Peering at her, she seemed to be slightly foreign-looking, partly Oriental, if you could be that, a rounded face with big dark eyes, although anyone's eyes would have looked dark in the Stygian ambience of Tut's. Who was she? His mind was trying to turn quickly over profiles of people he had fucked, fucked over, tainted or basically brassed-off but when she smiled at him the mild gripe of panic vanished from his stomach.

'You're very well known,' she said, leaning over, talking into his ear so that he could feel her breath prickling, although there was no need to come so close in the temporary silence.

'Of course,' he said, immediately on guard, thinking, Someone is selling something so watch it! 'Can I do something for you?' He tried to smile, hoping his nose was not running too badly, thinking, Too fuckin' right I could.

'A drink?'

He nodded. 'Happily.' He leaned forward to her ear, so that their cheeks were only millimetres apart and he believed he could feel the electricity crackle the downy hairs, could smell the shampoo in her hair, not yet drowned and pickled in smoke. 'But the cynic in me,' he went on, 'warns that you didn't seek me out for a free shandy, a quick fuck or a short lesson on pathways into journalism.'

'Or all three?' She had a mouth which crinkled and her eyes seemed to pulse, either an effect of the coke or the strange lighting. 'No. I want to effect an introduction.'

'Effect an introduction? Quaint language. You're an android, that's it, isn't it?' And then it occurred to him that, perhaps, English was not her first language. 'I'm sorry,' he said quickly, 'that was rude. Forgive me.' But her face maintained the same glassy unbending smile so perhaps he was right after all. 'What are you drinking?' he continued.

'Something that doesn't rust my carefully crafted insides,' she said, maintaining the same smile. 'Three-in-one would be fine.'

'Beer, if they haven't any?'

'Good,' she said.

He pushed back to the bar where he quickly caught the eye of one of the harassed bar women, regularity had its privileges, and ordered two cold beers. They came, with the tops knocked off, in the same tepid state as before. 'Sorry,' he said when he got back to her, 'I forgot to ask for a plastic glass.' She shrugged. 'So?' he said after taking a swig. 'Who is it that you want me to meet? Who is it that employs beautiful envoys? I suppose' – he rubbed his nose again, conscious of the dribbling – 'that rules out Rupert Murdoch or George McKechnie?'

Her smile slipped into a look of puzzlement. 'Sorry?'

'McKechnie edits the *Herald*, Murdoch owns everything else.'

'We have even heard of Mr Murdoch on the Planet Uranus.'

'I'm sorry,' he said again, 'you're right. I am an arse. But' – he held her arm as she tried to raise the bottle to her lips – 'who do you want me to meet? I'm not going outside for anyone, even you.'

'He's across there.' She motioned with her head somewhere over her left shoulder. 'He could help you. Be a good contact. He just asked me to ask you over.'

'He hasn't a name?'

'Sure. What he said was not to say. "I'm sure we can rely on the instinctive curiosity of the journalist."'

'He said that?' Thinking, another android. 'Right.' He nodded his head then turned to the person next to him, a young man with very close-cropped and gelled hair, tugged him by the sleeve and said, 'If I'm not back in half an hour, Jim, remember her face.'

'Couldnae forget it, pal,' the stranger answered, his face blankly unrecognising of McQuade. Isn't it fortunate, McQuade told himself, that one half of the population of Glasgow is called Jimmy

He followed her through the throng. 'Shite,' he said out loud, then touched her shoulder, causing her to turn, still wearing the same smile. 'I don't even know your name.'

'Ayshea.'

'Really?'

'No. Senga Agnes McMorrin.'

'Naw? Senga? I don't believe it. I'll call you Mac.'

She moved on and across to a table where a group of three young men sat watching them arriving; between them a champagne bottle peeped out of a bucket. Four glasses, McQuade noted. For her, me? Then, Christ, I didn't know you could get champagne here.

The face behind the bottle was disturbingly familiar. McQuade could not quite place it, but instinctively he knew it featured in a recent cutting he had looked at. He tried flicking through the mental Roladex but the clips were turning too slowly and vaguely. 'Dermot,' the man said, standing, smiling, holding out a hand which McQuade shook mechanically, feeling a lump on a finger which he took to be a ring, then motioned to a chair facing him which someone must have just dragged in. He sat down, still trying to place the face, then turned back to ask the girl to sit down, but she had gone. 'Where's ehmm – she gone?'

'She'll be back,' the man said, 'later.' He was pouring from the bottle into two glasses, one of which he pushed across at McQuade, the other he lifted in a toast before sipping from it.

'The others?' McQuade said, putting down his almost full beer bottle and picking up the champagne, nodding to the two bookends.

'Not on duty. Not,' he went on quickly, 'that they, we, are busies of course.' He sipped again and sat back, waiting.

The band were tuning up now, so McQuade had to shout, bending over the table as he did so. 'So who are you? I know your face, but I can't place it.'

'That's good.' The other man nudged the compatriot to his left, who grinned dutifully.

'But I will.'

'Don't bother, I'll introduce myself. Harris, Sean Harris. You recall now?'

The guy on the other side of the table was grinning and now that his eyes could see better McQuade detected the white trace of a scar on his cheek. The clippings fell slowly into place and the conversation with Ricketts. He narrowed his eyes and tried to focus on the picture in his head. 'Just the once, I think? Only the one picture. Something to do with' – he searched in his head for the headline – 'a shooting.'

'Alleged shooting.'

'Of course. And drugs? Correct me.'

'I got off.'

'That time,' the one on the right said, and they all started to laugh.

The one on the right had a scar too, a ragged chib mark. It was a sort of masonic sign of the crime world; the degree of severity marked your progress, added to the general air of malevolence. You just could not be taken seriously as a villain without a torn face and twisted mouth, although McQuade had always thought that it was not the ones with the damaged faces you should look out for, but the ones who put the wounds there. The latest innovation in slashings, he remembered, was to tape a coin between two Stanley blades so that the double cut was almost impossible to stitch.

Harris's scar was, he considered, thought-provoking without being awesome, a sort of Heidelberg of the genre.

'So?' McQuade said when the laughter had subsided, still not wanting to betray that he knew Harris's place in the pantheon, and also resolving to call Ricketts in the morning for an update. It occurred to him that, perhaps, he was meant to feel afraid. He didn't. Probably the drugs again.

'I've been reading your stuff,' Harris said. 'Some of it is surprisingly accurate . . .' The rest of the sentence was drowned in the booming beat of the band starting up.

Harris shook his head angrily, pushed at the meat to his left, who shuffled out of the bench seat, and motioned at McQuade to replace him, which he did slowly, pulling his glass across the table after him. 'Very intimate,' he said into Harris's ear.

'Knackers the tape recording, though.'

'I don't have a tape,' McQuade shouted back.

'I know. You were checked.'

Had he been? By her? McQuade didn't really care. 'So?' he said again. 'Continue.'

'You're very well informed, if only partially.' Harris took another sip of champagne, McQuade studying his right hand to see if there were any tattoos on the knuckles. There weren't. But he picked up the ring, a heavy gold number with what was almost certainly a diamond set in it. Even in the dull light it glinted. 'The polis, I suspect.' Harris looked at him enquiringly. McQuade shrugged and said nothing. 'Nothing wrong with that, although it puts a certain spin on it.'

'You,' McQuade shouted again, 'don't tell me, you're the counter-spin.'

'Could be.'

McQuade wiped his nose again. 'Look, let's not fuck about here – Sean. What is it you want, what's in it for you, what's in it for me?'

'I'm an impeccable source.'

'As long as you're cheaper than my regular, you're on.'

Harris smiled at the implication. 'No, information.'

'So.' McQuade gulped at his drink. 'Inform.'

Harris was shaking his head. 'This meeting is just to open channels. It isn't business.'

'But let me guess, what you want from me is information in return, yes? This information super-highway is two-way. You want me to inform. Well, sorry.'

He began to rise but Harris put a hand on his arm, so he sat back down. 'You flatter yourself. I don't think there's much you could tell me that I didn't know or would find interesting. If I tell you things, all I want is that they aren't distorted, that it's told straight and without emphasis.'

'I get it now, you're looking for a publicist.'

Harris leaned forward, pulled the bottle out in a rattle of ice and topped up both their glasses. 'You're being prickly, a smartarse. You want stories, that's your currency, I can provide them. I just don't want to be stitched up.'

'Or it might be reciprocated?'

'I didn't say that.'

McQuade plucked up his glass again and dug his mouth into the bubbles. 'Why me?' He wiped his mouth and his nose with the back of his hand.

'Your paper has more influence, clout, than the tabloids.'

'Mr Harris,' McQuade said, 'I didn't know you were running for office.'

Later, after the second bottle was halfway finished and the band had petered out, Mac reappeared – Harris called her Stick, but McQuade was not too drunk to appreciate that was almost certainly not her real name either – and sat opposite, occasionally bringing her foot up under the table and, with her unshod toes, playing with the inside of his thigh. 'If I didn't know for certain' – McQuade smiled across at her – 'that I was irresistible, I might begin to question whether this sudden show of affection was mercenarily motivated.'

'I think,' she said, smiling back, 'that under that hard-boiled exterior there's a sensitive, soft egg' – she raised her eyebrows, and her leg – 'or two.'

McQuade, drunk, airily out of it, realised that the two of them were now alone at the table. 'Do you think,' he said quietly, 'that androids have orgasms?' And to himself, And can pass on any anti-social or fatal diseases?

Ricketts yawned, reached for the vacuum flask, looked enquiringly at Blantyre; she nodded, so he unscrewed the top. The steam from the coffee cup perched on top of the dashboard condensed on the windscreen in a dappled haze. The sun was just beginning to come up, the sky streaked red and all shades of grey. He finished pouring and handed the cup to her in the passenger seat. 'We'll have to share, unless you want me to drink it from the neck. You first.'

He watched her take the white plastic cup in both hands and blow into it, the steam wreathing her mouth. She was wearing faded jeans, a heavy padded black bomber jacket and her hair tied back, perhaps in recognition of where she was, in a tartan ribbon, Black Watch, he thought. 'Good,' she said.

'How are you feeling today? Any better?'

She took her right hand off the cup and made a seesawing motion. 'My head's buzzing, like being a bit stoned—'

'Or so you're told.'

'Whaaat? Oh' – she smiled quickly at him – 'sure. I didn't believe in jet-lag before. So, shit, I'm reviewing all my discarded myths. You know, honour, decency, redemption – maybe there's even a Santa Claus.'

He rubbed his mouth, anticipating the coffee. 'Have you been here before? Britain?'

She shook her head, nuzzling the cup again. 'Nah. First time in Europe.'

'What do you think so far?'

'Mmhh?' She looked up again. 'Oh, your Holiday Inn is just wonderful—'

'Our policemen too,' he came in. 'It's a well-known fact, everyone says.'

'Do you ever give up, Ricketts?'

'Never. Dogged doggone Ricketts they call me.'

In spite of herself she smiled. 'Anything happening out there?'

Ricketts looked at his watch, then picked up the binoculars from his lap and looked out. 'The gate's still closed. But shortly, any time now.'

The car was parked in a lay-by on the edge of the wood, to the north of the gate, nose pointing south towards it and the city. Blantyre, the coffee finished, handed the cup back and Ricketts carefully poured himself a measure. It was strong and bitter and black, he felt it scald his throat and then his stomach as it went down. He had debated putting a few slugs of whisky in it but now he was thankful he hadn't. No doubt she would have reported him. His eyes came back up from the cup. 'Christ,' he said, slopping the coffee on his leg and the fascia as he tried to put the cup on the dashboard, then he quickly turned, put his left arm round Blantyre, bent over and pulled her towards him.

'What the fuuu—' she said, struggling, as he pulled her into the nape of his neck.

'A car, behind. Lights on, parking,' he said into her mouth, his lips a tantalising inch or two away from hers. 'We're winchin', remember.'

'We're what?' she said, removing his right hand from the leather patch over her left breast.

'Making out,' he whispered.

They both heard the engine turning over, the sound of the handbrake going on and then the motor dying. She hissed a whisper at him: 'Do you seriously think anyone's going to believe that a couple are going to make out in a lay-by a hundred yards from the front door of a fuckin' prison?' Her lips and nose screwed up. 'Did you have garlic last night?'

Mmhh? Yeah, sorry,' he said. 'That's the whole point. They're meant to know who we are, or suspect who we are, just so's they don't see our faces. We want them to think they're being followed and also that we're too stupid to mount discreet surveillance.'

'We do? Why?'

'Orders, don't ask me why. "Let them know you're about," was what they said, "just don't get found out." Maybe it's police harassment. Let's hope so.' His right hand went up behind her head and began to shake it slightly; her hair felt silky and newly washed. 'Simulated passion,' he said, 'for the watchers.'

He could taste the coffee on her breath as she leaned forward slightly and caught his nose in her teeth. 'You're enjoying thish,' she said slowly between her teeth, still holding his nose tight.

'That's sore,' he moaned, trying to pull his face away.

'Passhin,' she answered, before letting go.

Ricketts began to massage his throbbing nose with his free hand. She smiled primly. 'Is it marked?' he said.

'Hopefully. Too dark, can't see. So' – she wriggled in her seat again – 'what's your wife gonna say about the toothprints?'

'I'm not married,' he whispered.

'You're all married,' she said, shaking her head.

'I'll have to wear a false nose to go into the office, or a piece of tape, like Jack Nicholson in *Chinatown*.'

'Don't flatter yourself.'

They heard the engine behind kick into life again. Ricketts ducked his head. 'Can you see what's happening?'

'The gate's open' she said, patting his head then grabbing his hair and stopping him, adding, 'that's far enough.'

Ricketts, his eyes focused on Blantyre's crutch from six inches, heard the car go past. 'Haven't we,' he said, 'made some small but basic mistake here? A certain inversion in the traditional roles?'

'Mercedes,' he heard from above. And when he sat up and looked at the gates of the prison he could see Fat Boy with a package in his hands, looking round about him. Ricketts picked up the glasses again, fumbled in his inside pocket for a pen and began memorising the licence plate of the Mercedes which pulled up alongside Stark, the nearside back door opened and the prisoner, wearing a dark overcoat for his home weekend, after throwing in his package, climbed into the car.

Ricketts reached for the key in the ignition and turned over the engine, waiting for the Mercedes to move off before he engaged gear. When he had safely settled behind the tail-lights of the other car, so that they became like a hazy spot, a laser sight tracing the bends of the road about a quarter of a mile ahead, he began to relax. Blantyre was chuckling quietly to herself. 'What?' he said, after a few seconds, feeling riled and somehow knowing that he was the focus of it.

'What were you doing back there?' He could see out of the corner of his eye that she was still smiling.

'In case they recognised me.' He was trying to vary his distance slightly behind the other car, moving forward and back, so that it looked haphazard.

'It's okay that they recognise me?'

'You're foreign.'

'Right. I see. Bullets discriminate, do they? Anyway,' she continued, 'I'm sure they tune to the police band. Also, and surely to Christ, they know the number plates of all the local cop cars.'

'They are meant to suspect, not know for sure. It's hired anyway. The car. Along with the' – he nodded at her – 'the top gun.' He began to smile now too. 'It was instinctive. I thought that if I had kissed you, for cover, you'd have whacked me.'

'Too right.'

'So.' He shrugged.

'So?'

'Nothing.' Feeling embarrassed, not wanting to look across at her.

'Look,' she went on, 'I'm all for safe sex but, you know, cunnilingus with the Levis on?' She was tapping the glass of the passenger window, rimshots, obviously wearing a ring, and still laughing to herself.

'Right, right! Next time, in a stake-out with one of New York's finest I'll insist on a skirt on my colleague, whatever the sex.'

She continued tapping, not looking at Ricketts. 'Did no one tell you,' she murmured, 'we don't just have minds like steel traps?'

'Right,' he said, shifting down a gear going into a bend, 'I think I heard that once on *Cagney and Lacey*.'

They were silent for several miles, Ricketts tracking the merging yellow spots ahead, like a missile picking up the target. 'Any idea where they're going?' she said as the outskirts of the city began to drift past.

'Pretty shrewd guess.' He booted the car and slid through a roundabout. 'We are talking habituation here, in criminality, personal behaviour . . . so I should think it will be a check call to the old man, the ritual kissing of the cheeks and so on, then alcohol, sex, more alcohol, oblivion.'

'Although they know we are watching.'

'Particularly because they know we are watching,' Ricketts said, watching the tail-lights, convinced now that he knew exactly where the first stop on the route would be.

Chapter Seven

'**D**on't think I don't know what's going on.' He could hear
the fierce, whispered anger through his sleep. His mother's
voice was slurred, as it always was, but there was an edge
of bitterness and malice even he had never heard before. 'You've
got someone else, somewhere else too, haven't you? Haven't you!'
He could not hear the low reply but he knew that it must be from his
father. His mother began to cry again. 'What do you mean, "Look
at me?" I'm only what you've made me.' He tried to block out the
sounds of argument by burrowing into the blanket but the muffled
words kept finding a way past.

'Why don't you go to her then? Because she's someone else's, just
like you are? Is that it?' He heard the hard crack of a slap and then
the keening edge of his mother's scream which tailed down into a
low bubbling moan, then a door opening and her shouting, between
gulping sobs: 'And don't think I don't know all about you and what
you're up to. I know it all. All of it.' Then the sound of the outside
door slamming and he waited in the dark, behind the curtain in the
grubby, sweaty bedclothes, for the sound of glass jarring on glass
and then the rush of pouring and for the gulps and sobs to become
indistinguishable. And, finally, for the silence.

In the morning when he got up she was lying with her face
on the kitchen table, a dribble of blood or biddy on the edge
of her mouth, he didn't know which. He took away the glass
and located the bottle where it had rolled across the linoleum
and then he put on the kettle and waited, staring out of the
dirty scullery window, as the steam built up around him, until
finally he took a dishcloth from the peg, wrapped it round the
handle of the kettle and, although he felt the rage in him to
hurl the boiling water at her to rouse her or maim her, instead
he poured it into the teapot and added three heaped spoons of

tea, stirred the leaves into the brown water, replaced the lid and roughly shook his mother's loose arm.

Whatever had happened his mother never explained, but from then on there were not even any heated arguments in the night. A couple of weeks later they moved along the street to a bigger house, a two-room and kitchen just one up. There wasn't much to move. Three unspeaking men turned up, friends of his father's, with a cart for the broken furniture and the boxes of household goods and when all of it was cleared there were just the empty bottles, dozens of them in every cranny, and although it embarrassed him, his mother did not seem to care. It was as if she was parading what she had become as some bitter admonishment against her husband to the outside world.

'The factor will want it clean,' one of the men finally said.

'Well, let *him* clean it,' his mother replied, turning on the man, her face highly coloured, her mouth tight. 'Or his bitch!'

Then they closed the door on the house and walked slowly along the street. He felt eyes on them, knowing that they were being watched as they went, smirking and gloating behind hands or net curtains, little comments being made about the break-up of the Starks. He looked up to see but all he could take in was the glare of blank windows.

Apart from having an extra room to hold even more bottles, nothing much changed in the new house. He tried to ask his mother why they had moved but she would only say, 'Never you mind, son,' in a bitterly triumphal way. Only later would he realise that this was some tangible tribute she had extracted from her husband for his behaviour to her. She began to drink even more and money never seemed to be short, for cheap wine certainly, and although he did not know for certain where it came from, intuitively he realised that his father was providing. This also was part of the price she had extracted. For just what he did not yet know.

They had not been in the new house for more than a few days when there was a heavy knock on the front door. He reached up and unsnibbed the latch, his mother's voice shouting from the kitchen, asking who it was. He looked up over a profound belly garbed in black to the rich, round face of a priest. Although the

family were nominally Catholics none of them went to mass; all
that marked them were the crucifixes in the rooms and the little
dish, always empty, for the holy water.

'Is yer mammy in, son?' The priest was Irish, they all were,
and Johnnie recognised him, not from any spiritual surroundings,
although he had seen him several times in the chapel house, but
because he had often picked up his lines. The priest did not seem
to recognise him, despite patting him on the head and smiling.

'It's Father Miles,' Johnnie called ben the house. 'He wants to
see you.'

His mother arrived in the hall, stumbling into him, and then
pushing him away. 'I've heard of your trouble, Mrs Stark,' the
priest said in his rehearsed way. 'Is there anything I can do?' he
asked, putting on one of those doleful smiles the clergy regard
as bespeaking a state of grace.

'You shouldn't be round here asking me that. Did he put you up to
it?' she said, swaying on the door. 'Sent on an errand by an adulterer
were yi? Or did you just decide to poke yir neb in?' Johnnie could
smell the sweet decay on her breath. Then she pushed the priest in
the stomach, knocked Johnnie aside so that he went sprawling back
in the bare hall as she slammed the door shut, before slumping down,
her back against it, her head in her lap, too worn down even to cry.

Johnnie got up from the floor. The force of the drunken push
had clattered his head off the wall and he felt stinging tears in
his eyes but he was determined they would not spill, and looked
down at his mother. He realised that he felt nothing but shame
and he turned slowly and went into the kitchen to see if he could
find anything edible in the place.

'This is madness.' She was looking at the huge dirt-smeared windows. 'You must be off your head.' Despite what she was saying
she was smiling. 'Totally.'

'Where's the romance in your soul?' He was picking random notes
on the piano. 'Can't you see the possibilities?'

'Actually,' she said, looking up, 'not for the fifty years of soot
and glaur and doo shite.'

He sat down on the revolving piano stool and spun himself round.
'I can just see myself in a dinner jacket, black tie, greeting the guests.'

She began to giggle. 'A stage here' – he drew airily in the direction of the far corner – 'a big band. One of those birling balls . . .'

'Like the Plaza.'

'Like the Plaza only bigger. Hundreds of couples dancing, getting to know each other . . .'

'Paying the admission money.'

'Naturally. A bar or two on the floor above, where they can tap their feet to the music coming from below. Nice decor. Colours of the rose, of course. A year or two from now . . .'

'An impresario,' she said, beginning to walk from the centre of the huge floor towards him, shaking her long hair and smiling at him, 'a chain of dance halls, the record company – where will it end? Prison probably.'

'Well, so much for the grand gesture.'

She was standing in front of him, looking down, smiling. 'That stool looks like it hasn't been cleaned in years. You'll stand up and there'll be a great big greasy patch on those new trousers.' He continued to swivel on the rotating seat. 'What grand gesture is this?'

'We met in a ballroom. So . . .' He spread his hands.

'Yes? So?'

'So I thought I'd get us one of our own as a memento, where we could meet whenever we want.'

'Be serious.'

He leaned back on the seat and cupped his hands behind his head. 'Well, it was thinking about us meeting that sparked it off. I was standing outside looking at the Rose, thinking about meeting you in the Plaza, when you all but gelded me, and it came to me.'

'It?'

'That this was such a wasted asset. I mean, a dance school. In the Gorbals. If you don't learn to dance on the street corner then you're never going to pick it up in a place like this. It's been going downhill ever since I can remember. In the same family's mismanaging hands for years. And I thought, This has got a load more potential then the Tripe. You could get 750 in here easy.'

'With a crowbar, maybe.'

'Good music, reasonable prices, great atmosphere – equals profit.'

She unbuttoned the velvet top button of her suit, which fixed Stark's attention on her neck, and the high vee of her white blouse. 'You're not telling me,' she said at last, pleasingly conscious that his gaze had now dropped a few degrees, 'that this is yours?'

'It needs a few improvements. But Razzle's organising that. Plasterwork, a bit of paint – you can choose the colours – and I'll get round to the upholstery and the plumbing when the money starts to come in.'

'Goes down the pan more like.'

'I can tell that you're deeply impressed beneath that wry contempt. C'mere.' He put out his hand to grab her arm but she stepped back, smiling. 'He's very useful, your husband. I mean, if you want tradesmen at a reasonable rate who better to organise it than a trade union official? At least the comrades are not going to walk out on strike, are they?'

She had folded her arms and was leaning back on her right heel. 'I'm not sure he doesn't suspect.'

'No chance. Love's blind.'

'Not blind enough' – she paused and pointed round her back – 'to miss a huge bitemark on my bum.'

Stark began to rock with laughter.

'It's not funny,' but in spite of herself she was starting to giggle. 'You're always pushing things to the limit. I had to tell him I fell on a shoehorn.'

'A shoehorn!' He was spluttering, hardly getting the words out. 'Why a shoehorn?'

'It was the first thing that came to mind.' She was beginning to smile. 'I had just bought a pair of shoes.'

'A shoehorn? He believed that? Hedgehog maybe. Running spikes or a bag of rivets. But a shoehorn?' Tears were beginning to come to his eyes.

'He told me that it was my own fault.' She moved a couple of steps towards him, her chest rising and falling with gulped laughter. 'He said my skirts were too tight and my heels were too high and that probably caused me to fall over.'

'What did I tell you, love *is* blind.'

'I don't think he's ever seen a love bite before.'

She had moved forward another step and his arms were encircling her. He began to pick at the buttons of her coat. 'That figures.'

'I think he was virgin when I met him.'

He had all the buttons undone and was starting on the blouse, rolling the little mother of pearl buttons in his fingers, as if they were her nipples. The thought sent a shiver up her. 'And you?' he said and although she could not see his face she could tell from his voice that he was smiling. She did not answer. His hand had moved inside her blouse and on to her bare skin.

'You're not wearing anything,' he said, opening her blouse fully and putting his lips to her.

'I knew I was meeting you.' She grasped his head hard to her.

'What about below?' His voice rumbled on her breasts and both of his hands cupped round her bottom, rubbing gently.

'It's cold. You can only take the notion of seduction so far. If the mood's strong enough it ought to withstand a pair of blue bloomers.'

'I'll bet.' He stood, kissing up her breasts and neck as he went, then the side of her mouth and, with her eyes closed, she felt him behind her and pulling up her tight skirt hard over her buttocks. Then she was aware of him dropping to his knees.

'Not again,' she whispered as her pants came down.

'It's a sort of Benny Lynch colour now, black and blue,' he said and she felt his lips there, then his tongue gently sliding along in the crevice between her cheeks, which sent gooseflesh up her arms and legs. Her skirt was like a ruffled cummerbund round her waist now and, still with her eyes closed, she stumbled forward slightly, her knees catching the stool, so that she began to lose her balance and threw both arms out to stop herself falling. Her hands jolted on to the piano keyboard and in a loud, jangling discord he went into her.

As he pushed and as she pushed against him and struggled to keep her balance as his pitch grew, the cacophony from the keys grew faster and louder. 'What do you call it?' he panted in her ear.

'Jazz,' she mumbled, just before the accompaniment agonisingly terminated.

*　　*　　*

Dick Laughton's feet hurt. He had been walking most of the evening and he still had a few hours to go. He thought idly of a hot mustard bath for them when he got home, a large whisky, feet soaking in the yellow brine. It was as near to ecstasy as he could imagine, chilled through, drenched and corns threatening to burst out of the leather each time a big brogue hit the pavement. It was his own fault. He could have been sitting back in the squashy seats of a big Austin but that was not his way. That's what he told himself anyway. Getting close to it, making a presence, a statement, that was what was important. Never mind that he got car sick, a man of his age, he couldn't admit that, no chance. There would be the inevitable sheepshagger comments behind his back, of course, the puerile jokes about teuchters, donkeys and traps. Anyway, he enjoyed his own company for the most part, it was just a pity that the law demanded corroboration or he would never bother with a partner.

He walked up the big stone steps into the yellow, gas-lit hallway, nodded to the man on the desk and eased his big wearied feet up the stairs. He was wearing a three-piece tweed suit. Harris tweed suit. He probably knew who wove it, even the sheep who conceived it, the wry thought occurred to him. It itched constantly, particularly on the inside legs, so he had taken to wearing long johns in all weathers, but there were just some things in life a man had to do for the heritage and despite the privations. Well, at least he had not entirely lost his sense of humour. The suit marked out his difference too, his own uniform of distinctiveness. Noticeability was important in any walk of life.

The room was in its perpetual fug. That was another thing he had not entirely got used to despite the years, the concentrated haar a dozen or more dedicated smokers could produce when at least five of them puffed on pipes (Sherlock Holmes had a lot to answer for). This was something else which set him apart. A non-smoker. The others put it down to some Calvinistic aberration in his Wee Free background, the denial of pleasure or some such. But it was nothing to do with that. He had been an ill child through the period he might have started, pleurisy and other vaguely defined bronchial conditions, and when he went into the army in the war there did not seem much point in joining in, just to be part of the group. He wasn't and wouldn't be, so what was the use? His accent always marked him down as a big, gormless islander to them. Which he cultivated because it was useful, because people always underestimated him. Trusted him too, because of it, which was useful also.

He had reached his desk and he could see before he even sat down the scraps of ill-written notes, the piles of files spilling apart. No matter how tidy he left the desk – and he always did, this was another idiosyncracy – it was always raked over when he came back, although no one would ever admit to it. The senior officers, of course, he wouldn't dare challenge so, all in all, it was pointless to get upset about it although he always did. He sighed and sat down and tried to make tidy, collecting the messages into a sheaf, flicking through to see if any of them were important, none of which were.

When he looked up McKorkindale was looking down at him. 'Christ, man, d'ye always have to sneak up like that? Can't you cough a couple of paces away or say something?' he said quickly, chucking the notes down and sitting back in his hard wooden chair. 'Like, "Excuse me, Inspector?" Hmm?'

'Sorry, sir. Rather, excuse me, sir.'

'Just get on with it man.'

'Sorry. Right, sir.' McKorkindale was a DC, all of five months now, and great things were predicted for him, by whom Laughton had never established. He seemed to him just a daft, gauche laddie, too easily intimidated.

Well, son?'

'Sorry, Inspector.' He coughed, clearing his throat. To Laughton he looked barely old enough to have joined the force, although he knew he was twenty-five, and apparently university educated which, he had to admit, made him a sort of outsider too. The secret joy of not being part of the herd, he considered, was rapid ascent, so you could shit on them. He reminded himself, once more, to be kinder to McKorkindale.

'Sit down, son.' The DC looked confused, he reddened and glanced bleakly around. Strike kindness then, Laughton told himself, but eventually the boy found a chair and sat down on the other side of the desk. 'All ears, son.'

The detective coughed again and the movement of him putting his hand to his mouth to stifle it politely made Laughton notice that he was trying, pretty pitifully, to grow a moustache. 'We've got a prisoner downstairs, sir. Ordinarily I wouldn't bother you because he's a pretty minor offender, but the thing is—'

'Name!' Laughton cut in.

'Sorry?' McKorkindale was at sea again 'Oh, Sullivan, Francis Thomas. Breaking and entering, nothing violent.'

'Familiar name. From Brigton way, is he?'

'I don't think so, sir.'

'Just my wee joke. Sullivan. Catholic. Hardly from Bridgeton, hmm? Ireland, by way of the Bar-L, perhaps? I remember him, I think. Obnoxious little shite.'

'He was picked up by a couple of the beat lads with his pockets and arms full of whisky bottles, half cut, a couple of streets away from a pub—'

'Going about his normal unlawful business?'

'Exactly, sir.'

'So, why should we be interested in Francis Thomas?'

'Well, after he was charged he slept in the cell for a couple of hours and then he said he had important information, asked to see – ehmm, someone in charge.'

Laughton smiled broadly. 'So they sent you, Korky? To collect this precious information. I'm pleased to see ribaldry is still alive in the constabulary.'

'He wanted to make a deal.'

'There's a surprise. What did he offer, a couple of bottles of Glenfiddich?'

'What he is saying, sir, is that there's some fiddle going on at John Brown's, to do with the union subs. He seems very well informed. He got a start there a few months ago and seems to have been collecting information.'

'The first marker of an itinerant thief. Protect your back passage. Did you believe him?'

'Well, sir, yes I did.' McKorkindale leaned forward earnestly. 'Obviously I'm not qualified to judge—'

'False modesty is not becoming, son.' Laughton pointed his index finger. 'You want me to talk to him?'

'Yes, sir, if you would.'

Laughton pushed back his seat and got up, feet firing up in complaint again, the itch of movement beginning to nag. 'Lead on, Orpheus.'

'Sorry?'

'To the underworld, Constable.'

The cells in the basement had no natural light. There was a rancid, damp smell to the place, overlaid with the comingled stenches of urine and sick. The turnkey walked in front of them down the long corridor, between the huge dark cell doors, keys jangling on his belt with each footfall. Laughton thought of Tinkerbell.

The cell was second from the end and when the door swung open Sullivan, standing hunched over, was just finishing pissing in a pot. Laughton looked at McKorkindale, screwed up his mouth and shook his head while Sullivan finished. He was somewhere in his mid-thirties, Laughton guessed, sallow of face, with a crooked, probably broken, nose, from which a trickle of recently dried blood ran into a rough reddish moustache. His left eye was swollen and closing.

'What happened?' Laughton said, hands in pockets, nodding at his face.

'Wan o' yir bastards hit—'

His head rattled as Laughton hit him with his open left hand which had come up so fast that Sullivan had not even had a chance to prepare himself. But it was McKorkindale who gasped.

'One, they aren't! And two, they didn't. Right?'

Sullivan's head was coming back, a burst of blood on his lips which he dabbed at with his right hand. 'Right,' he agreed.

'So that's settled. Anything else you want settled?' Laughton's hands were back in his pockets.

'This charge—'

'Not possible.' He was shaking his head.

'Ah cannae go back in. There's people I owe.'

Laughton smiled. 'Tell me something I couldn't have guessed.'

Sullivan looked around him, still unfamiliar with his whereabouts, sat back down on the slight bench, six inches above the ground, which held the discoloured mattress. Discoloured, Laughton

146

thought, did not even begin to describe the smeared, dun material. He cautioned himself not to get nearer than his own height to it. He had read somewhere, either that or it was inherited myth, that fleas could jump six feet. Indeed, couldn't jump any less than six feet because they had some spring mechanism in their legs, however many legs they had, which always sent them the same distance. 'It's Broon's. The convenor's on the fiddle.'

'Really. Well, frankly, who the fuck cares? Why should that concern the polis? Take it up with the Movement or your MP.' All the same, something sparked with Laughton. For a few seconds he could not remember what. Then it came back, itching at him. The robbery and murder last year, which had clearly been abetted by inside knowledge and which they had never even got close to clutching a tendril of. And now here this was; well, a coincidence of corruption at least, which made this very interesting. A vein of corruption was always worth exploring, it might even produce the motherlode.

'His name's Dundas. I've been asking about him, checking up, you know.' Yes, Laughton knew, looking for exploitable information. Blackmailable information. 'He's doing very well for himself. Living above his means.'

'Maybe the wife's got a private income?'

'Even so—' Sullivan was smirking on the soiled bed, 'he's got some interesting connections.' He waited, but Laughton would not be baited. 'Stark. Mean anything?'

Laughton looked round at McKorkindale and smiled thinly, then back to Sullivan. 'Might do,' he said brightly, 'might indeed do.'

'You'll have to make a statement,' Laughton said at the end of it. Sullivan was beginning to shake his head, but Laughton put up a hand to still him. 'You've told us it all anyway, laddie. Two of us. We can use it in court, you know.'

The man on the mattress was sitting up, clutching his knees, thinking about cursing the two police but he was just bright enough to realise that doing that would not help his case whereas wheedling might and, anyway, cheek would just get him another backhander.

'What about me?'

147

'What indeed?' Laughton said, looking down, shaking his head. 'This is way it will be. You'll plead guilty to reset. We'll lose a few of the bottles, if you know what I mean.' Sullivan knew exactly what the detective meant and he cursed him inwardly. 'And I'll tell the PF that you are being considerably helpful in several linked investigations and we need you around, and he'll get you a non-custodial sentence. Okay?'

Laughton smiled, pleased with himself. Sullivan looked down at his knees and nodded.

'I wonder,' Laughton said, now looking at McKorkindale, 'if our man's got any previous.'

'I'll check, sir.'

'Makes me wonder how he and Stark got together.'

'Both fae the Gorbals,' Sullivan said.

'Maybe,' Laughton agreed. Then he touched McKorkindale's arm and motioned with his head. 'We'll be leaving you now, lad, to let your heid consider any other information that might be lurking in there.'

The door swung heavily on its hinges, making a sound like a heavy thunderclap as it slammed shut and the noise resonated in the amplifying bare corridor. The two detectives' boots clipped metallically on the floor as they went. 'What I don't believe in,' Laughton said, 'apart from the divine right of kings and the possibility of Partick Thistle winning the league, is coincidence.'

'Sorry, sir?' McKorkindale said, half a pace adrift.

'That raid at Brown's last year, you remember. They went at it like the HLI, well rehearsed and entirely vicious. A cashier, I think it was, got bayonetted. He bled away on the floor as our boys executed a waterborne evacuation. Not at all your everyday crime and one which needed a lot of local knowledge, don't you think? Now, who better to have the freedom of the Clyde than our man Dundas? Who better to study the byways and alleys, the times and places and goings and comings, than the union man? Clocking it all as he meanders about the yard winding up the workers and dreaming about the Glasgow Soviet. Christ!' He stopped so that McKorkindale bumped into him, quickly apologising. 'What a blow against capitalism, eh?' The young detective could see a broad smile on his face. 'And a bit more productive than walking the men out for a tanner.'

He set off again, with McKorkindale in tow and when they had cut through the fog in the CID room and made Laughton's desk the older man said: 'We'll have this Dundas bastard in, and you' – he swung down into his seat – 'we'll have none of that fancy fistwork this time!' He grinned up at the perplexed DC. 'This is a man of some substance. What we'll need is cunning detective work. Applied pressure of a subtle nature. So, we'll grab him by the balls and twist hard! I find that usually produces an anguished bleat of honesty.'

Dundas watched the room slowly compose. 'Hmmm?' he said. 'Sorry.' The radio was playing Scottish country dance music, a Strathspey, the odours of dinner were still hanging in the room, his head felt like damp heather. 'You say something, love?' Hazel was looking down at him on the couch, a grim set to her mouth.

'To see you.' Her head motioned towards the hall. 'Police.'

'What?' He sat up, rubbing the sleep out of his eyes. His stomach reeled with the music. Looking up he saw two figures coming into the room, one brawny, a drooping salt and pepper moustache, hair cut unfashionably short and brutal so that it bristled and tufted, the other much younger, late twenties against the other's late middle age. The younger one looked vaguely embarrassed, the older man was clearly enjoying himself, from the upward twitching of his moustache.

'Mr Dundas?' Razzle nodded. 'DCI Laughton, and this is Detective Constable McKorkindale.' The big man's hand went into an inside pocket and came out with a paper which he held up. 'We have a search warrant.'

'What?' Dundas stood up and held out his hand but the policeman shook his head and held it up so that he could read it. But he couldn't take it in. 'Carl,' he heard Hazel say anxiously, but he held his hand palm up to her to stop her. He could feel the blood raging in his face and he wondered if he was reddening. 'I don't understand.'

'We'd like you to come down to the station.'

'Like me to?'

'We have some questions.'

'What about?'

'Later.'

Razzle noticed that the other man was beginning to open drawers in the living room cabinet and was sifting through. 'You can't do this.'

'You can read, I take it?' the big Highlander said with an expression that was a kind of pleased grimace. 'The warrant says we can.'

Dundas was on his feet, wiping the sleep out of his eyes, his brain searching for something redemptive to come up with. Instead, he looked across at Hazel who was standing with her arms folded against the wall, her eyes levelled on him, burning. 'What am I supposed to have done?' he said at last. 'I'm entitled to know.'

'We are investigating' – Laughton drew the words out slowly, chewing on them – 'a robbery and murder at your place of work. I'm sure you remember it. Cashier killed? On Fair Friday?'

Dundas felt a wave of nausea begin in his stomach, his legs shuddered under him so that he had to slump back on the settee. 'Not me,' he said, shaking his head, looking up at the detective. 'Not me,' once more.

'If not you, then who?' The leering grimace again, the expression of some animal, Dundas thought, having just pulled a head from a carcase. 'Tell me, do you know, have you ever met, Peter Stark?'

Dundas looked up. Tiny fiery explosions seemed to be going off in the atmosphere between him and the detective, his head felt airy and his ears were full of the rush of his own blood. 'I met—'

'Say nothing,' he heard Hazel's voice cutting in. He looked up and she seemed, as she walked towards him now, ablaze in light. 'I'm sure these detectives were just about to tell you that you didn't have to say anything – and that a solicitor would be a good idea.'

She was beside him on the couch, her hand on him, apparently consoling, but only he could feel the painful hold she exerted as her fingers dug into his arm. He nodded. 'So, Inspector,' she went on, 'shall we phone now or from the station?'

He felt slow and dull, in a thick mist of unknowing. He did not need to be told the extent of the trouble he was in but it seemed not to register properly. He was in the back of the car beside the younger detective and he was not handcuffed, which gave him some comfort although he didn't know why it should. Everything seemed underpaced and oddly coloured. He focused on the material of the policeman's coat beside him, herring-bone, hairy, and the smell in the car of polish and stale tobacco, and it seemed comforting. He wondered if he were suffering from some kind of infection; it seemed so, sounds were fuzzy in his ears and he felt fevered. And although his stomach had settled he knew that he must be in some kind of shock. He had to stay quiet, trust in Hazel, but that would not be enough, he knew that. The police would not have taken him, he told himself, if they had not been confident they had enough evidence. What did they have? Nothing – it wasn't possible – that would link him to the robbery? To the rope! The idea dried his throat. Well, if they had said that just to frighten him or to soften him it had succeeded. He had nothing to do with it. But what was that phrase, 'accessory after the fact'? Was there such a thing or was that something he had picked up from the gangster pictures? What mattered was that there couldn't be any evidence to implicate him in it. Surely?

He kept going over it. What did they have? He closed his eyes and leaned further back in the seat. The detective next to him seemed to have pushed over on to him, to intimidate, he could feel the harsh material of his coat scratching at his hand as the car bumped slowly across the cobbles. Say nothing, he told himself. Remember that.

He could rely on Hazel. By now she would have contacted a solicitor. She would have – He sat forward sharply, and a pain tightened in his gut. No, not Stark. She wouldn't have talked to him. Would she? He thought about it. Why not? Wasn't it sensible to do that, to come up with some defence? He shook his head. He didn't even know what he had done – well, he knew that but he didn't know what they knew he had done. His head swam. Would they keep him in a cell tonight? The thought jolted him and he felt nauseous. He had never been in prison. Of course they would hold him, it was part of the intimidation process. It was Stark they really wanted, surely. But he was their only means to him.

The thick mist began to roll in behind his eyes again as he vaguely became aware of the car jolting to a stop. Well, if it comes to it, he said to himself, that's the way it will be. Hazel. Must protect Hazel.

He thought about their first meeting and craved to go back. All of it had been for her. Now, it all seemed absolutely futile.

151

*   *   *

As she sat in the taxi Hazel found herself surprised at her reactions. She had not felt in the least scared or intimidated. She had opened the door to the police and there had been an exhilarating burst of adrenalin, a racing of the brain, as if a great challenge, a contest had started. The air felt keen and energised. She had watched Carl stumble, falter, slither along the edge of tears and supplication and the feeling of superiority it had given her felt good too. She smiled to herself and looked up, catching the eye of the cab driver in his rear-view mirror. She stared fiercely at him until his eyes flicked away.

The cab was moving slowly; a thick cold fog had come in, foreshortening vision, providing, she felt, a flat cold logic to her life. She did not know what she could do for Carl – a lawyer of course, her strength for his – but this was of his own making, he had not included her, probably to protect her or for fear of her disapproval but, above all, she knew that she was not going to be embroiled in it. She was going to look out for herself. She wasn't going to become one of those squeezed-out husks in a shawl waiting for her imprisoned man to come home while life itself escaped.

Looking out of the window she thought they must be in Argyle Street. She could see headlights, yellowed and stained by the mist and soot so that they looked like the eyes of wild beasts slipping by. The cab crawled on, then the bleary lights of what looked like a picture hall, before it swung left through the coiling mist and now she knew where she was. She uncrossed her legs, her stockings crackled as she did so and she saw, or convinced herself she did, the white roar of static.

The cab stopped and she opened herself out from her slouch, picked up her handbag and let herself out into the night air which smelled of smoke and damp vegetation. She could hear the barking of ship sirens like animal noises from the river as she hunted in her bag for money and then, as the cab chugged away, for the keys.

'You shouldn't have come here like this' he said as the door swung open on him. 'You could have been followed.'

'No,' she said. 'The mist – it's like a curtain has come down.' She felt his hands round her waist, then on her back under her coat as he nuzzled at her lips.

'In a way,' he said, pressing into her, 'it has.'

* * *

Old Devlin had told him he must be able to see round corners
and he did seem to have a sixth sense which warned him to avoid
trouble; either that or it was some extremely heightened instinct
for self-preservation. He never seemed to walk into brawls, or beat
bobbies, or complaining punters. Maybe it was some change in the
atmosphere which alerted him so that his feet checked and he would
peer around a corner, or into a close, and usually find a cause not to
proceed, when any other time he would simply have waltzed round
it unthinkingly. It was uncanny, even to him. Now he could feel the
way was clear and he walked across the back greens, skirting the
washhouses where there was cover, and made for Crown Street.
He felt familiarly lop-sided, the money, coins mostly, in the right
pocket of his trousers, the lines, folded and stuffed as neatly as he
could manage, in his left pocket. It had been cold and wet for days;
the dampness hung on him, his nose ran constantly and the sleeves
of his grey jumper were even wetter than the rest of it, as he had
been constantly wiping the snot away. The constant chafing of his
wet trousers had brought wide red patches to the insides of his legs,
and his feet, soaked by the water from puddles which had saturated
the old leather of his boots, felt numb.

He had almost reached the dunny where he was due to meet
Devlin. But now he stopped, as the rain began again, hefty, hard
spatters into the puddles and scattered piles of dark rubbish around.
There was something wrong. It wasn't the same cautionary feeling,
not one of presence, but more absence, loss, some vacuum in the
air. Slowly he began to move into the dark close, ready to turn and
flee, letting his eyes adjust to the change in light.

Now he could see what looked like a large bag, or a discarded
bundle of rags against a door in the corner of the dark concreted
hall. Something was moving in front of it. His hand flew to the scar
on his face, knowing immediately what it was. A shiver shook him,
it seemed suddenly colder, as if a blast of freezing air had swept
through the place. He took a step towards the shape and as he
did the pricks of the rat's eyes disappeared. He heard it scrabble
away, and as the outline and detail in front of him became clearer
he realised that it was a slumped human shape. And he knew right
away who it was. 'Mr Devlin,' he began, then scuttled towards

him, the tacks on his boots chattering on the floor. He bent over him, shook at his shoulder, then dropped on to his knees beside the unmoving old man.

Devlin's head was slumped forward on his chest and now that he was so close he could see that the man's legs were splayed out in front of him, that he was not curled up in the corner, but almost jammed into it, as if he had been pushed there, bundled roughly out of the way, or had fallen. He continued to shake the old man but although the bookie's head began rolling loosely there was no other movement from him.

He was dead, Johnnie knew that, but he continued to push at him, unwilling to concede physically what he knew emotionally. With his cold hands he took the man's putty cheeks and pushed his head back, whispering to him, 'C'moan, Mr Devlin, get up now, get up.' Slowly he saw, even in the subdued light of the bleak, watery patch of illumination coming from the back entrance, that Devlin's throat and chest were saturated and although it looked just like the darkest shade in the monochrome of the gloom he knew that it was blood. The old man's throat, glistening wet and tuberous in the shadowing, had been slashed, so cleanly, wide and precise that it could only have been done by a razor.

Johnnie felt a retch start in his stomach. He sat back on his heels, looked around him and then at his hands. His fingers, and as he turned his hands over in front of his eyes he noticed that also the palms, were covered in blood. He got up, wiping them unthinkingly on his jersey, then his trousers and, catching himself doing it, looked down and noticed that his knees and lower legs were also sticky with blood.

The icy vacuum seemed to pass and he could see everything as if a floodlight had suddenly bathed the death scene, the splatters of blood on the wall in a mare's tail pattern, some of the droplets still slowly descending the dull whitewash, the heavy puddles around the man which had obviously formed when the arterial spurts had slowed to a pulsing flow, the soggy, wide, wet patch on his stomach, the final indignity, as if he had pissed himself. Which, if he had, had done nothing to dilute the gory mess.

Johnnie stood back, taking deep breaths, trying to quell the heaving of his stomach, to slow the racing thoughts in his head, work out what had been done and what needed to be. He felt hot and choking, his mouth dry, cheeks and forehead on fire. It must have been a robbery, he told himself, forcing a look at the old man's hands which confirmed, in the slashes which had opened them to the bones, that he must vainly have tried to hold his hands up protectively against the attack.

So like before, he thought, wondering if there were something in him which attracted such frenzied violence. He forced himself to crouch down beside the body and began to pat Devlin's suit and pockets, then slipped his hands inside them one by one, finding nothing; even the black leather notebook he kept tallies and the daily book in had gone. His hands came out sticky again; this time he wiped them on the dry sleeve of the old man's jacket, and then he stood up and away from the body.

Everything had slowed now and discoloured to a muddy mist in his eyes, but he felt calm at last. He could look at this with dispassion, from outside, realising what the conclusions would be if he were found here. He was covered in blood, the old man's blood, he had worked for him, the closest to him, and it would soon get to the polis, once they started asking around, that he had used a blade before. With such an easy suspect they would not look any further. Why should they? Who cared about a dead old bookie and a wee lad from a bad line in the Gorbals? They would not even begin to look wider. So, what he had to do – he was looking at the rain blowing in the back doorway – was somehow to get back home without being seen, or hide out until it got dark because *she* would never miss him, until he could get to the house and change, destroy the old clothes, rip them up and burn them bit by bit in the grate, soak and scour his boots – and himself, of course. The scrubbing brush, carbolic, boiling water in the tin bath.

He shook his head. That would be more suspicious than anything if he were seen, willingly going for a bath, but he knew that his mother would not see, even if she were there, and she certainly wouldn't remember. He was just an occasional shape in her nightmare.

As he turned to move away, his foot connected with something small and solid which skittered across the floor. He saw where it had ended up, against the far wall at the doorway, and at first he thought it was Devlin's tally book, but when he got closer to it he could see it was a partially torn package, dark, shiny paper catching the grey outside light. His footsteps on the floor moving towards it sounded like a shod animal's and when he bent down to look he felt a rush of elation. The paper had been peeled away from the beatific faces which glowed up at him, the purest of joy in this grisly place. It had clearly been discarded as worthless and when he kneeled down to pick up his picture he saw, still damp, the bloody print of a thumb on the gold background to the virgin and child.

For some reason he blew on it, and waved the little picture in the wet air, before he carefully bent back the heavy paper over it, slipped it inside his bloody jersey and ran out back into the rain.

Thank God for it, he said, his face up to the hard rain, for keeping the washing and the folk inside. And in a rush of water escaping from a rusty hole in a roan pipe he began washing his hands and legs until the water fell away clean at last.

All he wanted to do was have a hot bath, wash off the filth attached to him. He was cold, shivering, and he realised that soap would do nothing for him, but that was what he needed. Laughton had been so knowing, smiling and malicious. He had wanted to tell him everything, anything just to get away, and he would have if it hadn't been for Hazel's words in his head, even then if he had been alone much longer in the interview room. But the lawyer had arrived, a tiny swarthy man with strands of slicked hair flattened across his head, who had seemed relieved that he had not made a statement, and cautioned him to not to speak.

But the monologue from the big Highlander had shaken him deeply. Clearly the police had not had enough to charge him, at this point, but it was only a matter of time. They had been interviewing men at the yard, branch officials too, and Laughton had made it clear that his bank records were being examined. How would he explain the money? He felt only a sick panic. Laughton had kept waving the threat of the murder charge in front of him, conspiracy, the long years to come in Barlinnie. But they could not make that stick, could they? The lawyer, McGinlay was the name he recalled, was out of the room, talking to Laughton, presumably trying to find out exactly what they had on him, he hoped. He was the cat's paw in this to get Stark, he knew, but that gave him no comfort.

He wondered what Hazel was doing, his stomach took a sick lurch, but he knew that she would be working for him, coming up with some plausible defence. He smiled to himself and then sat up quickly when the door opened. Seeing McGinlay alone he relaxed a little as the lawyer sat down opposite him and the door swung shut behind him.

The oak table was scarred and burned, rough to the touch. Dundas's fingers drummed and itched at it constantly. McGinlay leaned slightly forward and began talking softly. His breath, Dundas thought, smelled of camphor, or lozenges.

'Sorry,' Dundas said. 'Could you repeat that?'

The lawyer sighed and shook his head slightly. Dundas noticed that he had placed a leather satchel on the table between them. 'It seems – and here I am just repeating what has been said to me, I offer no judgment – it seems that the police are very confident that they have enough evidence to put a recommendation to the fiscal that you should be charged with, well, basically theft, defrauding the membership. They have several statements. No' – the lawyer had his hand up in a blocking motion – 'let me continue, please. I'm just telling you what they have been telling me. Apparently they do have various signed, incriminating statements. I don't think that's bluster. It seems that they have talked to your bank, provisionally at this stage, I think, but they are confident of getting the full records, and there seems to be quite a lot of money in your accounts.' He looked up from his briefcase. 'Five thousand or thereabouts was the sum mentioned, I believe. They are now trying to collect and collate the various union books, bank accounts. In short, Mr Laughton seems very confident.'

Dundas was trying to assimilate what was being said. He felt hope sliding away from under him and a great gnawing anxiousness at his stomach.

'But there is a deal on offer,' McGinlay continued. 'I took the conversation to mean that. As I understand it, it's this. Peter Stark' – he looked enquiringly at Dundas, who nodded – 'they suspect of the raid on Brown's, the murder. They want him. You – well, let's say that Laughton doesn't seem greatly concerned about who does what to whom in the labour movement. Now, and this is unprecedented in my experience, they propose to lose or rip up the papers on the case in return for your co-operation. I expect you can imagine what they want from you.'

'A statement?'

'And testimony.'

Dundas shook his head, as if trying to shake the fuzzy elements in his head back into coherence. 'I can't,' he said. 'How can I, without incriminating myself?' He began to flush and stumble around his words. 'It's not that – I haven't done it, the fraud. I deny it. They won't charge me, is that it, but they want me to say I did it? In open court. No.' He shook his head fiercely, feeling on the edge of tears. 'That's not possible. How can they expect it?' He shook his head again and stared down at the desk.

'No, it's not that at all. Laughton thinks you saw Stark at the yard on the day. That's what he's saying. He only wants you to confirm that.'

'Or else.'

'Or else? Yes, that's it. Or else.'

Dundas rubbed his face with both hands, considering the two threats, explicit and implicit. With the one, Laughton's, he would simply go to jail; testifying against Stark would surely send him to the grave. 'I have to think about it. Talk to my wife. I just can't think like this.' He sat back in the chair which creaked and squealed as he did so. 'If I say no, now, will they charge me?'

'I'm sorry, Mr Dundas, I really can't answer that. I should have thought not, not immediately anyway.'

'If they don't then' – he looked at McGinlay, trying not to let the hope bubble through – 'I can go?'

'Yes, of course. But' – the other man spread his fingers on his briefcase – 'the police have clearly brought you here in, what shall we call it, a softening-up process? They had a search warrant, so they were clearly able to persuade the sheriff that they had a *prima facie* case. Well' – he smiled for the first time – 'that at least is the theory. I think,' he said in what seemed a summing-up, 'the police, having gone to this trouble, will want something from you before they let you go.'

'You said that Laughton seemed very confident?'

'Yes.'

'If he really is, then why shouldn't he let me go? If he feels that confident, that he can reel me in any time, then why rush? He can't hold me without charging me—'

'He may decide to charge you anyway.'

'No,' Dundas said, feeling suddenly confident, 'I don't think so. If he does that he loses his chance on Stark, there's no deal. He doesn't have to have me here to let me stew, does he? Much better, having given me a taste of custody, to let me go back to worry and brood on it in my own environment, make me appreciate what I stand to lose. Home and hearth, coupled with the worried wife thrown in. Potent that.'

'Possibly.'

'When he charges me, he's lost the chance of Stark. Correct?'

'Yes, probably.'

'So it really depends on how much he wants me? And Stark?'

McGinlay shifted in his seat, shrugged and held up his hands non-committally.

'Tell him,' he decided, 'that I am prepared to make a statement. But in the morning. After a good night's sleep. At home.' He had decided and it felt better, positive, whatever happened. 'Tell him that.'

He was out within the hour, Laughton showing him the door and looking no less pleased with himself than he had hours before when he first blearily swam into Dundas's vision. 'See you in the morning, Mr Dundas,' he said as he and the lawyer slipped out into the dark freedom.

They had almost reached the corner when he heard the voice, and the drumming of heels and turned as Hazel swept into his arms, covering his face with kisses. 'Well, I'll say goodnight,' he heard McGinlay say through the sighs and small talk.

'Mmmh,' he mumbled and waved with his free right arm.

'I was waiting inside,' she whispered, 'but when they told me they were letting you go I didn't want to see you again in there, so I waited on the corner.' She smelled clean and freshly washed as he nuzzled her neck. 'C'mon.' She broke away. 'We have to talk. Let's get a drink and work out the plan.'

159

'I can explain,' he began. 'The plan?' He felt dizzy on happiness. 'There is one then? Five- or ten-year?' The smell of the cell, all urine, sweat and staleness came back to him.

She smiled and kissed him lightly. 'I don't know what else you picked up in there' – she grabbed his hand and began pulling him – 'but the sense of humour suits you. Let's get a drink and discuss what we do.'

'Hazel.' He stopped, overcome by a surge of emotion. 'I love you.'

'I know.' She shook her head and a remote smile came. 'Tragic, isn't it?'

She got the drinks, which caused a ripple of looks from barman to barman, and planked them down on the table. She looked exuberant and happy, Dundas thought, which irked him. She pushed the large whisky across the table to him, saying, 'Go on,' and sipped at what he thought was gin and lemonade. He started to speak but she put an index finger to her lips and said, whispering, 'I know. I talked to the lawyer. Wasn't he a pompous ass?' She took another sip at her drink and he thought she looked strangely enlivened, charged.

He took a sulky swig of the whisky and said, 'Well?'

She leaned forward over the table. Her coat fell open and he saw that she was wearing a cardigan, loosely buttoned, with nothing on below. His eyes skipped to her cleavage and he felt himself start to get angry. 'They got nothing at the house, nothing,' she said, picking up his gaze and pulling her coat around her. 'What they need is hard evidence, not allegations from a few platers and welders. They need concrete proof, they need to show money was deliberately misappropriated, intent rather than incompetence, they—'

'Look,' he said, interrupting, and he leaned across the table and began whispering. 'I can get out of all this. All I need to do—' He stopped, realising properly now the ramifications of what it was he had to do. It wasn't just a few words of identification in the witness box. When Stark realised that he was fingering him, and he would know that as soon as the police lifted him, then it would all begin. He wouldn't be safe, neither would Hazel. His few words would send Stark on the steps to the gallows and he realised that the man would not go quietly. Peter Stark's influence was not contained by a prison cell, he knew that. And he would probably never even know the identity of those who came for him, but he was sure that they would. Testifying wouldn't just be the one death sentence.

A chill passed up his back, he clasped the glass and then drained the whisky in one gulp. What was he going to do? Move away, start again? He shook his head at the idea that he could ever have considered that testifying against Stark would wipe the slate, allow him to go back to the old life he had shunned. 'How did you find out?' he said finally, bowing his head.

'Carl!' Hazel was shaking his arm. 'Are you listening?'

'Sorry,' he said. And it didn't even end there. What was to stop Stark, in open court, making the same allegations the police were investigating. 'What were you saying?'

'Don't give up here.' She was smiling at him, shaking the sleeve again.

'They want me to grass Stark. I can't do it, and I can't refuse. There's no way of getting out.'

'Carl,' she said, smiling again 'you're not thinking. That polis, what was his name . . .'

'Laughton.'

'He told me everything, everything he claimed you had done. It's part of the psychology, the softening-up. Put the jitters up the "good lady", get her shiteing herself, falling apart, worried about her home and her man – patronising bastard.' She put her hand on his. 'They need leverage, don't they? They're going to have to prove that money's gone missing. How are they going to do that? Think.'

But in his mind all he could see were walls closing in on him so that the oppression made his breath catch in his chest.

'The books. They need the books, the ledgers, the contributions records. Where are they?'

'The safe,' he said, answering by rote, still seeing the blankness before him. 'Don't you mind?' he said, still hiding from her eyes.

She touched his cheek and smiled as he looked up. 'I'll protect my man, he got that right at least.' She pinched his cheek gently. 'At the yard,' she went on. 'Exactly. At the yard, Carl. They haven't been there. I asked Ronnie Glover. And he said no one else had the combination but you. Don't you see?' Her right hand was reaching for his cheek, as if to brush away a tear. 'The warrant didn't cover Brown's, I read it. So either they don't know where the books are, or they're slow. They need a new warrant and then they need someone to open the safe, don't they? We've got time, Carl.'

He nodded his head in agreement, not knowing what his assent was about.

'We need to get moving,' she said, draining her drink and standing.

'Where?' he said, then, 'How?'

She bent over him. 'Can you get in tonight without being seen?'

He smiled at last. There were innumerable runs and holes and pathways to get in and out – mostly out – to avoid being seen by supervisors and management. 'No problem.'

'So, we'll go.' She tugged at his sleeve again and he stood reluctantly. 'I'll wait outside, you get in, remove the needful from the safe.'

What did he have to lose? They agreed to take a taxi to Dalmuir, then walk. Dundas had wanted to take the bus – less noticeable, he argued, but really it was just to delay things – but Hazel argued for haste and to the cab driver they were just a young couple cuddling and giggling in the back, whispering endearments, although for most of the time it was Hazel stiffening his resolve, stifling his qualms and questions.

As they moved through the bleary lights, the raindrops on the windows separating colours into their four elements, Dundas finally accepted that he was not fitted for crime and intrigue – 'Capitalism at its purest,' he said under his breath – but that now, even if there ever had been, there was certainly no way out. He felt dismayed with himself.

'Here,' Hazel said in the dark, nudging him, the outline of her hand in front of him, followed by the faint tang of the peat. He took the hip flask, without saying a word, and tilted it back. The malt ran through his teeth, the delicious burst of cold glory as it hit his tongue. He coughed slightly as it scarred across his throat then rolled and burned in his stomach. 'Go on,' she said, pushing the flask back to him, 'just one more,' and he took another slower pull, squirting the whisky around his mouth before letting it fall. Hazel leaned across his vision and kissed him, her tongue dancing in the fire in his mouth.

When they got out of the taxi he stumbled and laughed as she paid and then, arm in arm, they walked towards the yard, him conscious of her guidance, her sure-footedness, her control. The alcohol had affected him in a way he had never experienced before. Tension, he told himself, but that was the least of what he felt now. 'Nothing,' he said softly, chuckling.

'Sorry, love?' she said, her left hand in his, deep inside his coat pocket.

'Nothing,' he said again, smiling, catching his foot on a kerb as he did, rubber-leggedly correcting himself as she helped pull him erect.

'Here,' she said, 'I'll hang about here,' as the yard's wire fencing came in sight.

'Be careful,' he said, moving off, treading slowly and carefully, waving back to her as he went. He knew where he was going, even if his route wasn't as direct as it might have been. He moved across the waste ground, inching exaggeratedly along the fence until he found the torn and bent-back strands. He squatted down, then slumped on to all fours, before crawling through, barely noticing the icy splat of water on his knees from the puddles. When he helped himself up, clawing the fence, he noticed that the knee of his right trouser leg was ripped, but it barely registered. There was a buzzing in his ears and a harsh, dry taste in his mouth. Fear, he told himself.

He could see well enough, a few gas lamps casting a dirty ochre glow. Mustard gas, he said on his breath, giggling and tripping again.

The door to his howff was unlocked and even in his inebriated state he could slip into it and move around in the tight dark. He slumped down in his chair and as he did so a string of lights began to roll up in front of his eyes, like cinema credits, but blurry and out of focus, no matter how hard he squinted. Waves of lethargy, like banks of fog, blew over him. He shook his head, scrabbling with the dial of the lock on the safe, his fingers splaying, rubbery, so that he could not feel the clicking of the combination tumblers. Once again he shook his head, slapped his hands together, trying to restore touch and circulation and this time, concentrating intensely, managed slowly to inch the dial clockwise and anti-clockwise so that, with the final heavy click, and then a turn on the brass handle, it swung open.

He reached inside, feeling the rough leather bindings, and as he stretched, lost his balance, and slipped forward, cracking his head on the edge of the desk as he went down. The sharp jab of pain temporarily revived him, although now he seemed to have gone blind in his right eye. On his knees, dabbing at it with his right hand, he realised he was cut, a flapping crescent of skin above the eye draining blood down into it. The pain was coming in erratic bursts, his ears felt muffled and dull and his mouth, his tongue, thick and blubbery.

The voice came from a long way up. From the heavens, he thought, and it seemed to reverberate in his head. 'It's too late for a two-step, Razzle,' just before he slumped forward again in a rush of breaking waves.

For slow moments he flittered in and out of consciousness, aware of arms on each of his, of being dragged forward, the ground inches from his face seeming to vibrate and pulse. At some point he was pulled into a hunched slump, his face blindly seeking the stars, raindrops prickling on his sightless eyes, something hard and flat pushed inside his coat, his arms now pulled around him to be crossed on his chest. And then he was tumbling away free, and it felt joyous, until the rush of breaking waves briefly revived then overcame him.

Stark watched as Dundas floundered slowly in his wet, enveloping clothing, his death shrouds tugging him down, the large metal-cased ledger adding weight. He waited until his hair, like weed on the water, finally disappeared, he waited until no more bubbles rose to the surface of the dock. The tides would take him. He might never reappear, but if he did, at Greenock or the Tail o' the Bank or washed up in Newfoundland, the decay, the chemical decomposition, would mask the alcohol mixed with the sleeping pills.

Then, thinking about Hazel waiting, looking at the gently lapping dark water where Razzle had gone, he felt as randy as hell.

Chapter Eight

'This is Paul,' the voice had said. 'From the Holiday Inn.'
'Right,' McQuade answered, twirling his pen in the coffee to move the sugar sediment.
'Something that might interest you.'
'Right,' he said again. He was putting the face to the voice, a young lad, no more than about twenty, with freckles and fiery red hair, a useful contact. A source in a top hotel was a must, he believed, to let you know who was coming and going, who was misbehaving with whom, and to give you particular access to celebrities who might – usually did not – want your company. 'Paul. How you doing?'
'Good. But listen, I can't talk here. Can you meet me at the Waterloo in about an hour?'
'Sure, I'll come prepared.' He tried to think where there was a cash machine on the way. 'See you then.'
The lad was sitting in a corner banquette seat, a trench coat buttoned up to the neck, over his uniform, McQuade guessed. He sat down opposite him. 'Drink?' The other guy looked at the orange juice in front of him, apparently untouched, and shook his head. 'Well?'
Paul took a deep breath and leaned slightly forward. 'The thing is, we have rather an unusual guest. A woman cop. From New York.'
'Yeah? So people take holidays.'
'Here? Anyway, she's not on holiday.'
'How do you know?'
'First off she phoned her office—'
'Her office?'
'Yes. She buzzed down to reception asking what she had to dial to reach New York. I said, "There ought to be a booklet there explaining," but she cut in, saying that she was tired and she just

165

wanted simple answers, so I offered to get her the number. She said, 'Fine,' so I did. I heard the answer – police department, or whatever. Plus later she got a message, to call back. I checked the number.'

'Good man.' McQuade winked at him and wondered where this was leading and whether he should order a drink. 'That probably does mean she's a cop, I agree. It doesn't mean she's on business. Why would she be?' he asked himself out loud.

'Don't know. Also, I checked, and the room was booked, indefinitely, by us, Strathclyde police. There's an instruction in the computer that the final bill has to be sent to Pitt Street, or any interim one. Except, drinks are excluded.'

'I'm glad,' McQuade answered, shaking his head slowly, wondering why a woman New York cop could possibly be in the city. 'Makes no sense. You didn't, I don't suppose,' he went on, 'happen to listen in to anything that was said on the transatlantic line?'

The boy shook his head rapidly. 'Too risky.'

'Sure.' McQuade regretted not having ordered a drink. It gave him something to play with while he thought. 'Anything else?'

The boy smiled quickly and nodded his head. 'She's really something. A-fuckin'-one.'

McQuade doubted that. Every female cop he had ever seen had looked like a sack of slops. 'No other calls, visitors?'

'I don't think so. But maybe a car called for her. I didn't get a number or anything. She was hanging about the reception, looking out like, then she dashed through the door.'

'Why on earth—?' he began to say, then stopped and fished in his jacket pocket for a notebook and pen. 'You got a name for her and that New York number she called?'

'Sure. Her name's Blantyre, Alice Blantyre. I wouldn't forget that. Mid to late twenties, tall, slim—'

'Okay, you can wank off later. The number.'

The boy produced a folded sheet of paper from below the table, which he had clearly palmed earlier, and handed it across.

'Great.' McQuade, gazed at it, then scribbled the number down in his book as well as her name. 'Look, Paul, I don't know if this is important or not, but I'm intrigued.' He put down his pen and notebook on the Formica table top and dug in his right-hand trouser pocket. 'There's a score to be going on' – he leafed off two fivers and a tenner from his wad – 'and if anything comes of this I'll square you for more later. In the meantime keep watching, particularly for anyone coming and going. Can you call me, or get someone else to do it, when she comes back, because I'd like to come round and have her pointed out?'

'No problem.'

'Is there a chambermaid or someone like that you can trust who could maybe help get a look inside her room?'

'I don't know about that.'

'Think about it, Paul. I'll square you up as well for that, you know.'

'Right.'

'And keep a note of the numbers she calls, you can get that from the computer right? And if you need me urgently' – he picked up his pen and scribbled on his pad, tearing half the sheet off and handing it over – 'that's the mobile number, twenty-four hours a day, excepting intimate moments and hangovers naturally.'

When he got back to the office he tried to reach Ricketts but he was out, according to the person who answered. 'No message,' he said and he slammed the phone back down on the cradle and cursed under his breath. When you didn't even know what you were looking for, where did you begin? He punched into his computer terminal to bring up the wire services and began browsing. After half an hour he gave up; nothing he had seen sparked off anything in his brain.

A New York cop, he said to himself yet again, why? He had checked out the number Paul had given and it was certainly an office of the NYPD. 'Why a New York cop?' he said at the screen. Spooks yes, secret service – the Lockerbie site had been crawling with them – but an ordinary cop? It didn't fit. If, of course, she was an ordinary cop? Whatever. There had to be some kind of joint operation for sure, but about what? It would hardly be terrorism. Intelligence? About what? 'Crime, fuckwit,' he said out loud. What kind of crime? Organised crime. 'Rather than the usual disorganised sort,' he answered himself. Then he cursed Ricketts again for not being around, opened a desk drawer and whipped out a half bottle of Bell's from which he poured a large dash into the smudge of cold coffee in the bottom of a polystyrene cup next to the keyboard.

There was no point speculating, he thought into the whisky vapours as he sipped, but one thing he was sure about, there was a story here. It just smelled right. Whisky-soaked, indeed. He leaned back and shaped words in the air, the big headline: *Polis and NYPD in* – in what? – *blank operation*. Blank. It was like that fucking game on television with the gnome from *Private Eye* and the smug bastard from a million voiceovers, where you had to fill in the crucial blacked-out word in a headline from the *Fish Breeder's Gazette* or the *Acton Mercury* or some such.

Right, he told himself, grabbing his address book, when in doubt do something utterly pointless and time-consuming like making random calls to contacts which, if nothing else, looks as if you're justifying your inflated wage and space on the floor. He began with low-level crime contacts, petty criminals, sheriff court fodder, the dregs he had met at countless cases but those who might have heard rumours or buzzes on the streets. Most of these, of course, did not have telephones, or if they did were out on the make, so most of the calls were to pubs and betting shops and after about an hour of this he gave up. There was Harris, of course, but he was reluctant to call him, he did not want to be the one who opened the first debit in the favours bank although, through Stick, he told himself, he probably had.

Next he tried the informal official approaches, first off with a source in the Scottish Office, usually helpful – one of the few – who, even if he couldn't be, was always honest. The source knew nothing of anything special happening in Glasgow. He thought of calling the police press office, Force Information as it called itself, but the big Highland heider who ran it was about as helpful as a heavy head cold. He remembered at Lockerbie being taken aside by him and being told, 'For your ears only, we're making absolutely no comment about this at all, and that's off the record!' So he didn't even bother punching the buttons.

Checking his watch, he worked out that it was almost 10 a.m. in New York. If he called the NYPD officialdom and asked why one of their officers was over here what would he get? Almost certainly nothing, but a warning would go out to her, so that line was not a starter. What else? He decided to take a leap into the dark and call the crime desk at the *Times* in New York, to try and horse trade on a story, if there turned out to be one, a joint effort. He talked to some bored woman, who clearly thought he was some hick from the British equivalent of Bumfuck Arkansas, but who said she would check out 'this Blantyre' and get back to him. 'Sure,' he said, then hung up. He drained what was left of the dark whisky puddle in his cup, got up and kicked the edge of the desk frustratedly. It seemed that he had nowhere else to go now, apart from to Harris, and he was determined not to do that. From the back of his chair he grabbed his jacket, figuring that he would go out for an inspirational walk, or a cold beer, and as he screwed round his keyboard to log off, it occurred to him. 'Why not?' he said, then scrawled a note on a Post-it and stuck it to his machine.

When he got home he closed the door on the bedroom to shut out the wreckage he knew lay behind and scrounged around the kitchen until he located the cafetière, roughly washed it out, turned on the kettle and ladled two hearty tablespoons of coffee into the glass jar. While he was waiting for the kettle to boil he switched on his Mac, dusted the screen with the back of his sleeve, then found the Laphroaig on its side among the pile of Sunday papers on the dining room table. The Mac was playing pretty *Star Wars* games with itself as he plonked down the bottle beside it, then the used glass he retrieved from the bookcase. When the kettle had boiled he slurped the water over the coffee, pushed on the lid with the plunger and took the mechanism to the computer, beside the other essential tools of the day, then remembered a mug, which he found in the sink. Vaguely he wished he still smoked tobacco. He poured a measure of whisky and plunged the grains of the coffee to the bottom and then filled his black and yellow mug. For a second or two he savoured the mix of the aromas, then began tapping on the keyboard. After a few seconds he got up, found a piece of paper and a pen, and jotted down the time. Then he accessed the Internet.

He was going to give it an hour or so, surfing the info or whatever the fuck the geeks called it, see if he could trace Blantyre anywhere, or any link to her. The problem was one of definition, there was so much information blizzarding about, much of it extraneous, arcane garbage, so that it was difficult to know where to begin. But at least with a name, which in theory ought to act like a cybernetic magnet, he had a beginning. For around half an hour he tried various combinations, her name against 'police', 'NYPD', every possible factor he could come up with, unsuccessfully. Then it occurred to him that he should search the newspaper libraries and, after pausing only to get his second dose of each brew, he suddenly came up with a line of reference to her, a major drugs seizure in which a 'Sergeant Blantyre' had apparently been put forward for a commendation. No first name? Tssk, tssk, he said at the screen, sloppy journalism. But he also felt a small surge of elation in his stomach which he hoped was unconnected to the artificial stimulants.

Then he decided to search by institutions and there, eventually, under the District Attorney's section of the City of New York, he found what he was looking for. Among the members of a high-powered investigatory unit set up by the DA to combat organised crime, and in particular drugs, was the name of the, obviously promoted, Lieutenant Alice Blantyre.

Beautiful, he told himself, sitting back and looking at the list of appointees, objectives and constraints, before he hit the print button for the hard copy. Then he logged off and toasted himself.

'Baroque,' Blantyre said.

'That's one description,' Ricketts agreed as he drove them back towards the city. They had followed the Mercedes to the house in Barmulloch where, and Ricketts had noted this, Blantyre's mouth had actually dropped open. Fat Boy's house abutted his father's, both had previously been owned by the council but bore no resemblance whatever to the way they had started out. What had previously been a building with four flats, 'four in a block', had been bought over by the family and transformed, into what it was not immediately apparent, but the two properties had been massively and, even Ricketts's low taste was able to discern, outlandishly transformed, with bolt-ons, additions, edifices and curlicues. The fronts had fake beams, there were two garages built in what were formerly the side routes to the back greens and Ricketts knew, from aerial pictures, that at the back huge extensions had been built on, even a swimming pool in a glassed-in atrium.

'Don't they have planning authorities here?' Blantyre had asked.

But what was undoubtedly impressive about the properties was the level of security. The cameras and the infra-red lights on the front were apparent but Ricketts knew that these were only the outward signs, that there were sensors on all approaches, constant video surveillance of all the surrounding approach areas, a laser alarm system which criss-crossed any potentially vulnerable points, that the windows were all bullet-proof, the curtains were blast-proof just like they had at important government buildings and that the doors would survive a medieval siege battering ram, or in fact just about everything short of a thermic lance or 200mm cannon round. When he mentioned all this she had smiled and said, 'State of the art, huh?'

Now they were driving to her hotel, relieved by another crew. 'Impressive but secure bad taste' he replied.

'God, I'd love to see inside.'

'No problem,' he said, changing gear and accelerating as they hit the Kingston Bridge. 'I'll get us a search warrant and you can pick up a few decorating tips. My bet,' he went on, 'is that the main room has a bar, plastic sixteenth century beams and heavy red tartan wallpaper.'

'You're kidding,' she said.

'Not at all. My guess is Hunting Stewart, or maybe—'

'The search warrant?'

'Of course.'

'Good.' She was looking out the passenger window, tracing a finger in the mist of condensation. 'I wouldn't want anything disturbed.'

'You?' he said. 'Sorry, I hadn't realised you were giving the orders.'

She turned, he could see from the corner of his eye, and was looking hard at him. 'You're right, I have no authority here. But just look on me as the mouthpiece of your superiors, their presence on earth. Check it out.'

Already have, he thought, but he said nothing as they came off the expressway approach and headed for the hotel.

'Look,' she said as he swung into the driveway, 'I'm just doing my job, you know, following orders just like you.'

He double-parked the car and pulled on the handbrake. 'Sure.' He turned and gave her a brief, cool smile.

'No hard feelings, right?'

'Not at all.'

She put her hand lightly on his shoulder. 'Look, sorry, I'll buy you a quick drink.'

'Fine,' he said, switching off the engine.

'Fuck,' she said as she got out, 'bang goes the assertiveness training. Why do I keep apologising to men?' as she slammed the door and smiled across the roof at him. 'And don't get any ideas,' she said, wagging a finger at him.

'Ballbreaker,' he said.

'And compliments won't do it either.'

Ricketts stared morosely into his mineral water as Blantyre beamed over her large gin and tonic. 'You could leave the car,' she said, taking a sip of her drink, 'and take a taxi.'

He shook his head. 'Someone would nick it and I'd be back pounding the beat.' He took a swallow and wrinkled his nose. 'This must be pretty boring for you after New York.'

'Are you fishing again?'

He shook his head and helped himself to a handful of nuts. 'Not at all.' He shook the nuts in the palm of his hand and began popping them in his mouth one by one. 'You're young to be a lieutenant, surely?'

'Maybe you're just an under-achiever, Ricketts.'

'Maybe we don't practise positive discrimination here?'

She took another, larger sip of her drink, undid the tartan tie at the back of her neck, shook her hair so that it fell down around her face and then said, 'Think what you like, it's no matter to me.'

She was preparing to leave, he could see that. 'I'm sorry. That was a stupid thing to say. It's just that I feel like the spare prick at this particular wedding. You know, a glorified chauffeur, not knowing what's going on, the dumb fuck in the driving seat.'

'That's not my problem.'

'I know. I'm just grousing but you can understand, surely? What, I wonder, have I done wrong to offend the DCS or the chief constable?'

'I don't think it's that at all.' She began picking at the dish of nuts. 'The reverse, I'm sure.'

'So, I'm the top man for the job?' He dipped his finger in the fizzy water and began drawing wet lines on the glass table top. 'This is how I see it. You don't have to confirm, although the occasional nod, smile or raised eyebrow would be helpful. Obviously there's some connection, a long white trail probably, between Stark, the Starks, and people on your side.' She shrugged, which he took as confirmation. 'So, that much is obvious. There's nothing I could see in the files about that. But, of course' – he looked her straight in the eyes – 'there's no reason why a drone like me should see everything is there?' He thought that he saw the edges of her mouth crinkle. 'The question is, I suppose, whether we're helping you or you us. I'm thinking out loud here . . .'

'And I thought it was the air-conditioning.'

'Here's the broader picture. The Colombians and all the nouveaux on the scene have over-supplied the coke and crack market in your place so the price has hit – excuse the pun – rock bottom, a couple of bits a pebble. So they're trying to open up new markets, like here, Europe, wherever. And since we disbanded the Customs controls with our wonderful open market at the beginning of '94 – open market, more like open vein – it's been the roll-on roll-off drug highway. Throw in the Channel tunnel and the fast trains and you've got a beautiful, ripe, underdeveloped market with almost instantaneous communication, no tariff barriers or serious interdictions.' He paused and took a sip of his water and made a face. 'Trouble with that scenario, as far as you fit into it, is that if you lot are helping us then, with respect, God help us because you haven't exactly got much to contribute, have you, based on how you did back home.'

He looked for reaction, but there was none. She smiled without warmth, took another sip of her drink and waited. He went on. 'Not that we're doing a lot better here with the injecting stuff. Coke and crack is expensive but heroin's plentiful, in good supply as ever and cheap. So we've both got saturated markets, but with different kinds of product. Your market, like any market, like here, is always looking for fresh thrills. Heroin's making its way back, it's got a different kind of cachet, if you forget the shared needles and the ODs polluting the public thoroughfares. It isn't as addictive as crack – these things being relative – and it has had a kind of romantic past. The creative types use it, jazz musicians, serious contemporary novelists and general detritus like that.' He toyed with an ice-cube in his glass. 'But with the crack pipe it's kids, single mothers in the Bronx, not the next Nobel laureate. How am I doing so far?'

She shrugged, sipped her drink again, put it down and ran her fingers through her hair at the temples. Ricketts thought, I wish you wouldn't do that!

'What a romantic soul you are, Ricketts. Junk is junk is junk. Period.'

He ignored the jibe and continued. 'So what we're getting here is attempts to transform both markets. They're almost mirror images of each other. So, we're helping you, I'm assuming that, and we're tailing Stark, which seems a fairly pointless and, given your exalted state, a fairly low-grade task. We've got heroin coming in through every port, it's coming from the Golden Triangle, from Afghanistan, from fuck knows where and we have Stark, and others' – he had dipped a finger in his drink again and was drawing arrows and islands on the glass – 'who have lots of H. But there is competition in the market, classic supply and demand, the price is so low that they try not to adulterate it so much, so the folks get a better hit, so that they keep the custom, but then it starts getting fatal too often, which certainly isn't too clever for business. And even with the better gear the price doesn't move up at all. So I'm back where I began, abundance of product, limited price and still a pretty limited market. What do you do in a situation like that? Classic capitalism again, look to fresh markets.'

He pointed his right index finger at her. 'Two things I can't work out, though.' He leaned back in the chair and folded his arms. 'How come Stark gets to be a big enough player in your manor that your side sends someone over to sort him out, if that's what you're doing?'

She smiled again, drained her glass and splayed her right leg over her left, showing off several inches of a highly tooled cowboy boot and up and beyond – Ricketts fought unsuccessfully to avert his eyes – her denim-encased crutch. 'Two, you said,' she replied, and he looked up to see her holding up two fingers. 'Two how comes?'

'How come you don't fancy me?'

'Goodnight, Sergeant,' she said, getting up.

''Night, lootenant.' He was looking up at her. 'I'll pick you up in the morning again, unless you have any other orders.'

'See you,' he heard her say as he watched her back.

'Points out of ten for the accuracy of my analysis?' he asked as she was half a dozen paces away.

She said nothing, continuing to walk and when she had almost reached the lift, still without turning back, he noticed her right hand come up clenched with the middle finger pointed at the ceiling.

The call got him on the mobile. He was heading through Kelvin Way at the time and as he chucked the phone back on his seat he put his foot down, crashed the lights and hung a hard left. The car he was driving was a company Escort, with uncertain gears and a dodgy clutch, and the marks of too-close encounters on the wings. His own car was one of the old, round Saabs, bottle green and as strong as a battleship with column change and little snash out of a grand a year to keep it running. It was probably just an affectation but he could not muster a liking for new cars, all aerodynamically correct and smelling of minted plastic.

When he pulled up he switched off the phone, pushed it into his inside pocket and from the glove compartment pulled out the camera. It was a Nikon, one of the automatic models with a motorised zoom, idiot-proof and almost journalist-friendly. He locked the car door and trotted into the reception, looked around for Paul, sauntered across to where he noticed him coming out from behind the desk with the regulation welcoming smile on his face.

'Table three to the right of the grand piano,' he said. 'She's wearing a leather jacket and she's with someone, a man.'

He nodded and began skirting the sunken area where the bar tables, dance floor and piano well were located. The perimeter was decorated with ficus plants and palms, all real, all requiring the services of a regular contractor no doubt, but excellent cover. He walked round past the lifts and ducked into what was meant to be a Hawaiian love seat, or something similar, a plaited, thatched hutch with two wooden perches, discreet but providing an excellent view through the foliage. He could see the table clearly and the woman; the man had his back towards him and seemed hunched over the table.

McQuade glanced around, retrieved the camera from his jacket pocket, made a viewing hole through the leaves and zoomed in on her face. Paul was right, she was stunning. He fired the shutter which was set on motordrive and caught three imperceptibly different images of her. Then he altered the setting to single shot, zoomed out and took a picture of the two of them and, although the man had straightened up a little, he could only get part of his profile. The cop, Blantyre, was standing up now. He fired off several more shots and as she came round the table and passed the seated man, he turned. McQuade had pushed the shutter twice before he realised who he was.

You devious bastard, he thought when it hit him, zooming in on Ricketts and pressing the shutter several more times. Business or pleasure? Then he began to smile. Ricketts was not following her towards the bedroom, so the answer to that one was clear.

Carefully McQuade pulled back from the shrubbery, put away the camera and sat down on one of the seats, which creaked and the plaited walls rustled. It's a jungle, isn't it just, he said to himself.

Driving back to the office with the film, McQuade considered what to do next. Here was a New York cop attached to a high-powered Mafia drug bust squad, in Glasgow, teamed up with Ricketts who was attempting to put the lid on a nasty little feud over the stewardship of supply. Discuss! He ground down the gears and booted the car though a gap between a lorry and bus in George Square. Clearly, he went on to himself, there has to be some supply deal between here and there. Obvious. So, a nasty little feud was the least of it. 'It is,' he said, shouting over the sound of Little Feat reverberating round the car, 'a fucking great feud which, in turn, is fucking great news. I wonder' – he was in top gear now and heading for an amber light – 'whether a Brit can win a Pulitzer or whether I'll just have to settle for Journalist of the Year?'

'Gimme the weed, whites and wine,' Lowell George was singing. 'That'll do,' McQuade said, sliding the car into a space and cutting the engine.

When the first print came off the dryer he grabbed and scanned it. 'Pin sharp.' He slapped Jake the technician on the back, who was looking at the second print as it dropped off.

'Aboot three out of ten for composition, though. Who's she? I'd give her—'

McQuade had grabbed the second print out of his hand. 'You'd give your eye teeth and a whole lot more and it still wouldn't do you any good.' He picked up the eyepiece and began scanning the detail of the print, now blotchy and grainy, for anything which might help. He didn't know what. Some identifying mark, some giveaway? There didn't seem to be anything. He noticed that she was wearing a ring on her marriage finger and a chunky diver's watch peeped out from just below her cuff but if these were clues they were lost on him. 'I want a blow-up of her.'

'Ah wouldnae mind a blow—'

'Chance'd be a fine thing.'

'Ah'll dae wan fur masel while ah'm at it,' Jake said, leering. He was spotty, indeterminately youthful, with a greasy ponytail in a rubber band, and nicotine-stained fingers although, as McQuade conceded, knowing nothing about the chemistry of the development process, these could actually have come with the job.

He left the darkroom and went down the two flights of stairs to the editorial floor, coming in one of the back doors away from the front bench so that he would not be clocked and asked to explain when he intended filing some copy. He took off his jacket – it was a rather svelte number, he felt, from Gap, with a faint check, over a hundred quid – and sat down. There were several messages stuck to his screen but he ignored them. He folded his arms and looked up at the ceiling, which was a dull mosaic of pegboard panels and opaque squares of lighting.

He had a story, no doubt about it. Top cop – well, hyperbole never hurt anyone – flies in to sort out city's drug war. Then: I wonder if the desk would pay for me to fly to New York for essential research?

He looked at his screen, shaking his head, and began unpicking the messages. There were, he noticed, two from 'Stick' – the name was underlined on the first and the second had question marks after it – both stressing that he should phone 'urgently', both leaving the same West End telephone number.

He sighed and decided two things. To phone her and to hold the story until he had done so, until he had done more research, until he had much, much more, until he was confident he had it all. He neither wanted to blow it prematurely or to let the opposition in on it. Writing the piece now would certainly do for Blantyre's cover, resulting either in her being pulled out or bottled up tighter than an ant's arsehole. A few days, some covert surveillance perhaps, would surely lead to a more fruity story.

And he had Ricketts, he had the goods on him, the leverage. He was a mate, well sort of, and mates talk. They do, he said to his screen, if they're undercover cops and they don't want their cover – and their gorgeous company over drinks in a top hotel – blown all over the front of a daily newspaper. He reached for the phone, trying to suppress a smirk.

Morse light was dancing on the face of the man in the box, falling from a window high in the roof, off and on, as the clouds scudded past on the wind. From the gallery, an unfamiliar aspect, looking down, he couldn't read the message flashing on the man's face but he already knew the sentence.

From here, he thought, everything seemed wrongly arranged. His memory of the last time, the only time, was gazing over the chest-high walnut surround with spiked-top railings, up and out, the two heavyweights in blue on either side occasionally pushing and prodding him to get up, sit down or move out. However, the smell was the same. Of floor polish, musty bodies, mildew and wig powder. With, he imagined, the far-off tang of blood. Blood was what he knew a lot about. Blood, indeed, was his business.

There was nothing to decipher in the man's eyes. Dark, shallow, staring ahead, somewhere far-off inside, where the crystals lay limitlessly. His hair was black, recently trimmed, gelled back over a bone-white forehead and long nose. The watcher, the man in the gallery, thought, I know everything I need to know about him. More than the jury. Far too much.

The accused's story, told haltingly, stumbling over syllables, had been that he had left the boy alone for no more than a minute, to go into the living room to get a cigarette. She was there, the mother, Anna, with two others. Shooting up. She had shouted at him to go back into the bathroom. He had. The wee lad was floating face down in the bath. Couldn't revive him.

'Wake up fur Cambi, son.'

He hadn't.

Of course he denied he had tried to prevent the mother calling an ambulance. 'Ah thought he'd wake up,' he said. 'It was only a few seconds. Thought he'd be aw right.' At the hospital the nurses and doctor who testified said that he had stumblingly denied what the mother had said about the delay and then he had gone out to get chips and when he came back he kept falling asleep. He was drunk, they said.

'How can yi eat like that when the wee wan's gone,' the mother in tears had screamed in the waiting room. She was twenty-four, six years younger than him. The boy was hers, not his; he wasn't yet four and never would be.

'Ah loved him,' he said.

Two forensic surgeons testified that the boy had not drowned, there was no water in the lungs, he had died of asphyxiation, consistent with his nose being pinched hard closed and his mouth covered. And there were marks and bruises on his genitals and his buttocks to indicate that he had been sexually assaulted. From the gallery the glossy colour pictures of Darren's body looked like fuzzy outlines, just as his short life had been.

Now he thought: You're supposed to be able to tell the jury's verdict by how they look or don't look at the defendant when they come back in. A myth. It had taken them less than five hours to reach the decision on evidence which had been unequivocal, but it shouldn't have taken them even five minutes. The foreman, a fat man in his fifties, chins rolling over a dingy white shirt, dressed in a brown shiny rayon suit which was too tight for him, delivered the verdict quietly. Embarrassed. It was 'not proven'. A breath pause of utter silence in the court and then gasps of anger.

Camburrini slumped down in the box and put his hands over his face, his shoulders shaking, sobbing in relief. All around people were on their feet, pointing, shouting. The watcher in the gallery did not move as the police waded into the mayhem, the judge hammering with his gavel and shouting unheard, and then they ringed Camburrini and moved him out, still in custody, but this time for his protection.

But the other man knew where he was going. Not exactly. But he would be easy to find. It was just a matter of following the glittering trail.

He got up and walked down the back stairs of the court and out into the late afternoon winter sunlight, which pinkly coloured the frosty grass in the park opposite. He was a big man, almost six three, with a short crew cut through which several white lines and arcs of scars showed. His eyes were the colour of bitter chocolate and his face was lean and muscled, as was his body, now covered by a leather, combat-style jacket and loose blue jeans. He turned and began walking north, not even taking in the spill of protestors, journalists, police and camera crews which had erupted down the court steps. After about 400 yards he turned left, down a broad, cobbled alley which followed the curve of the railway track above and then he found the café, the windows running with condensation so that the menu painted on the inside of the main glass was beginning to leach white tears. He ordered a mug of tea and sat down in the corner facing the door, ignoring the steam and the tobacco smoke and the mild arguments among the patrons, dossers or soon to be, and he waited.

Ten minutes later the door opened and an elderly man came in, in his late sixties, glasses, stooped and nervous, glancing around until he saw him. He shuffled across the floor, ignored the man behind the counter pouring tea from a massive silver kettle, stood for a moment and then nodded at the chair.

'Please,' the man said, and the old man seemed to deflate into the wooden chair. There were tears in his eyes, either from the cold or the crime, and he took off his glasses and rubbed at them with the back of his hands.

'Ah cannae believe it,' he said, shaking his head.

The other man said nothing but he motioned to the man behind the counter, making the sign of a 'T' with the index fingers of both hands.

The old man was still shaking his head when the tea was pushed under his bowed head. This seemed to bring him back. 'He wis a lovely wee lad—' He broke off and looked up, his eyes again beginning to fill behind his glasses. 'That bastard,' he said, both palms flat on the table, pushing himself up into a challenging position, 'how could they let him off?' The other man shook his head and shrugged. That was just the way it was. Then the old man seemed to remember why he was here and fumbled into his pocket and produced a heavy manila envelope which he pushed across the table.

The other ignored it. 'Take your tea,' he said. 'It comes already with milk and sugar.' The old man nodded and picked up the mug in both hands, sipping at the surface. 'Just to go over the rules once more,' he said quietly. 'If I pick that envelope up you've committed yourself, there's no going back. I want to make sure that you're truly aware of the consequences. This is a bad time for you, you're probably not thinking too clearly, but when clarity returns it will be too late. So – don't answer right away – just make sure this is what you want to do. I pick up the envelope, we're linked, as unto death. You understand what I'm saying?' The old man nodded. 'It's a bad time, as I said, I don't make threats but you do really appreciate all of the ramifications of our relationship, if I take it?'

He nodded. 'It's what ah want,' he said, tears now rolling freely down his cheeks. 'Ah'd huv given ma life fur that wee boay. Ah know whit yir saying an' it's whit ah want. Please, help me!'

The younger man nodded and picked up the envelope, stuffing it inside his jacket and when his hand came out again it was holding a small, spiral-bound notebook and a pen. 'I need some very simple information. This isn't going to be difficult. First, give me your name, address and telephone number. Don't worry, I'll keep it safe for as long as necessary.' The old man, Tam McBride, gave an address in Milton; he did not have a phone. 'Now, tell me where he's living, where he does his drinking and where he gets his supply? Because the first thing he'll do is go looking for a fix.'

'Ah heard he was living wi' some other junkies in some hoose in the Gallowgate, ah don't know where.' The younger man shook his head, motioning that this was not a problem. 'He drinks anywhere,

181

in Tamson's near the arcade a lot, and aw's ah know aboot his supply is that he takes taxis to Possil' – he pronounced it Poesil – 'a lot.'

The other man nodded, satisfied, and put away his notebook which he had not used since jotting down the old man's address. 'Just forget about it now. Forget everything.' It was a dismissal. The old man got up, tentatively put out his hand and then changed his mind, tried to say thanks, and then turned and left, his mug of tea still steaming on the Formica table top.

The big man waited for a couple of minutes then got up, shovelled through a jeans pocket, came out with a pound coin which he slapped on the counter, waving away the change. Outside, he put his hands in his pockets and began walking across Argyle Street to George Square. When he got to the main post office he stopped, pulled out his notebook and pen, the bulky envelope, then two pound coins which he dropped into the stamp machine. The cardboard-sided booklet dropped down, he tore out all the stamps together, licked the backs and stuck them on the envelope. Then, below, he copied out the old man's address in block capitals on to the packet and dropped it into the letter box, turned away and began walking across the road to the square.

It was ridiculously simple and predictable, junkies being noted neither for their subtlety or lasting sense of self-preservation. He sat in the darkness in the car in Saracen Street, occasionally driving round and re-parking in a different spot to avoid suspicious police or pushers' eyes, then he would get out and walk, the last time having come back with a parcel of fish and chips. He was eating the last of the haddock, the hot fumes clouding the window, when he saw the taxi draw up on the hill in Stoneyhurst Street and the figure get out. He quickly dropped what was left of his supper on the passenger seat and whipped up the night vision binoculars which he had bought for about 200 dollars in a market catering to *peshmerga* in northern Iraq, Kurdistan. Working tools. Quickly wiping the windscreen and peering through the bins he could see Camburrini clearly in the infra-red daylight. The man was motioning to the taxi, telling it to wait, after which he wheeled and went up the short flight of stairs to the close mouth.

Less than five minutes later he was back down, climbing into the back of the taxi which had its engine still running, the driver budgeting for a quick getaway if necessary. It then did a U-turn and came back down on to Saracen Street, indicating to go left towards the town. In the car Burns turned the ignition key and the Mercedes, with just the merest of tremors as it caught, began to move after the cab.

He trailed it to a pub called the Rock, just off Duke Street, where Camburrini paid off the driver. Burns parked opposite and got out as the man he was following went inside the bar. He trotted across the street and caught the door as it was slowly swinging back to close. He saw Camburrini at the bar, ordering. The place was fairly quiet, fewer than a dozen people at a quick glance, all men and most of them around the bar rather than at the six small tables or bank seats along the street wall. The barman finished serving Camburrini a whisky and a pint and came along to Burns. 'Tonic,' he said. 'Driving.'

The barman fired a splashy measure of tonic water out of the hose mechanism under the counter and put it in front of him. Burns slid a pound note across the damp surface, waited for his change, watching Camburrini in the mosaic tiled glass behind the optics, then pocketed the money, turned round and looked along. His man had swallowed the whisky and taken a great slurp of the beer. He was clearly edgy, his head darting around, scanning everything and taking in nothing. It would not be long now. Burns watched as he looked from side to side again, then put down his beer and headed to the back of the room, obviously to the toilet. Burns sauntered after him. Once again he caught the door as it began to close and stepped into the small, dark and empty toilet behind Camburrini who was now opening the door to the sole cubicle.

A quick couple of steps, Burns clasped both his hands, swung quickly and drove down with all of his considerable strength just below the nape of the neck, aiming for the bony protrusion on the spine where the long hair and Camburrini's jacket collar masked the target. The blow made a satisfying dull thud, like an axe in sodden wood, and the man collapsed forward, hitting the bowl and cistern and sliding to the floor. Burns stepped over him, bent his knees and hauled him around and up. The toilet seat was missing.

He lugged the loose body and jammed Camburrini's backside in the bowl, where the man lolled as if he had been filleted, head against the tiled retaining wall.

Burns kicked the door shut and slid across the bolt, then turned to check if Camburrini was still alive. He felt a fluttering pulse, then stood up and put his hand into his left-hand pocket, pulling out a pair of surgical gloves which he snapped on to his hands. Next, he began searching Camburrini, quickly finding his works and the plastic packet of heroin, which he tore open and scattered over the floor. He put together the syringe and needle and brought out a small capped pill bottle from a pocket, shook it to hear the liquid slosh, then pulled off the top. As usual he felt very calm. If any of the customers had even noticed the two of them going into the toilet they would not care about what was going on or how many came out, he knew that.

He watched the syringe suck up the liquid from the opaque bottle until it was full, then he stuck it, like a grotesque decoration, deep into the man's right thigh until he was ready. With little difficulty he detached Camburrini's jacket from him then struggled at his waist until he eventually managed to pull through the belt, then rolled up his sleeve and tightly knotted and twisted the leather strap just below the bicep, above the blue and black bruising and track marks, and tried to bring up a vein. As he bent over he could feel and smell the man's light breath, like rotten eggs, against his cheek.

When he had cajoled and plumped the vein he waited for a few seconds, hoping Camburrini would come round, but he did not. There was no point in prolonging it. He took the man's right hand, wrapped it round the syringe, pulled it from his leg and poked it into the swollen vein, blood spraying out in a fine mist over the gloved and ungloved hands. Then he gently pushed down the plunger, sending the household bleach solution into the bloodstream.

Only when Camburrini began to moan and convulse did he let go of his hand, pull himself up. Then, using one of the dying man's limbs as a step, he shinned up and out of the cubicle. He washed his gloved hands under the single cold tap, then pulled off the gloves, put them in his pocket and thoroughly rinsed his unprotected hands. After drying them on his jeans he went back out into the bar and finished his drink.

He waited until the barman was serving at the other end of the bar, and as a precaution, although it was probably unnecessary, he pocketed the glass, just in case the glasses were washed with the same regularity as the toilet, almost never. Next he turned and walked out, back to his car. It was then that the only flash of alarm hit him. Perhaps some kid had vandalised the paintwork? He walked round it slowly but the Mercedes looked untouched in the bilious sodium lamplight. He unlocked the door and climbed in and as usual the car caught first turn. It was, he considered as he drove off, a decent night's work.

Once they did the post-mortem, of course, they would work out that Camburrini had probably not engineered his own demise, but that did not really matter. Whatever else, there would be no great effort to find out who had. He slid in the Wagner tape and as the mechanism clicked and the Ring overture began he let his mind slide away.

Chapter Nine

He had only been to the principal's office once before without being beaten, when he was given the news of his mother's death. Father Conlon, unused to the uncertainties in life, was ill at ease, brusque when he meant to be sympathetic, not even looking at him when he tumbled it all out.

'It seems she met with an accident – errm, stumbled under a tramcar. Nothing could be done, no, nothing at all.' Perhaps he had expected him to break down but he did not. 'Sometimes it is so difficult to discern God's purpose.' He sighed. 'You'll want to pray.'

John said nothing. He had wanted to say, She'd have been drunk, which was his first reaction, but he remained silent. Not because he was afraid he would be beaten for that – he knew on this day he could get away with saying just about anything, stopping short of maligning God – but because he did not want to allow the priest to have any way of gauging how he was feeling. In truth, he felt vaguely relieved: his mother was only a complication, often a source of embarrassment to him and he was surprised to find that he did not even blame his father any more. There comes a point when you make your own choices and she had decided to drink herself to death.

'Can I go, Father?'

The priest dismissed him, perhaps with some pieties about the hereafter he could not remember, he had not been listening, and he was allowed the rest of the day off classes and housework. But the period of mourning ended at 5.30 a.m. next morning when he was awakened as usual with the rest of the boys in the dormitory by the shouting of the fathers and the clanking of the hand-held bell. Later, he had been taken to the funeral in a large black Wolseley, smelling of leather and tobacco, and escorted by Father Costa, a short, dark troll of a man, hairy in every exposed place and caught permanently in scowl, who was talked of in awe even by his peers for his unremitting fierceness in this harshly unforgiving regime.

It had rained. There were only two other people there, neither of whom he recognised and he watched the gravediggers a few yards away smoking impatiently, waiting for the short ceremony to finish so that they could top up the grave and find shelter.

That had been in about the second year of the war. Later he remembered lying in his bed at night hearing the planes going over, the crackle of ack-ack, seeing the thick beams of searchlights in the night and later the sound of explosions and the red light licking the sky. A couple of times large bombs had dropped nearby, shaking plaster free, fusing lights and breaking windows, but the holy fathers trusted in God more than the air raid shelter and, despite the siren warnings, there had never been any evacuations to the undergound bunkers in the gardens. Sometimes he wished for the bombers to come back, imagining that perhaps this time the walls might be blown in so that he could run out through the rubble and away, like in some Hollywood chain gang movie, but there had been no aerial activity from the Nazis for months now and the war seemed to be on the turn, from what he could pick up from the staff. But then they had been saying that from the beginning.

He had managed to escape three times, but he had always been found and brought back. Twice, it hadn't been too difficult. 'A rat always returns to his run,' is how Father Conlon had put it before lashing him. And, of course, with his inexperience of break-outs he had been entirely predictable, going back to the old haunts, the only ones he knew, and when he began to break into shops and houses, as he needed to for money, he was soon caught. But he had got away for longer each time and if the beatings had also been lengthened and got harder he knew that it was worth it. Not only had he learned a lot and put into practice the tips he had picked up inside but, more than that, it had made him realise exactly who he could trust. You only know a real friend when you're on the run, he had said to himself.

He had also picked up snippets of information about his father, and Hazel, their irresistible, bloody upward progress. His father was a hero in the streets, even inside the borstal, and some of it rubbed off on him. He was the Big Man. Boys from the Gorbals were the single biggest geographical constituency inside and everyone knew of Peter Stark. It ensured that most of the other lads backed down from him when trouble simmered, which made him angry. He wanted nothing from his father and had nothing to prove. The comings and goings of boys and relatives from the place meant that the gossip about his da invariably reached him. Peter, no doubt occasionally prompted by guilt about his neglect of his son, had tried to write a couple of times but Johnnie had destroyed the letters without even reading them. And once he had turned up at a visit, bringing some chocolates with him – with the rationing, these seemed more desirable than jewels to the rest of the boys and the masters – but he had walked out of the room, leaving the box on the table. He never knew what became of them.

The third time he had got away he got out with Joe Owens, Ownie, who had been brought up on a farm in the north, somewhere near Oban and who, to begin with, was laughed at and bullied and called a teuchter by the other boys because of his accent. But John had studied him in the metalwork and engineering classes and realised that he had a natural empathy with machinery, which he later learned came from him being used as cheap labour on the farm tractors, ploughs and harvesters and, later still, that his knowledge of the land and the country provided crucial survival skills. It had not taken him long to appreciate that Ownie was the perfect escape partner and so he took him under his protection and quickly the two boys, perhaps because they were so different or because they had integrating abilities, became close friends.

That third time they were away for almost two months and then they only got caught because John had insisted they go back to Glasgow. Using a stolen chisel and hacksaw they had cut their way through the grille on the first-floor bathroom window to get out and then clambered down the adjoining drainpipe, then over the wire fence and free. At first they had set out north, around the Campsies and beyond. It was summer, there were innumerable places to stay, barns, derelict buildings, and the eating was easy. Their upbringing had made them seem older than they were so they were rarely challenged about their ages and when they were they said they were due to enlist shortly.

They found work easily on farms: labour was short, the young men were away at war and the land girls were overstretched and so everyone's self-interest was served. It was exactly like an army living off the land, John kept saying, but eventually he had got bored with the long march round rural Scotland and persuaded his fellow fugitive to return with him to Glasgow where their tans and glowing wellbeing, as much as anything else, quickly gave them away. They were caught after less than a week in the city, three plainclothes policemen jumping on them as they came out of a close in Florence Street, clearly tipped off. John struggled and fought and even toppled one of them with a glancing windmill of a right hand shot, but it only doubled his beatings, one in the back of the Black Maria, the other when he got back to St Teresa's. Ownie had gone quietly and even the beltings from the brothers were less malign and lengthy, the tacit implication being that the poor boy had been led astray by his dangerous and evil accomplice.

To John it had been a small price, beatings every day of the week if necessary (and the regime fortunately did pause for the Sabbath, saints days and recuperation of the beating arm) for that blessed freedom. The sense of being alive, of life and hope crackling within you was never stronger than when you were on the run, when the next corner, or person, could bring it slamming to a close. But although he was beaten with as much vigour and holy commitment as usual, he sensed that the spirit infusing it was less wholehearted, that there was a letting go, a realisation that they appreciated that it was now pointless and wasteful, that he was beyond them, that he had already passed on. Pleasant as he found that, it did not provide the balm for his back.

And now he waited outside the headmaster's office, hearing the whispered chatter behind the closed wooden doors, building himself up for the rough leather strap or the cane. He had long moved past the idea of revenge, now it pleased him as a contest, showing them how much he could take; however much they beat him they never could best him – in the spiritual way that they wanted – and that gave him strength. He began to tap his highly shined boots on the brilliantly polished linoleum and shut out all thoughts except that of resistance, seeing past the pain to the triumph again.

The door suddenly swung open. 'Ah, Stark,' the voice said. The light was behind the figure and he could not, for a moment, recognise the speaker. Then, when his eyes adjusted, he saw that, although the voice seemed to deny it, it was Father Conlon. But somehow his manner had softened. Stark found this bemusing and concerning. He had prepared himself for anything but kindness. Then he realised where he was and shook out that thought.

'Father,' he said.

'Someone to see you. Come in.' For a moment John could not decode the tone, the atmosphere surrounding the words. Then he realised that the manner of speech, seldom heard, was the one the priest used for adults and for unction. Immediately he wondered what it was that the father wanted from him.

'Someone to see you.' And he was tugged through the outer office, past the flabby secretary, to the inner one, where it was not easy to see where the walls met the floor, where the grain of the highly buffed wood changed, the most reliable points of reference being the framed pictures of bygone Popes and our Lord and Lady in all their many manifestations.

The man standing with his back to the stained-glass window was, it was clear by his tense and upright stance, on official business. He was evidently not a policeman; John divined that immediately from his bearing, the cut of his clothes and because he had made no aggressive sound or movement to him on his entrance.

'Mr Arbuthnot,' the priest said. 'To see you.'

John waited for the priest to leave the room, or for the man to speak, but neither did. He began to reconsider his initial perception of the other man: perhaps he was a policeman after all. And then the stranger, who wore a double-breasted dark suit expertly cut, even John intuitively knew that, sighed and said, 'Sit down, on the couch there.'

John knew the couch well and for that reason was unwilling to sit on it. It had been where he had been draped, pinioned and prostrated while punishment was administered. He shook his head.

After a pause the man said: 'Well, what a business,' clearly discomfited. 'Uumm, I was your father's lawyer. Sorry' – he seemed to be stumbling over his words – 'I'll start again.' He sighed once more, a deep breath followed. 'Your father, I'm sorry to tell you, John, has been killed in action. I know this must be a shock. We don't have any details, I'm afraid we shall have to wait on those from the War Office in its own good time.'

He fished in the hip pocket of his tightly cut jacket and produced a silver cigarette case. 'I expect you'd like a smoke?' John shook his head, knowing in himself that what was being offered was complicity and that he should keep himself apart from it. 'I'm sorry.'

John looked first at the priest and then Arbuthnot. 'I don't understand. I mean, why you're here?'

'Mmhh? Oh. Yes, of course.' He had lit a cigarette with a silver lighter and was absent-mindedly picking at real or imaginary tobacco strands between his front teeth. 'I was your father's lawyer.' He stopped, as if John would immediately understand the implication. 'I handled his affairs,' he continued, then took a drag on the cigarette. 'There is an estate, a will, the bulk of which goes to Mrs Stark – rather, I'm sorry, your stepmother, ehhmm Mrs Dundas.' John nodded, waiting. 'However, your father did leave something for you in trust – actually, I'm the sole trustee – which you're to inherit when you come of age.' He smiled, glad that he had got it out.

John waited. 'And?' he said, after the pause had lengthened.

'Sorry? Oh, yes, the legacy. It's rather unusual' – he looked around at the priest, seemingly embarrassed – 'it's, umm, a dance hall. Called the Rose. In Glasgow. Are you aware of it?'

John nodded. He had trouble taking this in. Here he was, a borstal boy who had just come into a business, from a father he had barely seen, whom he had only barely got out of hating. He shook his head and started to smile.

'There's also a house. Well, a key and a tenancy to be precise, the rent paid up until six months after your sixteenth birthday. I expect your father thought you'd have a job by then. It's his house, where he lived with – ummmhh. Anyway, she has bought her own place now, Mrs – err, Dundas, so there you are. A house and an inheritance.' He smiled tentatively and, getting no reaction, went on. 'Well, I expect that's a big shock, Johnnie. No doubt you'll have lots of questions when you recover. Father Conlon has said that I can take you out for lunch today and discuss things through with you, Johnnie, and try to make provision for what you'll do when you get out of here.'

John looked round at the priest, and then back. 'Tell me, Mr Arbuthnot,' he said, 'what exactly do you know about running a dance hall?'

The man coughed slighly on his smoke and put his hand over his mouth before replying. 'Why, absolutely nothing at all.'

He could always tell when something big was coming up: there was a new intensity, an air of almost desperate abandon. Others laughed, but he had the nose for it. And it was twitching now, watching the dancers spinning through a tango, the dense shapes on the floor just a half-step too enthusiastic, the smiles held too long. Business had been dreadful all war long, except for the periodic flood of returnees trying desperately to cling to the present, or the fresh recruits glorying in their departures. But now the Rose was almost full, so full in fact that he could barely hear the pared-down orchestra over the squeaking of shoes, the clatter of heels and the clacking of the conversations. Definitely, he thought, a big push coming up.

From the edge of the scalloped dance floor, which had been half-heartedly laid in the vague shape of a petalled rose, he supposed, he could see that the bar was busy. Thrusting his hands into his trouser pockets he walked round the edge of the dancers to the bar, to make his presence apparent, and lingered for a couple of minutes watching the operation of the tills. Then he turned away and made for the door leading up to the office above. When he shut and snibbed the door behind him he bent down on the far side of the desk and dialled in the combination of the safe then pulled down on the metal handle, pushing aside the papers and the cash box and retrieving the bottle. The glass was in his top desk drawer; he found it and then held it up to the light, blew on the outside and then roughly polished it with his tie, after which he half filled it with whisky.

Jake Mullaney was running to seed: he had been a useful middle-weight, fighting on bills as far south as Belle Vue and even getting the length of a British eliminator, but his ambition outmatched his application, he was a poor trainer and his dedication could rarely take him past a pretty woman, a party or a pub. Now he was pushing forty, the parties and the women were spreading out, like his waistline; only the drink was staying true. His black hair, which was gelled hard down an his skull, was beginning to thin and patches of grey were breaking out around the ears.

He took a long sip of the whisky and sank back in the chair, looking up at the dense type on the fight posters, swivelling in his chair to take in with one long gaze his gradual rise up the bills and then the fall, so that his place on the first and last one was the same, bottom. Some of the fights he could not even remember, hardly surprising since there had been more than a hundred, although occasionally he wondered if the punches had blotted them out. Certainly they had caused the scarring round the eyes and the detached retina and partial deafness which had kept him out of the war.

A banging on the door disturbed the reveries. He threw back the rest of the drink and slipped the smeared glass back into the desk drawer. 'Who is it?' he shouted, turning to slam the safe shut and spin the combination.

No answer, only heavier banging.

On his feet now and striding to the door. 'Who the fuck is it?' he said, throwing the bolt.

'It's the fuckin' owner,' he heard as the door opened on Hazel Stark.

'Mrs Stark, sorry,' he said, trying to turn his head away so that she might not catch the booze on his breath. 'Sorry,' he mumbled again, 'ah wis just gonnae count the cash.'

She pushed past him and threw the door closed. He noticed her calves, the long tight skirt below the blue gaberdine coat and her hair, in a silver clasp at the nape of her neck. She sat in the chair and turned to face him so that he felt awkward standing at the other side of the desk, as if about to be disciplined as, he realised, he very well might be.

She continued to stare up at him. It went on so long, the silence pressing uncomfortably on him, so that at last he said, 'What can ah dae fur ye?'

'I'm glad you got that right,' she replied, ending with a cool smile. 'Me. What you can do for me. Now that's important. Remember it and you might just save your job.'

He glanced quickly at his feet and then back to her. 'Ah don't understand, Mrs Stark.'

194

She toyed with the little silver statue of a fighter on his desk. 'You wouldn't. Tell me, Jake' – he could see her eyes narrowing slightly – 'where do you think you could find another job like this?' He started to speak but she ran on. 'It's well paid, there are your own little rake-offs' – she raised her hand to cut him off – 'which I know about but I credit you with enough sense to keep in proportion to the turnover, which I suppose is a plus for you. You're your own boss, virtually. And I don't interfere.' He nodded his head slowly. 'And I'm sure you'd like to keep it that way.' He nodded slightly more promptly. 'Well, there are going to be changes about here, but I'm sure you want to help me make them as few and as easy as possible.'

'Whatever ah can dae—'

'I'm afraid,' she came in on him, 'that the Rose is now under new ownership.' She noticed the slow look of fearful bewilderment roll across his face. 'But it could be worse, because it's still family.' Actually, she thought, it could not be worse, not ever. 'My husband has left this place to young John.'

Hazel appreciated that Mullaney knew she and Stark had not married. First of all there had been the religious objection from the real Mrs Stark and, when that had been conveniently removed, Hazel had realised that she had no desire for it. But no matter, what Mullaney thought about it did not concern her. 'I'm sure he had his reasons. He was a sentimental man.' She searched for the slightest trace of mirth in Mullaney's expression. 'Everything else' – just so the implication was clear – 'he left to me. Now, of course, wee Johnnie' – Mullaney could not work out whether this was sarcasm or a crude attempt to persuade him she cared – 'is too young to have anything to do with this place and his present whereabouts make it difficult anyway, so there's no reason why anything much should alter in the short term. But I do want to make something very clear, Jake. I want to point you to where your loyalty really lies. Do you understand?' He nodded, loyally.

'I'm sure that you'll appreciate, if you think about it, that managers for a place like this are not difficult to find.' Pull up any stank, she thought. 'And if he was of a mind to, Johnnie could easily replace you. But you represent stability, for the time being and, for your sake, I hope for time coming. So why should he get rid of you, particularly if I lay on how well you've done in difficult times?' Mullaney nodded, clearly understanding what she was getting to. 'I hope I can rely on you to be appreciative.'

'In any way, Mrs Stark. There's nae need to ask.'

'Him and me are family, you understand? You, Jake, are not.'

'Anything, Mrs Stark.'

'And, of course, if you are appreciative and if something unfortunate was to happen here and it didn't work out with Johnnie, well, you could rely on me to look after you.'

'As ah said, Mrs Stark, anything.'

She put down the statuette and got up. 'Good. I'm glad. There's a Mr Arbuthnot. He's a lawyer and he's going to be the trustee until John's of age. He's a very busy man who, I'm sure, doesn't want to be overburdened with detail, as long as this place keeps turning a profit. And you and me will make sure that happens and things are presented to him in the best possible way, won't we?'

He nodded again. 'Absolutely.'

'Right.' She had moved round the desk and was motioning him towards the seat. 'Resume,' she said. Dismissed, he sidled back to his chair, glad that the tawsing had been light and almost subliminal. 'But don't take too much of the cratur so that you mislay or miscount the takings, eh?'

'Ah don't know what you mean,' he said, beginning to bluster and redden.

'Of course not,' she said over her shoulder just before the door closed.

He sat back and as he thought over the next measure, reviewed his options, Jake Mullaney swiftly came to the conclusion that he could do nothing else than be loyal to the widow Stark. Until such time, of course, as circumstances might change.

The dark was total, not even a chink of starlight penetrated the dormitory blackout curtains. Above the ripples of snoring he could hear the distant sound of bedsprings squeaking as someone masturbated himself to sleep. He could not imagine why it had not occurred to him before, the idea not the masturbation; it was all so easy as he turned it over in his mind again. The sense of exhilaration he felt was intense as he waited, trying to time the night. After what he calculated was an hour, he carefully unwound himself from the rough starched sheets and put his feet uneasily on the cold, highly polished wooden floor, then tentatively opened the squeaky locker next to his bed and took out his prison clothes. He dressed quickly, holding his heavy boots in his hands, then inched along the floor, his right foot out ahead probing for obstructions. When he had reached Ownie's bed, four down from him, he laid his boots silently on the floor, kneeled down beside the bed, clapped his left hand over the boy's mouth and whispered in his ear as he woke, 'It's me. We're going home.'

When he felt Ownie nod under his hand he released the pressure and then waited while he got up and got dressed. After he had done so Johnnie felt him move across the bed and then he heard the sound of tearing, and stitches giving, knowing that he was retrieving the key from the hard, striped pillow.

It had been made up in the metal workshop from strands of wire sawn from the springs of several beds, twisted and milled into a shape like a long L. Now they tiptoed across the floor to the locked door and Johnnie waited while the key scratched and probed in the lock and after about five minutes he heard a different sound, the heavy fall of a tumbler, then the moan of hinges as the door opened.

The hallway was bathed in a faint light falling from an arched and uncovered window high in the ceiling. The door closed behind them, Ownie turned back to it and after only a few seconds had it locked again. They slapped each other in triumph and then laced on their boots and crept downstairs.

'What now?' Ownie whispered.

'Conlon's study.' Both could have found their routes to it in any blackout but the watery moon made it simple; there were no locks to be picked so they got there within a couple of minutes. The room smelled of ash and old tobacco, and a faint light from the embers of the fire still glowing red cast a warm glow through the small latticed screen in front. Now they could talk relatively freely because they knew there was no one within a hundred yards of them.

'Well?' Ownie waited.

'You go down to the laundry and get us some of the brothers' clothes. I've got something to do here.' He waited until Ownie nodded and went, then Johnnie turned to the dark metal filing cabinets and began opening the drawers, searching for files. It was too dark for him to see properly. He glanced around until he saw the nearest brass candle-holders, tore a sheet of paper from a file, twisted it into a taper, grabbed the candlestick with the stub of tallow candle and then blew into the embers of the fire until he had enough of a flame to light the taper.

By the time Ownie came back with the clothes in his arms Johnnie had found the two files. They quickly buttoned up the dark clerical tunics over their grey borstal dress, Johnnie first stuffing the files under his jersey. 'These'll do until we get clear and then we can get other stuff. If we get stopped we'll say we're from a seminary somewhere . . .'

'Perthshire.'

'Aye, that'll do. St Thomas Aquinas.'

'We've got until daylight until they notice.'

'Maybe longer,' Johnnie said, picking up the candle and slowly waving it back and forward under his chin so that his face flickered and loomed grotesquely in the light. 'Look,' he said, holding the candle over a filing cabinet and opening a middle drawer, pulling out a half-empty half-bottle of whisky and then, putting the candle down on top of the cabinet, he uncorked the bottle and took a slug, passing it over to Ownie who gurgled down a measure then passed it back.

Johnnie took the bottle, picked up the candle and went over to the fireplace, where the candlestick still remained on the mantelpiece. He carefully dribbled a small amount of whisky beside the candlestick, then took the fireguard and laid it face down on the carpet. Then he poured the whisky over the carpet and fire hearth and left the bottle on its side in front of the black leaded grate. With the fire tongs he clamped a piece of dull red coal the size of a kidney, blew on it until it began to smoke and smoulder, then carefully placed it on the wet carpet, waiting only a few seconds for it to sizzle and then ignite into a thin blue flame before putting back the tongs.

The flames spread quickly along the carpet and as the two boys closed the door behind them dark, oily smoke was beginning to rise as the wooden floor and squares of linoleum caught and the fire began to reach for the wooden furniture and to skitter up the curtains. Johnnie made the thumbs-up sign as they headed for the stairs.

They did not say anything until they reached the large oak tree beside the grotto. Johnnie clasped his hands and gave Ownie a lift up on to the roof, above the rouged and garishly painted virgin, then he scrambled up, holding his friend's offered hand. First one, then the other, pulled themselves up into the tree, then inched along a lateral branch, before jumping out and over the barbed-wire fence, the air tugging at their tunics as they fell like plummeting gods into the long damp grass below, rolling over and over out of sheer excitement and happiness before they ended wrapped in each other below a hedge of wild bramble.

Johnnie had slightly sprained his ankle and he could feel a patch of skin below his right eye smart. He touched it and his hand felt sticky and bloodied.

'A matching pair.' Ownie motioned at his face. 'A scar on each side.'

John touched the palm of one hand to the cut, then the other, then held them up to Ownie. 'Stigmata,' he said. 'This is undoubtedly a blessed venture.' They made their way through the undergrowth towards the road, happy.

The light was beginning to come up as they reached the fountain in Cadder Road, where they washed themselves and wet their hands to sponge off the dirt from their outfits. John's face had long since stopped bleeding and after bathing the cut and touching it he knew it was nothing worse than a deep scratch which would heal without scarring. They could talk openly now.

'How far, do you think?'

'Maybe six miles. We could try and jump a tram but it's probably safer to walk all the way,' John said. 'Unless, of course, some good Christian should stop and offer us a lift.'

'Then we could throttle him wi' the rosary, drive off with the car and sell it,' Ownie said as they started to walk again towards the glow of the city.

'Aye, very subtle. If I had thought about it I would have brought a holy object as a bludgeon.'

'D'ye think they'll have missed us by now?'

'I should think' – John began to consider it with pleasure – 'they'll be more interested in fighting the fire and finding excuses for a drunken priest setting it rather than worrying about us.'

'They'll know we did it.'

John slapped him on the back. 'Course they will, but will they do anything about it? First of all, they'll think we died in the fire. Can you imagine the head counting that's going on right now, the panic? And then, when they begin to suspect, will they tell the polis? How does the whole thing look to them, if they enquire? Like Conlon gets guttered, knocks the bottle over, stumbles off to bed in a stupor and a spark from the grate sets off the fire. I mean, where did a couple of borstal boys get hold of a half-bottle of Black Bottle? Even if they had, they would have drunk it, wouldn't they? And how did they spirit themselves through a locked door and into the office? No, Conlon will keep his peace. Blame a spark or an act of God.'

The gravel was crunching under their boots as they walked and behind them they could hear the tremble of a car engine in the distance. They said nothing, trying to walk calmly as it got louder, then came alongside, seemed to slow, but it was only a change of gear as it checked, chuntered and then surged off on the upward incline.

'My guess is,' he continued, 'that they'll try to blame it on an accident, or one of the cats. I don't know how they're going to explain how we got out. But, after the first few days, I don't think anyone's gonnae be looking for us too hard. There's a war on, we've less than six months to do, so who the fuck cares?' He slapped his chest. 'It's a pity for them that everything about us got burned up in the fire, all the records, everyone's records.'

They were passing some farm buildings now and John considered whether they should try and steal milk, or eggs, but decided against it. His stomach was beginning to ache for food, but that was not an uncommon feeling and they would eat before midday, he knew, consoling himself that at least this morning he would not have to force down the lumpy cold mix like industrial slurry that masqueraded as porridge.

'We'll need some new clothes, John, and money.'

'Nae fears, we'll have both and more. Trust me.'

'D'ye have an idea where we can hide out?'

'Of course.'

They walked on for another mile, watching the houses thicken around them and the number of cars and vans and buses begin to grow as they neared the city. They passed very few people, but of those that they did none of them seemed to consider it odd that two young priests, one with a bloody tear to his face, should be walking purposefully towards the city centre. Trees and foliage lining the road had all but disappeared and ahead, as they turned a bend, they saw a small group of shops and, just behind, the steeple of a church. 'Let's try there,' John said, nodding towards the shops.

They walked along and around the shops but all were closed. There seemed nothing to scavenge, no milk or bread, and neither of them were yet at the stage of raking through the middens. 'All right,' John said, 'let's try over there next.' He was pointing towards the church, a large red sandstone building with a tidy garden in front. They walked the few yards, opened the gate and then tried the heavy, studded door. It creaked and swung open. Stark led the way into the dark and deserted nave which smelled of dust and years of devoted neglect. There was no one around but instinctively he ducked and made the sign of the cross, then he turned away from the direction of the altar and back towards the door. On a ledge behind the door he noticed the poor box. He took it, it felt heavy in his hand and when he shook it heard a substantial rattling inside.

'Divine providence,' he whispered to Ownie. The box was wooden, highly varnished, with a slot for money and a small brass padlock holding the bottom shut. John tucked it under his arm and nodded with his head to Ownie to follow him outside. They scuttled round to the back of the building, to the small, trimmed graveyard, ducking down behind a gravestone. John put the box on top of a marble stone set into the ground and looked around. A few yards away he noticed a carefully tended rock garden, dotted with heathers and ferns. He selected a large grey boulder, dug it out of the earth with both hands and pulled it up to his chest.

He could see that Ownie was looking at him oddly. 'It's a mortal sin.' His voice was wavering.

'It's for the poor.' John grunted as he pushed the large stone up in the air with both hands – 'What are we?' – then cast it down on the wooden box, smashing the wood and spilling out the coins. Then he quickly dug the silver and the pennies out of the splinters of smashed wood and counted the money into his left hand.

'More than ten bob.' He smiled and put his arm round Ownie. 'Cheer up.' He looked up at the sky. 'Look, no thunderbolts so far.

Think of it as compensation for some of the lashes and whippings and punches, and pretty poor at that.' His accomplice did not look any more reassured. 'Tell you what, Ownie, I'll tuck a ten bob note in your pocket before the coffin lid's nailed down and you can square it upstairs with the man on the gate. C'mon.' He pulled his arm. 'Let's get a tram or a bus and find some new clothes.'

'I feel pretty strange,' the other boy said. 'It's no' right.'

'If you feel so bad about it we'll send the money back here, okay, when we've got it? Will that make you feel better?'

'Aye, it would.' They had reached the gate and were walking again towards the back of the shops. 'That gravestone,' he continued, 'that you smashed the box on, did you notice the name?'

'No.' John could feel the comforting movement of the money in his pocket against his right leg. 'Can't say I did.'

'It was Stark.'

'Aye? Well, I doubt if I wakened him.'

'Ye cracked the stone.'

'I doubt if that'll bother him.'

No, Ownie thought, but it does me.

Master Sergeant Angelo Guiliano stepped down on to the platform and into the smell of coal smoke and waved away the old porter with the barrow. He looked up at the vaulted iron ceiling and the wheeling pigeons, sighed and slung his kit bag over his shoulder and began to walk to the barrier. He was in his late twenties, thickset and dark, with his beard coming through again although he had shaved before boarding the train. He was wearing Army Air Force uniform. After the heat of the empty first-class compartment, and although he was now wearing his greatcoat, the sudden chill made him shiver. He showed his ticket to the inspector at the barrier and pushed out through the clots of passengers with suitcases, the entwined lovers, the waiting relatives, out into the main concourse of the station and began to walk purposefully towards the exit, although he had only the vaguest of ideas about where he was going. A taxi, he thought, would be a starting point although he wasn't quite sure if they had them this far north in a war.

'I've got what you're looking for, Sergeant.' He turned and noticed that a boy, a teenager, had fallen into step beside his right arm. The lad was thin, about five eight in height with a scar under his left eye. Guiliano motioned him away, but the boy continued to walk. 'Whatever you want, Sergeant, I've got. Whatever you're looking for, I have.'

'Go away, kid,' Guiliano said out of the corner of his mouth.

'We're allies, Sergeant. You're a guest here, let me help you.'

'Did you hear me, son?' Guiliano stopped and turned round, the boy stumbling into him.

'I'll be your escort, show you around.'

Guiliano fumbled in his pocket and found a packet of gum. 'Here you go, kid, now just leave me alone.'

But the boy shook his head, rejecting Guiliano's outstretched hand. 'I want to make it up to you, Sergeant.'

Guiliano knew that he should not ask, but he could not resist the question. 'Make what up to me, son?'

'Well, it's just that you saved us in this war, Sergeant' – he paused for effect – 'so' – another pause – 'I saved my sister for you!'

Guiliano, in spite of himself, smiled. 'You're good, son, very good.' He held out his hand. 'Angelo Guiliano. What can I do for you, Mr. . . ?'

'Stark, Johnnie Stark, Angelo. I noticed you come off the train and I thought, a man in a strange town, what he needs is some company. I can offer my own – show you around, point out the sights, perhaps get you some rare-to-come-by products, a game of chance if you're gemme – or arrange for a rather more sweet companion, or companions. It's up to you.'

The American smiled. 'You thought, there's a Yank with too much cash and an itch in his groin who's made for me.'

'Something like that,' Stark agreed, grinning.

'Okay, let's you and me see if we get on in each other's company first and then we can talk about the other items on your menu. Is there some place we can get a coffee or a drink around here?'

'Just step this way, Angelo,' Stark said, making a sweeping motion with his right hand towards the side exit of Central Station. He grabbed Guiliano's kit bag and threw it over his shoulder, saying, 'Let me.' Once you have the luggage, he said to himself, the lug is sure to follow.

*   *   *

203

Johnnie had learned enough to know that it would be foolish and extremely hazardous to return immediately to his old parts. If there was a hunt it would be at its most intense in the first few days and would then die away, he was sure of that. But if the two of them were not being sought for arson or fire-raising, and he believed he knew enough about the psychology of the priesthood to believe they would not be, then there would not even be a proper search, probably at best a message passed along police lines to watch out for them. The only way they would be caught, he reasoned, would be either to bump into an inquisitive policeman or to be given up, which was another reason not to go back to the Gorbals right away.

The problem was that John did not know much more of the city; he even knew the surrounding countryside better. So they had taken the red Lawson's bus to Dundas Street and then walked down to Paddy's Market, buying some torn and patched old clothes, including two long and baggy tweed coats for a couple of shillings, then they had checked into a model lodging house in Calton run by a local Protestant church. It was called the Alexandria, with pictures of Egypt all over the foyer because the chairman of the trustees had served there at some time. It would do, the dormitories were clean, although the sheets were thin and stained and smelled of cabbage and lysol, Johnnie thought.

When they had arrived, there had been some vague but unprobing questions about them, although the turnkey seemed only to be going through the motions required of him by his employers. Orphans, they said, just turned out of a home in Perthshire, come to the city looking for work in the yards. The man, who was bald and sweaty and constantly itched at the sleeveless cardigan he wore each day, nodded and turned away. They did not even have to pay until they found work, just suffer the soup, the staple along with the morning porridge, and the prayers and hymns and sermons which prefaced the eating.

'It'll do for a few days,' John said to Ownie as they bit into the stale bread which accompanied the Scotch broth. 'Until I get us something better sorted out.'

John had been thinking a lot about the dance hall since the visit from Arbuthnot, but not in any kind of romantic or hopeful way. He believed that his thought process was entirely pragmatic, considering all the problems and the dangers, but particularly what his stepmother would be thinking and planning. Perhaps, having inherited everything else, she would allow him the Rose? But he quickly discounted that as one of the odd and romantic sprigs of an idea which, for his own protection, he could not allow to flourish. From what he knew of her, what his mother had slurred out bitterly, what, more trustworthily, people on the streets had said, she was a hard, unforgiving and sagacious ticket with big plans in which, he was sure, she would see him only as an obstruction.

She had never attempted to visit him or write, he had only ever seen her in passing and she had not even admitted to his existence, which made him think he could hardly turn up at her door for help. He even wondered if she had been behind the previous recapture.

All of which meant that if he turned up in the Gorbals he was sure that she would find out about it and almost certainly turn him in. But information was power and whereas he knew a great deal about her and what was, had been, his father's business operation, she knew nothing – and had made it clear that she wanted to know nothing – about him. So he concluded that she was not going to get to him unless he was extraordinarily foolish, which he did not intend to be.

Looking back at his previous life he realised that, while he had thought that he was being completely unemotional about her, he had, of course, failed. He held her responsible for breaking up his family, for the death of his mother but, and this is where he tried not to let his feelings colour matters, he had striven to bring a fiscal view to it, to reduce it all to a balance sheet and calculate how much he had lost financially because of her, what he had failed to inherit. He knew about the moneylending, although not its worth or extent, the shebeens – at least eight of them which had been operated by his father under proxy – the girls that were run, even their names, and he had an idea of the blackmarket contraband, the clothes and nylons, the chocolates, the tinned meats and, most valuably, the alcohol.

He considered, thinking about it for some time, that it had been foolish of his father to allow himself to be conscripted and so to permit Hazel to take over, a foolishness which had been justly rewarded, in his view, although the consequences were messy and deeply unfortunate for his next of kin. Him.

And then there was the dance hall once again. He was legally the owner but she was effectively in control. And although profits were supposed to be put into trust for him he knew that she would ensure that the books would show, when he eventually saw them, that there would be nothing, indeed that the place had apparently been running at a loss. She might even run it into the ground, although he thought that unlikely. Why destroy something which is turning a coin for you? Particularly when you intend to have it yourself, as he was sure was her intention?

But, he continued his musing, when you don't know anything about the opposition, you are not properly armed and you are vulnerable. He was the opposition, she barely knew his name, and despite his apparent lack of power he felt strong and he vowed once more that all that had not been fairly left to him he would take back.

She slowly turned the dial, the lustre on her deep red nails glowing in the lightly lit room, and listened with satisfaction as the tumblers fell. This never failed to give her pleasure, much more than gazing at a bank book could. It was almost sensual and a tangible reminder of her success. She turned the handle and pulled open the heavy door, about the only exercise she got these days, she thought. The envelope she had sealed earlier lay on the shelf next to the ledgers. It felt satisfyingly bulky in her hand as she turned back to her desk and sat down on the swivel chair. The man in the seat on the other side had not moved, she noted. He sat uncomfortably, hunched, as if unused to sitting still for any time, or, she thought, perhaps not familiar with the surroundings of civilisation. Or could it just be that it was her who was unsettling him? She hoped that it was that.

She put the envelope on the desk between them and slowly, with the red nails scraping on the green leather surface, pushed it across towards him. He made no move to take it. 'Fifty pounds now, all in ones, one hundred when you complete.'

Slowly he leaned forward and picked it up, folding it over with the fingers of his right hand before slipping it into the hip pocket of his jacket. He was wearing a grey herring-bone suit, the full shoulders of which could not properly drape or disguise the width of his chest. He was small, less than five foot six she guessed, but although he was broad it was apparent that the bulk was all bone and muscle. She knew, because she had had it checked, that he had been a regular soldier, invalided out, although he showed no sign of carrying a wound or any other ravage of war, and she would have put him at about forty years old although she realised that while she did not know exactly the effect combat had on the body clock it was a reasonable bet that it accelerated it.

'Complete what?' he said at last.

'Do you have scruples about what you do?'

'I've taken the money so does it seem so?'

'Yes, you're right. I'm sorry, I'm not used to this.' She tried a flirtatious smile but if it registered with him he did not let it show. 'I need you to get rid of a problem for me . . .'

'In my experience problems are usually human, so there's no need to beat around—' For the first time he smiled, at least his mouth pulled back to reveal gold-filled teeth. 'Is that it, do you want me to beat someone around or were you thinking about something more serious? You're certainly paying for whatever solution you want for your problem, as you put it.'

'You're right. It always seems better to me, too, to deal with things head-on,' she said.

'Always the best policy, saves trouble in the long run. So who is he, or she? And is it to be painful or just quick and neat?'

'This is business, not personal.'

He nodded. 'Fine.'

'His name is . . . .' She paused, ill at ease for the first time. 'This isn't what you think, he's no relative of mine. His name is Johnnie Stark. I was the' – she chose the word carefully – 'partner of his father,' she paused momentarily, 'who was killed in action.'

'Fine,' he said again. 'Where do I find him?'

'I don't know, that's partly why I'm paying you. But it won't be too difficult, the Starks don't stray too far from their own mess. He's young, about fifteen or so – is that a problem?'

'Makes it easier as far as I'm concerned.'

'Until a few days ago he was inside, well, borstal, approved school, but he got out. I've been expecting him to turn up here, but so far he hasn't, obviously.'

'Any picture at all, anything like that?'

'No, nothing. But he's well known. I'll give you a list of names of people and places to try, but there is one place I know he'll turn up at eventually. The Rose. It's a dance hall. You don't have any objection to hanging around a dance hall for a while, I don't suppose?' He leered his sparkling smile. 'The manager there will tell you all about him, the people he goes around with, but it should be very easy because he has an interest in coming there, coming to you.'

'He does? That's good,' he said. 'And I don't suppose it would be stretching this bargain too far to ask whether I could mull over the occasional drink while I'm waiting for him?'

'I'll arrange that, provided the mullings are occasional.'

Chapter Ten

McQuade broke another unbreakable rule and decided to work on Saturday. He woke, remembered that Stick, as he now called her too, was beside him, ran his hands down her body until she began to shiver and complain, had sex quickly and brutally which both of them seemed to enjoy, then showered.

As the tepid water sluiced over him he recalled that he had broken another unbreakable rule. A Saturday and no hangover. Well, only the mildest inflammation of the brain, which did not count at all. He gave his balls and cock a particularly lengthy soaping – well, you could never be too sure – after the usual examination. One thing he was not going to do, he told his aspiring erection, was to fool himself about Stick. He had not quite worked out what her relationship to Harris was, except a clearly subservient one, but he doubted that she was being an infiltrator. Actually, as he remembered it, she clearly was being that, given the rapidity she had gone through his clothes getting them off and, at a crucial moment, had also rammed an undetermined but forceful digit up his backside but, when he was dressed, he told himself there was nothing for her to find out.

So, if there's nothing of importance to find out about me, why? Perhaps she was just a gift, to be later recalled in kind? 'But if I should feel guilty about that, and I should, I don't! Anyway, even if I knew anything helpful, which I don't, it would undoubtedly be dangerous to someone. I'd become an accomplice, an extra name on the conspiracy charge sheet and, much as I relish the long, encompassing legs, the flawless skin, the perfect juicy pout and the unmatchable oral excellence, I do not fancy long nights in a scratchy bunk looking at the sky through bars and watching the blankets come up on remembrances of a few hot nights with a henchperson of Sean Harris.

He turned down the shower dial a few notches so that it ran colder.

When he had finished he dried himself quickly and found an old pair of jeans and a polo-neck sweater neatly folded in the top drawer of his cabinet. It was fortunate, he considered, as first he pulled on pants and socks, that he had Aileen to do for him, tidy up, iron and generally stage-manage, or he would be in deep, permanent, cotton-encrusted shit.

Stick was lying with her right leg out, the duvet pulled round her and over her face, and with her olive backside quite definitely challenging him. He considered, briefly, getting his own back on her for her unexpected but immensely enjoyable one-finger exercise but cautioned himself that there were more important things than having torrid sex with a beautiful woman. He struggled to think. Well, a rip-roaring exclusive would do until he could come up with the others. So, regretfully, he shook his head and hopped across the floor, putting on his shoes, grabbed a denim jacket from the cupboard and went into the kitchen.

If you can't stand the heat in the bedroom, get into the kitchen, I always say. He boiled the kettle, made a jug of filter coffee, downed two cups without milk and sugar and considered briefly how odd he felt. It must be normality, he told himself, shaking his head and wondering why it did not hurt.

The plan, simple as it was, seemed an eminently sensible one. He would follow Ricketts and the Yankee cop for a day or two, the weekend, and see what happened. If nothing else it would give him the opportunity to get more photographs and stack up some mileage on expenses, but he did not believe there would be nothing else. It seemed logical that you didn't call in the services of a foreign agency and then have it sit about on its expensive – and apparently perfectly-formed – backside for days watching the slum scenery and the parade of chib-marked ne'er-do-wells, numpties and psychotics which comprised the local crime scene. No, he was extremely confident that tagging along behind the beast and beauty – he looked longingly at the bed again as he packed his pockets with camera, film, tape-recorder and mike – would unquestionably lead him to an exclusive. He considered for a moment the sad sight of the average British woman's arse in comparison, then ran his fingers through his damp hair and let himself out quietly.

Ricketts, he already knew, was working. He had called him late last night and asked him out for a drink today, maybe go to the game. Ricketts had grumbled that he couldn't, hadn't said why, but when he had pressed him about work he had said that he was on from eight in the morning. It was now just after seven; Ricketts's flat was only five minutes away in the West End. He fumbled the key in the lock of the company car, a Sierra this time, which Ricketts would certainly not recognise and then turned the engine over.

Eventually his man came out of the close, one of these renovated numbers with a walnut door and an entry mechanism, just after quarter before the hour. McQuade waited until Ricketts got into the Cavalier before turning on his own engine, slipped it into gear and then tucked in behind the other car as it headed for Hyndland Road. McQuade was sure he knew where Ricketts was going, the hotel, and as he let his car drift behind as they headed past the university and then down on to Charing Cross and beyond, his certainty was confirmed. Ricketts parked in the driveway, McQuade drew up across from the distinctly ugly hotel building, universally out of character throughout the world so that you knew exactly where you were, and waited. He swore at himself for not buying the morning papers to pass the time but Ricketts was out of the hotel with Blantyre within a minute.

She must have been in the lobby, McQuade told himself. Smart lady, avoiding the chance of Ricketts coming up to her room. He knew enough about the man to know that he would have tried it on with her and, from the signs and the body language he had witnessed, it clearly wasn't going too well. As their Cavalier moved off he started his engine and reassured himself that if there was one thing the polis did not expect it was to be tailed.

Ricketts's mouth was dry and his head throbbed. He had drunk too much, out of anger and pique and depression and self-pity, he supposed, and now he needed something to wash out the shit and re-hydrate his system. 'Hold on,' he said, pulling in beside an Asian newsagent, letting the engine run as he got out.

Blantyre was wearing the same clothes she had on the day before, clean underwear naturally, and a fresh woollen crew neck, and for the first time since she had arrived she felt her body was back to normal. She had slept right through, wakened early, had a swim and

211

a work-out in the gym, actually in the reverse order, and then one of those help-yourself breakfasts, coffee, toast and juice, again in reverse order, before reading the newspapers. One of the pleasures of being abroad, or just in a strange city, was that feeling you got of being parachuted into someone else's problems without having the responsibility of caring or doing anything about it. Except, in this case she reminded herself, it was different.

She could see the outline of Ricketts's head behind the glass at the counter. He was all right, pretty good-looking and not even that persistent, but there was work to do, definitely no place for anything more which, she knew from experience, would only get around if – and she wouldn't – she had happened to do anything beyond the rules. For sure.

He got in the car, blaming her silently for his hangover. He was holding a white polythene bag, out of which he brought a bottle of Irn-Bru and a tube of aspirin. He fumbled with the cap, poured three or four of the pills into his left hand, stuffed them into his mouth and unscrewed the bottle top. The lemonade was warm but the scouring, gassy bubbles raging through his mouth and throat made up for it. He waved the bottle at her, she shook her head and he took another swig before re-capping it and then lobbed it on to the back seat.

'Our other national drink,' he said.

'Sorry?'

'Made from girders.' She shook her head. 'Advertising slogans. Like "I heart Noo Yoick". Irn-Bru, that's what you take when you're feeling a wee bit wabbit.'

'You know, that's the first time I've noticed you have a wisp. And I didn't put you down for a pet owner.'

'Wisp? Oh, good, lisp! Not rabbit. Wabbit, ehhm, under the weather, a wee tait overhung. Irn-Bru's the medicine you take after. Saturday and Sunday mornings you can't hear yourself think in this city for the clink of Irn-Bru bottles hitting the dentures.'

'Wabbit, tait? You have your own language, right?'

'Yep, about the only thing your lot haven't colonised. Tait, as in little bit.'

'You have a hangover?'

He put the car in gear. 'See, no communication problem at all. And you,' he went on, 'what did you do last night?'

'Oh,' she said, looking out the window at the quiet streets, 'very quiet. Nothing special. Meal in the room, fuck movie on cable and the dildo.'

'As long as you weren't too bored.'

'I feel good about today,' she said stretching in the passenger seat.

'I feel good about the overtime.'

'Yeah, it's always good to get time and a half.' A light rain was beginning to fall. 'He's due back in tomorrow so my guess is that it'll happen today.'

He looked round quickly. 'What will?'

'I mean, if anything does. What we're looking for is some connection to be made.'

'You know something? People from your side perhaps?'

'Maybe. There's some information that – that a particular family of ours have been negotiating over here. Italian naturally. A couple of foot-soldiers flew out – flew in, to London a couple of days back and maybe they might just turn up.'

'Flew in a couple of days back, when you flew in a couple of days back also? So that's why we're on our way to relieve the night shift?' She did not answer. 'Do these henchmen have names, or will we just recognise them from the deep tans and the Palermo City football shirts?'

'Palermo, as in Sicily.'

'Exactly?'

'They have names. Do you want the street names or the real thing?'

'They have both? Well, they would.'

'Modesta, Sergio, he's known as the End, on account of that he's as big as a brownstone and because that's what he does for a living, and Franco Strattani is the Angel, probably because he went to a seminary for just a bit longer than it normally takes to steal the silver.'

They were close to the Stark township now. 'At last, a little bit of trust.' He swung the car round a corner, avoiding another of the barking mad mongrels. 'You think they'll turn up?'

'One way or the other,' she said. 'Probably.'

*   *   *

Camburrini's death had only made a paragraph or two in the papers. When he had been found, which was not until closing time, there had been no identification on him. The assumption was that it was simply another drug OD and he had been shipped to the city mortuary while the police thought slowly about how they would go about tracing him. There was no missing person fitting his description, none of the uncooperative bar staff had seen him in the place before, allegedly, so officers would, after the real business of the weekend was over, get round to fingerprinting the body and checking the dental records if no one came forward looking for a lost junkie. On Monday his body would be retrieved from the cold store and the post mortem would extract the chemical and biological truths. Until then he would remain in the rubber body bag with the colour-coded label round his right, dirty, big toe.

Blantyre and Ricketts were going to see it right through to the close. Fat Boy had not come out of the house until after noon, he had gone in next door and come out with his younger brother Owen, twenty-one – calendar years and IQ, it was said – and they had driven into town. The two cops, acting the part of lovers, holding hands at Ricketts's instigation, had discreetly trailed them around on a shopping spree and then back to the Ponderosa. Neither of the police had eaten properly, just crisps and drinks as they went, and now they were sitting in the dark along from the house, waiting again. Just so that there would be none of the too obvious clues about their identity, the Cavalier did not have a police radio, neither did Ricketts nor Blantyre. He had a mobile phone, which he had been careful to keep charged in the cigar lighter gizmo as they drove, and now that they were parked he watched its greeny-blue blink as it looked up at him from beside the gear stick.

He checked the time on the digital clock on the dashboard. Six fifteen. Christ, he thought, how much longer? Do we sit here until all the lights go out? What if he goes to a club, are we going to be boogying around to rave music in our street clothes until dawn? Actually, when he considered it, and still blind to the hopelessness, the togetherness part with Blantyre was a not unpleasing prospect.

He jumped up in his seat, for a moment confused about what had startled him. It was the phone screeching. He grabbed at it, dropped it, fumbled around his feet, found it and then breathlessly hit the send button. 'Ricketts.' She watched him nodding at the phone in the ochre shadows cast by the street lights. 'Right,' he said, then looked round at her. 'Copy.'

She shook her head at him. 'Well?'

'He's made a reservation, for four, at an Indian restaurant. Eight o'clock.'

'How do we know, a tap?'

'Didn't say, I suppose so.'

'For four. Promising.'

A taxi arrived at fifteen minutes to eight and a young woman got out. Ricketts shook his head, indicating that he did not recognise her. The taxi remained with its engine running. The woman went up to the door; it opened before she knocked – 'Pass, friend,' Ricketts said quietly, guessing that she had been spotted on the surveillance cameras – and a bulky shape came out, Fat Boy he presumed, although it was difficult to tell at this distance and in the light. The two embraced and then walked back to the taxi.

Ricketts turned the ignition key and, 200 yards back down the road, so did McQuade. And the odd three-car caravan, only one of them knowing that this was what it was, headed for the city centre.

'Christ, I'm hungry.'

She made no answer.

'I could dive in and get a carry-out – takeaway. Just generally check out who he's with?' She said nothing. 'You haven't seen anything of them – the two, you haven't seen an angel, witnessed the end?'

'Nah, just the occasional flash in the sky and spot of ethereal music.'

'What do you think, about me checking it out? Getting some food?'

'Does he know you?'

'No. Definitely not.'

'I'll think about it.'

She had hardly said a word to him all day. He did not really know her, of course, but it was pretty obvious that something was going on in her mind. He could tell from the hunched silences and occasional facile expressions that she was worrying at it. 'Is there something wrong?' he said for the umpteenth time.

'Leave it,' she said, slouched in her jacket, both hands buried deep in the pockets. 'Blame it on the time of the month if you like.'

They sat in silence for several minutes. 'Right.' He slapped the steering wheel. 'Unless you strongly object, I'm going to check out Fat Boy and his company in the restaurant and I'm going to get something to chew on. Anything for you?' She shook her head. 'Watch the phone, okay?' She nodded. 'I need the air.' She nodded again.

The Café India was one of the newer and more upmarket Indian restaurants. There were more Indian restaurants in the city than anyone could reasonably count. Curries had been the most popular ethnic food in the city for more than twenty years, the main choice for eating out, but most of the restaurants were functional, flock wallpaper, warbling music through tinny speakers, although the food was usually good; what the Café India had done was marry excellent food with an expensively designed interior and had attracted the young and wealthy who had either grown out of Indian food or had put it down as the preserve of the proles, the kind of people who jammed it in between ten pints of lager and an up-and-downer with the wife.

The interior was bright, with lots of angled, shimmering glass, strips of wood and even a fountain in the lowered foyer where an old gentleman dressed as a maharajah, or a Delhi dustman for all Ricketts knew, welcomed you.

'The manager please, police,' Ricketts said quietly and was shown up a short flight of illuminated stairs to the bar area where a slightly chubby Asian man in his late thirties wearing an immaculate white tunic and turban walked towards them, smiling. Ricketts put out his hand, the other man shook it warmly. 'I'm a police officer,' he said softly. 'I don't want to pull out my warrant card here, in public . . .' The manager nodded agreement, motioned towards a wooden door marked 'private' at the end of the bar. 'Nothing to worry about,' Ricketts added as they walked.

The office had a parquet floor with a dark blue Indian rug in front of the glass and metal desk which a computer dominated.

There were two leather sofas. 'Sit down, please,' the manager said.

'Won't take a minute,' Ricketts muttered, shaking his head and turning his identification under the man's gaze. 'I'm looking for someone who's in your restaurant. Don't worry, I'm only checking, we're not going to make an arrest or anything. Stark, I think the booking would have been. For four?'

The manager walked over to his desk, picked up a telephone and said something, in Urdu Ricketts presumed, and then after nodding a reply hung up. 'That's right. Table 12. But that's a table for two.'

'It is? Okay. Could you describe just where that is on the floor and maybe how I could get a look at it, discreetly.'

The manager beamed. 'That is simple. It is the table against the wall, two before the toilet, the gents. You can't miss it.'

'Great,' he said, shaking the manager's hand again, 'I do need to make a visit. Oh,' he continued as if it had just occurred to him as they walked together to the door, 'any chance of a small carry-out, maybe pakora, chicken tikka?'

'Of course,' the manager said, opening the door, 'and it's on the house.'

'I couldn't,' said Ricketts rather unconvincingly.

'Of course you could,' said the manager, stepping back to let him pass.

McQuade was worn out from walking and sore from sitting and his throat felt raw and deprived. He needed a drink. Once more he shook his head in wonderment at his ability to predict entirely wrongly the course of events. What were Ricketts and the NYPD rear over here doing following Stark all over the place? What were they expecting? Or had the surveillee clocked them and was he leading them on, taking them for the grand tour?

Now here we all were, he thought, sitting outside a curry shop waiting for him to show again after his tea. Or for something to happen other than the numbing ordinariness of just another Saturday. Granted, even this would be somewhat out of the ordinary for Stark Junior, after the last few years in the pokey, but you would think that his ambitions for liberty stretched further than a few new shirts from Gap and a biryani and lager soup in Glasgow. Criminals lacked imagination, he concluded.

He twiddled with the scanner on the seat beside him once more, seeing if it had strayed off the police band. It hadn't. He had taped a list of the police incident codes inside the glove compartment but nothing of any note had happened in the time he had been listening, certainly nothing about the Fat Boy. He wiped condensation from the window and noticed the door of the Cavalier ahead open and Ricketts get out. For a second a little flare of expectation went through him, convinced that an arrest was about to happen, but the other door remained closed, which ruled it out. 'Probably going for a piss,' he said softly, thinking that if something dramatic did not happen in the next hour – he glanced at his watch but could not see the hands properly in the darkness – he was off. There would still be time to take in a few beers and find out if Stick had stuck around. He smiled. 'Maybe she really likes me?' He thought about it for a couple of seconds. 'Nah.'

Ricketts had taken in exactly what was going on at Stark's table, which was nothing, and a lot. Nothing interesting or suspicious, nothing but a great deal of holding, touching and curry-aromaed kissing. The girl was deeply good-looking – he felt a pang of resentment as he peed against the cubicle wall – with long dark hair and a tight, dark-coloured top on, scooped out at the front so that as she leaned over the table her breasts swelled against the rim of the fabric. Fuck it, it wasn't fair. He told himself to concentrate on the job but his mind went into free association, blow-job, hand-job . . . 'Stop it,' he said out loud, drawing a look from his neighbour. He zipped himself up, then washed his hands and smoothed his hair. May as well keep hope alive, he thought.

As he walked back down the passageway past the table he saw that they had made little progress on their main course, but that they were now into a second bottle of champagne, the first one dead and neck-first down in the melting ice in the bucket. Bastard, he thought, walking past, what kind of punishment system allows a major villain out for the weekend to suck champagne and fuck a beautiful woman? He paused only to pick up his free meal in a polythene bag from a smiling waiter.

The day, he considered, had been entirely wasted. Stark had done nothing even marginally illegal, not even a used sweet wrapper dropped in the street, far less a drug deal. It was a prosaic shopping trip stocking up on fashionable goodies, no doubt to impress his jail colleagues. Now this, a randy meal out, no sign of the other two visitors, just Stark and some pretty brass walloping down the champagne and tickling each other under the table, prior to rogering each other rotten, no doubt, all the way into the Sabbath while he and the ice blonde performed abstinence in their metal cell outside.

As he skipped between the cars with the bag, Ricketts tried to retrieve some positive elements, some consolation from the long day. There were still a few hours to go, it was possible something might still happen, the two gentlemen from Little Italy might still turn up, perhaps the arrangement had been changed, hence the meal for two rather than four? As he opened the door his stomach sank at the prospect of a Sunday spent like this.

'Sickeningly normal,' he said, slumping into the car seat. 'They're just getting a sheen on for a night of sin, it looks like.'

'Well,' Blantyre said, sitting up in the seat, 'this is the point where we tiptoe quietly into the darkness.'

Ricketts was rummaging in the bag to see what was there. 'What?'

'We're off the case. The call came when you were inside.'

He looked round. 'Sorry? You mean we're being relieved?' It both pleased and angered him.

'Yep, that's it. It's all off. We're out of here.'

'But why?' Letting the bag of hot food sag in his lap. 'You mean we've fucked around here all day for nothing and now we're being pulled, before the stake-out's even over?'

'That's it. Orders from above, ours not to reason . . .' She pushed his arm. 'Look at it positively. We can go somewhere, grab a few beers and pig-out on this.' She nodded at the bag.

'We can?'

'Yeah. Let's lighten up. And I'm sorry, y'know, for being such a pain in the butt.'

'Forget it,' he said, handing her the bag and searching for the car keys, not understanding anything. 'And lightening up is something I do pretty expertly.' The engine coughed and started and he put the car into gear and eased it out and away from the brightly illuminated restaurant. 'It doesn't make sense. Are you sure you got that quite right?'

'Exactly right. I assure you I can understand Scotch English. Orders from the chief constable, so it was said. I didn't think I should argue the case. Anyway, Ricketts' – she winced slightly and straightened up in the seat – 'how's about you show me the bright lights of the city?' and she wondered whether the pistol in the quick-release holster strapped tightly under her arm would leave a bruise on her ribs.

'Shite! Shite!' McQuade slapped the wheel, quickly turned on the engine then found himself racked with indecision. Should he follow or stay? He banged the wheel again and began bouncing on the seat. Why had they left? Was the shift over, had a relief crew arrived he hadn't picked up? He looked around, not remembering any other car pulling in, but then he hadn't been looking too closely.

That must be it, he almost convinced himself. There had not been any communication on the radio as far as he could tell, but that did not necessarily mean anything. He decided to wait, to follow Stark because – because? Because he was the original target, that seemed logical and, besides, his mind could not cope with any more intrigue. If Ricketts and the cop were off on some other gig that was just too much for him. As I've started, he said to himself, I'll finish.

It was almost 10 p.m. when Stark and the girl came out. He might have missed them had he not been expecting an ordered taxi. When he saw a black cab pull up and the driver get out with the engine running he rubbed his hands over his face and switched on the engine. They came lurching down the steps. McQuade was not sure whether they were drunk or whether it was the difficulty of walking when the two of them were all but mounting each other as they went. The door slammed and the taxi did a U-turn and took off. McQuade guessed they were going back to Fat Boy's place. There were rules, he guessed, which insisted that prisoners on home visits, or training for fuckin' freedom or whatever they called it, had actually to be at home. There were probably rules preventing them getting guttered and shagging too, but Stark didn't seem to be observing those ones.

The cab was easy to follow. He imagined what the two were doing in the back seat, what the driver was thinking about it, and he thought about Stick again. Well, it looked as if he'd had that for the night, if not for ever. A front-page splash beats a quick dip any day, he uttered to himself without any great conviction. There was a bottle of champagne in the fridge and when he got back he decided that he would try her mobile. Why not? She could only say fuck off.

It came to him: I could phone her now, and then it went from him, he'd forgotten to bring his address book.

But he recognised where they were, on the long approach road to the Ponderosa, so he let the car hang further back, convinced now that they were certainly going home. And when he saw the taxi had pulled up he braked and slid into a space about 200 yards away on the opposite side of the street, jammed on the handbrake and left the engine running, then checked that all his doors were locked. When he looked round the couple were still behind the cab, probably arguing the fare with the cabbie through the passenger window, either that or buttoning their clothes up. Then the taxi slowly drew away and left the two of them entwined, one dark shape with four legs, it seemed, before they split slightly apart and began to walk towards the gate.

It seemed to happen like in a silent movie. Black and white. There were no colours in the dark. The noise of the engine running, the background squabble and static of the scanner, and then two other shapes in the frame behind the couple. Stark Junior turned his head back, perhaps at the sound of a shout, then broke into a stumbling run, the woman running furiously away. The lead figure behind raised an arm, pointing, denouncing perhaps. McQuade noticed a small sparkle of brightness in his hand. Under the street light the person, a man certainly, seemed to have fuzzy short blond hair, but later McQuade wondered whether that had been a trick of the light and it had been a nylon stocking. He was only a few paces behind and then Fat Boy stumbled, seemed to struggle to keep his feet, as if the pavement had iced over, then pitched forward on to his face, before trying to scratch at it to get up again.

The man with the gun – it came to McQuade in a rush of fear that that was what it was – walked up over the rising man, his arm shook a couple of times and then he and the other figure turned and ran away. The only noise McQuade heard in the whole scene was the squeal of tyres and the howl of the engine as the car slithered past him and away.

Without knowing why McQuade put the car lights off and then the engine. He could not see the girl any more, she seemed to have de-materialised in just a few seconds; it was almost as if his mind had suddenly written her out. Now, he realised he was holding his breath and that the roaring in his chest was his heart.

He kept watching the body on the pavement, still not quite believing, and now it was moving again. McQuade felt a wash of insane relief, it was not what he had thought, his dried-out brain had been hallucinating. He wiped his mouth with the back of his hand. Now Stark was on his knees, then his feet until, his balance clearly gone, his upper body was propelling him over and towards the gate of his father's house, while his legs hopelessly sought traction below. McQuade watched as he fell through the gate and into the garden and then another figure arrived, bending, holding him, then another, and still there was no sound except now a gaggle of electronic voices on the police band.

One of the figures ran away. McQuade wanted to roll down the window to hear the sounds but he was too frightened; he wanted to turn on the ignition and get out but his hands felt like water. He slid lower in the seat in case he could be seen. Then after a few minutes a car pulled up between him and the house and he saw heads bobbing frantically behind it, shadows getting in, then that car too tore away and McQuade noticed that the body had gone and that the road was just like it had been only a couple of minutes before.

They'll take him to the Royal, he thought and then, as exhilaration chased out the fear, I've got this to myself.

He kept repeating that as he switched on the engine and began to make for the hospital.

He did not get home until after 4 a.m., and still he was dry. There was no sign of Stick; he didn't even bother looking for a note or any sign of her passing. He retrieved the Laphroaig from the cabinet, poured a horse tranquilliser-sized measure, switched on MTV and slumped into an armchair.

Stark had been dead on arrival at the Royal, that much had been obvious, although it had taken more than a couple of hours to confirm it. McQuade had lurked in the background, among the stab-wounded, the battered, the drunk, bloody and tearful, the RTAs, the few bemused, innocently injured and the police officers who attempted to keep order and the belligerents apart. No one even asked him who he was, or probably even noticed, assuming, if he even swam into notice, that he was waiting on a victim.

The old man was there, Stark Senior, dressed in dark trousers and a white shirt, the front of it soaked in his son's blood, and the younger brother, Owen, and another one, in his early thirties, carrying the characteristics of a minder, broad shoulders, a few battle wounds and eyes of chipped ice.

McQuade had been too scared to approach old man Stark, whose countenance hadn't changed throughout, even after he came out from the meeting with the doctor where he must have been told that his son was clinically dead. The three had merely whispered to each other in a corner of the raucous casualty waiting room and then walked out into the rain and dark. McQuade had followed them to the door, to the ambulance bay, and then watched the lights of their car disappear. Then he had gone home.

Now he was sipping the whisky, watching the bright, jumping images on the screen, the rap music booming round and about him and he was shivering. He felt about six years old, afraid of the dark and the shadows and in need of company and comfort. He took a gulp of the whisky and realised that his teeth were clicking against the glass. He had the story all right, but he also had serious trouble. Now that he could think it through he appreciated that he was a material witness to the shooting, the killing, and how disturbing and potentially dangerous that was. Apart from the curvaceous girl who had disappeared and, it seemed reasonable to consider, may well have been part of a set-up, he was the only other eye-witness. Not only would that be of great interest to the police, it would be even more so to Stark's father because, if there was one thing McQuade knew for certain about him, it was that he would not be waiting for the police to bring the killers before the bar.

The music was not bringing companionship. He got up and rang Stick's mobile number but got the metallic message that the phone was off. He realised how pathetic he was being, how his life looked in fact, phoning up some chippie so he could blubber over her. He took another small sip of whisky.

Then, of course, there was his part in it, and hers. How did they fit, why had Harris cast them together? It would appear now, if it got out, that he was deeply embroiled with the Stark opposition, and he had no faith in Harris not to let it do so. Had he engineered it, was that part of it? 'Part of what?' he forced himself to say out loud so that the words hung in the room against the staccato backdrop. 'Part of the set-up,' he answered. There was not much doubt that Harris was involved in the hit; who else could it have been after the recent events, who else had the motive?

His mind could not let go of the small pinprick of light in the killer's hand and he wondered what it was about this that was familiar and disturbing.

He began to retrace his day from waking up to see if there was anything that seemed unusual, if there was a pattern leading to the shooting. But it seemed even more mundane in retrospect. And then he got to the wait outside the restaurant. He tapped the glass, recalling Ricketts going inside, then coming out with a package and then the Cavalier disappearing. The song had changed now and some ancient, smudgy concert footage of Joni Mitchell replaced the rappers, her paving paradise once more.

'The Cavalier disappears, the police surveillance is called off and less than two hours later Stark is stiffed.' He was talking at the screen. 'Coincidence or not?'

I woke up this morning an observer, he said to himself, and I am going to bed a target.

Stark's body was lying on a table in a dimly lit treatment room, a uniformed constable standing in front of the door barring entrance. The body was naked; the clothes which had rapidly been pulled off or cut away when he was brought in were now carefully stored in a large plastic bag under the table. There were three wounds on the body. A shot to the head had entered through his left cheek, shattering three teeth, tearing a lump out of his tongue and then through the right-hand corner of his mouth where it gouged the cheek and lip. It had not been fatal. Another shot had passed through his fleshy upper right thigh, avoiding the femur and exiting leaving a hole the size and the rough shape of an old threepenny bit. It had been a minor wound. The third shot, which was actually the first, had caused a small entrance wound in the lower back, then, striking the pelvic basin it had fragmented and ricocheted and channelled upwards, tearing through the aorta, the trachea and embedding in the heart. It had been remarkable, if surgeons had any longer been surprised about the resilience and will to live of the human body, that he had managed to get up and had staggered a few yards before collapsing. The first shot had been fatal from the moment the trigger was pulled on the light .22 handgun.

Police forensic surgeons had now cordoned off the street in front and around the Starks' houses and were beginning the search. Two cartridge cases had been quickly found in the street, their positions had been circled and photographed and they had been bagged for further analysis. A faint patch of blood, all that was left after the rain, had been found and a rough outline of where the body must have been, marked on the pavement. Uniformed coppers were searching the gardens and the street, the photographer was taking long shots of the cars and the house and detectives were starting to interview adjoining householders, none of whom, entirely predictably, had seen or heard anything through their dense sleep.

Peter Stark had given the briefest and most bland statement: 'Came out, picked his son up, took him to hospital, had no idea why anyone should intend to harm him, saw nothing.' It could have been written in advance by any of the coppers.

At just after 4.30 a.m. the body of John Stark Junior was carefully lifted by two orderlies wearing plastic gloves, and under the instructions of the forensic surgeon, into a black rubber body bag and then into a drop-sided enclosed trolley and wheeled out to an ambulance, two uniformed constables in attendance. The ambulance drove the mile or so to the morgue at the river and the trolley containing Stark's body was wheeled into the reception area. The details were noted by another orderly, the body bag was tagged and sealed and the trolley was wheeled away by an attendant. Stark was then stored, for the post-mortem on Monday and thereafter for as long as it might take, in the chilled cabinet next to Camburrini who, through a labyrinthine route and several profit-takers, had actually been one of his customers.

225

Chapter Eleven

Every day after Ownie had disappeared John would walk across town to the Mitchell Library. He always wore a muffler and an old torn cap which he hoped would mask his youth. The library was warm and smelled of varnish and damp clothes. He read the papers and then moved to the reference section where he hoped to find something about his precious picture, but, although there were many books on religion and religious treasure, there did not seem to be anything at all to help him, so he strayed into what caught his eye, histories of the clans, parish council records, old manuscripts about the city, travel books, dictionaries and encyclopaedia, even valuation and voters' rolls. Then, around lunchtime he would walk back down to George Square and south to Argyle Street and to the Clyde where he would wait for Ownie.

Sometimes his mate did not arrive until it was dark and John would have come and gone several times, to shops and shebeens, anywhere to keep warm. It did not take long to build up the information, John jotting it down in a notebook as Ownie recounted what he had picked up on the streets, and it had not been difficult. Malice and envy were great tongue looseners and the outlines and colourings of Hazel's businesses – his inheritance! – were sketched in. She had bought a house with a garden in Langside, there was the street name but not the number; however John was able to fill that in from the valuation roll in the library.

One wet Tuesday waiting on Ownie, the daylight charcoal-filtered, he wandered along the bank of the river and came across a stables. The smell reached him before the noises of hooves and snorting, the gates open, a cobbled yard beyond marked with dung and a couple of poor looking specimens being unhitched from long carts. John went into the yard and up to the nearest carter who was bending over the rigging, back to him, the reek of coal dust surrounding him. 'Excuse me.' The man turned, white eyes glinting out of soot skin, and it occurred to him. 'You wouldn't have a start for a lad, would you? I'll no' cost yi much.'

The man looked him up and down. 'You look fit.' The horse behind him had its head down staring at the cobblestones, clearly expecting only to slump to them. 'How much is no' much?'

'Whatever you think is reasonable. I could give you a day for free, so's yi can try me out.'

The man coughed, turned his head and then spat out a stream of dirty phlegm. The clothes he was wearing were so dark and coal-soiled it was impossible to tell what they had once been, they hung on him formlessly, and round his shoulders he had folded and tied a coal sack, for protection, John assumed. 'Yi' look worth the risk, son. Quarter to seven here the morn; if you're no' here I'm no' waiting. This is where we pick up the cuddy and the cart and then we go tae the depot tae pick up the coal – well, it's mostly briquettes – and then off on the run. It's hard work, mind and if y're no' up to it then I'll soon tell you and y'll have to make your own way back.'

'I'm up to it. I've had plenty of experience of manual work.'

'Fine,' the man said, turning back to the horse.

'What's your name, in case I don't recognise you in the morning?'

The man turned back. He smiled, showing more splashes of white. 'Wae a clean face, y'mean? Gerard, just ask for Gerard Queen.'

Ownie was waiting for him when he got to the rendezvous point at the suspension bridge. 'I've just come up with something,' he said, unable to keep the excitement out of his voice. 'Don't laugh. I'm going to be a coalman.'

Ownie looked at him and shook his head, failing to understand.

'Think about it. No one notices a coalman, do they? They just come and go, never recognised, covered in keech and camouflage. It's perfect; once my face is covered in coal dust like a chocolate minstrel no one will ever recognise me. I won't look like a lad, as well.'

'But why?' the other boy said.

'I've got to go back, Ownie' he said.

Gerard Queen was self-employed. After having been thrown out of the army with no trade he had been on the Means Test for more than a year before he managed to get a start as a foundry labourer at Beardmore's. He had a wife and two kids but Agnes, the younger one, just five, had taken scarlet fever, burning up in her cot, them unable to afford a doctor and proper medicine, and had died, her breath just stopping in her wee racked throat. It had hit him really badly, he had started to drink fiercely and one morning in Beardmore's with a severe hangover and a foreman riling him he had punched the man with all of the pent-up hatred that boiled within him and smashed his jaw to fragments. He was out of a job and could have been inside for the assault, but charges hadn't been pressed. It was his word against the foreman's, lucky to get away with just losing a job, he was told. After that he walked around for three days, pretending to be at work, until something eddied into his consciousness from somewhere, a barely remembered conversation in a pub about the coal business and a carter's on the Clyde. He had put his wage and the week's lying time into loosening tongues and then hiring the horse and cart and buying the coal from the yard in Scotstoun. That was it, he didn't know what to do next, just let the horse amble on, figuring that horse sense was as good as any, waiting to see where the old nag took him, the remembered steps it would pick out as it crossed the bridge. He just took up trying to sell coal where the horse pulled to a halt, screaming, 'Coal, coal briquettes', on the second day bringing along a big brass bell which he clanked before each announcement.

On the fourth day he ran into the trouble he expected. Two coalmen, him on their regular run, came running up shouting and pulling at the horse's bridle. He jumped down, fighting for the lost lassie he hadn't been able to save and for the last one, Jean, felling the first man with the blunt hatchet stave, turning on the second one, swiping and swearing and kicking and punching with the left hand too until the man ran off. Then he calmed down, looked at the downed man next to the cart, his face a splash of red on black, holding his nose and mouth, blood bubbling through the coal-streaked fingers pressed to them and he said quietly, 'I've got weans.'

Through his broken teeth the man mumbled into his fingers. 'So huv ah.'

Now he was gently slapping the reins on the back of the old horse with the strange boy beside him. Johnnie was a sturdy lad who didn't seem to notice the exertions of humping sacks on his back, or a tray of briquettes, and trotting up the stairs. Something about the lad was difficult to resist: he seemed to carry with him a determination which brooked no resistance, which others might find threatening but which he found appealing. Queen had tried to interrogate him gently about his life and family but the boy had quickly shut up and he had not tried again.

He sighed and slapped the reins. There was no doubt that the lad was useful, that they were getting round in less than half the time it normally took – he was past fifty-five now so that ought to be no surprise – but, nevertheless, there was still the additional cost of him.

'It's not much of a living, son,' he said.

'I don't intend it to be,' he replied. 'I'll have my own soon.'

'Is that right?' Queen turned to the lad as the horse drew to a stop. 'So maybe it'll be you employing me, then.'

'Could be,' Johnnie said, swinging down from his seat to the ground.

Queen had tried to lead conversations around to personal matters, even asked him directly about his parents, friends, where he lived and what he did in the evening, but the boy had managed to shrug off the questions with some wisecrack or a grim smile. Well, if he did not want to talk that was up to him but, Queen suspected, there had to be a powerful reason for his reticence, either that or he was running from it. Queen suspected it was the latter. 'Could me taking you on get me into any trouble, son? Ah'm no' saying I would necessarily want to avoid it, but I'd just like to know if it wis coming and where it wis coming frae. You understand.'

When he said this Johnnie had his back to him and was adjusting the bit into the mouth of the broken-down horse called Patsy. Queen watched him pause, then turn. 'I'm an orphan, my ma died a couple of years back and my da a few weeks ago in the war. I was in borstal then. I ran away with a mate, I only had a few weeks to do. I'm living in a model and I'm thinking of enlisting.' It came out in one long breath. He gazed unflinchingly into the man's eyes, holding on to the bridle with his right hand, the horse's head nodding slightly.

'And what did you dae, to go inside?'

'I wasn't going to school. And I was fighting.'

'Stealin'?'

'Aye, a bit of that too, I can't deny it.'

'Now?'

'No, no' now.'

'Well,' Queen said, 'okay. Y'd better no' be.' He turned away. 'Get along now, we're behind.'

Next day, it would have been their fifth or sixth together, John turned up with another boy. 'It's all right,' he said quickly 'you don't have to pay Ownie and he's strong, we'll have it aw done by lunchtime.' Queen said nothing, just nodding and twitching the long whip at the horse, allowing the two boys to scramble up.

They were almost at Eglinton Toll before a word was spoken. 'So, John,' Queen said eventually, 'what's behind all this?'

'Well, it's like a demonstration and a proposition. We both need to work, to pay for our digs. I thought that if we could show you how much use we could be you'd maybe agree to getting another cart and round, sort of double your business.' Queen said nothing, just clucked his tongue at the horse as the cart creaked and rattled over the cobblestones. 'We could split the additional profit,' the boy added.

A tramcar overtook them in a cacophony of grinding and scraping and a shower of blue sparks. 'Well, that's interesting right enough. You know, until today I didn't even realise I had a business. I thought I was just gettin' by, making wages.' He shifted on the bench seat, turned up his collar as a smirr of rain drifted softly in, prickling on his eyes and face like the touch of cold, fine hairs. 'Suddenly I'm a businessman and here, before you know it, I've got partners as well. This has been a pretty surprising day so far, I huv tae admit. Mind you son, from the little I know you, I would have thought you'd have set your sights a bit higher than being a caul howker.'

'Maybe so,' John answered, 'but at least you're out in the open, no' locked up like a beast. Eh, Ownie?' The other boy, clinging on behind the bench, nodded. 'But this'll all be a bit new to you, teuchter, after the peat cutting.'

'And the sheep shagging.'

'I was just coming to that.' The horse pulled up outside a close on its first unimposed stop, the two boys jumped down as Queen rang the bell and called and then quickly began to load up the briquettes.

When they were back on the cart and it was moving again Queen asked, 'And what kind of division were you thinking about?'

'Evens,' said John. 'That seems fair.'

'Aye, it does. But why cut me in at all? Why not just hire the cart and do your own deal with the coal yard?'

'It's no' a career I've got in mind, Gerard. I just need some money and a bit of flexibility for a few weeks. Anyway, even if I wanted to and I had the money the carter wouldn't hire out a wagon to boys like us, would he?' The horse, head down, was wearily pulling up again. We'll make you some extra money, if just until the end of the summer. We can finish the morning runs by lunchtime, you can louse yerself and have a couple pints and we'll meet up with you later and take the cuddy back.'

'There's more to it than you're letting on,' Queen said, watching the two lads spring down again, thinking that the longer that he did not hump the briquettes up the stairs the better it seemed and the harder it would be to go back to. 'I'll think about it,' he said, picking up the bell.

The houses were red and grey sandstone, bungalows mostly, set back from the road and usually shrouded by bushes or rhododendrons which, for some reason, always seemed funereal to Johnnie. His step-mother's house had a straight paved path running up to the door, the window frames had been painted a dull green and to the side of the house a gravel driveway led up to a pebble-dashed garage, its wooden doors the same shade of green. They had stopped the cart outside the metal gate framed by two small pine trees. Johnnie nudged Ownie. 'On you go,' he said.

The sky was the dark grey colour of a faded bruise and a small shower of rain had blackened the pavements. Johnnie watched as Ownie walked up to the door, first rang the bell, waited, then pounded on closed storm flaps. No answer. Johnnie swung down from the seat and hefted a sack of coal on to his back, feeling the muscles strain around his stomach, then made his way up the drive, the stones crackling under his boots, Ownie moving round the side of the house ahead.

The back garden was formally neat, a precise rectangle of grass, narrow, carefully hoed seedbeds on three sides filled with meticulously planted roses and deep in the fourth side, in what would have been the vegetable garden (Hazel was clearly not digging for victory) was an oval-roofed, corrugated-iron air-raid shelter. The coal bunker was set against the back wall of the house, next to the back door. Ownie pulled up the wooden lid, noted that there was space inside; Johnnie adroitly swung his sack round and tipped the coal in a black landslide into the maw, then slid back the lid and dumped the empty jute sack on top.

'The house?' Ownie asked.

'Naw, look at us. Too much mess.' They were soot-stained from head to foot, only the steel tips of their boots showing dully through the dirt.

'Let's have a quick look at the shelter.'

The two of them skipped across the grass and while Ownie picked at the large padlock holding the door, Johnnie looked around. The garden was totally enclosed in high privet hedges with a line of mature trees, rowan and beech, at the bottom, the gently waving branches against the sky and looming over the shelter.

Ownie had the lock open in seconds; the door creaked as it swung back, the light catching three wooden steps leading down into the gloom. It took their eyes a few seconds to adjust, the milky backlight spraying into the long bevelled room.

'Jesus Christ,' Johnnie said, picking out the boxes stacked floor to ceiling. He moved towards one of the smaller columns, around six stacked wooden cases and rummaged in the top one, feeling the cold touch of a bottle and pulling it out. 'Whisky.' He rubbed at the label, then looked up at what was clearly an illicit stockroom.

Ownie was moving along the central passageway. He had struck a match and was crouching, crabbing forward, taking in the labels and slogans. 'Gin, brandy, wine – God' – the match flickered and died – 'there's got to be at least a hundred cases.'

Johnnie turned back towards the door. 'Time enough. Just leave everything as it is and let's go.'

'Can't we just take a crate or two?'

'No, we'll come back to it.'

'One case? She'll never notice.'

'Don't you believe it, she's probably got a stock list.' He looked back down at the vague shapes in the ill light. 'So what if she does miss one, who cares?'

Ownie grabbed a case of whisky and, with both hands, under-armed it to Johnnie who caught it to his stomach, rattling as it arrived. 'I'll stick the sack over it while you lock up here.'

He checked back across the lawn, looking behind to ensure that there were no traces of their visit in the grass then retrieved the sack, pulled it over the box and swung it over his shoulder like swag. Ownie joined him and they made their way slowly round the side of the house again and back down the drive to the cart, burying the sack among the rectilinear stacks of briquettes and the lumpy bags of coal. Johnnie threw another couple of empty sacks over it as further disguise, then picked up the reins and set the horse going with a gentle ripple of the leathers on its back.

'A fortune,' Ownie whispered, 'there must be a fortune in there.'

'Ours' – Johnnie nodded his head back – 'in there.'

He turned the cart left round a corner and stopped at a narrow run, a little wider than the cart, which was delineated by low wooden fencing and overgrown with grass, that clearly had not been used since the war began. 'Wait here a minute.' He vaulted down again, quickly glanced both ways before burrowing into the lane.

Anyone who had noticed him would assume he was going for a pee. The lane was a jungle of overhanging branches, long, extended grasses, briars and tall nettles. He moved through it, shielding his face with his right arm, picking out the path and checking on the territorial limits of each house as he moved along. It was as he had thought, an access and service route to the backs of the houses, which ran along for about a hundred yards before meeting another path at right angles. Moving back, he stopped where Hazel's house began, pushed aside the shrubbery to see a low brick wall overgrown by rambling vegetation and a wooden gate sagging on its hinges. Burrowing a bit more, ignoring the spikes of briar plucking bloody trails on his cheeks, he picked out the air-raid shelter through the trees, and the back of the house beyond. Perfect, he thought, and pushed himself out of the shrubbery and started to walk back to the cart.

*   *   *

Guiliano lay soaking in the tub, a large tumbler of Scotch on the edge of the bath next to his hand. The bathroom was huge and ornate, cut-glass light fittings, which sent down bluey shards of light, gold filigreed work picking out the ceiling, the walls washed a light ochre colour, and illuminating the massive gilt mirror were two angels of some sort, holding glass torches which spilled a warm glow on the glass. The water was hot, as was the bathroom, indeed the entire suite. About the only fault he could find was that there was no ice for the Scotch.

He picked up the glass again, which was running with perspiration, took a sip and felt the whisky curl and seethe in his stomach. 'Cheers,' he said, looking down at his knees looming out of the milky water like two large land masses. Reluctantly he stretched his right leg and sought the chain with his toes, pulling at it so that the plug came away and the water began to gurgle and sough in the drain. He splashed his way out and began towelling himself on the hot, knobbly towels before pulling on the cream dressing-gown.

The main room had a lit coal fire, with an immaculately clean brass bucket shaped like a medieval helmet, tongs for the coal. The curtains had been drawn, heavy maroon velvet running from floor to ceiling, across a window bigger than a cinema screen. The furniture was big and bulky, a chesterfield sofa in some dark floral material, matching armchairs, a walnut radiogram, Chinese screen, two tables, a grandfather clock, pictures on the wall of hunting scenes, mountains, stags and great hairy cows. Guiliano smiled, took another sip of the whisky, silently toasted the boy. He surely knew how to arrange matters, he thought, this was truly lordly. He sat down on the armchair, shuffled it around a little so that he caught the heat of the fire on his damp legs and settled back, just the hollow ticking of the old clock and the crackling of the fire.

He must have sunk into a deep reverie, the heat and the warmth of the whisky blanketing him, so that the first gentle knock on the door barely registered, then the second, slightly louder, and a mumble behind. 'Be right with you,' he said, putting the glass down on the hearth, tightening the dressing-gown around him and going to the door.

The waiter was barely visible behind the trolley with the huge stainless steel dome, just a head all but obscured, eclipsed by it.

Guiliano stepped back and the man, stooped and grey-haired, dressed in chocolate and navy, tight waistcoat, white shirt showing, dark trousers, patent shoes, heaved the trolley into the room then expertly flicked a white tablecloth over the larger table, quickly set one place, opened the dome and with spoon and fork moved in like a surgeon and produced steaming salmon, lightly roasted potatoes and vegetables. And then a dull plop, the expert uncorking of champagne, the breaking sound of bubbles in the glass then the creaking of ice as it went back into the bucket. Seconds later the waiter was gone and the room was as it was, save for the additional sound, as Guiliano moved to the table, of the exploding bubbles.

He shook his head amusedly and sat down, tasting the champagne which burned beautifully and chilly in his mouth, then the salmon, moist and flaky, with the vaguest hint of dill. Truly excellent, he thought, truly classy. He had taken two mouthfuls and a second taste of the champagne when the door rattled softly again. Putting down his fork and quickly wiping his mouth with the starched white linen napkin, he got up and padded to the door. 'Mmmhmm?' He could smell wood polish on the door, the brass handle was cold to his touch.

'Room service.' A giggle, female.

He pulled open the door and discovered he was wrong. There were two giggles, two young women, shoulder-length hair, one in a dark suit, close-fitting, pinched at the waist, the other in a dress, green print with brown scalloping at the neck. 'Well, the entrée,' he said. 'Come in,' closing the door on the inquisitive hall.

Looking at the two of them standing in the middle of the room he did not even want to think what ages they might be. Both of them were little more than children, that not even the powder and ruby lips could conceal. They huddled together in the way shy adolescents do, still giggling. He shook his head. 'Names, ladies.'

'Morag,' the one in the suit said. She was slightly taller than the other one, brunette, with a seductive curl lapping her right eye. Her eyes were huge, he thought, although her frame seemed scrawny under her jacket.

'Shona,' the other one said. She seemed more self-assured, more heavily made up and slightly pudgy in the cheeks. Puppy fat, he thought. She had a real or painted-in beauty spot on her right cheek, long, blood-soaked nails.

'Can I get you a drink? Morag? Shona? I can offer champagne or whisky. Or I can ring down for room service.'

'That's cute,' Shona said, him thinking, she got that from a movie. She giggled again. 'Whisky, please.'

'Can I have champagne?' the other one said, 'I've never tasted it. They say it's like lemonade.'

'It doesn't come with a cherry,' he said walking into the bathroom to retrieve the toothbrush glass. 'Only the one glass,' he said, pointing towards the table, then pulling out the bottle which felt like a cold dead limb, then sloshed the champagne into it. He handed it to her, then picked up his own glass, topped it up and banged the bottle hard down into the melting ice.

'Cheers,' he said, clinking his glass against hers.

'*Slàinte*,' Morag said, sipping at the bubbles.

'Now,' he said, 'is anyone hungry?'

It had taken four bottles of whisky to fix the manager. That is, nothing. Hazel's whisky could open any door. And no doubt Guiliano would be handsome with the tipping so the serving staff would benefit too. Everyone wins, he said to himself. As his step-mother probably hadn't paid for the bottles either, she was not even losing. Another bottle had gone to Gerard, in his role as guide, taking Guiliano to Molly's, the shebeen on Crown Street and, through Queen again, another to the proprietrix for the introductions, two young and pretty girls who wanted to make some quick money.

First they had taken a taxi ride out to Campsie Glen, to where poor old Benny Lynch used to have his training camp. Johnnie had brought a small flask with him and they had exchanged nips from it as they walked into the glen, the sky looking like cleanly wiped metal, the day cold but fresh. The taxi driver slumbered in the cab while they walked.

'Do you normally hang about railway stations, young man?' Guiliano said, smiling and handing back the flask.

'Usually only at weekends. In the week I'm working.'

'Yeah,' the American said. The ground was gluey underfoot and mud was sticking to his boots as they sauntered. 'What do you do?'

'Sort of buy and sell.'

They had reached the burn and Guiliano sat on a rock looking up towards the waterfall. 'From what I've seen there isn't much of that to do.'

'There's always good prospects in shortage, if you know how to find things.'

'And you do?'

'I'm learning.'

Guiliano dug out a pebble with his muddy heel and picked it up. 'You do seem to know your way about.'

'And you, Angelo, what do you do, when you're not saving mankind?'

The soldier smiled and chucked the pebble towards the burn. 'Oh, work in the family business, buy and sell, a bit like you.'

'Are you here on business then, the buying and selling business?'

'Well, I suppose that depends whether you have anything in mind. I guess I came because I met a girl once who said I should look her up if I ever got to Glasgow. So, I'd never been in Scotland, all I knew about the place is what you're carrying in your inside pocket. I had a few days off and it seemed like a good idea except, the nearer the train got the less good it seemed. By the time it reached the station I knew she was either married, pregnant or dead. So I figured I might check out Loch Lomond, have a quiet weekend, just so I could tell the folks at home I didn't spend the entire war fuckin' the womenfolk of absent heroes and interfering with the army's supply lines.'

Johnnie, standing on the hillside, looking down at the Yank and past him to the smoky outlines of the city, offered, 'But I don't suppose you'd want to give up the habits – just because you're on a kind of retreat this weekend – of satisfying some throbbing womenfolk and perhaps even diverting a few more of the enemy's supply lines.' He grinned. 'My enemy, that is.'

'Hell,' he said, 'you're a long time dead, why be a monk in the meantime? What have you got in mind?'

'I can get hold of a lorryload of spirits, whisky mostly. Can you market it?'

Guiliano got up, and put his arm round the boy's shoulder. 'Did Babe Ruth ever hit a homer?'

*　　*　　*

'You're not serious?' Ownie was washing his face in the cold water in one of the sinks in the bathroom of the model, the ingrained grime and dirt on his face now streaked with white. He and John were the only ones in it; the other residents were hanging about the hall, smoking and listening to the wireless behind the wire grille in reception.

'Where are we going to get a lorry and a driver, one that isn't going to clipe on us?' Johnnie was sitting in one of the cubicles, already washed, drawing his tacketty boots across the slabbed floor, occasional blue sparks flitting across between his legs. This was, so he claimed, to mask the sound of their conversation but Ownie knew it was really because he loved the clatter. 'Queen cannae drive, and neither can we.'

'We cannae carry out a' – he dropped his voice to a whisper and moved closer, dropping a line of dirty water across the floor – 'a fuckin' robbery wae a horse and cart! It's no' the fuckin' wild west. Talk sense, a horse and cart, we'd be—'

'The laughing stock of the criminal classes?'

'Too true. Christ, can you hear them hooting in court? We'd probably get extra time for causing actual bodily harm to the jury, having them aw in stitches. Jesus!' He went back to his sink and began running in more clear water.

'I didn't say it was ideal. But we cannae drive, you cannae hot wire a car can you? These are major gaps in our education – so it's about the only method of transport we've got available. Unless, of course, you've got a better idea.'

Ownie looked round, water dripping from his face, running clearer now. 'I have. Let's forget it.'

'Not a chance. I'll do it myself.'

'You cannae do it yourself.'

'I'll find someone to help.'

'You would as well.'

'Too right I would.'

He grabbed the rough towel from the hook and began furiously rubbing his face. 'Christ, Stark, you're a bampot.'

'I'll take that as a yes then.'

'Don't you think someone's going to think it's a bit suspicious? Two coalmen, rather than unloading the stuff, are walking out with boxes and piling them up on the cart? Don't you think some nosey old biddy behind the net curtains is going to think it's a wee bit suspicious and phone the polis?'

'Sure, I would, if that's the way it was going to be, but it isn't.'

'How is it going to be?'

Johnnie stopped kicking his heels and grinned. 'I've got it all worked out, trust me.'

It was raining hard and the dusk had fallen as they turned the cart into the dim street. Not a curtain twitched as they moved through the faded yellow puddles of light from the gas street lamps. Both of them were well wrapped up, with not only all the clothes they possessed on their backs, but old newspapers stuffed down between the layers. Johnnie pulled on the reins, drawing the horse to a halt, then passed them to Ownie and jumped down. He drew a knotted length of sacking across the horse's eyes to blot out its vision and then manoeuvred it slowly backwards. Although they had practised this dozens of times, inching the horse and cart back between oil cans and old tyres, it was extremely difficult. Ownie was behind the cart now to provide guidance instructions as Johnnie gently pushed the old horse back in the traces.

Here, it was almost pitch dark. Earlier the two of them had shinned up the nearest two street lamps, pushing torn wet sacking through the small lamplighter's windows and extinguishing the flames. And now, just the darkness and the awkwardness of the job of inching the cart back into the narrow alleyway and the thrum of anxiety in the chest as the wheels crunched into the metal stanchion post.

Johnnie pulled the horse forward several feet.

'About a foot to your right,' Ownie hissed out of the dark.

Johnnie tried again, gradually moving the horse back, the cart wheels breaking over the pavement and then a soft crunch as the back wheels found the damp ground of the lane. 'Steady,' he heard coming at him, 'that's it fine, keep it like that,' and then he could feel the atmosphere change and the smell; tendrils clasped at his face, he felt the scratching of twigs and briars as he kept soothing the horse over the uneven earth until finally he eased it to a halt and looked back, seeing nothing of where they had come from.

He heard Ownie crackling through the undergrowth, inching his way along the side of the fence and the cart until he reached him, slapping his arm and taking in deep breaths.

'Quiet!' he said in a low voice. 'Sound carries at night.'

'It's hardly gone teatime. Naebody'll hear us above the scraping of pots and the crashing of dishes being thrown into sinks in time to the Scottish country dance music on the Home Service.'

They seemed to be in a leafy, wet bubble. Johnnie climbed up on to the bench seat of the cart, feeling his way carefully in the dark, until he shinned on to it, felt it under his feet and then he inched over the back and on to the flat bed beyond. The cart sagged slightly to the side again, which he assumed would be Ownie climbing up. They had brought several dozen empty sacks which lay in a pile, as well as one full of hay for the horse. He fumbled around until he found it.

His worst fears about the whole thing concerned the horse although he had not, of course, admitted this to his mate. It was a sorely abused bony beast which he had never heard even utter a whimper, but what if it started braying at the moon, or began pawing at the earth and snorting? Worse, what if it had a heart attack and dropped dead in the traces with a load of contraband booze on board? How would they get out of that one?

He inched back along the wooden flooring and back across the seat, crawling across Ownie's legs as he did so, then to the ground, feeling for the horse's head. God, he realised, he had even forgotten to take off the blindfold! He dropped the feed bag and pulled off the sacking, the horse shaking his head lightly so that the metal in its tack rattled. John grabbed the bridle, hooked on its supper, patted the horse on its neck and uttered what he hoped were a few reassuring words: 'Good boy . . . There there . . . on you go.' The horse chomped its thanks, or so he hoped and believed.

The way he had planned it, he was going to uncouple the horse from the harness, so that it could stretch or lie down, but now that he was here, in this dark and impenetrable cave of vegetation, he realised this was completely impractical. The beast spent its life standing around, a few more hours wouldn't kill it. Hopefully. He patted the horse again and climbed back into the seat.

When he sat down he realised for the first time, from the soggy feeling in his seat, that he was completely soaked through. He nudged Ownie with his elbow and whispered, 'Over the back,' to him, beginning to climb again on to the wooden floor of the cart. The answer was obvious. He scooped up an armful of sacks and eased himself off the edge and back on to the ground, ducking under the boarding for protection and laying a carpet of jute under it. 'Come on,' he said softly, 'shelter, under the wagon.'

He felt Ownie move in next to him. 'Do injuns hunt at night?' he said in his ear.

'It's the polis y'want to watch out for.'

'What are we going to say if they come along here?'

'I don't know. The horse went lame – we got caught out for time and didnae want to drive in the blackout – I give up. Here' – he hunkered down with his back against the inside of the right-hand front wheel and pushed some sacks at Ownie – 'wrap some of these around you and try and keep dry.'

Ownie tumbled over his legs, took the sacks and Johnnie could hear the sound of him making a bed near the front of the cart. 'What if a winching couple come duking in here for a quick shag and in the middle of it Dobbin here leans over an' licks the wan on top's arse?' Johnnie could feel his smile in the dark.

'There's worse than that,' Johnnie said, grabbing some sacks and moving away from the wheel towards the back. 'All of these oats have got to end up somewhere tonight . . . and what if he's got diarrhoea?' From the scurrying sounds he knew that Ownie was coming towards him.

He was stiff and cold and wet when he woke. It was still dark but he had no idea what time it was although, as he looked around, the darkness did not seem so intense; he could see the outline of the wheels and the legs of the horse. He kicked out with his foot at Ownie who groaned and then sat up quickly, banging his head on the underside of the cart.

'I think it's getting light. We'll need to move quickly.'

They scrambled on their hands and knees out from under, stretched and made for the back fence. Johnnie went first, pulling his jacket around his head and slowly levering himself over the fence and through the hedge, the branches cracking like tiny gunshots. Then he held out his hand and helped his accomplice through.

Ownie had picked through the padlock before Johnnie had properly pulled the candle and the damp box of matches from his clothes. Inside, they pulled the door behind them and lit the candle which cast a faint and flickering glow.

'Thank Christ,' Johnnie whispered to himself. Another of his unmentioned fears had been that they would get in to find that the stuff had already been moved. He inched down between the boxes with the light and identified the spirits, marking out the area where the boxes of whisky were stacked. 'Let's go,' he said.

They worked quickly, carrying two cases each at a time to the back fence, where they stacked them up. After they had made about ten runs the sky was noticeably lighter. Johnnie was getting uneasy, there was something about this which jarred. And then he realised that it was the unnatural sound in the city, to him, of birds chuntering. 'Right, lock up, that'll do.'

'One more?'

'No, now.'

He made his way quickly to the fence. Looking back, the form of the house seemed to be slowly emerging from the darkness like a photographic positive developing. He jumped through the under-growth and over the fence and then began taking the crates from Ownie as he lobbed them over, trotting back to the cart and slinging them aboard on the floor, which he had roughly sound-proofed with sacks. He was sweating, the breath was sore in his chest and his thighs ached. As they worked the two of them seemed to be making a huge racket, their panting like bestial howling at the dawn. At least that's what Johnnie hoped it would be mistaken for.

And then, when the milky light had given way to the hard outlines of the day, they were finished, Ownie leaping over the fence, catching his foot and tumbling face down in the dirt, then coming up with a huge smile on his face.

They scaled the back of the cart and began throwing sacks over some of the boxes, putting other cases inside the wet bags until they were confident that the consignment was sufficiently disguised, then John quickly climbed into the driving seat, let off the handbrake and ruffled the reins on the horse's back. It did not move. He tried again. Same thing. Then he noticed that the nose bag was still on it. Quickly, he slithered off the seat, unhitched the bag and pulled at the bridle. The horse shuffled its feet, flicked its head back but still did not move. Please, he thought, not now! Maybe its joints have seized? Maybe the load's too heavy?

He moved back along the side of the nag, not quite knowing what to do next. Then it seemed to wince, stumble and finally lurch forward so that he had to scurry in front of it again to keep out of the way, into the street, with the cart rumbling and squelching after him. When he looked back he saw that Ownie was in the driving seat, confidently holding the reins in the halflight, so he let the rig come alongside, trotted beside it for a few steps to judge the pace, then pulled himself up on to it.

'How did yi manage to start it?'

'Ah,' Ownie mumbled out of the side of his mouth, cracking the reins along the horse's back, 'you learn a bit about animal psychology on the croft – after I found it didnae have any ba's to hack, I howked its tail hard.'

It was almost daylight now, although the street lamps were still lit. Johnnie looked back over his shoulder, but not only could he not see his stepmother's house any more but, better, he could see no one else in the street, no sign of discovery or pursuit.

'Never again,' he heard Ownie say.

'What? I thought it was great. This must have been how they did it in the old days.'

'Not with a horse and cart, I mean. Next time it's a grown-up burglary, wae a car, and masks rather than just mockit faces like cut-price highwaymen.'

'Let's just finish this one first before we start reminiscing and fantasising.'

'I'm going to get one of these suits with the broad stripes.'

'Well, just don't incriminate me.'

'No' that kind – one wi' the big shoulders, pinched waist, turn-ups, like Spencer Tracy.'

Half an hour, Johnnie thought, and they would be at the house. There was a delicious irony in storing his stepmother's stolen booze in her old house, where she and his father had been, which was certainly the last place in the city she would think of looking for it. He smiled, imagining how her face would be when she dicovered the missing cases, how it would be in the future when he was older and running the dance hall.

'I'm going to take some dancing lessons,' he said quietly, over the back of the old horse as it clopped over the cobbles, wisps of steam dribbling from its sides and shanks.

The euphoria of success had gripped him and wouldn't let go. He needed something to do, some way of celebrating, of coming down from it. He felt immense, untouchable, capable of acts of greatness and impossibility. It was the best feeling he had ever experienced, adrenalin still pumping through him like high-octane fuel. 'I'm going out,' he said.

'Where to?' Ownie asked him.

He shrugged.

The two had checked out of the model and into a working man's hotel on the hill above Sauchiehall Street. It was cheap and clean with the smell of soup cooking and carbolic and they had their own room with two single beds, the sheets and blankets faded and darned but free of fleas and bed bugs. The landlady, a Mrs Jackson, had looked them over suspiciously to start with but Ownie's Highland accent had turned her, brought a wee fond smile to her outlined lips. 'My man, God rest him, was from Tain,' she said. They both nodded sympathetically. She had even trusted them with the rent. 'No later than Wednesday,' she said. It was Friday.

'I've got something to collect,' John said.

'Where from?' Ownie asked but Stark was already picking his jacket from the hook on the back of the door and turning the handle.

'We'll get fish and chips for our tea and then we're off out,' he said over his shoulder.

The streets were wet but a watery sun had come out and the clouds were clearing so he decided to walk. He pulled the cap out of his pocket and down over his eyes, trying to cover the youthfulness of his face now that the muck was off it. He walked down to the river, then along the Broomielaw to the Jamaica Bridge. There were several ships moored alongside the quays and warehouses and cranes were pulling crates and bales into the air as he passed. He was going back to the Gorbals. It was almost like a return in triumph, he thought, although he could not let on about what the achievement was. When he reached Crown Street he kept glancing around for faces that he knew, or those that would know his, but he saw none. It had been so long since he had left.

He made his way to the old street. A wind had started and it smelled like ash and cinders and decay. He pushed through some girls playing peever at the close mouth, then past two men playing pitch and toss just inside. The remembered smell of urine and faeces surprisingly made him queasy. He had to wait until the toilet was vacated, sitting on the top step of the stairs at the landing, cradling his head, hand just under his nose so that the faint smell of soap from it would cut the foul atmosphere. When he went into the cubicle the toilet was choked and crusted with shit turned green and black, the floor was puddled with piss. He dug into his pocket and pulled out his knife, stood up on the edges of the toilet, trusting that his footing was secure, and began working the blade into the broken plaster and brickwork near the cistern. A fine red and white speckled mist fell as he worked. Quickly he reopened the gap and got his fingers in and began levering at the brick, then chipped away some more with the knife around it. He gave a hard wrench and it came away in his hand. Carefully he slipped the brick into the toilet pan, so that the muddy liquids would not splash his legs, and burrowed his right hand into the wall. His fingers touched the outlines, the waxy paper and he slowly inched out the package before slipping it into his inside jacket pocket and jumping down on to the floor.

His feet left urine footprints as he went down the stairs and into the street where a knife sharpener had drawn up and was perching on the flat bed of a cart, grinding the edge of a blade in a shower of blue and red sparks. John walked to the corner and then turned and looked slowly back. For the last time.

As his steps took him away he could feel the warmth of the Madonna and child through the folds of paper and coarse material next to his heart.

Chapter Twelve

When he woke on Sunday at midday McQuade was clear that his duties as a private citizen were outweighed by those as a journalist. That, at least, was how he decided that he would pompously present it if he had to, which he sincerely hoped that he would not.

Self-interest and a vicarious excitement were more like it but he felt fuelled as he dressed and drove the company car back to work. He was newly showered, he wore a double-breasted suit and a denim button-down shirt with a dark tie and he felt dressed for serious business.

A brief faxed press release from the police was taped to his screen. It was one main paragraph and it intimated simply the death of John Stark Junior at the Royal Infirmary, the time, his age and the usual guff about enquiries continuing. A second off-the-record guidance paragraph below detailed his relationship to John Stark Senior and carried an oblique reference to the drugs feud. There was a further briefing press conference to be held – he checked his watch – now. He was sure that nothing would come out of that but, anyway, it would be covered, he was not due to start until two, so another hack would be picking it up.

He switched on his terminal, logged on, then went across the newsroom floor to the vending machine, firing thirty pence into its gut and taking back a black coffee. It was going to be a simple story to write, he would dress it up with qualifications, parenthetical 'allegations' and 'it is understoods' shovelled in, but what it would describe, after the usual punchy intro, would be all the detail he had witnessed. Seen, of course, through anonymous, third-party eyes. The story would allege that Stark had been under constant police surveillance until just before the killing and that he had been shot dead immediately after that had been removed. It would question why this was done and how the killers became aware of it.

He would say that Stark had probably been shot by a rival drugs gang, that he had been shot three times from behind at close range, that he had died in his father's arms and would go on to speculate that police believed that three or more people were involved in the hit and that a car had been seen speeding off back towards the city centre. Then he would reveal the existence of Blantyre and the US connection – he paused over the keyboard; on reflection that would come much further up the story – then finish off by weaving in a few coded but non-libellous paragraphs about the father's history.

That was about it bar, of course, the holocaust to come. The police would be round at the building, or on his doorstep, as soon as the paper hit the street. So, after he wrote the piece he would talk to the desk, get them to agree to pay for a night or two in a hotel, then talk to the lawyer. All that he would be saying to the police, and in the lawyer's company, was that his story came from several impeccable sources which, naturally, he had no intention of revealing. After that it would be up to the polis and the PF.

The first draft took him less than half an hour. He intended to fill in additional parts after he had talked to whoever had been at the press conference and after he had made a couple of calls. Draining the dregs of his coffee he scrolled back to the top and began reading it through.

Ricketts found it difficult to work out why Blantyre's mood had so improved. She seemed to be smiling to herself as they drove back to the Holiday Inn. He walked with her into the hotel reception and a few paces from the lift she turned and checked. 'Something more comfortable, I think,' she said, looking down at her clothes then smiling at him. 'Why don't you wait in the bar?'

Naturally, he thought, turning away and heading in the direction of piano music and expensively ringing tills. Still, he was off tomorrow, didn't have to check the car in until Monday so, he decided as he walked into a leafy bower, he would either leave it in the hotel car park until then or phone up one of the lads to ask for it to be collected, keys at reception.

He ordered a large vodka and tonic, pushed a ten pound note

across the bar and did not dare count the change when it came. I should have put it on her bill, he thought and then realised that he did not even know her room number.

Upstairs Blantyre had thrown her jacket on the bed, taken off the gun and holster, pulled her top over her head, noted that there was a raw and tender patch on the ribs just below her left breast, unhooked her brassiere and discarded it on the floor, pulled a low-cut silk blouse from the wardrobe which she slipped on quickly and then wrapped the holster ties round the gun and buried it in the back under her suitcase and hanging clothes. Hardly official procedure, but there you go.

Ricketts was on his second drink at the bar, munching on the nuts, when he saw her coming out of the lift. God, he thought, beautiful. She was striding across the marble floor, her heels clicking as she walked – he imagined this part because the piano drowned it out – wearing a short skirt, darkly checked, a loose, unbuttoned white blouse and a long dark coat, similarly open, her hands thrust deep into its pockets. She had brushed her hair out and as she got closer he could see that she had put on serious make-up. He could also see that she was smiling at him mischievously.

'Very nice,' he said, getting up to offer her a bar stool. 'I'm embarrassed. Me in my Marks and Spencer suit.'

'I'll have a glass of white wine,' she said to the barman who had immediately appeared, then turned to Ricketts. 'It's just fine, Harry, the suit. Hardly a gravy stain to be seen.'

'*Harry*, well, well, well.' He shook his head.

'Isn't that what your friends call you? Or is it Dirty for short?' Her eyebrows were arched and she grinned over her drink.

'Not recently.' He looked at her through narrowed lids and raised his glass to her. 'So we're friends.'

'Sure, the day's over.'

This turnabout was confusing, but certainly not unwelcome. 'Why d'you think we were called off?'

She shrugged. 'The day's over, Harry.'

'I know, but it doesn't make sense.'

'Police work rarely does, don't you find?' She swirled round on her stool so that Ricketts caught her perfume in the backdraught and noticed for the first time, as she faced him, that she was quite clearly not wearing a bra. 'Talk about something else. You, tell me about you. And here, Scotland. But before that – I was thinking, the curry, it'll be stone cold and the car will be smelling like downtown Bombay so . . .'

'Shite, I forgot all about that.'

'So, let's either dump it or maybe grab it, and a taxi and go back to your place? We can heat it up and you can change into something more comfortable. Right?'

'Right,' Ricketts agreed, thinking, Wrong! There is something very strange going on here but undoubtedly, after a few more drinks, the boundaries between the two will be pleasantly blurred.

The rasping in his ear wakened him. An unfamiliar ceiling swam into view and a familiar pain behind his eyes. He grabbed the phone. 'Mr McQuade,' an unfamiliar voice whispered with urgency in his ear, 'I thought I should let you know that the police are on the way up.'

He threw down the phone and scrambled out of bed, trying to locate where he had discarded his clothes. The banging on the door began as he was stumbling into his underpants.

'McQuade, open the fuckin' door. Pronto, pal.'

He recognised the voice. 'What do you want, Harry?'

'I want to clean the fucking room – what the fuck d'you think I want?'

McQuade ran his hands through his hair, then sighed and turned the lock. Maybe because Ricketts was present they would merely beat him about the body.

The first thing which surprised him was that Ricketts was alone, the second was that he was wearing casual clothes and, putting the two together, as quickly as his tortured synapses would permit, he deduced that this was not a business visit. Also, Ricketts was holding the newspaper up in front of him, rather than an arrest or search warrant. But then he pushed him in the chest back into the room and closed the door behind.

'We need to talk. For our mutual good health.'

'We do? In that case I'll wash and dress. You can order the coffee and croissants.'

He took his time showering, trying to work out why Ricketts was here. Looking for a favour rather than a body obviously, or he would have come in behind a sledgehammer. He brushed his teeth, rubbed at the mirror to check his tongue and eyes, like congealed fat and raw eggs as usual, then put on the courtesy dressing-gown.

'How did you know how to find me?' he said when he went into the bedroom.

'Oh, it was really difficult. The Holiday Inn! Deep cover. It took about half a dozen telephone calls once I realised you had gone to ground.' He was sitting in the room's one armchair, the newspaper carefully smoothed out on the white sheet of the bed. He nodded towards it. 'So, tell me about it.'

McQuade went to the wardrobe and pulled out a holdall and then a clean pair of pants and a shirt. 'Did you order coffee?'

'Yes. But go on.'

'There's nowhere to go. Are you saying there's something wrong with my story?'

'There's plenty wrong with the fuckin' story, principally because it's so right. They're going mental at the ranch, searching the statute books for any charge they can throw at you, however humble, from conspiracy, obstruction, withholding evidence to the Abuse of Solvents Act. This is how they are working it out. "Either he did it, which seems very unlikely given his relatively minor criminal transgressions in the past over banned substances and the Road Traffic Act, or he sure as fuck knows who did." The mistake was all that detail, some of which was even news to them, like three shots. At first they thought you were full of shit, because only two cartridges had been found at the scene up until then, and then the chief constable—'

McQuade looked at him doubtingly.

'No! The fuckin' chief constable says to the DCS on the Serious Crime Squad, "Check the body. Personally." And sure enough they find three holes in the Fat Boy, and all this prior to the autopsy.'

'A lucky guess.' McQuade's stomach was churning.

'So then you can work out the next bit, they all sat down and had a jolly good laugh about it!'

'You were not – being a humble flatfoot – privy to these discussions?'

'No.'

'So the tale could well have got garbled in the transmission?'

'No chance. I know the chief constable's secretary, she told me everything.'

McQuade had dressed in jeans and a green cord button-down shirt and was now scrabbling in the holdall for socks. 'Tell me, Harry' – he was consciously not looking at Ricketts – 'why are you here? Oh, and how's your close friend Alice Blantyre? Has it got beyond the sharing a carry-out curry stage yet?'

When he looked round he could see that Ricketts, despite him trying to bite down on his jaw, was shocked. 'So were you just naughtily going *hors de combat* for a quick one at the time – we are referring to the time when Fat Boy was being sent to the great penitentiary in the sky, of course – or were you following orders? I'm sure my readers would love to know.' Ricketts did not reply, so he went on. 'Shall we start again then, Harry? Over that coffee perhaps?' He smiled, which broadened when he saw the hate and confusion in Ricketts's eyes.

'As I said,' Ricketts said again, as I see it we have an alliance of interest here—'

'Get on with it, Harry,' McQuade cut in, you're sounding like a bloody politician or a building society manager. Just tell me exactly what happened.'

'I don't want to become a scapegoat—'

'That's certainly a common interest.'

'And, well, I think you're right. I don't want to believe it but I think he was set up. Stark.'

Me too, McQuade was thinking. 'So why do you care? "Drug baron gunned down," as the headlines put it. I suppose you find it an affront to your notion of justice?'

'It's not that.'

McQuade waited. 'Well?'

'Self-interest, I suppose.'

'That's more like it.'

'Look, I'll start at the end.'

'That's the way you usually do it in the polis. Find the body, form a conclusion and work backwards, grind the clues into the carpet.'

'We tailed – as you know – we tailed him all day.'

'Ditto.'

'I see, now.' Ricketts poured milk into his coffee and then two heaped teaspoons of brown sugar. He was still in the chair; McQuade was lying stretched out on the bed with his hands cupped behind his head. 'So we're schlepping about all day, the two of us, masquerading as winchers when we had to and her face is grim, hardly says a word. Nothing happens, not on the street, not in small talk. Then when we're outside this restaurant—'

Café India.'

'Right. Of course, you know. Anyway I pop in to check out the suspect, see whether he's got any company—'

'Collect a freebie from the management.'

'Two Sicilian hoods were due to arrive, according to her; maybe they didn't fancy the ethnic menu. And then when I get into the car she tells me HQ's called on the mobile—'

'The mobile. That explains it, why I heard nothing on the police band.'

'—and the message is that the gig's off. No explanation, orders from above. And then she's as nice as can be. She gets changed, made up, we go back to my place, we talk, we drink—'

'But you don't fuck.'

'How the fu—' Ricketts put down his cup and saucer on the dresser. 'How did you know?'

'Hack's intuition. I don't reckon that if you had got cosy with her on Saturday night and Sunday morning you'd be round here first thing this morning unburdening yourself to me. Would you now?'

'Well, about four, five o'clock in the morning, just when I'm warming up the great seduction moves, she suddenly switches off, puts on her coat and she's off. Quick peck on the cheek, you've been wonderful company, all that sort of shite, and away. Then first thing this morning—'

'Twenty-four hours later your ego still throbbing, your gristle still tumescent . . .'

'I got a call from the station, asking if I'd seen your bloody paper. Asking me if, and why, the surveillance had been called off and telling me I had to go in immediately to make a full report. Jesus! I didn't even know he was fuckin' dead until that call. From what I can work out, the sub-text, the official position, is that no instruction came to pull the watch.'

'You just took her word for it?'

'Why not? It didn't seem to be any great deal.'

'So, the first thing you did this morning, after your alarm call – pun intended – was to try and contact Blantyre and then, of course, you discovered she had gone.'

'How did you know?'

'Checked out early Sunday morning.' McQuade reached over and picked up his black coffee. 'I have a contact.'

'I checked the register and sure enough she had. And then I saw a booking for another punter, made through your paper. So I checked it out.'

'And then you came hot-foot up here.' He blew on the coffee and then took a sip. 'She flew out yesterday afternoon, by the way.' He felt a lot better now, it was always cheering to know that someone was in at least as bad a fix as you. 'So, Harry boy, the way it looks to me is that if pushed, and eventually reluctantly, your employers will admit that there was an unfortunate breakdown in communication, that surveillance was withdrawn mistakenly, that no order was given, the Fat Boy was then stiffed shortly thereafter and that this was all down to the fault of an individual officer.'

'I was hoping I was being paranoid.'

'My advice is say nothing and get a good lawyer. Which, coincidentally, is the course I'm following. More coffee?'

Ricketts shook his head. 'They'll come looking for you and it won't take them any time to find you here.'

'I guess. Anyway,' he sighed, 'I'm going to have to talk to them soon. Only, of course, in the presence of a solicitor. What I'll say is that I got it all from sources, anonymous calls, divine assistance or whatever. No names, just sources, and nothing else. I rather think they won't arrest me. What for? There's no evidence.'

'But you saw it.'

'Are you wearing a bug?'

'Of course not.'

'Not much. Not enough to identify anyone. It was dark, I was tired, it happened so quickly, I was too far away – all I got was a vague impression of the shooter. It could have been you for all I saw, but for the vague impression I got of blond hair, and if I didn't now know you were trying, like King Kong, to mount New

York at the time.' He poured more coffee. 'It has just occurred to me that if there was a call on the mobile, there'll be a record of it, so that bit can be checked out all right by ringing Cellnet or Vodaphone, right? You've done that?' He looked at Ricketts, who stared straight back. 'You haven't got the phone, have you?'

'It was in the car, but the car isn't downstairs any more. It must have been taken back. I didn't call it in.'

'She hasn't left many loose threads, has she? And now she's flown the territory.' McQuade walked over to the window and looked out at the grey buildings below. 'So, what happens? You make your statement saying exactly how it was, how you took her word that the surveillance was off and how much shite are you in? Back on the beat, or what?'

'I don't—'

McQuade cut in. 'Of course, they're going to contact her, aren't they, get a statement. How much worse is it going to be if she says, "What, me? A guest in another country taking command calls? No, sorry, didn't happen." What then?'

'Why would she say that?'

McQuade turned from the window. 'And why, Harry' – the more he pushed at Ricketts the more plausible it began to feel, he could almost hear the pieces dropping into place – 'would she be part of a set-up in the first place, which is what we're saying, isn't it? Blood all over the place, so she would hardly stop at a little lie, would she? And I think that we also can work out – I don't know quite how to put this, Harry – that fairly early in this conspiracy you became expendable.'

'You know what we're saying?' Ricketts was sitting straight up in the chair, looking very sombre.

'I think so. It didn't just happen that she got pissed off sitting around in a cold car with an overheated colleague, although I can understand how that could get to you, or got a temporary flush for him so much that she unilaterally decided to call the thing off. Totally implausible. So, if that didn't happen, what else? That there was a plan to murder Stark, either by persons unknown, or by persons known very well to you, the communal you, the force. I know which of these suspects I'd put my money on, but then I've never been very close to your lot since that incident over the peck of coke. At the very least there must have been collusion.' He paused for a few seconds. 'Particularly because she just disappears within hours. Who checked her off? You know, where's the fury to get after her, to get her back here to explain her side? No, she's gone and they knew she was going. Check her flight booking, when it was made, who made it, hmm? Go figure.' He looked across at Ricketts, sitting in the chair looking up at him. What I can't work out is my place in all this.'

Jim Radcliffe looked down at the dirty water in the dock and then up at the dereliction beyond, the roofless warehouses, many of them burned out, the graffiti on the walls and the diamond glitter of abandoned scrap in the overgrown grass and the muddy walkways. The helicopter was hovering a few feet off the ground above the helipad, the pilot presumably checking the stability of the beast or waiting for air traffic control to clear any further ascent. Radcliffe did not know and did not want to. He hated flying. He was wearing a pair of headphones which partially muffled the noise, but the chatter in his ears of technical conversations helped too.

'All right?' For a moment he could not relate to the voice in his head and then he looked round at the pilot, a civilian, who was looking enquiringly at him.

He nodded. 'Yes,' he shouted into the microphone in front of his mouth.

'Here we go,' the voice said again and the chopper began to move up and out over the dull water and towards the sky, the city falling away around him. The pilot was wearing dark blue trousers, a white shirt with epaulettes, captain's presumably, and a dark tie with a helicopter motif on it. Although the uniform was correct it looked as if it had been quickly retrieved from the boot of a car or the bottom of a laundry basket, which did nothing for Radcliffe's confidence as he considered whether the man's general sloppiness transmitted to his flying. Radcliffe was not qualified to tell, although the ride seemed smooth enough.

The pilot – 'Kidd' he had introduced himself; Radcliffe couldn't recall his Christian name. 'Captain Kidd,' he had continued with a big grin – looked to be about forty, with tangled, too-long, unruly hair and a scruffy short beard. He had arrived in a fast, but beaten-up Audi, and uncurled himself from the driving seat in a cloud of wispy smoke so that Radcliffe was reminded of a stage trick. But it was tobacco, not conjuror's or hemp-based; at least Radcliffe wanted to believe that and hadn't gone too close because the alternative, that he was now being ferried by a stoned pilot, was too horrific to contemplate. At first he had assumed the man was a technician, or a steward, not that the company had anything larger than choppers, but when he jauntily rolled up struggling to fasten his tie and alternately offering his hand Radcliffe realised his mistake.

'Jim?' the pilot said, rolling the tie under his shirt collar. 'Just tell me what you want. After all, it is your funeral,' and then he grinned and shook Radcliffe's hand warmly, cupping both of his hands round. 'I forget, what's your rank again?'

'Assistant chief constable,' Radcliffe replied stiffly.

'Right, of course. I shuttle your boss around a lot.'

Radcliffe had said nothing.

Now they were at 1,000 feet, so Kidd was saying, and they were heeling over to starboard - the earth and the Clyde had canted to forty-five degrees without any of the water spilling – before they levelled out and headed eastwards.

'Let me check this with you' – Radcliffe was pleased to see that the pilot was looking ahead and not at him – 'we fly over to the house, then follow the cortège to the cemetery.'

Radcliffe nodded, then realised about the microphone. 'Yes, that's it. We're supposed to be patched into our communications system so that I can talk to the guys on the ground and they to me.'

'Okay. You just tell me what to do. I'll pick up the procession and stay about this height. The other chopper's got the camera gear hasn't it?'

'That's it.'

'You must be expecting something to happen, going to these lengths? Who's going to interfere with a funeral?'

'Just precautions,' Radcliffe said, 'but you never know.'

Radcliffe had not been keen on the maximum security approach, he felt it merely helped to glamorise a gangster, but the chief had been adamant. The funeral would be all over the TV, radio and news-papers and a very visible police presence, the governor argued, would show the public that they were firmly on the case. Plainclothes and uniforms would be interviewing mourners for information, others would be taking contemporary pictures of the notables to update files, the high-resolution eye in the sky would get the video pictures and generally the whole operation would irk the underworld.

Radcliffe thought it was a load of expensive bollocks which would achieve nothing. In his view they should not even have returned the body until they had someone for it and no matter how long it took, despite all the forensics having been done and the fact that Fat Boy wasn't going anywhere anyway and could always be dug up any time from his forthcoming repose. If you don't have a funeral, he had said, you don't have a *causus belli*.

But the chief had made a production of it, all leave was cancelled, the busies were everywhere, checking the route and even the drains below, running sniffer dogs over the entire vicinity, restricting and removing cars as if it were Belfast. At the planning meeting someone had even postulated that home-made mortars might be used, rigged up on a lorry nearby, which Radcliffe thought pre-posterous but the governor had even taken that seriously hence, in part, the overhead surveillance.

The main part, of course, was that the chief was in the thrall of high-tech policing, or executive toys to Radcliffe's mind, and the crucial sub-text was self-interest. That in the unlikely event of some spectacular taking place the likelihood, the certainty, was that the prospect of the chief's ritual knighthood would blow up with it. What this expensive charade was entirely about was safeguarding the chief constable's future appointment with the sovereign.

'There we go,' he heard in his cans and looked to see Kidd pointing down, and now Radcliffe could see the knot of people, a couple of hundred at least, he estimated, on the pavements on both sides of the street.

They hung in the sky above for a couple of minutes. Radcliffe looked around and could see the city petering out towards the Campsies. He remembered how, as a boy, he took the blue Alexander's bus out to the glen and then the climb up the hill to the waterfall where he would splash, or bathe or fish for minnows. He had been back to the glen recently and it had disgusted him. This was where Benny Lynch had based his training camp for his later fights and the major battle against booze, where generations of Glasgow folk had started out discovering the hills and now, typically, the old houses and byres had been revamped, gentrified, turned into coffee shops and potteries and weaving sheds, all owned by English people no doubt.

'Mr Radcliffe, sir!' The voice broke into his reverie. He glanced round at the pilot before quickly realising that the tone was different.

'Yes,' he replied, feeling slightly foolish that he was talking into the unknown.

'DCS Finch, sir. Sir, we have a Code 36.' Radcliffe understood immediately that this was murder by shooting. 'The chief constable is requesting your attendance, sir.'

Requesting? The choice of the word amused Radcliffe. 'Indeed,' he replied. 'The chief constable does appreciate where I am at the present moment?'

'He does, sir. We're organising a car to meet you at Glasgow Green and it will take you to the scene.'

'I see. We'll be there' – he looked round at Kidd who held up a spread palm – 'in about five minutes.'

'Very well, sir. Ask the pilot to put you down as close to the People's Palace as possible.' Radcliffe caught Kidd smiling and nodding. 'The scene's only a few minutes away. Over and out.'

Radcliffe gently shook his head. At least he was getting down to the earth and out of this damned contraption and back to doing real police work.

The road had been cordoned off with blue and yellow tape and posted uniformed police officers. The usual crowd of gawpers had gathered. Radcliffe and Finch climbed out of the back seats of the Granada, joined from the passenger seat by Gordon Chisholm, a chief inspector. Rarely had the detectives of the Serious Crime Squad seen as much top brass on any investigation. The three men ducked under the blue and yellow tapes and began walking towards the car.

'We were clearly looking in the wrong place,' Radcliffe said.

'He's got bottle, I'll give him that.' Chisholm had his hands in the pockets of his trench coat.

'And he'll have the perfect alibi too,' Finch chipped in.

The car had been screened off from view and telephoto lenses by a three-sided screen, although, as all the newspapers had been tipped off at about the same time as the police, trying to conceal the scene was pointless. A forensic team was still working on the car and the bodies were still inside, one in the front passenger seat slumped against the window, the other occupying most of the back seat. Radcliffe leaned over a man in dungarees who was trying to lift fingerprints from door handles. There was a lot of blood, he noted, the grey upholstery fabric was dark with it, indicating that they had probably, but not certainly, been shot *in situ*.

The car had been traced and it was not stolen. It belonged to – had belonged to – the man in the front seat, Joe Hatton. He was twenty-four and well known, a heavy, armed robber, enforcer and drug courier. The body in the back had been Tom Gower, two years older, but with similar credentials. More importantly as far as Radcliffe was concerned were their social histories: both had grown up a few streets away from the Starks and had run around with the Fat Boy in his bloody ventures; both had defected to Harris.

Radcliffe turned to Finch. 'Well, evidently others marked them down as suspects as well.'

'Any idea how long they've been here, John?' Radcliffe asked.

'The best estimate is since the early hours. We've talked to a few locals who say that, to the best of their knowledge, the car has been there since before 5 a.m. One guy, coming back from his work, is pretty sure it was there at 4 a.m. and several others are certain it was there at 7 a.m.'

'Who found them?'

'A man out walking his dog. It stopped to pee against a tyre. He was a bit embarrassed, you know, he thought the guy dozing in the front seat might get really pissed off, so he went closer to knock on the door to apologise and then he saw the two of them had been topped. Nearly had human shite on the pavement to join the dog mess.'

'We don't know yet how long they've been dead?'

'No.'

'Well' – he shook his head and looked away from the car – 'it's pretty obvious, isn't it.'

'Tit for tat.'

'Very symbolic, on the morning of the son's funeral.'

'Want to bet, sir, that Stark spent the night at the wake sitting beside the boy's coffin and that there are half a dozen other witnesses to corroborate, at least two of them being a priest and a monsignor?'

'No one would take that bet. Right' – he turned and motioned Finch after him – 'we're going to a funeral. No wonder they call this the graveyard shift. And afterwards, after paying our respects and sympathising with his loss, we're going to spend a fruitless couple of hours asking the old man questions he won't respond to.'

'It helps to be an optimist in this job, doesn't it sir?'

Chapter Thirteen

Mullaney turned the key in the lock. Before pulling the door open he looked around him. A figure pushed itself out of the shadows and walked a few steps up to him.

'We're no' open, son,' he said, pushing the door.

'That's all right, I'm not a customer.'

Mullaney turned, blocking the doorway. 'No? So what are you, then?'

'I'm the owner,' the boy said, touching his shoulder, clearly indicating that he should move over.

For a moment Mullaney hesitated, then shrugged and moved aside, allowing the boy to walk into the hall. Cocky bastard, he thought, following him up the stairs. They walked into the dance arena. Stark paused, hands in pockets, looking around, taking it in. 'First time here, is it, son?' Johnnie nodded. 'Well, you've obviously come for something, so why don't we go up to the office and talk about it?' The boy nodded and followed.

Mullaney was conscious as they sat opposite each other that the lad was not really concentrating, he seemed nervous and to be going through something in his mind, staring past him, his mouth trembling in the corner as he worried at the inside of his cheek with his teeth, his hands jammed in his jacket pockets. 'You shouldn't be here, son. It's dangerous.' The boy continued his stare. 'I heard you ran away, is that right?' Johnnie nodded again. Mullaney flattened his palms on the desk and leaned slightly forward in his chair. 'You're saying nothing, son. What is it you want?'

And then the boy smiled, wide and bright and utterly without warmth, his eyes seeming to char with their focus. In spite of himself Mullaney felt a tremor and he thought how old and completely without pity the look was. 'I want to see the books. And I want to make an arrangement.'

'I'm no' sure, I mean I think maybe I should talk to your ma – rather, Mrs Star – your step mother—' He took in a blur, a quick movement from the boy and then a bang on the desk and, when he looked down, he saw Stark's hand and, below it, between his own thumb and forefinger, a knife driven into the desk. Instinctively he pulled his hand away.

'I told you, *I* own this place so you'll talk to me, no one else, or you'll be looking for a job.' And slowly he pulled the knife out of the wood.

Mullaney's heart was pumping, he felt like lashing out but while he knew that he could take the boy he knew that Stark would not back down and that it would be extremely bloody before it was conclusive. And also, if he laid a finger on him he realised that he would be out of a job. 'You've got a pretty good eye,' he said, smiling, trying to defuse the tension. 'How is it for figures?' He turned away and moved over to the safe and began to dial in the numbers.

When he had removed the cash books and the bank book and had put them on the desk in front of the young man with the tight mouth and the clawed scar in his cheek he sat down again, leaned back and tried to look as helpful and unthreatening as possible. 'You said there was an arrangement, something like that?'

Johnnie, who had opened the first ledger, looked up. 'I want to meet someone here tonight, discreetly, and have a wee bit of a celebration.'

'Of course.' Mullaney was already calculating what he would do. 'That's no problem. Of course we'll have to keep you out of the way of the punters, you being a bit young and a bit hot, but you can use the office here if that's all right and I'll arrange for some sandwiches, if that's what you're after.'

Stark shook his head. 'Champagne, maybe some chicken.'

'I don't know where I can—'

'You can get it, Mullaney, just make sure you do.'

The man shrugged. 'I'll try. How many bottles, how many folk?'

'Three of each, probably. And some beer, that shouldn't be a problem. Tell me' – he looked down at the ledger again – 'what column are you putting down backhanders to the polis in?'

They spent more than an hour going over the books, Mullaney explaining the double-entry system and the artifices and creative nooks and crannies – or most of them – where the various small caches of money were salted. There was not a great deal of surplus, the business was entirely dependent on the vagaries of the war, it appeared, swelling markedly when there were visiting boats and returning and recuperating heroes, ebbing when the boys were at the front. 'Still,' said Mullaney, 'it'll be a gold mine when it's all over.'

Stark nodded non-committally. He was still trying to come to terms with all the figures, which buzzed in front of his eyes and then seemed to disappear. He was no nearer to understanding the business and its cash flow than when he had sat down. Closing the ledgers he stood up. 'About nine?' he said. Mullaney nodded. 'I'll see myself out,' and he turned and left the room.

Mullaney listened for the footsteps dying away, then he picked up the telephone.

He felt woozy and light-headed from the perfume, the champagne bubbles exploding in his veins, the knowledge of what was inside the brown paper parcel Guiliano had handed over. 'Go on,' he said to Ownie, 'have a drink.'

The other lad shook his head again and then leaned over and whispered in his ear. 'Be careful.' He was looking around anxiously, which made Johnnie giggle. 'This is just stupid. We should never have come here.'

Ownie was trying to brush off the arms of an older girl who was deliberately trying to embrace him and to embarrass him. Her name was Cheryl and she was about seventeen. Johnnie had given Mullaney two five pound notes to fix up the girls. His was called Sadie, she was heavily made up, dark hair caught at the nape of her neck, her blouse unbuttoned from the neck showing plump cleavage and she carried with her, under the cheap perfume, the sickly sweet smell of concealed poverty.

At least she had, John recalled, before he had put the first glass or two down his throat.

She was rubbing his stomach, occasionally the insides of his legs and his erection was constant and extremely noticeable. He had never been with a woman, or even a girl, but tonight he would be and the thought of it filled him with trepidation as well as excitement.

'We should get out of here,' Ownie said again, 'before it's too late.'

Johnnie responded by kissing Sadie roughly on the lips, tasting the lipstick, feeling her tongue squirm for his. He began to run his hands over her breasts as she took her mouth away and began biting on his right ear, sending shivers down his back. 'Let's go somewhere,' she said, pulling away from the lobe, breathing the words in.

'In a wee while.' He was still sober enough to be concerned about the act to come, so he picked up the glass from the puddled surface of Mullaney's desk and drank again. 'Where's Angelo?' he said over the shoulder of the girl.

'Dancing, at the bar, I don't know. Fucked off back to base maybe?'

'Hope he drives carefully, he'll have a bit of a load on.' Johnnie was aware of his face burning, the alcohol pulsating in his cheeks and now it was beginning to feel a little sour in his stomach. 'About a hundred cases.' He tried to giggle but he was hiccupping through it.

'I'll see you later.' Ownie was fighting off the tentacled persistence of his selected mate and was opening the door. 'I'll see you back there.'

'What about . . . ?' He motioned with his hand at the other girl who did not seem to be in the least concerned about her proposed partner's disappearance. Ownie shrugged and closed the door behind him. 'Fuck it,' John murmured under his breath and began to busy himself with the unbuttoning of Sadie's buttons. He had them undone to the waist and was putting his hands inside when he felt a pressure on his right knee, then a scrabbling at his flies and when he looked down he saw that Cheryl had him undone and was bending her head into his lap. He shivered as her lips slid over him and her tongue began to play with him.

'Come on,' he heard her whisper in his ear. 'I know somewhere mair private where we can go.' Cheryl had raised her head and was smiling at him, licking her lips. 'Let's grab a couple of bottles and go.'

He stumbled up, pushing his erection away, buttoning his trousers, smiling sloppily at both of them, his head seemingly full of echoing spaces. 'Right.' He grabbed the brown paper parcel, pointed at the bottles on the table. 'One each, girls and let's go.'

They were giggling, stumbling into him as they went, occasionally cuddling him, spilling down the stairs, which seemed to yawn and widen, and then out into the cold air which rushed over him. He felt himself totter, then right himself, the girls were on either side of him, arms round him, holding on, laughing, going forward over the rough ground. They were propelling him, he did not know where he was going, the stars above were pulsating, the air seemed to be slapping him in waves. He was, he realised, extremely drunk.

Now they had gone into what seemed a long dark pend. 'Not much further, darling,' one of the girls said, he could not recognise which, their arms still around him, the two bottles of champagne clinking together as they weaved forward and then the arms detached, he heard the hurried crunching of footsteps and he stood alone, swaying slightly, peering around him in the dark, slowly realising what was happening when it was too late to get away.

He turned, was aware of a milky white smear of white in front of him like a face, a downward crescent of blurring light and then nothing.

Park and Dunbar moved through the street, avoiding the rubble from the ruined houses and the dead livestock. The place smelled acrid and sharp, of fire and high putrefaction. The only close sounds were of the crunching of their feet on the debris and the occasional crack of a burning round going off in one of the smouldering ruins. The advance was more than a mile ahead of them; they could see the puffs of smoke on the skyline and the oily clouds over the action, and what came back to them was the dull catarrhal rumble of artillery. It had been more than an hour since they had seen a plane overhead, a lone American Mustang, which had come in low and soared away towards the front line. It had been weeks since they had seen any German planes. The Luftwaffe was either destroyed, or what was left of it was pulled back to defend Berlin.

'Have you any water left, Mick?' Dunbar said to him, raising his voice so that it crossed the street.

Park slung his Lee Enfield over his shoulder, detached the canteen from his belt, and lobbed it overhand like a grenade across to

267

Dunbar who caught it with one hand as it fell, then put down his weapon while he twisted off the cap and drank from it. Park glanced around him and then walked across to his colleague.

'They must be all around us,' he said 'people, civilians,' collecting the canteen and taking a swig. 'Hiding in the ruins. Probably think we're going to put them up against a wall.'

'I could do with puttin' a woman up against a wall.' Dunbar was grinning, his teeth bright in his dulled and dirty face. 'The last time I—'

'What's that?' Park said, cutting him off with a wave of his hand so that the other man stumbled over his rifle in a panicked haste before retrieving it. 'Aw, nothing,' he said as Dunbar brought the rifle around, 'just my imagination.'

'My imagination's got better things to think about.' Dunbar was in his mid-twenties, from Edinburgh, a big gawky lad with ginger hair and a propensity to blush, who had recently been promoted to lance-corporal.

'Don't I know it,' replied Park and they both began to move off again. They had reached a corner and were swithering about going left or right, although there seemed nothing to choose between the two because both options looked similarly derelict, when he stopped again and inclined his head.

'Not again,' Dunbar said, also pulling up.

'Listen. Hear it, an engine.'

Dunbar listened and heard nothing. He began to draw back his mouth to curse Park when he heard what sounded like the faint mechanical cough of a motor turning. 'Aye,' he said, 'that way,' pointing with the barrel of his rifle down the street to his left.

They broke into a heavy run, their packs jiggling sorely as they went, until they reached the corner and the coughing grew louder and more persistent and finally tore and rattled into a deep engine reverberation. When they peered round the edge of the pockmarked building they could see, about 200 yards down the street, what appeared to be an agricultural lorry, very old, sagging to one side, flat-bedded, with a lumpy tarpaulin tied down with ropes. It was facing away from them, oily smoke belching from the noisy exhaust.

'Let's go,' Park said, anticipating the command, breaking into another shambling run, Dunbar a few paces behind. They had gone about a quarter of the way when the lorry started to move forward. 'Stop!' Park shouted, forgetting the German command. He dropped into a crouch and pulled his .303 up and aimed at the back of the cab. Dunbar pitched forward on his face, came up on his elbows, pulled back the bolt on his rifle and fired.

Park could not see where the round went, he was not sure of the allowable procedure here, but fuck it, he thought, sighting on the driver's side of the cab and squeezing off a round. He saw a tiny puff where it hit the metal, pulled back the bolt, ejected the cartridge and got his second shot off just after Dunbar's. The lorry seemed to accelerate, then it slowed and moved lazily to the left before running into a pile of rubble. The two men started to run towards it again and as they did, vaguely noticed a pair of legs arrive under the body of the lorry, then a few bright points of starlight.

Park felt the air move around him before he heard the stutter of an automatic weapon. He threw himself down to the left and began rolling behind part of a broken wall where a bloated dead horse, its belly huge and round as if it had been blown up with a foot pump, lay half in and half out of the cover. Pulling his rifle from under him he checked the sights and then was aware that sweat was running into his eyes, but when he touched his left hand quickly to it and looked, it was bloody. Christ, not another scar, he thought.

He smeared away the blood coming from a cut above his eye which, he thought, must have come from the tumble rather than a round. When he sighted his rifle on the lorry and then looked quickly to his left he could see that Dunbar was still in the middle of the street, but he was moving, wriggling on his stomach, trying to seek cover. Park began squeezing off rounds at the body of the truck and below it until the magazine was empty. As he began to reload he could see that Dunbar had made cover and lay slumped on the other side of the street among boulders and debris and what looked like a fallen shop sign.

'Give up, ya fucker,' Park shouted at the lorry, before he began firing again. When he had reloaded once more he rolled on to his back and detached a hand grenade and then realised that his heart was thumping and rolling and what he felt was a fierce angry pleasure rather than fear. Although he knew that he could not reach the lorry with the grenade he pulled out the pin anyway and popped up and hurled the thing overarm as far as he could.

The bullets ricocheted off the wall as he got back down and then a couple of seconds later the grenade went off and when he peered round the side of the broken stonework he saw the dust storm where it had exploded harmlessly in the street more than thirty feet short. 'Shite,' he said, rolling into the firing position and peppering the lorry with another six shots.

'How y'doing, Hugh?' he said when the angry frenzy had abated and he was reloading. 'Can y'hear me?' Still no reply as he cocked the rifle. 'Shite,' he said again, staring down the sights of the weapon and waiting for an indication from the target where he, or *they*, he thought with a tremor of anxiety, was hiding. Think about it logically, he told himself. They're out in the open, I've got the better cover and if I wait this out long enough I'll either get lucky or a tank'll come along. One of ours.

The only problem was Dunbar. If he was alive he was clearly in a bad way, if he wasn't, well, that had ceased to be a problem. 'Dunbar,' he shouted, then waited a few seconds. Nothing.

The blood was trickling into his eye again. He fired one round at the back wheel, hearing it zing and splinter off the metalwork. No answering fire. 'Hey, Deutsch. *Sprechen ze Englische?*' No answering fire. 'How d'you say fucked in German?' he shouted along the rifle, grinning with the incongruity of it all. 'Because that's what you are. Fucked. We've got a great big bastardin' Centurian – a tank, *Panzer* – about a quarter of a mile away. We're the scouts. And when it rolls up here in a few minutes it's gonnae blow you back to Berlin in bubbles and tiny bits of Spam. So get yourself a bit of sense, son and chuck out your Schmeizer and come out wae your hauns up.'

There was no reply, no sign of any life from the lorry. Park squinted at the driver's door, thought that he could see what looked like the top of a head in the glass just above the door, so he blew out the glass where the head seemed to be, then drove a couple of rounds into the door where the soldier's trunk should have been. Still no return of fire.

'Hughie?' he called again. Nothing. Shite, he thought, this is stalemate. He was considering whether he should pitch in another grenade just to relieve the boredom and keep the adversary on edge when he caught sight of something arcing high over the lorry then falling to the ground in front of it. He focused on it. It looked like a weapon. And then a shout, something he could not decipher, then a crouched figure emerging from behind the lorry, hands on head, stumbling and dragging himself almost like a beast. Wounded, Park thought to himself, fuckin' marvellous.

'Here,' he shouted, 'keep coming this way.' He debated dropping him with a round when he got closer but he decided that would be short-sighted. A live prisoner gave him a better chance of a medal. 'This way. Keep your hands like that!'

As he got closer Park picked up the dark patch and the flapping fabric on the man's thigh. He had taken a bullet and had clearly endeavoured to bind the wound and stop the bleeding. Either that had failed or the movement had opened the wound because the field bandage, he could see through the ripped-open trouser leg, was glistening with fresh blood. Park took his left hand off the stock of his gun and touched his hand to his own wound which felt caked and crusty. 'On your face,' he shouted to the German, a sergeant, he noticed, nodding his body forward. The soldier, who was wearing dress uniform rather than fatigues, looked at him, then got the meaning and grunted as he first shuffled forward on to his knees and then flopped on to his face where he lay, whimpering, hands still clasped behind his bare head.

Park moved on to his knees then, watching the lorry intently as he went, sprinted for the other side of the street. Dunbar was lying on his side, face in his arms, his helmet off beside him and, Park could tell from the rippling of his upper body, that his breathing was fast and shallow. He knelt down beside him, glanced back to see the German was still prone, dropped his rifle, then carefully pulled him by the arm so that he came over and he could see that a bullet had torn away part of his jaw and mouth. From the mess it looked as if it had splintered and exploded its way through the lower face. It was messy, he had lost a lot of blood, but it was not a fatal wound. Or wouldn't be if he could bind it up and get him back to the field hospital. He fumbled at Dunbar's pack, spilling out tins and pans and clothing until he came to the bandages. He tore open the wrapping and wound the bandage round the wreckage of broken teeth, bone shards and torn flesh. Dunbar, who either had a phobia about it or a premonition, had been scared of being wounded and bleeding to death and had traded cigarettes for morphine with an orderly and on almost every day since had reminded Park about it, about what to do with the stuff if he caught one. So, Park shrugged, pulled out the needle and syringe and the small bottle of morphine and sucked out the drug and quickly banged it into Dunbar's leg through the rough serge, then he sat back on his bottom and wondered what to do next. There was a bleeding German lying face down in the street, his pal with half his face blown away now slipping from a shock coma into a drugged one and who knows what, or who, at the lorry?

There was nothing he could do for the time being for Dunbar. He certainly could not carry him all the way back and manage a wounded German as well. Then, looking down the ravaged street, it occurred to him. The lorry, if it was still serviceable, could take them all back. He bent down to listen to Dunbar's breathing, which seemed slower and more regular, then he threw off his own pack and ran quickly to the German, splaying himself down beside him and, prodding at him with his rifle barrel, pointed towards the lorry. He was no more than a boy, about fifteen Park thought, and for a moment he looked as if he would burst into tears. He pointed down at his leg. Park looked at it, shrugged his shoulders then drew back the bolt on the rifle. 'Move,' he said again, 'move,' motioning with the gun towards the lorry.

Park had to pull him to his feet and half carry him, the boy hopping and moaning, Park trying to get behind him for cover until, halfway there, he stopped, slung his rifle over his shoulder, grabbed the German by the tunic, pulled him off his one leg and dragged him by the arms to the lorry. He was unconscious by the time they got there.

Park looked up, wiped his face and glanced up at the hillside ahead on the horizon which was still blooming with explosions. He caught sight of himself in the wing mirror of the truck, his face grimed and filthy, a long black bubble of a scab on the forehead, the deep scar in the cheek, then opened the passenger door carefully.

The driver, an officer, sat hunched and jammed between steering wheel and door, what was left of his brain splashed over what was left of the windscreen, a few spiked and reddened shards. His uniform was dark with blood, as if buckets of the stuff had been cast over him. Park complimented himself on his marksmanship. There was no one else in sight. He smiled ruefully at his undue caution, the earlier performance, then walked round the front of the lorry, pulled open the driver's door, noted that he had caught the officer with at least one bullet to the body, then pulled his left arm so that the body spilled out and hit the dusty ground. Blood, probably sweetened with urine, puddled the seat. Park stood back and considered.

The two Germans must have known that the Allied advance had passed them. So, where were they going with this lorry? Why was the officer driving when there was an enlisted man around? What was in the back?

'No point in speculating,' he said out loud, then pulled himself up on the truck. He pulled out his bayonet and quickly cut through one of the retaining ropes, then knifed into the tarpaulin. There seemed to be three cases, boxwood, he noticed as he peeled back the heavy material. Each had a lid nailed shut on top, the first of which splintered easily under his gun butt. He pushed aside the pieces of broken wood and rummaged inside. There were several shapes, wrapped parcels. He pulled the first out. It was covered in a heavy brocade, like curtain material, about a foot square. He tore off the covering and held it in his hand. It was a religious painting, an icon, done in dark, melting colours, the Madonna and child leafed in gold. He smiled at it almost familiarly and put it down, then delved again, pulling out an angular object, which he undressed, and saw that it was a gold Orthodox cross. He re-wrapped it, did the same with the icon and put them back in the box. Next he drove in the lid of the second box. The same brocade, another flat shape on top. It was a painting, he did not know from what period but it was old, probably Italian, he thought, of a man with an extravagant bouffant hat, a loose ruff at the neck. He wrapped that and put it back in the box.

When he jumped down from the lorry the young German was still unconscious. He knelt down beside him and began slapping him around the face, then when that did not work he poured some water from his canteen over him and repeated the slapping. The German, who had a thick stubble of blond hair and a hint of moustache, rolled his head, coughed and came awake. Park looked down at his leg, sopping with blood, and realised that it wasn't going to be much use to him in future.

'Lorry,' he said, 'machine? Where from? Where to?' Then he shook his head crossly, angry at his lack of German. The boy looked far-off and mystified. Park grabbed him by the collar and pulled him, screaming, to his feet where he hung to the tailboard. 'This,' he roared in his ear, pointing at the load, 'what is it?'

The boy gagged, tried to be sick, but nothing came up. '*Russisch*,' he said softly, '*der Russe*.'

'What?' Park said. 'What?'

'*Der Russe*,' the boy said again, then, '*Russki*.' He sighed: '*Das museum*,' then blacked out and fell backwards.

Park stood back from him. 'Right,' he said. 'Of course. The lieutenant or the major or whatever the fuck he is – was,' he corrected himself, grinned, recalling his excellent marksmanship, 'was trying to get away with his souvenirs of the Russian front. Although Christ knows where he thought he was going to take them to.'

He looked around, then up at the sky, noticed a swarm of neatly spaced black dots against the cloud, a flight of bombers, probably on their way to harass the German retreat, and saw that he was alone, apart from an injured German and a comrade slowly bleeding to death up the street. He put his rifle down, propping it against a rear tyre which he noted was unpunctured. A quick scan showed the rest were the same. Then took off his tunic top and spread it over the soggy mess in the front seat and climbed into the cab. He turned the engine, which ground and coughed and eventually grumbled into life, then he jumped down beside the mutilated officer, moved towards the back of the lorry and pulled out his bayonet.

It sounded like metal driven into gravel as it plunged into the ribcage of the unconscious soldier. Park pulled it out, wiped it on the dead man's tunic, then sheathed it. Looking around, he spotted the machine pistol in the dirt about ten yards away. When he had picked it up, he checked the mechanism was free of dirt, slipped off the safety catch and walked back towards Dunbar. He lay in the same position, the bandage he had wound round his face now looking like a bright red muffler. Park shook his head and sighed, then fired a quick burst into Dunbar's body, knocking it into a grotesque slithering motion.

He looked around. Still no sign of life. The irony of that made him smile wanly. He wasn't quite sure where he was going to take the lorry and where he was going to store the trophies but after he had found a place and gone back, told the story of the ambush and how Dunbar was killed, how he had eventually killed the two Germans after losing his comrade, he would probably get a medal. Another trophy.

Chapter Fourteen

The figure loomed out at him, from the shrubbery beside the entrance door.

'Christ!' he said, flinching.

'It's me,' she said. 'Can't you see?'

McQuade's heart was rattling like a sewing machine.

'Have you been trying to avoid me?' she said.

'I've been busy – no,' he said, searching in his pocket for the door key, 'all right, the truth is that you worry me. You, and your connection.'

'Sean, you mean?' She was wearing what looked like a dark trench coat, and he could smell her familiar perfume above the tang of the rain. 'Can we talk about it? Inside?' She tentatively touched his lapel, then withdrew her hand. 'I'm soaking.'

'Right,' he said, recovering. 'But if you've got nothing on under that coat, it's off – I mean, for you.'

'Wishful thinking,' she said. 'Do you want to look inside or frisk me before we go in?'

He shook his head and tried to avoid a smile. 'Let's go,' he said.

When she did take off her coat she was wearing a wool suit underneath, navy blue, very short skirt, a brooch on her chest holding the neckline together, beneath which she was obviously naked. He went into the kitchen, tried to ignore her as she followed him in, opened the fridge and pulled out two bottles of Budvar. 'It's all I've got,' he said, pulling off first one top, then the other with his teeth as she winced.

'I wouldn't say that, entirely,' as she took the bottle, nodding it at him in a toast, then took a swig.

He walked into the living room, she followed him again, he bent over the stereo, found a CD by Mary Chapin Carpenter and stuck it in the tray and hit the button. Then he slumped in the settee as the piano came in, then the guitars. She cocked her head, listening to the first few bars, standing in front of him. 'Is there a message in this?' she asked. 'Everything we got, we got the hard way?'

He shook his head, and took a gargle of the beer.

'Look, I'm sorry. What did you expect?'

He shook his head again.

'Well then, what's to lose?' She took a couple of steps towards him and then stopped. 'Do you mind if I sit down?'

He shook his head again.

'C'mon, McQuade, grow up. Stop sulking. What is it you want?'

He sighed. 'We've got two lives, the one we're given and the other we make.'

'Right. You said it.'

'No, she just did,' gesturing at the stereo with his bottle, then he grinned at her, patted the sofa beside him.

Stick sat down and put her left arm round his waist and clinked her bottle off his. 'This doesn't sound like your kind of music, McQuade.'

'That indicates how little we know about each other.'

'Don't get sombre on me again.'

'Betrayal, broken hearts and confusion . . . tell me, about you, about you and Harris.'

She sighed and drew away from him. 'Why, exactly?'

'Because, professionally, I don't want to be used; privately it's just fine, of course. Because all of this – you – this may sound pompous, but it compromises my impartiality.'

'Don't let it.'

'Go on, tell me. You know that he deals in drugs, and kills people too, so the story goes. Not that I know for sure, of course.' He took another quick swig. 'But I will.'

'I know all about the rumours.' She cupped the bottle in both hands. It made him think of her holding him and he shivered. 'My mother's Indonesian, my father's from here. He's a businessman – was. He died about eighteen months ago.' McQuade tried to offer the ritual condolences but she shook her head and went on. 'I was studying in London. Media studies, actually. When he died I had to quit. I met Sean at a party. I was depressed – I don't know – that's rationalisation, I was wild. I slept with him, I enjoyed his company, we had a good time for a couple of weeks. I didn't know anything at all about him then. He was . . . kind, I suppose. Now I know about his reputation, but he was.' She looked round at him. 'I'm not ashamed. These things happen.'

He nodded, trying to look sanguine, mature, but his stomach was moving.

'He wanted to loan me money. He said he would pay for me to finish college, but I couldn't accept that. Then he offered me a job.' He nodded, as if he understood. 'No, you don't know. It's not like that at all. He has a couple of bars, he's not the licensee but he owns them. I look after one, the Dominion, in Shawlands. D'you know it?'

He shook his head and took a deep swig of the beer. 'Do you?' he took a harsh breath, tried putting on his reporter's persona – 'still sleep together?'

'McQuade' – she put her left hand on his knee – 'I'm not sure that's any of your business. But yes, occasionally. When we're both—'

'Lonely?' he cut in. 'Don't give me that.' He felt the sour bubbles from the beer in the back of his throat.

'Horny, I was going to say. And when there's no one else.' She had withdrawn her hand.

'So, now we know the sexual history. What is it he wants from me?'

'. . . *shouldn't I have all of this, and passionate kisses* . . .' Carpenter's voice was booming in the silence.

'I can't answer that entirely. I don't suppose you'd believe me anyway. Part of it, certainly, is vanity. Him feeling that he's at the centre of things, controlling events, donating information, you might say. And' – she rolled the bottle in her hand – 'I think he enjoys the fame, the notoriety, picture in the paper, being a celebrity. It gives him a buzz. The rest, I don't know. You'll have to work that out yourself, between yourselves.'

'What did he say about me, about why he wanted you to make the introductions?'

'You don't expect me to answer that honestly.'

'Not really, but go on.'

'He said that it was easier, that you would react quicker to me.'

'To a pretty face.'

'All right. He wasn't interested in a long—'

'Courtship?'

'C'mon, McQuade, grow up. And stop fuckin' interrupting. He wanted to meet you, quickly, and in the right circumstances. I made it easier.'

'That's right.' He put the beer down on the carpet. 'I must say, he's a pretty shrewd judge of character. Did he tell you to sleep with me?'

'I don't think I want to talk like this any more.'

'Us reporters,' he said, 'always read the positive into no comment.'

She put down her bottle on the carpet and stood up. 'I'll go,' she said, picking up her coat.

'I wish you wouldn't,' he said, against his better judgment.

'. . . *passionate kisses, from you . . .*'

She looked at the stereo deck, shrugged and sat back down.

Burns woke at 6 a.m., as usual just seconds before the alarm. He slid out of bed and walked through to the kitchen where he poured a large orange juice which he drained in one long gulp. Then he went back into the bedroom and retrieved his running gear from the jumble on the chair. He opened the blinds and saw that the day outside was streaked with rain clouds. After he had dressed in the tracksuit and put on his training shoes he set up the coffee filter machine so that it would be ready when he got back. He was drawing the bolt on the front door when the phone rang.

He took it on the hall extension. 'Hallo?' He waited for a reply but all he could hear was what sounded like faint breathing. 'McPherson, is that you?' The faint breathing continued. 'C'mon, man, speak up. It's okay. I'm listening. C'mon, let me hear you.'

After a few seconds the breathing grew into a sigh. 'I – I'm sorry to bother you, sir. It – it's, well . . .' he tailed off.

'I know what it is McPherson and it's no bother. Look, I'm just going out for a quick run and then I'll have a shower. Then I'll be having coffee and croissants, toast if you prefer, so I'll see you about seven, all right?'

'No, sir, it's all right—'

'McPherson, it clearly is not all right. Seven a.m., that's an order.'

'Very well, sir. And thank you.'

Burns hung up.

He checked his mailbox as he left but it was empty – the postman did not come for another hour and his services had clearly not been needed throughout the night – and then he began to run along the canal system towards Firhill football ground and to Maryhill. His footsteps splashed in the mud, his white trainers were clatty inside a minute and gobs of dirt stuck to the inside of his training pants. McPherson, he thought, would be better after a bit of firm emotional bolstering, some reminders of times past but, more importantly, to show him how these events had shaped him for what was to come, to show him a future. The lad had been caught in a nail-bomb attack in Lurgan on the patrol, his mate Windsor, who was closer, catching most of the blast, so that he was left like a flayed corpse on the pavement, except that it took him several minutes to die. McPherson had taken nails, or rivets or nuts or whatever they used in these infernal devices, in his left hand, leg and upper arm. Another piece of the metal had sliced away half of his cheek. Burns had been leading the back-up patrol which arrived five minutes later, with Windsor already dead and McPherson dragged into a shop doorway where a paramedic was sticking needles into him as fast as the blood seemed to leak from dozens of different holes. Burns hadn't given him more than half an hour, but somehow he had hung on and pulled through, if it could be called that.

That's what they all had done, he thought, that just about summed it up. Pulled through. All over the country there were hundreds of men, thousands more like, men like McPherson and him, men who, if they were not crippled physically and mentally, were somehow impaired because they had had their – reason to live was too strong – choice of way of life summarily terminated. Without appeal. Men – okay there were women too but hardly any at all – men who were highly skilled, who had immense ranges of intense and obviously now redundant technical skills, who were supremely fit and dedicated, loyal and trustworthy, who had not just their proven valour but management abilities and huge dollops of innovative nous and who should have been the core of the country's future, but were just rusting away.

It made him angry again, so that he turned on the pace to punish himself. Fuck the brass and the crap-hats, he intoned to himself as he did it.

When he had got his 'Dear John' from the ministry it hadn't so much stunned him as made him seethe and boil. Pensioned off at thirty-five, it was ludicrous. His peace dividend was a miserable cheque, a meagre monthly stipend, his medals boxed up and a pat on the back. He wasn't the sort who could slip into a nice job in civvie street with a merchant bank or Highland estate – wrong accent, wrong background – so he seethed and boiled for several fruitless months and then he did something about it. He did what he had been trained to do, he went back to war, he went back to killing people. He became – although he didn't like to use the word because of the connotations it evoked of sloppy-waisted, over-armed right-wing braggarts – a mercenary.

There was always demand for a recently discarded British officer, but unfortunately the money was rarely sufficient. The CIA were the real payers, funding the assorted wars and warlords, but since they had pulled back their horns after the collapse of the USSR and its satellites, small conflicts in large dusty countries, no matter the emotional rewards or the presidential thank yous, did not cover the mortgage.

So he had sat down again and thought through what he should do. He had considered a survival school, joking that a city-based one was what was really needed nowadays, and then discarded the idea because there was so much competition. He contemplated signing on as a security consultant for one of the failing Arab Gulf states, but the idea of remorseless sand and torture and pink gins into middle age appalled him. He had made contact with some middle-ranking British officials who seemed to be acting for Dubai – it was denied of course over tea and sandwiches in the Connaught. But, whatever he had done, he had clearly come to the notice of officialdom, or some maverick outpost of it, because he had been recruited several times for black bag jobs, deniable affairs, which had involved a couple of minor break-ins to peace groups, bodyguarding some visiting businessmen and minor royals, as well as two returns to Ireland to act as leader of the guard in covert meetings between British civil servants and the IRA.

It was passing exciting, but it still was not a living. Then slowly it came to him that what he should do was to collate and collect some of those dispersed skills wasting around the country and put them to use. So he had put out the word, bought the computer and compiled the database of ex-soldiers and their particular skills. It was a loose liaison. He fed back to his handlers and into diplomatic conduits the fact of the existence of the group, he supplied advisers to various sheikdoms, which was well paid, he sent men to South Africa to supervise the setting-up of the new secret police, exceptionally well paid, and he sent the adventure-thirsty to Bosnia and Belgrade, Liberia, Afghanistan – wherever people were shooting at each other, which was on large tracts of the map. He regarded this almost as a social function for his friends and fellow former colleagues, rather than a way of making money. But it ticked over and it prospered.

The group did not have a name, of course, but over a few beers with a group of the lads one of them, Gus McFadyen, a former Para, came out with, 'Know what this is, it's the severe Burns unit!' And now, under his tracksuit top as he ran, Burns had the tee-shirt with that legend on the front.

Still with time on his hands, he set up a small security company and a detection agency. The work was pretty mundane, guarding army installations, stewarding football matches, spying on errant husbands, tracing hire-purchase debtors, but these companies ticked over too. And through them, also, came the unofficial jobs, the ones that could not be handled by the companies because they shaded the law – well, often totally over-painted it – but these were usually the fun ones, or the morally correct ones. He did not take on any job which offended his own code and those he did take on were usually the ones where the law had totally failed. Sorting out persistent wife beaters, increasingly child molesters, warning off the moneylenders and usurers, helping out old ladies terrorised by local tearaways. Chastising the unpunished, as he justified it to himself.

He had passed Firhill and he decided to make a right and run up into Ruchill and Possil and observe the pond life which digested or spat out the stuff which was poisoning the city. Drugs.

Chapter Fifteen

Guiliano was drinking at the bar, toying with the thinned Scotch in his mouth. So obviously watering the whisky, he thought, was not the way to keep a clientele. That would be the manager's doing. Another tickle, another squeeze, another buck. He made a mental note to tell young Stark, recommend an early retirement. He smiled over the insipid whisky. The lad certainly was one operator. What age was he? Sixteen, eighteen? No, he couldn't be eighteen or he would have been called up. He took another sip of the whisky and turned his nose up. By the age of majority Stark would surely own the city.

The place was getting busy. Guiliano turned round, leaning his back against the bar, looking out for any loose. But it seemed to be couples everywhere. He turned back to the bar and stared along, seeing the only other single person there, a smallish man, early forties, who was drinking what looked like lemonade or water and was studying the stairs to the upstairs office. Interesting, thought Guiliano, got to be a cop. He looked around for his company, his partner, but could not see anyone else who looked like the heat. So, he continued to himself, is this a bust or is it just observation and is he the look-out?

On a shelf below the gantry he noticed a telephone. He motioned to the barman, leaned across and said quietly, 'D'you have a line here to the office?' The man shook his head. 'Okay,' he said. To go up the stairs now would be giving himself away, although maybe he had been spotted earlier. He looked along at the other man who continued to stare at the stairs. No, he didn't think so, the watcher showed no interest in looking his way. Maybe there was someone else checking on him, but that didn't seem likely.

He was considering whether he should go up the stairs when he noticed Johnnie's mate come stomping down and then disappear out of the door. The watcher at the bar made no attempt to go after him, neither did anyone else. A few minutes later Johnnie appeared, cocooned by two young girls. He could hear the laughter from them above the piano, trumpet and drums. As he expected, the man pushed himself away from the bar and followed in the slipstream of lust and cheap scent.

Guiliano left about fifty yards between him and the other guy, who was following the youngsters by around the same distance, feeling conspicuous in the open to the slightest glance over the shoulder. He shook his head as he walked; this was either a very raw cop, or it wasn't, a cop that was. So if not, what? The answer to that was pretty obvious. Trouble.

The kid and the two girls had now disappeared into a large alleyway. Guiliano knew this plot. He quickened his step, moving on his toes, breaking into a jog. This, he appreciated, was unnecessary behaviour, it was none of his business; the kid was good, almost a transatlantic image of what he had been, but that was no reason to put himself to any risk. There was the money, though, he thought, wondering if this was just rationalising his involvement. He had the whisky, Stark had the money, the deal had been done so it shouldn't matter what happened to it, but somehow he seemed still connected to it, that the loss of it would be a robbery on him, an affront. At least that is how he rationalised and convinced himself.

When the two girls broke away from Stark he knew more than the plot, he could read the final credits. He broke into a run just as the sap came down on Johnnie and by the time the man was picking up the package he was on him, spiralling a kick with venom and plenty of backswing into his right thigh and when he dropped, the leg useless, the parcel falling from his grasp, he put a rapid tattoo of kicks into him fiercely with the hardened toes of his co-respondent's shoes. Eventually, when the ribs were done for, he stamped down briskly on the bridge of his nose, enjoying the crunch of cartilage and bone.

The man lay barely breathing, sounds of anguish gargling in his throat, as Guiliano went through the pockets. Nothing, no sign of identification, just, in the right-hand jacket pocket, a length of strong wire, with tight woven loops at each end. A nifty ligature, thought Guiliano.

It made sense. Theft was simply the bonus. The way the watcher had rehearsed it was first to down Stark, reduce the risk of mis-lassooing or simply to cut out a prolonged struggle, then take what the boy had on him, perhaps make it look like a robbery, before whipping halfway through the neck with the cheese wire. Guiliano found it a rather arcane way of murder, although it did have a certain artiness to it. Admirable plan, he conceded, unfortunate execution. Well, no execution now, in fact.

He slipped his hand into the inside pocket of his double-breasted jacket and retrieved the flask which he uncorked and then poured half the Napoleon brandy over the head and clothes of the man on the ground who was gagging and squirming and drawing rattling breaths which sounded like gusts of wind tearing at loose metal.

He bent down beside him. 'I'm only going to say this once, then I'll start breaking your fingers one by one. Understand? So, who was it that put out the contract on the boy?' Johnnie was still lying motionless, a dark shape on the wet muddy ground next to the watcher. He leaned over him and checked his breathing, which seemed regular. 'Speak up.'

The man was trying to say something but all that was coming out was a bubbling in the throat. 'What's that you say?' Guiliano was resting on his heels, knees bent, the badly-injured watcher on his left side with his knees drawn up to his chest. Guiliano leaned over, picked up his right arm and took hold of the index finger. 'Just write it down. In the dirt there.' He jabbed his finger into the marshy earth. 'You can write, can ya? If you can't, the broken finger won't spoil your signature.' Slowly the watcher began drawing his finger up and down in the dirt next to him.

'What's that say? M-U-M,' he read out. 'Mum? His fuckin' mother?' The body seemed to quiver, which Guiliano took for confirmation. 'Jesus Christ, this is Shakespeare we got here.' Then he kicked him once more viciously to the body.

Johnnie was still out. Guiliano leaned over him and ran his fingers over the large, rising swelling on the back of his head. His fingers came away bloodied. The weapon was lying between the two bodies, what looked like an abbreviated police baton. He took out his linen handkerchief, briefly considered soaking it in a puddle, which seemed like an unnecessary waste, so he took out the flask again, doused the material in brandy, padded it and began dabbing at the wound and at Johnnie's forehead. It took a couple of minutes before the boy began to move, moaning and coughing. Guiliano pulled him into a rough sitting position where he began to retch and throw up. Guiliano wiped his mouth with the handkerchief. 'Do you know where you are?'

Johnnie shook his head and began moaning again.

'You think this is bad,' Guiliano said, 'wait until the hang-over kicks in.' Johnnie retched again but could bring nothing up. 'Tell me your name, son.'

'Mmmhh?'

'Just say your name for your Uncle Sam.'

'John . . . Stark,' he said slowly.

'So, at least some of the synapses are working.' He shook his head. 'Well, you've been a foolish boy, Mr Stark. But in a strange way this has been your lucky day. Someone – the someone in the pile next to you – hit you over the head with a baton and was about to separate your chin from your chest until I intervened. Saved your life, you could say. No, no thanks, please! But I'll expect a substantial discount on our next deal. Now' – he heaved under Stark's arms and lifted him to his feet – 'we need to get out of here. Can you stand?' Johnnie weaved on the spot, Guiliano holding him by the shoulders. 'Guess who put our friend here up to it?' He took John's face in his hands and gently shook it. The boy grunted. 'Well, I don't know what you've done to offend her – maybe not washing enough behind the ears – but according to our friend here's last testament, it was your mom. Which reminds me . . .' He let go of John, so that he staggered on the spot, then knelt down beside the watcher, grabbed his head by the hair, put his two arms round his neck in a choke hold and, without any apparent effort, snapped his spine, which cracked like a rotten bough.

'That make any sense? Mom contracting on you?' he said, standing up and brushing off the dirt from his right knee. 'C'mon' – he took John's left arm, threw it around his neck and put his own right arm around and under John's armpit – 'we need to get outta here.' They started an unsteady progress towards the street. 'And you should think of gettin' outta this city until you get some serious resources.'

*   *   *

The pistol jerked in his hand. For a moment he felt nothing but a dull thump on his thigh and then the pain flooded in, pulsing and roaring, boiling in the flesh, making him cry out. He had fired the shot through a wad of torn tunic and rags to catch the cordite and when he pulled off the material he saw the blood bubbling out of the neat hole in the inside leg of his tunic. Tears were running down his cheeks as he bit on the pain.

Carefully he lifted the wounded leg and looked underneath at the flapping serge and the ragged raw exit wound filling with blood. His leg felt huge and fiery, waves of pain rolling out from it as he began to cut away the legging and dab painfully at the wound with the gauze before he bound on the field dressing. When it was tight he picked up the limb of wood he had ready and prodded at the ground as he got himself on to his feet. Then, hopping on the good foot, he hurled the Luger as far as he could into the middle of the river. The pain roared again as he stumbled. He scooped up his pack, strapped it on with difficulty, and began hobbling back along the bank of the river.

When he reached a road, after about ten minutes, he began to move in what he thought was a south-westerly direction. The road was broken and rutted; he was moving through what was once clearly farming country, but was now overgrown and wild and abandoned. Ahead he could see what was, or had been, a group of farm buildings which had been bombed or shelled, because the roofs seemed to be missing and even at a distance he noticed the pockmarks in the grey walls and the blackening of fire.

Park stopped, pulled back the torn leg of his trouser. The bandage was dark and heavy with blood which was also leaking down his leg, some of which had dried and darkened but most of which was new and wet. He felt dizzy, his sight was swimming, the pain seemed to have dulled to a manageable torment, and a series of shivers trembled through him. Blood loss, he knew. Get on, he told himself, stumbling forward once more towards the farm buildings.

A hundred yards nearer and he heard the soughing and then the deep roar of a heavy engine starting up, then the unmistakeable clatter of metal and first the barrel, then the dark grey shape of a tank, emerge from behind one of the farm buildings. He strained to recognise it as it rumbled out and on to the road, swinging round towards him. He stood mesmerised, trying to focus on the cranking grey shape, unsure where to run, towards it or for the scrub around him, and then he picked out the star on the bodywork and relief flooded through him like a narcotic. He stumbled on to his good leg, waved his stick at the approaching tank, and began laughing, before he lost his balance and pitched forward on to his face.

He was aware of arms grabbing him from above and a buzz of voices. 'Easy, fellah,' he heard and when everything finally came around and was in equilibrium he saw that two helmeted GIs were grinning at him, one with a bright white cigarette clutched in the teeth of his smeared face. A canteen of water was pushed at him and as he gulped at it he felt fingers poking at his wound. 'We'll tidy this up, kid, and get you back to your unit and home.'

He nodded, feeling faint now, cold and tired, the leg, by contrast, hot, sore and pulsing. 'The war's over for you.' The voice was rich and humorous. 'It's all over. And you won. We'll ship you out and the Yanks'll take over.'

'And claim the credit,' he slurred, hearing the laughter as he slipped into the black.

The conspicuousness he felt in the new suit lasted until about Rugby, when he joined the other bunch in their new civvies, and as the whisky began to go around his embarrassment evaporated so that by the time the border came up he felt sharp and almost sophisticated. It had been, he mused, slumped in the seat now, the waves of whisky lapping back and forward in his head, a great war. Just brief enough not to pall and sufficiently packed with incident and the learning of skills that it had never become boring. It had satisfied all his boyish fantasies and now there was a vague emptiness wondering about what was to come.

He had been a sapper, an explosives expert; the eloquence with which he could plan and lay a charge was almost breathtaking, even to him. His affinity with dynamite, gelignite, timers and charges had come as a complete surprise, but it had clearly been what his previous life had been leading up to.

He looked out of the window of the stuttering train at the first hills of Scotland, the patches of heather and bracken around the bare rocks. There had been nothing like that in Germany, just mud and destruction, then sun and more destruction. Forget the elements, he thought, and enjoy the elemental.

As the train rumbled on he kept talking to himself, recalling a rapid succession of days which culminated in the same way, either a series of barely perceptible explosions which took away the legs of a bridge, or the massive harrumph which atomised a gun emplacement, an explosives dump, the walls of a barracks or culvert.

But it hadn't all been obliteration, although that had been the best part of it. He had learned about electronics, the workings of the internal combustion engine, he could build or refashion weaponry, given a lathe, the materials and the welding gear, he could plot exactly the trajectory of a mortar shell given the elevation and a couple of co-ordinates – he had been expertly trained, he appreciated, to do absolutely nothing constructive with the rest of his life.

He sighed and looked across at the other three jocks in their demob suits sleeping along the bench seats in the carriage around him. He was not, he realised, cut out for peacetime. He was already beginning to feel bored and fractious days into it. He missed the single-mindedness of his old job, the precise result achieved, success or failure – rarely failure for him – and the instantaneous pleasure. Clocking in, firing rivets into the iron entrails of some big ship, a few bevvies in the evening, would never be for him.

He wiped at the mist on the window where his breathy musings had condensed. But, of course, it would not come to that. He thought about Johnnie again. He had heard nothing about him in the last few months although he had been a part of the same advance, the 51st Highland Division roll which had started at El Alamein and ended up in Berlin, although Johnnie and he had come in on the finale. He knew his china had wound up with the Seaforths, rather than the HLI for some reason, the arbitrariness of the army no doubt, and some days, when he had been dodging sniper fire on his face with his explosive bag towed behind, he had expected to look around and see him peering out from beneath a nearby tin lid. But they had never bumped into each other. He did not even know if Starkie had got through it, but he felt that somehow he would have known if he had not.

Ownie yawned and snuggled his neck into his tight collar and began to fall asleep. There was one place for sure where he would find out. Coloured images of turning dancers and closely wrapped couples moved around in his head before he slept.

The jolting clatter of the train stopping woke him up. The four men, the former soldiers, shook and groaned and stretched and got up. Shapes were moving past the window. He looked out and recognised the station.

'We're here,' he said, as much to himself as anyone, then pulled his kit bag from the netting above, slung it over his shoulder and pulled open the sliding door of the compartment. He jostled his way along the corridor and then stepped down on to the platform. Only then did it truly hit him that it was over, he was safe and a civilian once more.

Mechanically he joined the queue of people pressing towards the barrier, dug out his cardboard ticket before he got to the collector, handed it over and squeezed through onto the concourse. He walked a few paces then stopped, looking around and up, taking it all in slowly, then he moved forward again. The ragged notes of a band starting up made him pause; he saw a guy with a squeezebox, one with a saxophone, a boy with a snare drum round his neck drilling out the rhythm and an older man, a trumpeter, licking his lips and putting the mouthpiece to his lips.

'Jesus Christ!' He stopped suddenly, someone bumped into him from behind, his kit bag tore from his shoulder.

'No need to go down on your knees,' Johnnie was saying, smiling hugely, his arms wrapping round his neck. 'Welcome home,' into his ear, before kissing him on the cheek. 'Oh,' he went on, 'do I have plans for you.'

'I'm no' sure which knife does what.' Ownie said.

'Disnae matter. Eat wae your fingers if you like; we can do what we like, I'm paying enough to make sure we can behave in any way we want.'

Ownie felt conspicuous again. A dinner suit, brand-new, a flower in his buttonhole, his hair newly cut and pomaded, all around him gleaming cutlery, white linen, a bottle of champagne peeping out of a gilded bucket, waiters in brown hovering discreetly on the periphery.

He felt more than conspicuous, he felt ridiculous. Johnnie pulled the uncorked champagne from the bucket in a rattle of ice and splashed a foamy measure in each of the two glasses, crunched the bottle back and handed Ownie a glass before picking up his own.

'So,' he said, brandishing it, grinning, 'did you have a good war, old man?'

Ownie took a swallow, feeling the bubbles exploding in his throat. 'Actually' – he gasped slightly – 'I did. I shouldn't say it, but terrific. You?' He took another drink.

'Exceptionally . . .' Johnnie paused, savouring the taste and the correct description, 'profitable.'

Ownie glanced around the lavishly furnished small room, at the eyes of waiters in the shadows awaiting a summons. 'You must have. How?'

Stark smiled over his glass. 'Never you mind.' He raised his arm and a waiter cruised silently towards it. 'You can start now.' He turned back towards Ownie. 'I just stumbled into good fortune. I'll tell you about it some day. Got a DCM too, for gallantry, and a ribbon as well, probably for the wound that I'm too much of a hero to talk about. Although, of course, technically that's not quite true. Actually it's not true at all. But I've got the medal, even if it's in someone else's name.'

'You got wounded? Badly?'

'Nah, hardly anything at all. Although I've probably lost my chance of playing inside-left for Celtic. But fortunately not my ability to sire a half-back line.'

'I forget exactly, what was your name again?'

Stark reached for the bottle and topped up both their glasses. 'Michael Park. You were McArthur, weren't you? Tony?'

'Tommy.'

'The original Tommy – the unoriginal Tommy, I should say.'

Ownie drained his glass, feeling himself beginning to ease once more into his changed circumstances. 'Christ, I enjoyed it, most of it. It was a bit like being a kid again.'

'Look at the old man, barely shaving.'

'It was a bit like you were playing games, though you were actually doing it. I've learned a lot, too.' Stark was filling the glass. 'Not a lot of it much use. There's not a great deal of call for someone who can bring down a sixteenth-century bridge with a few pounds of dynamite.'

'On the contrary, I know just the fellow who needs a man like that.' Two waiters were ladling soup into their bowls and Ownie was looking pensive over the choice to be made from the array of cutlery. 'And you've just passed the interview, even if you can't tell a soup spoon frae a soap dish.'

'Aye?' he said, looking up. 'What are we going to be doing?'

'We're going to be going into the specialised banking business.' Stark picked up his soup spoon and brandished it for Ownie. 'The withdrawals side of things.'

Johnnie knew that under Gerry Queen the Rose was being run honestly. Other than periodic visits and conversations the place demanded little of his time. But it did not provide a proper living for him. It was in the wrong place, the Gorbals was still regarded as an exclusion zone from the city by most of the population, and rationing and austerity meant that although there was celebration in the blood after the victory there was little in the pocket for good times. There were still a few US servicemen around and their contributions basically kept the place in financial equilibrium but they were going home and the dance hall would shortly be listing into debt. John had to generate additional sources of income.

When he had wakened from the beating he found that he was lying in a bedroom of a small flat in the West End, his neatly wrapped parcel beside him. The money. Only later did he find out that he had been unconscious for most of thirty-six hours. His head was bound and it ached but he was able to get up and get dressed. Guiliano was not around. He did not remember how he had got here, who had treated his injuries or where, but his clothes had been washed and ironed and when he left the room and walked into the living room a middle-aged woman, in a floral cross-over pinafore, got up and handed him an envelope. He tried to question her about the previous hours but she just shrugged, as if he were speaking a different language, and went out into the kitchen.

The letter did not help much. It was a brief goodbye note from Guiliano wishing him well. 'Had to leave you. If you're in New York look me up. Similarly I will if I'm back here. If your noggin' isn't too scrambled it must be obvious who set you up and why and what you should do. Aren't families wonderful! I cleaned up the immediate problem. Look after yourself.'

He hadn't felt like eating so he walked out and up into Byres Road. It was strange, he hardly knew this part of the city so it felt anonymous to him and him to it, despite the bandage, almost like another country. And it felt safe. He walked up to the Botanic Gardens, which were closed, but he moved round the perimeter fence until he found a lower part, he shinned up, making his head pound even harder, and dropped down into the empty parkland.

As he walked around, realising how lucky he was to be alive, appreciating how foolishly predictable his movements had been and what he owed to Guiliano, it quickly became apparent to him what he should do. The Yank had said that he had got rid of the immediate problem, the guy who had attacked him, the guy Hazel had clearly put on him, but there would surely be others. He could not take them all on, he was not up to taking even her on in his present state, so he had to get out of the way, either until he was forgotten about or until he had built up what he vaguely remembered Guiliano calling 'serious resources'.

If Hazel had set the monster on him, how did he find him, who had set him up? It seemed staringly obvious. Mullaney. He was her appointee, he had most to lose with a new regime, and informing would obviously have brought him credits. He kicked at a lump of mud on the path. Emotionally he felt like physical revenge, but pragmatically that was stupid. Anyway, he could always get even later. What he should do was hit him financially. Get him sacked from the Rose. For a moment he was undecided about how much he could trust the lawyer but when he rationalised that too he realised that no matter how much Arbuthnot would counsel him to give himself up, he would not actually turn him in. Lawyers' masonic rules were fairly strict on that. So, he would call him and tell him to jotter Mullaney, whose replacement was already forming itself in his mind. He could trust Gerard Queen, he had not known him more than a few hours before that became clear, and it was a better job for the man, better paid, better than heaving hundredweight bags up stairs all day, much better to employ someone else's muscle in the heavy work.

He nodded, agreeing with himself as he walked, imagining Gerard in a dinner suit and stiff shirt-front, patent shoes, striding across the dance hall floor.

But now he was starting to shiver. He felt slightly sick and his head was sore and hot. He had to get away, and so did Ownie because he was also at risk. Hazel, he knew, would not hesitate at getting at him through his friend, or even wiping him out of the way just because it pleased her. So, where should they go? Money was not a problem, he had that well taped and sealed in the room. Now that he was beginning to look around call-up age made him increasingly noticeable among the old men and the bairns. What to do seemed obvious. Go to the busiest, most anonymous place possible where he would be surrounded by young men and become invisible. Into battle. Enlisting anyway, when he thought about it, was probably a lot safer than around here.

They, he and Ownie, would need papers, ID and ration cards, but that would not be difficult. The cash from the whisky deal would buy stolen ones, or perfect reproductions of the real thing.

He felt better. The pain had eased a little and a watery sun had slipped out from behind the cloud cover. You could read signs into that.

'I thought there was meant to be rationing?' Ownie was carefully cutting a chunk of steak, pink in the centre and dark on the outside.

'Not for returning heroes.' Johnnie was motioning for more wine. 'You know, I vowed never to drink again after that night at the Rose.'

'D'ye hear from Guiliano?'

'We've had a dealing or two.'

You owe him—'

'I'm aware of it,' Stark cut in. 'Anyway, I've had a bit of legal advice. I wanted to know what would happen if I owned up to everything – well, not everything exactly, but if I went to the police and turned myself in, confessed I'd absconded and then had enlisted, under-age, with false papers.'

He motioned towards the brimming glass of red wine. 'Go on, try it, it's French.' Ownie sipped and tried to look approving. 'Good? Well, I suppose the real reason was that I didn't want to be called up for National Service again after having defended my country so stoutly and at such great personal cost.' He swigged the wine like lemonade and grinned.

'You said it was a flesh wound.'

'It was, but it can pain me profusely when called upon, particularly in front of authority.'

'So?'

'So, the lawyer, Arbuthnot, reckons I'd – we'd – get off. That they would take our glorious service into account and if charges were pressed at all it would end up in a small rap on the knuckles or a minor fine. I mean, did we not show such reformation of character that we went willingly into battle for the country whose laws we had transgressed. Something like that.'

'Stark, the way you're talking, you sound suspiciously like you have read a book since I last saw you.'

'It's good advice, expensive advice. We can clean up our past misdemeanours at one go. So, I'm turning myself in. You should come with me.'

'This is one of the big plans you have in store for me? A spot in the Bar-L.'

Johnnie shook his head and drained his glass and a waiter materialised at his elbow to refresh it. 'This is a land fit for heroes – even teuchter heroes – I heard that the other day. We're never going to have a better chance to clean the record.'

'I'll think about it.' The second gulp of wine tasted better to Ownie, he didn't even have to block his nose for it. 'But you were talking earlier' – he leaned across the table and lowered his voice – 'about banks. I urgently need to make a withdrawal from somewhere because I'm totally boracic.'

'It's all in hand, we're going on a tour tomorrow. But in the meantime we're going to have decoration with the pudding.'

'Decoration?'

'All I can say is that yours is in the business you were recently in.' He smiled. 'You know, demolishing erections!'

Ownie shook his head and his face reddened.

'I gather from that you're still a virgin.'

297

Chapter Sixteen

azel had done well out of the war and the peace was shaping up even better. There were shortages of everything, but particularly money, which she could supply at a rate, to buy the rest of the things which she could also supply, the booze and the foodstuffs, the clothing, the nylons for the women, silks, sweets for the kids, in fact all that rationing could never provide. Her alliance, too, her Yalta accord she liked to call it, had been inspired.

Chris Webb was the biggest bookie in the city and she had met him by chance at a function in the City Chambers, a fund-raising concert for war blinded, when he had introduced himself to her after catching her eye several times across the room. He was fairly plain, big and bluff with receding red hair and running to fat, but they had, it seemed to her, contiguous business interests. He ran books in some of the streets she controlled and he paid for that, but she did not have any real direct gambling interests, whereas he had nothing in the other vices like booze and cigarettes and women. So she flirted with him. She was still attractive and slim, she knew, with only a few puffs of white in her hair which were easily masked and she had about her a musk that few other women in the city had, dangerous power.

He was married, to a small and stupid little woman with too much make-up and bad hands, which had obviously seen their share of sinks. Hazel knew that it would not be difficult to hook him. She was surprised, but he was excellent in bed, and bigger than any man she had ever been with. Over drinks after the concert, while his wife was powdering her sagging flesh, she had told him that she had a business proposal to put to him and indeed she had. It seemed obvious to her that there would be a massive public building programme in the country after the war and she wanted in on that, so she suggested a meeting over dinner. To avoid any misinterpretation of her intent she suggested she cook him a meal, although of course she would get people in, and he accepted. She could tell from the sly smile that he had correctly understood her meaning.

Her proposal had been simple, that they set up a joint company, under nominees if necessary, hire a contracts manager with contacts, probably from the Corporation, and then buy up the entry needed – a couple of bailies, the planning convener, or chairman of public works, whoever was necessary. 'They always come cheap,' she said. 'But the beauty of this is that it gives us a business to become legitimate in, then to be able to live in a proper manner without having to disguise wealth or worry about awkward questions about where our money is coming from. I don't know where you put your cash now but it would be better working for you. Didn't Attlee mention "homes fit for heroes"? Well, someone's got to toil heroically to build them? Someone's got to get rich and why shouldn't it be us? Now isn't that a beautiful idea?'

She had been wearing a low-cut black dress, she had produced a bottle of champagne to propose the deal, he had muttered something about her being beautiful and how he could think of a proper way to seal it, and then he was on her. At first she had thought it was just something necessary she would have to en-dure but as he stripped her standing up, the fire warming her buttocks and the backs of her legs, as he moved his hands over her and in and out of her, with her eyes closed and drifting, the warmth of pleasure grew. She began to unbutton his shirt as he unbuttoned his trousers, then she kissed his surprisingly hairless chest, his chubby belly and as she slithered down on to her knees his trousers and pants dropped to his ankles. 'Fuck,' she said as it sprang free and up at her.

'Of course,' she heard him say.

She smiled. Blow-jobs, she thought to herself, are the way to a man's heart, but this was going to give her a flutter or two as well. She wrapped both her hands round him and there was still plenty to spare for her mouth. And then later he put her down on the floor on her face and came at her from behind, endless thick strokes, she pushing her bottom up at him until the tremors roared over her and she collapsed, him still thrusting, before he finally stopped, then pulled her on to her back, pushed her legs wide and came into her again in a pumping frenzy so hard that another orgasm tore free before she felt the final push and him coming before he slumped on to her wet chest.

That was six months ago and the arrangement was working out well, the sex and the building business both. The company was called Webb and Co and after tendering to the Corporation, a bid that they knew would be accepted as both the city chamberlain and the building works convener had assured them over separate meals and tidy piles of money, they had started on a 100-house scheme in Linthouse. The company was taking on tradesmen and subcontractors in platoons and had tenders in for three new projects involving 500 houses and a small shopping centre.

It was clear to Hazel that Webb was completely infatuated with her; he was taking greater risks with sex, demanding it in the most public places which excited her too, even staying over, as he was now. She never asked him what excuses he made to his wife – she could not even recall her name – because she did not care. He was here now, in the bedroom getting ready for work, dressing, whistling as he did so.

She was buttering toast when she heard a gentle rapping on the door. The whistling above stopped. She dashed into the hall and up the first few stairs, noticed him at the top, in trousers and shirt, neck open. She put a finger to her lips in a hushing movement and motioned him back into the bedroom. Then she adjusted a smile and opened the door.

'It's the wicked stepmother.'

For an instant the smile quivered, but he did not seem to notice. 'What do you want?' she said, looking through him. Then: 'Shouldn't you be careful about the police?'

'Shouldn't I be in prison, you mean. That's all right' – he smiled with no warmth – 'it's sorted.' He looked closely into her face. 'But is the other business? Ours?'

'What do you mean?'

'C'mon, Hazel, can I come in?' He pushed past her without waiting for an answer.

'You're up early.' She followed him into the living room, wondering vaguely how he knew where he was going. 'Aren't you afraid of the early birds?'

'Is that the best you can do, Hazel?' He had his back to her, facing the crackling new fire she had set in the fireplace. 'Quite nice,' he said before turning. 'My father provided well for you.'

'Not him, me! I did it all myself.'

'Oh yeah? Isn't a good war a convenient thing?'

'What do you mean?'

'Him getting killed, you inheriting everything.'

'The Rose?'

'Except, of course, for a broken-down dance hall. But it's interesting you brought that up. You know that I was beaten up, could have been killed, was meant to be killed, there.'

'Were you?' She smiled. 'That would have been a pity now, wouldn't it?'

'You know all about it.'

'About what?' She smiled again.

'I don't have time for all this. You tried to have me killed. I just wondered whether the intention was still there or whether you've given up on it?'

'I still don't know what you mean.'

He stepped forward so quickly she thought he was about to hit her, but he stopped, his face a few inches from her face so that she could feel his breath on her cheeks. 'Mullaney said. In fact it was about the last thing he did say. He told me about the toerag you hired, hanging around the bar for me, and about his calls to you. Now I can overlook that once, maybe, but not again.' He stepped back. 'You've done well for yourself out of death, haven't you? First my mother, then my father and then you pick up the pot. I think you should recognise your good fortune and disperse it a bit more favourably, in a family way.'

So that was it, he was just looking for a hand-out. She felt more comfortable about the situation now. He was cheap. 'Your father gave you more than you deserved.'

'And my ma?'

'She got exactly what she deserved from him,' she said, unable to suppress a giggle.

'What does that mean?' he asked, very calmly.

'Oh nothing,' she said, still giggling.

He seemed to smile too, then she was aware only of a fast blur out of the corner of her eye before she lost consciousness.

When she came to, colours pulsated in her eyes, swimming in and out of focus, the side of her face ached and as her vision cleared she realised that somehow she was staring at the carpet from just above it, her limbs and body immobile although she struggled to rise. She lifted her head and saw him standing next to the fire, still smiling. She craned her head round, unable to get up, taking in her naked shoulder, then back round, seeing that not only was she naked but she was lying face down on the large coffee table, bound by what looked like strips of her own clothes, tying her by all her limbs to the table legs. Again she tried to struggle to move her hands and feet but her own bodyweight pressing down on the table defeated her.

'Now,' he said, 'we can talk. And don't think we're going to be disturbed because your gutless boyfriend's in a similar state to you upstairs. Did you not think I'd notice the extra cup?'

He walked towards her, picked up a cushion from the chair then disappeared from her view. She felt a hand slip between her legs and lift her by the stomach, and then a cushion slipped under her, which she collapsed on to.

He came into her vision again. 'Now, I want you to tell me everything.'

'Fuck off,' she said, dribbling on her words, feeling tears not far away.

'I know a lot, but not everything. You're going to tell me.' He grabbed her hair at the crown and lifted her head. 'Look. At the fire.'

At first she could not see what he meant and then she caught sight of the poker plunged into it. He picked what was left of her jumper from the floor and wrapped it round his right hand, then he pulled the poker from the fire, brandishing it briefly, smoke curling from the glowing red and white point. 'You're still an attractive woman, you know,' she heard as he disappeared behind her again. She felt panic rush through her and then his voice, softly saying, 'Just keep absolutely still or you'll be scarred for life,' then a powerful heat on the outside of her vagina. 'Don't even tremble,' he said, followed by a singeing crackle which, it took her a moment to realise, must be from her pubic hair.

Now she began, in spite of herself, to tremble and chitter.

But the heat had gone, so he had obviously moved the poker

away. 'I don't intend to ask supplementaries. The first wrong answer or hesitation and you get the Edward the Second treatment, the white-hot suppository, but I'll start at the larger opening.' She nodded vigorously. 'What happened with my mother?'

'Your da—' Her jaw was trembling and her teeth clashing. 'She wouldn't divorce him. Catholic. And he wanted to marry me. I didn't want that but he did. She fell under a trolley bus.'

'Convenient.'

She felt the heat on her again. 'I don't know for certain, honest to God I don't. She was drunk and maybe there was a little push as well.'

He thought about it, knowing that it was not beyond his father to organise. 'Why didn't you want to marry him?'

'I had been married. I didn't want to do it again. Please,' she was snivelling, 'let me go.'

'This poker's cooling down, I may have to heat it again.'

'I'll do anything. Please, just let me go.'

'So he made a will leaving everything to you. Almost.'

She nodded hard. 'But I made one for him too.'

'Whose idea?'

'I can't remember' – the heat again – 'honestly,' she screamed as if it had been torn from her. 'Because he was going to war, that was why.'

She was trying to think clearly, to anticipate the questions, where they were leading and how much he knew. Did he know about Razzle's brothers, their part? Did he know that she had told them how Peter had confessed to her that he killed her husband to have her, that she could not live with the memory? How could he? How Billy, in the same regiment, had shot Peter in the back in the middle of action? No. But if he asked about it she knew that she would tell the truth, or shape it in a way to suit her survival, whatever the consequences.

She heard him chuckle. 'So,' he said, 'is it all over between us? The bad blood?'

'Of course,' she heard herself say, too quickly. She gritted her teeth. She would get him for this, make sure that he died slowly and painfully.

'Just keep out of my business.'

'I will. Definitely. You can depend on it.'

She heard that chuckle again. He enjoyed violence, she knew, was renewed by it. Then the door slammed and she struggled to look round, trying to ensure that he was gone and that it was not someone else coming in.

'John?' she said. No answer.

It took her more than an hour to get free and by then her arms and wrists were bruised and cut. She felt disgraced, violated, ashamed. She began to cry. Her dressing-gown was in the kitchen and she ran for it and wrapped it round her. She was going to have a long bath and think about how she was going to get back at him. Only when she was upstairs and running the bath did she remember about Webb, just as she heard the low calling of her name from the bedroom.

He was trussed up on the bed in pieces of torn sheet, the mattress and pillows had been ripped open and spilled feathers and down, and Webb lay among it, like a trussed animal in a nest, with a pair of her old knickers jammed tight over his head.

'Yes,' she said, 'of course,' and went down to the kitchen for a sharp knife.

When she had cut him free he dressed quickly, barely looking at her, not even going into the bathroom to wipe away the crusted blood from his nose, mouth and left eye. She followed him down the stairs as he went, her arms folded around her. 'I'll need to take your car,' he said. 'I came by taxi last night. I'll leave it at the office.'

'The keys are on the mantelpiece.'

He did not attempt to kiss her as he left, or say anything, or even look back. She watched his slumped shape disappear down the garden path and she knew that all of it was over. There, in the doorway, slumped against the side, dazed into docility and hopelessness, she waited, for some reason, for the car to leave before going back in. Oddly, she felt a rising sense of relief.

She heard the car door slam, a few seconds later the engine cough and turn over, then she became aware, rather than heard, that the dull grey morning had gone bright, then red and oily black. The roar hit her, she ducked too late to have any defence, as shards of metal and glass exploded and tore through the foliage in the garden. The after-shock hit her and when she finally looked up she felt a burning in her left hand and right leg, looked down at both of them dripping blood, then up, at the pieces of car and flesh and sinew dropping to earth through the dense black smoke.

And she just knew, when she saw what looked like a large raw, round, torn hunk of flesh on her lawn, that it was Webb's head.

She started screaming and crying and rocking in a ball on the front step because she knew that it should have been her.

Everyone wanted to have fun and a little adventure. That was the business principle. Whether what you did was legal or not depended on the mores of the time, but there was always a demand to be satisfied, a perversion it might seem to some, but businessmen like him did not make moral judgments. Sex, drink or something a little heavier, it was no matter. He could supply it.

At first Johnnie felt pleased that this was a small city, that you could know everyone who counted and you could find out a route to anyone with just a few phone calls or a little bit of pressure. But after a few years he saw the limitations, that the corollary was that anyone could find out about you in the same way and get to you, and it began to pall. It was also too small a market for him. A million people was not enough, neither was the larger one, London. He saw the future and it featured sea and travel, burgeoning foreign territories, all with the same cravings, emerging markets – France, Germany, the United States, even Japan – and how important it was to think internationally. So he began to develop a strategy. He withdrew from the front line and he became a sponsor, insulated from the action by intermediaries and fear, funding and bankrolling projects, taking his percentage. He set up nominees and nominee companies, he controlled pubs and illegal gambling, moneylending and prostitution, although he had to give credit to Ownie who had proved as adept at adapting the machinery of commerce – the bypasses and the trip switches, the conduits and the circuits – as he had with cogs, wheels, rotors and, of course, high explosive.

Legitimately, well almost so, he had inherited the Webb and Co building contracts, picking up and greasing the same levers of control for just a little bit more money to each of them. The company, which he had re-named Adams and Eve (he liked the whimsy of it, and that all the principals had got screwed), was now one of the largest contractors in Glasgow with an annual turnover of more than five million pounds, although none of the profits, or even any of the equity holding, could be traced back to him. It was not necessary to have a legal title to something when it belonged to you purely by might. Anyone who worked for him, who took and dared to try to double it elsewhere by selling him out, would not have lived long enough to make the bank or to get the first drink to their lips.

'He was the first of the sophisticated villains,' said Ricketts, recapping to McQuade his reading of the early history. He had gone in to work with a large sports bag and loaded it up with dozens of antique faded files and the newer blue ones, shuttling between the desk and the car three times to get them all out. It was against regulations. But then regulations were against him, it was clear, and possession might give him some kind of leverage.

He had already had one interview with the DCS, which had not gone well. In response to the first questions about the incidents on the night when Fat Boy was killed, and what happened between him and Blantyre, he had simply told the truth. At the beginning the DCS was sceptical, pointing out that a statement from Blantyre clearly contradicted what he said, that she had told him the surveillance had been cancelled.

'I see, sir. You say statement. That seems to indicate to me that this could be a disciplinary matter' – the DCS said nothing and blew slightly between his arched fingers – 'in which case I'm entitled to representation' – again the DCS remained silent – 'which I'm now formally requesting.' The meeting was postponed, to be reconvened officially seventy-two hours later, and for that period, although he was not formally suspended, he was asked not to come in. Which gave him almost no time at all to find out what was going on.

McQuade was interviewed by two senior Strathclyde detectives in the presence of the company solicitor. He was friendly, but his stock response to questions about the sources of his story was repeatedly 'as a result of information received from a contact', always declining to reveal the identity of his sources, which pissed off the police while leaving them helpless, short of charging him. He was half expecting them to turn up on his doorstep with a search warrant so he had, firstly, got rid of all the drugs – regrettably not by ingestion – and then loaded his car with the computer, the laser printer, scanner, phone-fax, reams of paper, some personal files and a few items of clothing. And some purely medicinal drugs because – although when he had told Ricketts that he had cleared the flat of illegal pharmaceuticals and this was true – what he neglected to say was that he had held back a few amphetamines to bring with him in the travelling bag, to get him through the nights in front of the screen.

What the two of them were endeavouring to do, in a mere three or four days, was to reconstitute the past of Johnnie Stark, to turn up – and here there was hope more than real conviction – a crucial key which would open up what was happening now. There would be, McQuade was sure, something in the files that would be a kind of skeleton key that would ensure their freedom. What he was afraid of was that he would not recognise it when he found it.

McQuade blagged a few days off from the newspaper, researching the next piece, he said. He was ahead of the pack on the story (the newsdesk did not realise how integral to it he had become) so he had no problem arguing for the time away. From the office he phoned up the manager of the Turnberry Hotel and convinced him that he was doing a major feature on the place – 'the world's favourite golfing hotel', he crawled – and needed a long weekend there to soak up the ambience.

'Brilliant,' he said, more about his deception than in thanks, adding, 'of course, the photographer will be with me . . . No, no, a suite with two single beds will be fine. Honestly! Yes, I'm looking forward to it too. Must look out my clubs.'

The suite faced out on to the raging sea, the dark hump of Ailsa Craig to the south, and the golf links all around. None of the staff even looked sideways at them as they channelled the gear up in the lift. The shockability factor in top-class hotels, Ricketts noted, is not high. The porters were then brushed off with folding matter and the Do Not Disturb sign hung out on the external door knob. McQuade plugged in the fax and phoned up Adrienne in the library – whom he had once fallen into bed with at the end of a leaving do and it had evidently gone well enough that she still spoke to him, albeit amusedly – and asked her to help. He had already brought the newspaper's Stark cuttings file with him but the library was largely automated, with the usual loss of staff, and for the last four or five years all the information was stored somewhere in the discs, tapes, chips or electronic bowels of some remote mainframe.

'Fax me any reference at all – you'll have to go through the switchboard here – ask for the Open Suite, it's extension 240, and then you can stuff it down the line. Also, I'll probably be coming on to you about particular dates or incidents or people, I'll need a bit of research on that . . . Yes, of course, Sandy's approved all this – look, I'll buy you a meal afterwards . . . All right, this is on condition I don't buy you one! I'll make a donation to your favourite charity, Blind Dogs for Librarians or – no, I'm not calling you a dog. I'm just agreeing that after that night you thought you needed one. Love you too.' He hung up. 'Bitch.'

Ricketts dragged a large table from the bay window – 'the view's too distracting' – and set it against a wall so that the outlook was of swirling Sanderson. He put the various pieces of equipment on it and was now hovering. 'You'll have to set it all up,' he said. 'I don't know what goes where.'

McQuade tipped the contents of his bag on to one of the two beds, doubles in themselves, and rummaged around until he came out with a manila foolscap envelope. He opened it and guided two yellow pills into his hand – Ricketts made a show of putting his hands over his eyes – then popped them in his mouth, going into the bathroom to flush them down, head under the central tap.

'Right,' he said coming out, rubbing his hands, 'let's go to it,' and he began plugging in the cables of the machinery. 'We'll do a chronology of events, flow charts, biogs of all the main characters, family trees, notes, gossip, informed speculation, we'll cross-reference it all, press a button and "hey presto", that'll be it – a malfunction.' He looked up at Ricketts. 'Have you any better ideas?'

Johnnie had decided to remain in his father's house, the council house. Ostentation was bad for business and, anyway, questions would only be asked from the wrong areas about where the money came from if he bought somewhere else. The only business that he had which showed anywhere, the legitimate one filed by his accountant on his tax return, was the Rose. He was taking a small salary from that and Ownie was also on the books as deputy manager. Everything else, all the legal profits as well as any others which could be disguised, were ploughed back into the place and other ventures and endeavours.

By the end of the 1950s the place had been extended to twice its size by building behind and to the side – although this required substantial baksheesh spread among the politicians – by knocking down adjoining tenements and developing the sites. It helped, of course, to have a building company on tap.

It had seemed natural, too, given the rate of slum clearance and redevelopment, to have a demolition company. There was money in pulling down and removing the debris of the sandstone tenements which had been built to house the huge influx of new citizens in the middle and towards the end of the last century, Irish from the famines, Highlanders from the benighted straths and glens.

There was money in land reclamation and in-fill sites and there was also money in haulage. This part of the business, run by a cousin of Gerry Queen's, had grown from just the one lorry after the war to an operation employing nearly 300 people. That first lorry had gone into Germany in 1947 carrying humanitarian aid, generously contributed by the city council and the people of Glasgow, collected and stored in the Rose and then shipped out with flags, cheers and good wishes. Johnnie went with it, waving diffidently from the passenger seat as they left. This was the first time his picture made any newspaper. When the two men came back the paper, the *Glasgow Herald*, was on his desk in the Rose. The picture caught a serious young man framed by the window of the cab. 'Look at this,' said Ownie, 'it says how you're a war hero and how we should be magnanimous to our defeated enemies, and what better example?' pointing at Johnnie.

'It must be true then, if it's there in black and white.'

The lorry had come back with nothing except the humble thanks of Germany, and three soil-stained boxes recovered from a grave in a packed and overgrown cemetery south of the Rhine.

'I suppose I should have realised before, that ninety-five per cent of police information is made up of innuendo, gossip, paid-for tips of doubtful provenance, veiled suspicion and downright lies.' McQuade was staring at the screen. 'And the rest is the bits you make up.'

'Get on with it, McQuade.' Ricketts was lying on a bed, head propped up by several pillows, his shoes off, a cup of coffee balanced on his chest, a file open in his hands. 'Just log it.'

They had been at it for more than eight hours and although the speed was still residually working in his bloodstream McQuade's eyes were sore and bleary. 'What about you taking a turn?'

'Sorry, I know how these files work, what the codes mean, what's important and what to sift out. It's the computers and the typing I'm iffy on.'

'Codes, bollocks.' He got up. 'I'm having more coffee and a wash.' He walked across to the pot with his cup and refilled it. 'I suppose I'm breaking the law by doing this. It'll be reset or a breach of the Official Secrets Act or something. Do you think they'll notice they've gone?'

'Not yet.'

McQuade sat down on his bed. 'I've had an idea. What if I run a story in the paper that an anonymous thief has claimed to have broken into Strathclyde headquarters through an open window and got away with a load of files? That would cover it up. Remember Fettesgate when a burglar broke into Lothians and Borders headquarters and then went to the press with some of the embarrassing material?'

'I think we'll just keep that one in reserve for the time being.'

'Suit yourself.'

Ricketts looked around the suite, the curtains now closed and the soft, subdued lighting casting a warm and discreet glow over the room. 'I have to hand it to you, McQuade, you do these things in style.'

'Shall I order us something from room service?'

'As long as you ply the tip this time.'

McQuade sipped from his cold coffee. 'You know, after all this I'm beginning to think I know Stark personally. But there's just so much about him and so little substantiated it's difficult to know what to filter out and what to believe. That first reference to him, the chibbing when he's just a wee tot in the Gorbals. I mean, did that really happen? It seems a bit far-fetched.'

'I'm convinced by that. The intelligence was pretty good. It was the talk of the steamie. People lived in the streets then, didn't they?

They weren't tucked up behind curtains watching the telly and everyone knew everyone else's business, even if they didn't tell the polis everything. There's a lot more corroboration here than for some of the earlier local tales, like the Commandments.'

McQuade punched in for room service. 'Could we maybe have a couple of steak sandwiches?' – he looked over at Ricketts, who nodded – 'a bit of salad and a bottle of white wine. Anything dry'll do. Great!' He put his hands behind his head and stretched out. 'So, his mother's a soak, his da runs off with someone else's wife, someone who comes to a pretty unlikely end, and then the mother walks under a tramcar or a trolley bus.' He shook his head. 'Does that last one ring true? Did these things go fast enough to hit anyone? I don't know, I wasn't alive then. What was the annual fatality rate from public transport in Glasgow? Probably about the same as lightning striking, or good fortune.'

Ricketts took it up: 'Meanwhile the boy has been dodging the truant troops, avoiding school, running lines for a bookie who ends up getting topped in a back close. Did he kill him? If so, why? For the contents of his book? I don't think so. Unless he sold it on to someone else. And meanwhile his father sets up with the fancy piece, whose husband has conveniently drowned, then he gets shot in the back in what looks like – what's that macho Gulf War term – a blue on blue? Poor old Sonny Jim gets the short end of the inheritance and stepmummy gets the pot.'

'It's true, not many get out alive in this plot. It's *Hamlet* with glottal stops. And then a car bomb goes off outside new mummy's door, turning her latest beau into vermicelli.'

'We know, but can't prove, that friend Owens, trained at great expense by the Royal Engineers, has laid the charges aimed at the wicked witch of the West End, but collateral damage is inflicted on her bidie-in.'

'Stepmother may have been left the pot but young John grabs it when everything blows up in her face. Racy dialogue, don't you think? I should have worked for the *Sun*.' McQuade swung off the bed. 'It's a pisser, this flow chart I've organised on the Mac continually ends in small exploding stars, the characters disappearing into the pixels.'

Ricketts was staring into space. 'And he has the dance hall. That's the one constant. He's left that when his old man gets shot, when he's in approved school. Then he enlists, under age . . . what's that all about? A thirst for heroism? Hardly.'

McQuade sat on the edge of the bed, looking out at the curtains where the ocean tossed beyond. 'Escaping from something, perhaps?'

'Honing their skills, him and Owens, maybe?'

'Something happened, I'm sure of that, and then he signed up. I'm sure if we had all the police records for all the divisions for the few days or weeks beforehand we could work it out. Sure of it. Whatever happened, and it must have been pretty serious, they had to make a quick exit. And not because they were on the run, I don't think so. They enlist. He and Owens must have got hold of real papers, or pretty convincing forgeries, must have done. Anything in the files about that?' Ricketts shook his head. 'So where did the money come from to pay for it all? We're not talking about the kind of dross that comes from screwing a sweetie shop here.' He looked across at Ricketts. 'Then he comes back as a war hero. It doesn't compute, as us Trekkies say.' Staring at the endless curl of faxes on the floor. 'Let's check the hard copy.'

He only realised when he was much older that he had been born out of his time. The music of his youth had passed him by, big bands, crooners and torch singers, none of it stuck. He did not hum melodies, he did not associate particular times with particular tunes, he had no musical accompaniment to his past, only silence. Then rock and roll arrived and he knew he had been born too soon. It wasn't just the music and the abandonment, it was the courage of it, it was the complete antithesis of the cordial, arranged and scripted stuff which limped through the Rose, it reeked of bodily odours and hope and conflict and, of course, sex.

He was pushing thirty when he heard 'Rip It Up' by Little Richard and it stunned him, stopped him dead, literally, in the street when he heard it come scrapping and bleeding out from a record store in Buchanan Street. A great truth revealed in the most pernicious of circumstances. Driving rain, a love affair which had just died, the rumour of a vendetta pursuing him, which seemed to be some family connection to Hazel and which he did not take too seriously, and then the song. It stopped him in mid-step; he stood there until the end of it, unwilling to move in case something irreplaceable shattered, and then, completely immersed, like a baptism, he walked into the shop utterly changed. At least to the extent that he now liked music. What it was, he said later, was discovering his ears for the first time.

He bought a box of the 78s (the other side was 'Ready Teddy') and called a taxi and went straight back to the Rose. He had time to think about it on the journey, but not time enough to change his mind. Instinctively he knew that the music at the Rose was of a dying generation and that this was the authentic post-war music, the first music of the new generation. He had never been more sure about anything. The Rose had to change. The problem was that he knew nothing about the music, did not know how to change. When he got out of the taxi, clutching the brown box full of records, looking up at the neon sign with the name of the dance hall and the posters for Derek Brown and his Band of Renown, he realised that did not know where to go from here.

McQuade started at the bottom of the snaking fax and tried to read the reproductions of the faded cuttings. There was a news story about Stark taking some lorryload of food to Germany. Why? Wasn't there rationing in Britain still? The next cutting, or series of cuttings, was about trouble at the Rose. He was thankful now that he had sent Adrienne a list of core names and places to hit and cross-reference because Stark's name did not feature in any of them. The cuttings were about rock and roll riots at the Rose – it sounded like a song title – and the objections of the bailies and the licensing committees to renewals of drinks licences, none of which ever seemed to stick. Surprise, McQuade thought.

'Shrewd bastard,' he said to Ricketts, who was licking the last of a sandwich off his fingers. 'He changes the place around, kicks out the old farts with war wounds and pensions, starts bringing in rock bands, a new young clientele. Money—'

'And drugs.'

McQuade kept unravelling the cuttings fax. 'And then this' – he brandished the roll to Ricketts – 'he gets six months for supplying cannabis through the place. That seems pretty remiss of him. Unlikely, I'd say, in an otherwise careful chap.'

At first he tried out rock bands on a Monday night when the place was at its quietest. He had the city centre fly-posted and he hired local kids to scoot round the pubs handing out flyers and complimentary tickets. The Rose became Glasgow's first rock venue. He developed it gradually, balancing between the older audiences who came for the big bands and whose cash was necessary to keep the place afloat, and the younger, busier audiences with less money who came for the groups. But gradually rock took over and the 'Over 21 Nights' began to be slotted in mid-week as the popularity of pop music grew.

He hooked up with a London promoter, Terry Solomon, who supplied most of the acts and he also booked other venues in Scotland, usually subcontracting the promotion, so that he was able to shave the prices and have a hook in other cities in the country. A succession of bands on the cusp of success trooped through the Rose – the Beatles, the Yardbirds, the Pacemakers, the Rolling Stones and too many less successful to recall – as well as faded Americans, like Jerry Lee Lewis and later Little Richard, the man who had started it all off for him. He even asked for a signed photograph.

Then the local bands began to come through the place, usually in a cacophony of raucous music and similar behaviour, like Alex Harvey's band, his brother Les's Kinning Park Ramblers, the Poets, the Gaylords and later the Beatstalkers and Pathfinders. There was a brief summer of traditional jazz but the music melted back to its middle-class ghetto somewhere on the South Side and Johnnie could not even bear to be in the same building as it in these months.

What the new music brought with it was young girls, most of them still at school, but enough older ones to make it satisfying to be around, even if he was a decade or more senior. His sex life became vigorous and varied, confusing and often messy. And then there were the drugs. He tried dope, but he didn't smoke and the feeling of dippy helplessness wasn't for him. Seeing the effects of heroin made him contemptuous of the users but pills, uppers and downers, helped him get through. He could also see the business angle in the recreational attachment between the musicians, the music, the fans and the drugs. It was a burgeoning, inter-related and inter-dependent new market.

He brought the stuff up from London secreted in the lorries but the market was unsteady and the prices fluctuated wildly, which offended his business sensibilities. It was important to control his own market. There was an obvious source, when he thought about it, and an equally obvious method of delivery.

From the office he could barely hear the music, just the pulse in the floor from the bass notes. The TV was on silently in the corner, the *Lucy Show* it looked like; he was counting the takings and separating the notes into their own piles with Ownie when the door, which was locked, started rattling. They looked at each other. No one would have been able to get there by dodging the bouncers, the stairway was protected.

'Yeah?' he called.

'It's the polis, open up, Stark.'

'Minute,' he said, ignoring the renewed rattling, while he and Ownie scooped up the cash and bundled it into the safe, then spun the dial. He opened the top drawer of his desk slightly, just so he could see the handle of the gas gun and finally he sauntered across the floor and unlocked the door.

It flew open. He recognised a local detective inspector, Jim Shields, and another man, a sergeant, he thought, whose name he could not place. 'Gentlemen,' he said, grimacing on the word.

'Yir pal can fuck off,' Shields said, nodding at Ownie. 'It's the organ grinder we're efter, no' the monkey.'

Stark felt himself redden. He held out both arms at his sides in case Ownie went for him. 'I don't like your attitude,' he said slowly.

'No?' Shields pushed him in the chest. Stark could smell drink on him. The detective, in his late forties and fat with greasy thinning hair, was sneering at him.

'Trying to provoke me?'

'D'you want to come down the station and answer questions or dae it here?'

'Here, naturally. Questions about what?'

'Get yir man out, okay?'

Johnnie looked at Ownie and nodded. He left, glowering at the police as he went.

'So, questions then.' Johnnie walked back to his desk, sat down behind it and casually shut the top drawer. Shields walked over and sat on the edge of it, his comrade leaning against the door to prevent anyone else coming in.

'You were warned, Stark.'

'I was? About what?' He knew what was coming.

'You were told that the levels of contribution were going up. It's inflation.'

'My arse. Greed, you mean.'

'We know exactly what's going on here, how much you're taking and what you're not declaring.'

'Sorry, I thought you were the polis, not the Inland Revenue.'

'You're taking the piss.'

You're so perceptive, Inspector, I can see how you got on so well in detection.'

'We could have you shut down—'

'Aye? That would be really bright, then you'd get nothin'. And then you'd really be in the shite with your bosses.'

Shields leaned forward towards him. Stark lazily brushed at the air between them as if dispersing unpleasant fumes. 'We know exactly what you're doing here.'

'I've said it before but I'll say it again. Jings and crivvens, it's a fuckin' dance hall. You're right, what deadly perception.'

Shields swung at him with his right hand but Johnnie caught his forearm in his left and squeezed his fingers hard into the flesh. He said quietly, 'But a pity about the lack of control.' Then he released the detective's arm.

The other man rubbed at his jacket on the spot where the bruising was beginning. 'You've had a good run—'

'I'm a good businessman,' he cut in.

'Naw. You're just another fucking crook on the make.'

Stark shook his head. 'Obviously the irony of this situation has escaped you, Detective Inspector. And your geography too, about just where exactly the fucking crook on the make is located, is pretty far out. About three feet to be exact.'

Shields eased up from the desk. 'No second thoughts?'

'I don't think so.'

'This is going to be very inconvenient for all of us.' He tapped his jacket pocket. 'I have a search warrant.' Stark said nothing. 'It wouldn't surprise me to find – in fact, I'm sure I'll find, a quantity of drugs on your premises. Enough, in fact, to lay a charge of intent to supply. An old policeman's nose never lets him down.'

Even then Stark could probably have got out of it, if he had shown penitence and paid up, but he was still seething. Instead he said: 'It's probably to do with your neb being too near your guvnor's arse.'

Shields sighed exaggeratedly. 'Sergeant!' Stark caught sight of something being thrown towards him and instinctively he put up his hands to grab it and save his face. 'Excellent,' he heard Shields say. And when he looked at what had been thrown he saw that it was a block of cannabis, about the size of a paperback book, wrapped in cellophane and now with, he appreciated, his fingerprints all over it. Both policemen were smiling.

'He pleaded guilty,' McQuade said. 'Strange.'

They had slept for four hours, had a breakfast sent up and now Ricketts was yawning and rubbing his eyes, holding an open folder. 'That seems to be the only conviction. There's nothing else recorded here. He obviously made sure he wouldn't be caught in possession again. Seems to have done the porridge without a problem, got time off for good behaviour. There's an informer's report here from inside the Bar-L says he ran the drugs operation in his brief stay, that others deferred to him. Then out he comes again having paid his debt to society.'

McQuade poured another cup of coffee and began filing through the windows on screen. 'What was the name of the cop?' he said.

'Shields.'

'Know what became of him?'

'Nope.'

McQuade reached for the phone. 'I'll get Adrienne to run a check on him, see if anything shows in our library or on the database.' When he had done that he finished his coffee and went back to the screen, punching back and forth looking for connections, anything that he had missed.

'You know that the manager's invited us for dinner tonight?' Ricketts said.

'We'll have to go, I suppose. But I hope he doesn't start asking you about composition, or the finer points of a Nikon F against a Canon, or the prismatic properties of good lenses.'

'I know a bit about photography,' Ricketts replied. 'I've taken the odd excellent snap, usually a prostrate body and a few chalk marks and quite a lot of fill-in flash.'

'They must love you in Boots. Well, I know they love you in anything – except your top brass of course.'

A couple of minutes later the phone rang four times, then the fax burped and cut in and shiny paper began to inch slowly from its mouth. Ricketts wandered over, craned his neck to watch it dribble out and when the machine had signalled the end by bleeping again he tore off about three feet of paper of what was a series of photocopies. 'My, my,' he said. 'Shields. A year or so later, 1963, here he is spread all over the *Screws*—'

'The year sex was invented, good timing.'

'—featuring in a sex orgy with a couple of pros, complete with pictures.' He turned the page round in his hand. 'Low marks for composition but top for candour.' Ricketts giggled. 'Headline is "Cop Your Whack" – one of the girls claimed he liked a bit of slap with his tickle. Naturally, he claims it was a set-up. Surreptitiously filled him with drugs and cheap champagne, so he says, the usual story.'

'It can happen,' McQuade was stretching on his seat.

'Then there's a couple of paragraphs in one of the more serious sheets alleging he's being investigated for corruption, something to do with unexplained amounts of money sloshing about in his account and an anonymous telephone call. Then, a few months later, there's a piece about him killing himself. "Top detective at the centre of corruption probe tops himself," you know the kind of thing.'

'Amazingly neat,' McQuade said. He turned to the computer. 'I suppose I can now wipe him from the floppy disc of history.'

'It's intriguing you should say that because what happened when Stark got out is that he seems to have hung about for a bit then disappeared for about five years.' Ricketts was sifting through loose papers in the file. 'There's a record of a passport application and

319

some speculation that he went to the States. But nothing, until he arrives back with wife and child.'

'Nothing at all? Don't you have connections with Interpol or the FBI or something?'

'A blank,' Ricketts said, throwing down the file on the bed and walking towards the window. He took a deep breath. 'It smells.'

Burns slipped down his swimming trunks and towelled himself off. It took little effort to dry his hair, it was so short. He dressed in front of a mirror, checking out his body for any signs of thickening. It was still in excellent shape, tanned to his trunks' line from top and bottom, apart from the white and pink scars from the bullet wound, and the later and newer ones of shrapnel. He swam at least a mile every day, tried to use the gym at least three times a week, other than the four hours he spent in the *dojo* with the master, forced himself to go running once during the week and once on Sunday, the Sabbath outing always being more than ten miles. Others might have called him obsessive, had there been others, but to him it seemed simply part of the business of staying alive.

The pool was in the basement complex of the renovated warehouse block in which he lived, overlooking the city and the Firhill Basin. When he had finished dressing he walked up the stairs carrying his training bag and retrieved his mail from the brass letter box in the nest inside the glass security door. The day looked raw outside. He flicked through the letters, pulled out the padded envelope he was expecting, and slipped it into the deep inside pocket of his thigh-length leather jacket, then he walked out into the day.

Inside the Mercedes he tore open the envelope, shook out a key with a blue numbered tag which he put into a trouser pocket of his jeans, throwing the envelope on to the back seat next to his bag. Then he pulled out his own car keys and started the engine. He drove down to the Round Toll and on through Cowcaddens, skirting the bus station, to Queen Street station. He found a parking meter in the warren of streets around the university, stuffed it with twenty pences, locked the car and broke into a jog as the rain started. He made for the left luggage office, dug in his pocket for the key, checked the number, located the box and opened it. Inside was a green Marks and Spencer carrier bag wrapped around a large box of chocolates.

He tucked it under his arm and then walked out into the concourse again and then through and down into George Square.

When he reached the car park in Mitchell Street he hit the button for the lift and when it arrived empty he stepped in, pressed the button for the top floor and pulled out the box from the bag, opening the lid and slipping out the sheet of paper under the drawings of the contents. The writing on the paper said: 3/L295DPG. He put the lid back down on the box and pushed it back into the carrier, waited until the lift stopped at the top floor, then pressed '3'.

It only took him a couple of minutes to locate the car after he had torn the paper into scraps and thrown it like confetti out off the balcony where the pieces caught on the eddying winds and scattered.

When he got to it he took out his skin-tight leather gloves and put them on. The door of the car, a beige Peugeot 306, was open. He climbed in, put his package on the passenger seat, opened the glove compartment and scrabbled for the keys. When the car was started he looked around him, checked the mirrors and then pulled over the bag, taking out the box and laying it in his lap. He opened it again, crumpled the glossy menu for the chocolates and saw the other sheet of paper and the name and address. He memorised that and then again crumpled the paper. When he delved further in he was a little surprised to see that the gun underneath was only a .22. He shrugged, put the car into gear and moved off down the incline.

Sammy McSween finished his drink, put down the pint glass, then pulled on the dog's lead. It was a mongrel, mostly a collie, with two chewed ears and an irascible temperament. He pulled it after him and walked out into the street. The rain had stopped, the patches of grass strands in the mud outside hung bedraggled, the puddles had spread back from the drains and into what looked like a large bowl of water in front of him. He began to curse and move round it. It reminded him of a year before, when the torrential rains poured down from the hills and built up against the new road, causing a flood which spread back and up so that in parts of Ferguslie Park the water was over seven feet deep, higher than the cars, almost up to the ceilings in the ground-floor flats.

He stopped on the corner, tugging back the dog, so that he could light a cigarette, throwing away the used match into the huge puddle. He was cold, his feet felt wet and he hoped that Margaret had the dinner on, for her sake.

The dog padded after him, jerked along on the rope lead, as he moved with his head down, swaying slightly, along the pavement. It took him only a couple of minutes to reach his gate, or the space where a gate had been. A broken pram and a torn old mattress lay in the mud of the front garden.

'Is that Sammy, Sammy McSween?'

He looked behind him. A man was standing outside a car, engine running with its passenger door open, someone else in the driving seat. The guy was big, upright, looked a bit like a polis, Sammy decided, particularly with that other gent in the front. 'Eh?' he said, spitting out the end of his cigarette. 'Who're you, like?'

'I'm looking for a deal.'

'Oh aye? Deal? About what? I don't know what you mean.'

'Sure you do. Fancy a chocolate, Sammy? Hard or soft centre?'

'Whit?' The guy was smiling, opening a big box of Black Magic. What the fuck was this all about? Then he saw the gun.

Burns had been taught to aim for the trunk, even if there was a chance that the subject was wearing a flak jacket, which seemed highly unlikely in this case, and so it proved when the small slug slapped into Sammy's chest, knocking him back, and then the second put him over. Called a double tap in the trade. Burns walked up to him where he lay spread on the concrete path, right leg feebly kicking, and although it looked completely unnecessary from above, slapped another double tap into his napper.

'Definitely soft centre,' he said, then carefully, so he avoided getting any mud or the seeping blood and shredded cerebellum on his polished shoes, he walked back to the car and slid into the passenger seat. 'Hit it, Paton,' he ordered.

He walked up the long, round, twisting tunnel like the neck of some huge bird and felt spat out in the arrivals lounge. The sun was streaming in through the high windows, it was humid and he was tired and stressed. He had never had any reason to fly before and an eight-hour trip was rather a prolonged and unpleasant baptism. He had not liked it, not the food, the buffeting, the feeling of having his life in someone else's hands – he had seen what pilots got up to off duty in the Rose and his faith in their defeat of gravity was for ever compromised by their total lack of aerodynamics – and the feeling it gave him of sheer helplessness. He could not stop remembering that between his feet and six miles of free-fall to solid earth or the Atlantic was a ridiculously thin metal membrane. He was only grateful that Ownie wasn't here to work out how little it would take, probably only a few ounces of explosive or the sharp beak of a high-flying bird, to send him spiralling down to oblivion.

The life-jacket routine only made it worse. His mind was screaming out the question, 'How many jet airliners have ever crash-landed in the sea and the passengers got out?' but fortunately his mouth refused to open, realising that the answer was one his ears did not want to hear. Forget the return half of the ticket, he told himself, he was sailing back home and keeping the dinghies nearby.

In the terminal he spotted the chauffeur first, in black glasses and skipped cap, then the sign with his name on it and when he moved towards it, smiling tentatively, his eyes flicked past and there he was. 'Angelo,' he said, seeing the heavier, greyer version of the man he knew, and then holding out his arms to him and walking into the other man's.

'My friend,' he said gravely, 'it was my intention to come here to dedicate my life to you because you saved mine' – a smile broke through – 'to serve you faithfully like a slave. But unfortunately I had to make certain prior promises and also a few accommodations to several spiritual parties on the way here, owing to the horror and the turmoil of the trip, but nevertheless I can probably still buy you a good meal.'

'That'll be fine,' Angelo said, releasing him. Then: 'You've changed.'

'That's true,' he said. 'Last time you saw me I was unconscious and in a coma. A change for the better, at least as far as I'm concerned.'

Angelo put his arm round him and led him off. 'I definitely preferred you when you didn't answer back.' He stopped and looked at him, allowing the driver to walk on. 'I'm glad we kept in touch.' They had reached the revolving door. 'I heard you did some time.'

'I didn't do it. Time I did, sure' – he pushed through the door after Guiliano, the heat hitting him like a slap – 'but I didn't do it, at least not what they got me for.'

In the car, a stretch number which seemed to Stark as long as the aircraft he had just left, Guiliano asked him what had happened. 'The police, they planted a couple of keys on me because I wasn't prepared to play, to thicken their slice. I mean, as if I'd have a wedge of cannabis lying around my office, rather than working for me. Anyway, I'd never mix my interests, compromise one with the other. There were no drugs in the place, at least none that I brought in. But the sheriff believed them and that was it. The chokey.' Ahead he could see, through the tinted glass, the skyscrapers of the city, a gradation of colours down them. 'It was all right. But I made two vows, which I have kept. The first was to be more accommodating – to pay up, within reason, y'know, there's always enough for everyone. The second was to get even.'

'Mad and even. Sound business practices. And how did you do it, get even?'

'It was pretty easy.' He stretched out and began to yawn. 'His colleagues didn't much like him anyway. I got hold of his deposit account number, paid in rather a large lump of money, then I had a flat rented in his name through a friend and a couple of tarts installed. This all happened over a couple of months or so. He was divorced, lived alone and was a bit of a boozer. His name was Shields. He had a regular session after hours most Wednesdays in a pub in the Calton I knew. Well, I know them all. He always got legless and took a taxi home. So this night I arranged the taxi for him, also a nightcap, one for the road, which was a bit more powerful than he expected. He went blissfully to sleep in the back of the cab. The rest was simple. Drove him back to the tarts' flat, shipped him in and undressed him, slung him into bed with them, had a few shots of him taken face down and side-on on top of a naked whore, the other one doing unspeakable things from behind to him – you know the score. When he woke up he didn't know where he was—'

'Heaven.'

'The girls said something like, "Come off it, darling, you were all over us last night." I suppose I expected him to storm out of there, the photographer and reporter were staked out in the car waiting, but instead he decides to give the pair of them a right good seeing to before he does. So it worked out fine. He was guilty, by one remove. Pictures inside, outside, sworn statements by the girls to the paper, not just with intimate descriptions of his private parts and body marks but what he liked to howl while he was in the saddle.'

Guiliano gurgled with laughter. 'Wouldn't it have been easier just to have had him killed?'

'Yeah, but not nearly as much fun.'

Through the darkened windows of the car Stark could see the glinting blocks and spires of the New York skyline pressing in. Just like the Naked City, he said to himself.

'Johnnie,' Angelo said, opening the built-in bar and offering him a Coke, 'this is going to be a little more than a holiday or early retirement, I know this.'

'I have a few ideas I'd like to discuss with you and your colleagues.'

'It's discussion, then?'

'Of course. Sure. Mutual co-operation. What else? You thought I was going to set up a clan? To muscle in on the families? C'mon Angelo, Scotland is a very small part of the world.' He winked. 'Mind you, so is Sicily.' Then he hugged Guiliano, kissed him on the cheek and both men burst out laughing.

Chapter Seventeen

Burns packed the gun back into the chocolate box and the M&S bag and, after he had dropped off Paton in Govan, drove back to Queen Street and posted the package back in the same left luggage box. Then he drove back to the car park and left the car unlocked in a vacant space on the fourth floor, the left luggage key in the glove compartment. He stretched, got out, then walked to his car. As usual he bent down to check under it, having to bring out a pencil torch from his inside pocket to run the beam over the floorpan. Then he got up and put the key in the lock. Fuck, he said to himself: someone had run a key or a knife along the door paintwork, leaving an ugly metallic score in the dark blue paint.

As he eased the car through the quiet street he switched on the radio, hunting for the local news. He was almost home before the newsflash came through.

'A man was shot dead tonight in Ferguslie Park, Paisley in what is believed to be another drugs-related killing. The man, who is not being named until after next-of-kin are informed, was shot on his doorstep shortly after 7 p.m. Witnesses say that three or four shots were fired and that the killers – believed to be two men – then fled in a dark-coloured saloon car. Police are appealing for anyone who was in the area this evening or who saw anything of the incident to get in touch.'

Burns stopped the car at the gate, rolled down the window, slipped his identity pass into the machine and, when the gates opened, drove into the complex, parking the car outside next to the canal. Inside the lobby of the building he put down his sports bag, checked his mailbox, retrieved a manila jiffy bag and slipped it into his pocket. He took the lift to the fourth floor, automatically scanned the hallway, then walked along to his door. He could hear the cat scrabbling and mewing behind. He turned the key in the lock and walked into the flat.

When he had fed the cat he took off his jacket and pulled out the envelope, ripped open the top and poured the money out on to the low table. From a quick glance at it there seemed to be about £5,000, which was just right. Then he walked over to the Linn hi-fi and searched in the rows of vinyl beside it for the one of the Rings.

The waves were white-capped and the water looked cold and deadly. McQuade and Ricketts walked along the shore, occasionally skimming stones or kicking lumps of seaweed, out of frustration as much as to keep warm.

It hadn't worked. They had combed the files, typed and scanned in everything which seemed relevant, but if there was an answer to be found, they had overlooked it. Sure there was plenty of supposition and informed speculation there, but nothing which would crack it open, get Ricketts off the hook and rack up the exclusives.

McQuade looked at Ailsa Craig, swimming in and out of the mist. It was pretty clear that Stark had come back from the States to take over again when Owens was killed, in what seemed like one of those random acts of good fortune. A gang fight had broken out in the Rose between some of the Tongs and the Fleet, the bouncers had moved in to stop it and in the mêlée one of the kids had peeled off and stabbed Owens, who was directing operations from the edge of the dance floor, in the heart. He had died immediately. The boy who had done it, John McGurk from Maryhill, was seventeen and had no connections to crime other than to his street gang. He went to a young offenders' institution for the maximum sentence, 'at Her Majesty's pleasure'.

Stark had taken over again, running girls and drugs. He had become the major supplier in Britain according to the police, although he was never again convicted. It had settled down cosily, a lucrative fiefdom, until he had moved over at the end of the eighties and let John Junior take over. And Junior, Fat Boy – McQuade picked up a large stone from under which a tiny sand crab scuttered away – was clearly not strong enough for the responsibility. War had erupted, unfortunately for him. McQuade threw the stone high into the air and watched it plunge into the water, throwing up a huge spout.

It came rushing back at him, that dark night outside the Stark spread and the shivering fear, then next day the newspapers full of it. Followed by the deadly message, the other shootings presaging the funeral. The headlines tumbled through his head. 'Do you know what I think?' he said to Ricketts after a while. 'I think your stuff on Stark has been doctored, or filleted. Either that, or what we've got is just the low-grade stuff and the major material is elsewhere. Possible?'

Ricketts nodded. 'Possible, sure. But what makes you think that?'

'I don't know, it's just that important pieces seem missing. I mean, these years in the States. It's not credible that nothing at all should be known about that. There must have been some communication between here and the NYPD, the FBI? Stark's off the scene but clearly is still active. There's this blank, and then he saunters back in with a wife and a child and – Christ . . .'

'What is it, McQuade?'

A newspaper picture from Junior's funeral had stuck behind his eyes and had refused to budge. '*Cherchez la femme!*' he said. 'Jesus.' He started walking back towards the hotel. 'C'mon. I'll bet she's crucial. Trust my nose, Harry, there is a faintly remembered smell there. What fuckin' time is it in New York?'

He spent more than two hours making calls, to newspapers, the boroughs and city halls, the mayor's office and got absolutely nowhere. He was looking for a marriage certificate or a notice, a small ad in one of the papers about an engagement or an announcement, even a small contemporary story. Ricketts continued to plunder the files, looking for any reference to Stark's wife and a maiden name. But their initial enthusiasm had slowly dissipated.

He called the library and asked Adrienne to check out the death notices and the tributes in the paper for the days around Junior's death, to see if there was any reference to grandparents, nephews, nieces or cousins. The two paced around for half an hour before she rang back. Plenty of detail and doggerel about the boy, flowery tributes and broken hearts, but nothing about Stark's wife's lineage.

'Shite,' he said quietly into the phone. 'Adrienne,' he said, 'you're French—'

'You're so quick, McQuade.'

'You've got a kid, haven't you?'

'Don't worry, it's not yours.'

'I'm trying to be serious here. Your old man was Scots, yeah? You were married, weren't you?' He looked over at Ricketts, nodding his head slightly. 'On your kid's birth certificate, what does it say about you?'

'That's a strange question, are you trying to cover something up?'

'No, no. This is important. As well as your married name, does it give your former name, your maiden name?' He closed his eyes in silent prayer.

'I think so.'

'You think so? I need to know for sure. Can you check that for me with a registry office, if including the wife's maiden name automatically goes on the form, and phone me back?'

'At your service,' she said, hanging up.

McQuade forced himself to sit in a chair by the window waiting for the return call. It took less than five minutes. 'Yes,' she said, 'definitely. It gives the mother's maiden name.'

'Adrienne, I'm going to buy your kid the biggest present he's – right, *she's* ever had. And, as well, I swear I'll never write anything rude about you on the wall in the gents' toilet again. Love you too. Can you transfer me to the newsdesk?'

He explained to Tom McCallum, the deputy news editor, what he needed. He gave Junior's birth date, from one of the death notices. 'Can you send someone right away? Andrea, if she's in. She's at least competent. Great. Thanks.'

Ricketts was making a pot of tea with the in-room kettle and refreshment service. 'How do you know this'll lead to anything?' he said through the steam. 'Her maiden name's probably Jane Doe from Boise, Idaho.'

'Nah, there's something. I just feel it in my water.'

'And your water never lets you down.'

Alas' – reaching for his cup – 'frequently.'

McQuade thought that the hotel staff were beginning to look at him strangely. Little wonder, he was supposed to be writing a piece about the hotel complete with sumptuous pictures and the two of them, the supposed authors of this wondrous puff, had been stuck in a suite for forty-eight hours, apart from a brief walk on the beach and continually opening the door to pull in room service. Probably think we're a couple of gays on a bender, he thought. He was in the sauna passing the time while he waited and he was alone, which he considered was probably significant. The sweat was pouring off him which he hoped was purging his impurities, at least some of them because he didn't have enough time or bodyweight to deal with all of them.

When he thought about it, he did not know why he felt so hopeful about Mrs Stark; perhaps because it was all he had to go on. Ricketts was probably right and she was nobody important, somebody he met in a shopping mall in Manhattan. He watched the sweat drips from the end of his nose plop on to his bare thigh. Nah, that didn't fit at all. His spirits rose slightly, he was still clinging to the belief in the importance of Mrs Frances Stark.

After a few fragile lengths of the pool – it had pissed him off that he had forgotten to bring trunks and had to pay twenty quid for a pair in one of the bijou boutiques (still, he'd negotiate it through his expenses somehow) – he towelled himself and dressed. When he got upstairs Ricketts was playing computer games. 'Phone the newsdesk,' he said, without looking away from the bright bursting shapes. 'Oh, and there's a note from the manager, requesting a meeting.'

'Right.' He dialled the freephone number and was put through.

'Hold on,' McCallum muttered at the other end of the line, 'Andrea's got something for you.' Then: 'I hope there's a fuckin' story in this?'

'Of course.' He rummaged in the mess of food on the bedside table for a pen and notebook.

'Well?' Ricketts asked him when he came off.

'Francesca Strattani. Mean anything?'

Ricketts shook his head. 'No. What about you?'

'Nothing.'

'There is something familiar about it, though.' Ricketts was peering up at the elaborately corniced ceiling. 'The name.'

'Your first girlfriend was called Francesca?'

'No, fuckwit! Strattani.'

'Well?'

'I'm thinking.' He got up from the seat at the computer and walked

over to the window. 'Yes,' he said, clenching his right fist. 'Strattani
was one of the names Blantyre mentioned in the car, one of two
Italians supposed to be meeting Junior for a Ruby.'

'At the Café India?'

'Him and someone called Modesta, colloquially known as the End
apparently. But they didn't show.'

'What did she say about them?'

'Emissaries from one of the Italian families, reputedly.'

'What else?'

'That was about it. She said the two had been traced flying into
London, or planning to, but on the night they didn't show. Junior
was at a table for two with some woman, clocked the face, and
she was clearly a close friend.'

McQuade was now at the computer and was killing the destruction
game and punching in, looking for their Stark files. 'Who was she,
d'you know?'

'Never saw her before, face wasn't familiar.'

McQuade recalled the shapes on the pavement outside the
Ponderosa. 'She's the one who shot the craw when Junior was being
shot in the craw. She vanished like smoke, like she was expecting the
whole thing.' He remembered that he had just looked round and
somehow she had disappeared. 'Would you recognise her again?'

'Yeah, probably. Would you?'

'Not a chance. Too far away, too dark and too scared.' What he
was thinking was, was this another leggy one from Harris's stable
provided as the relaxant? 'You didn't check the photo books and
the wanted posters?'

'Didn't have a chance.'

When he had cruised the files he turned back to Ricketts, who
was sitting on his bed. 'No mention of any Strattani here in your
files. Are you sure that was the name?'

'Certain. Strattani, known as the Angel.'

McQuade eased himself out of the chair and went to the phone,
dragging it on to his chest as he slumped on the bed. It took him
only two calls to locate Strattani in the New York crime pantheon,
the second call to a crime corr he had talked to in the past on the
Times city desk who told him that the Angel was a well-known foot
soldier, bodyguard and close confidant of an Angelo Guiliano. 'He's

a cousin, or something, but then they're all cousins. Guiliano is one of the best known, y'know, of our Italian-Americans – philanthropist, big fan of the opera, loves his mom and the Mets.'

'A mobster.'

'Oh, Grade A.' Michael Berry's voice was metallic and slightly delayed on the line. 'I love him. But for him and others like him I wouldn't have a job.'

'Ever hear of him having an association with someone in Britain called John Stark?'

'Didn't hear. Who's Stark?'

'One of the ones here who keeps me in a job.'

'I see. Doesn't mean anything. What's it all about?'

McQuade thought about it, what it was about, whether he knew what it was about, whether he should unburden on Berry. He sighed and told him that Stark seemed to have married into the Mob, that there was clearly some transatlantic co-operation going on between them. 'There's some kind of federal task force looking into this.' He mentioned Blantyre's name and sketched in that she had visited Glasgow. 'Can you maybe make a few calls and see what you can find?' He gave him his work telephone number.

'Sure,' said Berry. 'Anything in it for me at this stage?'

'I don't think so. But I'll keep in touch.'

When he had put down the phone he ran through the conversation with Ricketts. 'Now,' he wound up, 'although I believe in the fuck-up theory of history it is just not possible that Mrs Stark's previous life is not known about, that there's no intelligence in these files. So it all must have been weeded out and that's either as part of a cover-up or' – he pointed at Ricketts – 'deliberately to mislead someone.'

'Too many movies,' Ricketts said, shaking his head, a little unconvincingly.

'Why is there nothing in all of this dross then? Stark married into a family and our lot don't even know about it? Come on. When he brought her back immigration, the Home Office, would have looked into her, wouldn't they?' Ricketts nodded. 'And they wouldn't have asked their American friends about her? Balls. Of course they would. It's *de rigueur*, isn't it, the exchange of intelligence material. So how come there's nothing in the Strathclyde polis files about her antecedents, like she's some ordinary wee herrie from Brigton?'

Could' – he began to consider the possibilities – 'could Blantyre have removed some of the stuff?'

It's possible.'

'Could this stuff just be the leftovers? I mean, could the files be weeded, a composite prepared, the top-grade intelligence put on computer files – I don't know – and that, whatever, given, sent, to the Yanks. If this was a joint operation between the Home Office and the Justice Department, it would be our spooks and theirs, wouldn't it? MI5 and 6, FBI and CIA.'

'This is beginning to sound like paranoia,' Ricketts said, unconvincingly.

'Fuck off, it is. Are you telling me that the chief constable and the chief of the NYPD wake up one day and decide, just like that, that the drug business is getting a touch out of hand and just unilaterally decide to call each other up about it and form a joint initiative. Of course not. It would be government to government, wouldn't it, with the police acting as the footsoldiers, the MacPlods, providing the personnel and the resources for the humdrum jobs. No?' Ricketts nodded, agreeing. 'There is no way, then, is there, that some gallus Glesca bobby is going to be allowed to come into possession of any sensitive material, now is there? Well?'

'I suppose.'

'You suppose? You mean you're embarrassed to admit that you're only a mere drone in all this, don't you, Ricketts? Let's get out of here,' McQuade said, getting up to move over to the computer and log off, 'if we can get past the praetorian guard in reception.'

It took about forty-five minutes to pack up the gear. McQuade had the computer in his arms when the phone rang. He looked at it and then at Ricketts. 'The manager?'

'Answer it.'

He dumped the computer on the bed and picked up the phone.

'McQuade?' It was McCallum. 'I thought you'd like to know that the police are crawling all over the office and, particularly, your desk, armed with search warrants. They seem to think you're in possession of stolen property – police property. Now, what the fuck is going on!'

McQuade booted the Saab out of the driveway and on to the main road heading for the city, the high hedgerows blurring past.

'They would raid my flat, wouldn't they?' he said.

'Certainly.'

He tried to remember if he had left any criminal traces, like drug residues or pornographic paraphernalia. 'McCallum was phoning from the pub so they don't know he's contacted me, where we are. Just don't ask me where we're going, I'll just keep driving until we come up with something.'

'They'll have a watch out on this car and it's pretty distinctive.'

'You're right. Where else will they be watching, usual haunts, stations, airports . . .'

'I doubt that.'

'We can't go back in this. I'll stick it in a car park on the way and hire a car. What are we going to do about the files?' He was trying to recall whether he had touched any of them, whether his fingerprints would be on them along with Ricketts's. 'If we get caught with this lot it's first stop Barlinnie for certain. Maybe we should dump them? Or burn them?'

'Jesus, McQuade, I wish I'd never met you.'

'That's great.' He jammed the Saab down a gear, booted the accelerator and lurched out from behind a lorry and clipped in ahead. 'Stick together in adversity, eh! We're the only ones who can help each other.'

Ricketts said nothing for several miles as McQuade attempted to exorcise his aggression on the road. 'The files are signed out to me,' he said. 'There's no way of getting out of this. They've got Blantyre swearing it was me who said we should stand down, and then Junior gets stiffed.' He slumped further down in the seat. 'Set up for that, and now this. Or maybe this was just opportunity, born out of stupidity on my part.'

'What we need—'

'We need a good lawyer is what we need.'

'Yep. But leverage, that's required. Something to trade.'

'Yes, I know. Me, for you!'

McQuade slid the car off the main road and on to a slip road towards Ayr. 'C'mon, Harry, buck the fuck up. Get mad and get even, as my old daddy used to say.'

'Didn't he used to beat you up? And didn't he run off with some other woman?'

'Jesus, Ricketts, always so literal. That's the policeman in you.'

'You mean ex!'

He changed down a gear. 'Let's pull some stunts of our own.' The traffic was beginning to thicken. 'I've got an idea, my own small counterweight to all of this, a trade-off maybe. So shut up while I think.'

He sat down wearily on the couch and slowly unravelled his black tie, then threw it across the room where it caught on the arm of the leather chair. Slowly he unbuttoned the white shirt at the neck and then ran his fingers through his short grey hair. Through the wall he could hear the slow murmur of conversation and the smell of smoke, cigar and cigarette, was seeping into his atmosphere, tainting his memories. It reminded him of death. It reminded him of fires, of being young, of wars, of escape, of dance halls and, always, of money.

He got up and walked over to the window and, although it was cold outside, pulled down the top part of it, letting in the damp air of the street. He tried not to think about the boy in his box in the dark wet earth. He tried not to think at all, because there was only pain.

The helicopter was still hanging about, he could hear it faintly slapping on the air. He breathed deeply once or twice then turned away and went back to the settee. From here he could see his shrine. The icons and the relics glowed in the gloom of the room. He fixed on them, trying to exclude everything except consideration of the pictures, as if expecting something. There was nothing, except a shiver of cold now in the room. He focused on the Madonna and child, which had started it all off, he peered at the eyes of both, hoping for even just a breath of compassion, a relief of feeling. But their smiling joy was personal and exclusive.

After they had taken the boy to hospital and had come back, his foot had kicked against the icon where he had dropped it on the floor in the lobby, sending it spinning away. When he had picked it up he had not at first noticed the droplets of Junior's blood on the surface, tiny dried splashes on the face of the Madonna, a trail of bloody tears. Only when he had gone to put it back up on the wall had he noticed and then, and now, he could not bring himself to wipe them off. They would age to ochre and black and he would never remove them.

He had never prayed in his life that he could remember. He stared at the wall. It was too late to start now. And prayer involved repentance. It was too late to start now. He could not even remember how to cry.

Turning away, he looked at the long low table where the coffin had been and at the scratch marks, the only traces left. The boy had lain there all night and he had been here with him. For most of the time. What he had hoped for, he supposed, was some religious experience. He had lit two dozen candles under the icons so that their images shimmered and weaved in the heat and the smoke and he had waited, but there was no sense of the soul. Nothing but an occasional spatter of falling wax, the smell of tallow and the body of the boy who had once been his son.

He looked back once more at the Madonna and child and wondered why the picture had had such a hold on him. But perhaps that was all religion was? How different, he thought, would his life have been if he had walked away from the old Jew's room, if he had not taken down the picture, if he had not stolen from a murdered holy man? Maybe these circumstances invoked a curse. Perhaps from the moment he took it down from the wall predestination set in which – he looked at the solemn face of his dead son – resulted in this? And what was still to come.

He had shaken his head and got up. There was no point in speculating, he was being stupid. Let predestination take its course.

Now, he shook his head again and tried to blot out consideration of anything which could weaken him.

When McQuade was signing for the hire car, a Cavalier, it occurred to him. After they had driven round to the car park, transferred the gear from the Saab into the new car, he drove down to the harbour and parked. 'Fancy some coffee?' he said.

'That's your best suggestion?' Ricketts said, staring out the window.

'You're a moody bastard, Harry,' he said. 'No wonder they chose you for the fit-up,' diving out of the door before Ricketts could reach him.

'Is there anyone still there you can talk to, who's a friend?' he said after Ricketts had climbed out of the other side in a rage.

'Of course.'

'Who wouldn't shop you?'

Ricketts took a deep breath. 'I suppose it would depend on what I was asking. What are you thinking about?'

'The car which picked up Fat Boy from the holiday camp . . .'

'The Mercedes.'

'Did you ever check it out, the licence plate?'

Ricketts had closed the door and was leaning against it, hands on top of the roof. 'I gave the number to Blantyre to check. I don't remember she ever told me anything about it.'

'Have you still got the number? In one of your notebooks?'

Ricketts nodded and was already moving towards the boot as McQuade chucked the keys across.

After he had retrieved the notebook they walked across into the pedestrian precinct and found a coffee shop, a place with an electric train running on a raised platform round the wall above head height. 'Never had a train set as a kid, Ricketts, did you?' McQuade said, looking at the menu. 'Do you want to use the mobile or that public phone there?' he said, nodding to the wall behind Ricketts.

Ricketts looked over his shoulder and then got up. 'I'll use that,' he said. 'Cell phones are too easy to bug.'

McQuade ordered two coffees and two jam doughnuts while Ricketts huddled around the phone. When he came back to the table he threw his notebook down next to his cup, sat down and grimaced. 'Nothing. At least, nothing we can get at. According to the PNC the number belongs – belonged, to a Ford Sierra which was written off a few months ago.'

'You didn't get a bit of the number wrong?'

'Don't be stupid, McQuade.'

'Your pal on the other end of the line wasn't spoofing you?'

'Definitely not.'

'So what does it mean? Some car ringing operation?'

'I doubt it. It looks like disguise. A Q-car, a cover-up.'

'Yeah, but anyone can get a plate made for any number they like.'

'Sure they can, but not anyone can find out a number for a car that no longer exists.'

'It could be coincidence.' The dying froth on his coffee looked up at him. 'Or, maybe there's a scam going with someone at the DVLC to provide lists of dead numbers for hot cars?'

'Possible.'

'Unlikely. You're right.' McQuade poured more milk into his coffee and watched the train trundle over his head. 'Did you get any gossip, any word about you?'

'The word is that I'm out, of the force. That'd be the good news, if that was all of it.'

McQuade's mind drifted to thinking about his flat, whether it had been raided and what they might have found. He decided that he would ring the desk from the car and find out the latest. 'It's just occurred to me – oh, Christ, the tape. Your lot, they tape all incoming calls.'

'Don't get paranoid. It's only emergency calls. And I called on a direct line to a mate.'

McQuade nodded and silently contemplated his coffee once more.

'So,' Ricketts came in again, 'what was this bright idea of yours?'

McQuade swirled his spoon in his cup. 'Through an intermediary, the paper maybe, we try and do a deal. "While admitting nothing" we say "we might be in a position to locate these missing files. Also, we could be persuaded not to spread the picture of the gorgeous departed Blantyre over our front page, telling who she is and what she was up to and the consequences," etcetera.'

'You've got a picture?'

McQuade nodded. 'A beautiful paparazzi shot from the under-growth – wherein yours truly skulked – in the Holiday Inn, while you, like a lounge lizard, were trying to slither yourself between her sheets.'

'You bastard.'

'Don't you mean, your bastard?' He took another sip of the coffee. 'Think it might work?'

'I don't know. I suppose it depends on whether this operation, whatever it is, is over and whether it's deniable for them. What else have we got?'

'Exactly.'

McQuade turned the car off the roundabout and left the A77 heading for Edinburgh. He had decided that it was too risky to return to

Glasgow and when he phoned the newsdesk and talked to Sandy
Bell he arranged to meet him in Edinburgh, in the bar of the Bank.
Then he dialled the place, a pub with a few rooms above which had
been converted from a surplus branch of the Royal Bank, or the
other one, he could not remember, and booked two single rooms.
He knew the landlord and could trust him to be discreet.

The paper's main office was in Edinburgh anyway, and he needed
its resources. He made a mental note to buy something exotic for
Adrienne, lingerie (he only had a vague memory of her proportions,
which consisted of handfuls and armspans he could not properly
describe to any shop assistant) or a book token or maybe a couple
of tickets to a concert.

When they had dumped the car and checked in, he and Ricketts
sorted and prioritised the files, impounded several carrier bags and
loaded them as well as the sports bag and walked across to the
office. They went in through the back door and up to the library
– it was Adrienne's day off – commandeered the photocopier and
began work.

While they were doing that, fifty miles to the west a police
roadblock was stopping every northbound car on the A77, causing
a ten-mile tailback.

They broke off after four hours and wandered back to the Bank.
McQuade had booked a table for three in the restaurant and when
they opened the door he could see Sandy Bell was already there,
drinking white wine. He ordered a bottle as he passed the bar.

'I take it they didn't find anything?' McQuade said after he had
introduced Ricketts.

'I'm not sure that's even what it was about,' Bell said, 'more
just general smug harassment.'

'What about my flat?'

Bell dug in his pocket and dropped a padlock key on the table.
'I don't know what they've taken, they're preparing a list, but
they broke down the door. There's a temporary padlock on it.'
He nodded at the key. 'And of course they want you to get in
touch.' He drained his glass. 'Look, McQua – Dermot, I'll say this
as reasonably as I can.' He leaned across the cutlery and hissed,
'What the fuck is going on here?'

The waitress had arrived with the wine in an ice-bucket, providing a temporary pause while she splashed the wine into both glasses and then filled Bell's again. When she had gone McQuade recounted all that had happened. It took him about ten minutes and Bell kept shaking his head. When he had finished he leaned over the table again. 'This is all just supposition.'

'No, it's not, it's informed deduction. There's a huge difference. What I know for certain is that I followed Ricketts and Blantyre, I saw them going off duty, I saw Fat Boy being stiffed. I mean, who is she, Blantyre? What was she doing here? Why has she disappeared? If I didn't have a picture of her I bet the police would be denying she existed. She wasn't even checked in at the hotel under her own name. They would probably say it was all a story Ricketts made up to cover his arse.'

McQuade looked at Ricketts, who was looking grim and pulling on his drink. 'Don't worry, Harry, this is the news editor as devil's advocate, does it all the time. Underneath he trusts me implicitly.'

'Like fuck,' Bell agreed.

'Look.' Ricketts put his glass down. 'I know I was set up. She fixed it, she was the one that said we had been called off and then' – he snapped his fingers – 'the round-the-clock surveillance just goes like that. And then minutes later Stark gets shot. Coincidence that is not. She must have known, got some kind of sign, that a hit was going down. Either that or she set it up . . .' His voice tailed off.

'Oh, come on—' Bell started to say.

'Why not?' McQuade came in.

'Our police—'

'Wonderful, I know.' Ricketts cut him off again. 'There's no reason why anyone, apart from the chief constable and maybe a deputy, would need to know anything about it. Let's say everyone is just told that this is a highly sensitive operation and Blantyre has carte blanche to do what she wants, and if anything seemingly untoward comes up and anyone's worried it's to be referred back to the chief constable.'

'Which must mean it's politically inspired or approved, surely?' McQuade came in, jabbing his finger at the news editor. 'The Home Office, probably. And it's led by the security services, the upper-class twits and Cambridge buggerers.' Ricketts nodded supportively. 'They're at a loose end, aren't they, the demise of Communism, the unfortunate cessation by the IRA of our indigenous terrorism, so they have to find a role to justify their existence, their huge secret budget and their vast ugly fuckin' building on the Thames. What they are going to do is to burst organised crime and cut off its lifeblood, drugs. Even if a little of life's blood has to be spilled in the cause. God, you can just picture our slimy Home Secretary keeping his hands clasped in his lap as the spooks are telling it, pressing down on his erection.'

'Oh come on,' Bell said again.

'Sandy, I saw the shooting and I saw who did it and I saw the American cop lady and what's more I have her picture.'

'You saw – you have?'

'I did. I am,' he said. The waitress was hovering over them, waiting to take their order. McQuade winked at Ricketts and settled back in his seat.

When they had ordered Bell leaned forward once more and said: 'You actually saw the killers? You can identify them?'

'That's the story I'm going to write – and illustrate with the delectable Blantyre. Unless—'

'Unless what?'

'Unless the polis agree to drop any potential proceedings against him and me and allow him to resign, honourably, and keep his pension rights. Hey' – he smiled widely at Bell – 'we could do with a highly experienced crime corr on the paper. And, of course, they get to take back their property. Sundry well-hidden items.'

The waitress was despatching plates in front of them. Bell was clutching his knife and fork so hard his fingers had gone white. 'Don't think you're going to use the paper to conduct a private vendetta.' And then, too loudly, 'What fucking property?'

'It doesn't matter, Sandy. Later. Just enjoy your steak.'

'Steak?' he said and with his knife he made a stabbing motion at his heart.

Chapter Eighteen

The quarry near Tyndrum had produced sand and aggregate for over a hundred years, for house-building and roads, and although it had been shut over the war the new house-building programme had revived it. It was now working six days a week – it would have been seven had it not been for the religious sensibilities of some of its neighbours – and there were even plans to put on a second shift, although the problems both of finding additional labour and of lighting the area properly had so far thwarted the ambition. It closed at four thirty every afternoon, after the last lorry had creaked down the rutted, unmade-up track to the main road, and there was no security or night watchmen, partly because of cost but principally because there was nothing to steal. Who was going to pinch half a hillside?

Stark eased the car slowly up the track in the dark, lights off, his eyes screwed up, searching for the bends and bumps.

'I hope you had your carrots today,' Ownie said from the passenger seat. Then: 'Shite! D'you know it's a sheer drop at my side?'

'Christ, if you talked this much with your regiment it's a wonder no one put a live squib up your arse.'

'Can't we just put on the sidelights.'

'Lights carry for miles out here.'

'Aye, so does the sound of a car bouncing a thousand feet down a rocky gorge.'

'We're almost there.'

'You can see through solid rock, can you?'

'I've been here before. I've rehearsed this over and over. Trust me.'

A few seconds later the car seemed to put its nose down and the upward plane they were on levelled out. 'We're here,' Johnnie said, cutting off the engine. 'Bring your gear.'

343

Ownie silently saluted in the dark, grabbed his haversack from the seat behind, opened the door and got out. 'I suppose it's okay to use a torch, is it?'

'You mean you haven't been training blindfold or with a balaclava over your head?'

Ownie rummaged in the bag and pulled out the light, clicking it on and shining it around, enhancing the faint moonlight. They were on a large, muddied plane bevelled with the tracks of turning lorries. He could see the skeletal outlines of diggers and cranes and earthmoving equipment and what looked like, behind, a huge cave, a half hollowed-out hillside.

'Over there,' he heard, shining the light round on John, whose arm was pointing to the left, 'is the main quarry, so don't wander off.' Then he tugged Ownie's arm and led him in the opposite direction, taking the torch from him. 'It's over here,' he said, pointing down at a rutted path.

The shed lay about a hundred yards away up a slight gradient. It looked to be about eight feet square and as Johnnie shone the light on the door he picked out the dull yellow of a brass hasp on wood. 'Christ, you could do this yourself.'

'It pays to employ professionals,' Johnnie said in his ear as he bent over to look at the padlock. 'I don't want anyone to know we've been here.'

'Don't you think they might twig when half the gear is gone?'

'I don't want them to know for sure when it happened.'

'So you don't want me to pull it off, you want me to pick it?'

'Exactly.'

Ownie pulled out a ring of picks from the bag. 'Here's one I taught Harry Houdini. Hold your breath and it'll be open before you exhale, as they used to say to Harry, who didn't always listen.'

'Are you thinking about going into fuckin' show business?'

'Gimme.' Ownie grabbed the light and examined the metal keys, then the lock. 'There ought to be a law against this.'

'There is.'

'You know what I mean.' It seemed only to take a few shakes of the wrist and the lock clicked open. 'Okay, let's go.'

He moved inside and waved the light over the inside, then moved closer to the haphazardly stacked boxes and kneeled down. He removed the top two in a pile of four, then passed the third one down to Stark, before shuffling across on his knees and picking up a smaller box about half the size, around a foot square. 'That's it, let's go.'

'You're sure? Sorry.'

When they reached the car Ownie opened the boot, slid in his box and asked for the other one. 'You're sure they'll be all right in there?' Ownie took the larger box and said nothing.

Stark drove the car even more gingerly down the track but as they neared the main road he switched on the headlights, bumped up on to the tarmac road and swung the car left. Neither of them spoke until the car was climbing up towards the Rannoch Moor.

'D'ye smell something?' Ownie said. 'You know when gelignite starts to weep and become unstable it gives off a smell a bit like rotten eggs.'

Stark's nose wrinkled. 'Oh Christ, I can smell it. What are we gonnae do?' In the dull light from the dashboard his face looked ochre-coloured. 'Shall I pull up or will that set it off? What d'you think? What'll I do? Will we ditch the car and make a run for it?'

He picked up on a choking sound from the passenger and suddenly Ownie was gurgling with laughter then screeching. 'What is it? What's tae laugh aboot ya numbskull? What is it?' He took his left hand off the wheel and grabbed Ownie's lapel so that the car slewed across the road, then came to a halt.

Eventually, wiping tears away, Ownie said, 'I farted, that's what.'

Dingwall is one of those douce, grey Scottish towns where the severest forms of social disapprobation, like blank stares, follow unpardonable acts, such as hanging out washing on the Sabbath. It was just after 2 a.m. on Sunday morning when Stark nosed the big Austin along the predictably deserted main street and wheeled left and around into a small car park. He nodded towards the windscreen and towards the back of the building and then both men got out, leaning back into the car to retrieve their bags. They were both wearing their regimental battledress jerkins and had streaked their faces with soot, from a little bag carried in the car, not so much for camouflage but to cause fear and alarm in the citizenry, should any of them still be weaving home, much delayed, from the pub.

Ownie shone the lamp on the big oaken back door of the bank. It had two large mortice locks and, he deduced, probably a cross bar behind. He could see them locking the back door, drawing down the bar and going out of the front. He motioned to Johnnie who was standing a couple of yards behind, looking around, as he moved along the side of the building to the front. After half a dozen paces he felt his arm being grabbed. 'What are you doing?' Johnnie whispered in his ear.

'I'm looking to see which is the easier entrance.'

'It's in full view.'

'I know that. How far away is the police station?'

'I don't know, quarter of a mile?'

'You're the one who's supposed to have checked this out.'

'Quarter of a mile. But it's not manned twenty-four hours a day. It'll be closed now.'

'Right,' Ownie said, pushing Johnnie against the roughcast wall. 'Just stay there for a couple of minutes.'

He slipped round the corner of the building and to the front where he stopped and began to smile. The bank had a shingle driveway and crescent-shaped front garden on which some care had been lavished. The bank manager was either a gardener or was bent on keeping up appearances, and along the front wall a high screen of birch trees and rhododendron shielded the forecourt from the road and the houses opposite. You could hide a Sherman tank behind this foliage. He checked the door which was made of light walnut and was protected by only a Yale lock and a small mortice. A hefty kick would push it in. Unslinging his haversack he retrieved his picks, worked on the mortice which sprang easily, then pulled out a thin oblong of tin from a pocket in his blouson and slipped the Yale. He picked up his bag and stepped into the dark lobby of the bank, closed the outside door behind him on the Yale, then switched on the torch, following the beam through, under the counter and the desks and chairs, to the back door. There was no bar mechanism on it. Playing a hunch he ran the torch around the perimeter of the door looking for hooks and keys then, on his tiptoes, ran his fingers along the shelf above it. His hand caught a heavy object which fell to the stone floor and gave off a metallic crack. He picked up the key, tried it in the first lock, it turned, and without even trying the second lock, with his left hand resting on a panel, the door swung open. Talk about high security.

'Pssst.'

He saw Stark's outline tremble in the dark. 'Shite,' he said 'how did you get there?'

'Bring in the stuff, will you, then keep a watch out the front.'

The safe was in a back office, a huge, ancient steel and cast-iron affair, at least eight feet wide and about the same in height, which must have weighed tons. How did they get it in? he wondered. With a crane? Or did they just build the bank around it?

He stood looking at it, playing the light over it, judging the amount of explosive he needed. Not that he had anything to go by, never having blown a safe before. His calculations in the past had never had to be that critical; the object had been to blow something apart, bring it down, atomise it, not a job like this, knocking off the door without burning out the contents or mincing them into confetti.

'What do you think?' Johnnie had put the boxes down on the floor next to him.

'I think it's a big bugger.'

'I can see that.'

'And I've never done this before.'

'I thought you . . .' Stark let the sentence trail off.

'Underground bunkers, bridges, reinforced gun emplacements, yes. But unfortunately they don't let you train at blowing the CO's safe apart in demolition school.'

'It's not too difficult.'

'No, it's not. I'm worried about giving it too much and ending up with just a few specks of soot left floating on the breeze and a crater where the bank was.'

'For fuck's sake.'

'I was joking, slightly.'

'I wish I could help.'

'You can.'

'Aye?'

'Shut the fuck up.' They kept staring at the safe, the light trained on the lever mechanism. 'Are you no' meant to be keeping look-out?'

'If I'm inside and the door's closed it looks normal.'

'All right, but just let me think for a bit.'

Another thing he did not know about safes was the strength of the internal components of the lock and what they were made of, the same with the hinges. Amazing the things you don't get taught in borstal, he thought.

He looked at it hard, the name London Pride in gold on gilt glinting, and then decided. 'Okay. I'm ready,' almost to himself. And then, to Johnnie, 'Do something useful, you're making me nervous.'

The artistic approach is what he had decided on. He unpacked the explosive in the heavy greaseproof paper, smelling of marzipan, pulled off a couple of chew-size bites which he squeezed into the lock. Then he extricated a tin of cow gum from his bag and a paintbrush and painted the glue in a circle around what he thought might be the perimeter of the lock mechanism under the plated steel. He waited a few minutes until it was tacky and then stuck a chain of gelly to it. Then he split a fuse, implanted the two ends in the two sites, and led it back out and around a brick wall to the tiny toilet. Stark was standing at the back door, pressed against it. 'That's it,' he said, 'I think.'

'What about the noise?'

'Put your fingers in your ears.'

'Outside, I meant.'

'I know. Hopefully the neighbours will think it's either thunder or some intimation of the Lord's displeasure with them for having carnal thoughts in the early hours of the Sabbath, which should keep them inside in both cases. A prayer would be useful as well.'

He pushed Stark into the toilet, closed the door behind them, pulled the matches from his tunic pocket and lit the fuse, watching it spark and sputter as it disappeared under the door. Ownie was trying to work out how much fuse he had used and the burning time and why the explosion had not happened when the door rattled and shivered and the reverberations of the blast hit them.

'Not as bad as I thought,' said Stark.

'We haven't looked yet.'

The room was thick with dust and cordite and the smell of burning when they ran in, coughing on the atmosphere. Ownie swished his way through the haze, noted the scorch and gouge marks on the face of the safe and pulled at the handle. It did not move. 'Too cautious,' he said and kicked the door. 'Let's get out of here.'

'No,' Johnnie said, grabbing his arm. 'Try again. And let's hope what you said earlier about the noise is right and that the holy willies stay in bed.'

'You're kidding? That would have wakened the graveyard.'

'Let's just rely on the sleep of the righteous being a deep one. Most of them will be paralytic drunk anyway, let's hope.'

Ownie was searching in the swirling, smelly haze for his materials. 'Get outside and keep a look-out' he said firmly, pushing Stark towards the door, imagining he could hear police sirens, thinking, This will probably set a record for the shortest time ever someone has spent in civvies between one uniform and another.

But as he worked there was no screech of an arriving car, no whistle, nor even the creak of an old upright bike. He tripled up his charges this time and for good measure placed three pounds of gelly under the safe. This one might be crude but it would surely be effective. And just to be sure he led the fuse all the way out to the back yard and the car. Johnnie followed him as he ran the fuse along the gravel.

Afterwards both would recount how the safe seemed to exit through the roof of the bank before disintegrating in a black cloud and casting a shower of bank notes like autumn leaves all around them. What actually happened was that the explosion seemed surprisingly quiet, muffled partially by the walls of the building in the milli-second before the front windows blew out in a spray exhaust of powdered glass, the front wall bowed and then collapsed and the front angle of the roof tilted and then collapsed in a rain of slates and tumbling timbers.

It did not look too bad from behind in the car park; the building seemed to shudder deeply then recover, but as the two men ran inside for the safe they stopped, looked at the room and then out where they could see the wooded front garden framed on three sides by the walls and floor of the bank and above this the moon, in front of which paper blew like flakes of snow in the light.

'Christ,' said Stark, 'let's pick up what's left and get out of here.'

'I think I've worked out the correct amounts now,' said Ownie.

'Great,' said Stark digging in the inside of the torn safe where singed and bound heaps of money still remained, 'we can do Beauly and Inverness before dawn and by the time we get to Fort William you can have written the manual.'

'You're joking?'

'Only partly,' answered Stark, 'but I don't think anyone has ever done three banks in a weekend.'

'Can you hear a police siren?'

'No, can you?'

'No. It's a miracle.'

'Well, it is the Sabbath.'

Chapter Nineteen

The clatter beating on the windows wakened him. He sat up in bed and realised that the glass was vibrating, there seemed to be some kind of machine outside and downstairs he could hear banging and shouting. Frances had the bedcovers pulled up to her chin and was burrowing into her knees. The bedroom door swung open and Owen and Helen rushed in, her in nightgown and dishevelled hair, him pulling a dressing-gown around himself. 'Look outside, Da!'

Stark got up, as casually as he could make it appear, and went over to the window and pulled aside the curtains. 'I don't believe this,' he said, shaking his head and peering out into what seemed to be the cockpit of a helicopter. It was hovering in the street facing the bedroom window and when he looked down from it he could see blue-clad policemen in flak jackets scurrying everywhere, taking up positions with rifles and handguns in his garden, behind hedges, and white-painted police cars with flashing sirens. And downstairs the banging was continuing.

He knew what he would see when he opened the front door, a search warrant in his face and several bulky figures behind in protective armour.

He did. 'This for the media, isn't it, lads?' he said, stepping out of the way.

'We have a warrant to search here, Stark,' the one in the lead said, one he did not recognise, one with an English accent. He was in his late forties with side-parted greased hair and he, too, was wearing a blue police flak jacket over a dark suit. Stark shook his head and walked into the living room and sat down in a chair. The place filled with police.

'It's okay, hen,' he shouted, 'it's just a few uninvited guests who arenae waitin' for breakfast.' He looked at the clock. It was just after 7 a.m. 'Just what are you looking for?' he asked the one in charge. 'And who the fuck are you?'

'My name's Dickenson and that's all I need to tell you. I have a warrant here duly sworn out by a sheriff if you want to query it.' He offered a further sight of the warrant. Stark shook his head and settled back in the chair. He was determined not to be provoked.

'You're no' the polis are you?' he said. The man who called himself Dickenson ignored his question and began directing the milling blue throng in the living room. Frances, Owen and Helen had come into the room, angrily pushing through the policemen. 'Sit down on the settee,' he said to them, 'and sit this charade out.' Then: 'Show us your warrant card, Dickenson.' The man ignored him.

'What are they looking for, Da?' Helen said from the edge of the settee.

'Publicity. Isn't it obvious? Before they've come out they'll all have set their videos to see if they can catch themselves on the evening news. It's pathetic.'

The four policemen in the room, searching through drawers, the record collection, videos, pulling back the carpet on hands and knees, ignored him.

He smiled across at his family and remembered. They could not retrieve evidence from the mind, nothing they could get to there, he could revisit whatever he liked without incriminating himself. And he remembered just four days before, sitting in the candlelight in the evening beside the boy's body, then the respectful knock on the door. He knew who it was because Owen had already checked on the security screens and given the all-clear. It was Gerry Malone, one of the many who had stayed loyal to his lad, although Harris didn't know that. He had appeared to be a defector, one of several, he drank with them, hung about with them, even went on jobs with them, but the information had always been filtered back. 'Ready, Mr Stark,' he said.

Owen had wanted to come but Stark had refused him. 'No, you're staying here with me.' He winked at his son. 'Just watch the telly and answer the phone and tell me everything about what happened here this evening later.' Then he put on his bulky overcoat and shouted to Frances: 'Got to go out for a bit, hen. I'll see you later.'

She had come out into the hall, her face etched in grief, eyes red still and she had hugged him tenderly – it wasn't like her to show public affection – and had whispered, 'Take care.'

He had pecked her on the cheek – 'Nae problem' – and gone out into the night. Malone drove him through the streets for about fifteen minutes until they came to a patch of waste ground beside the new road extension workings. He saw a car drawn up next to a workman's shed. 'They say anything?' he asked Malone.

'Just denying it aw the time.'

'And you're sure?'

'Aye.'

'Good enough for me.' He patted the lad on the shoulder.

Three men got out of the car as they drove up, Andy McIntosh, Shug Breen and Terry Brady. He nodded to them. Brady pointed to the boot of the car. 'Half-pissed and wholly restrained,' he said.

'Open it,' Stark said, fishing in the pocket of his coat for gloves which he pulled on. In the faint light from the lamp in the boot he could just about see the two, trussed with wire and with mouths taped, jammed in together so that limbs were impossible to allocate to bodies. He looked down at them, then slammed the boot lid. 'Right, let's go.'

The streets were quiet as they drove, carefully observing the speed limit, Stark and Malone ahead, the three in the car behind, plus the two in the boot of course. Neither Stark nor Malone talked.

When the car stopped Stark did not recognise the street, although he knew the area well. 'Just along there,' Malone said, pulling up the handbrake. He meant the Bon Accord. Then he put on woollen gloves, Stark did the same, and leaned across and opened the glove compartment. He pulled out a small pistol, and sitting back into the driver's seat again, he rummaged in his right trouser pocket. Stark saw the glint of metal and then Malone screwed the silencer on the gun before handing it over. Both men got out and looked at each other in the street lights. Stark, holding the gun down by his side, patted the lad again with his free left hand as the following car quietly drew up.

353

He slowly glanced around the street and up at the tenements and gap sites but could not see any lights. The cars were parked opposite a hole in the buildings. 'Okay,' he said.

The boot of the second car was unlocked and two of the lads, Stark couldn't be sure which two they were in the half light, pulled out the first man and carried him round to the nearside of the car and threw him in through the open doorway on to the back seat. Stark walked round and looked in, the bulb in the roof of the car casting a mist of faint light down. He recognised Hatton, who was struggling to bring his body round to face him. Stark trained the gun on him.

'Cut him free,' he said, stepping slightly to the side as Brady leaned in with the wire-cutters and sheared the trusses, carefully picking up the frayed lengths of wire. Hatton began to squirm, trying to make himself as small as he could in the corner of the seat and door. Stark leaned in and pushed the barrel into his forehead between his eyebrows then, with his left hand, he pulled off the tape over his mouth. He could see the glaze of panic in Hatton's eyes, until he pulled the trigger quickly twice and his head shook back, spraying blood over the window behind, which looked like molasses in the night light.

'Okay,' he said again.

This time, when they pulled Gower out of the boot, they cut him free before carrying him to the front seat and tearing off the tape. He was burbling something unintelligible, the speech muscles seemingly as impaired as the limbs, when Stark smiled and shot him, first in the groin, and then in the head as he bucked forward.

The sounds of the shots were like small stones dropping into still water from a great height, Stark thought. 'Grand,' he muttered to the four lads around him, 'thanks a lot. It's home now.'

Now, home, he looked around at the police officers and Dickenson, as he came into the room, and said: 'I take it you're not arresting me?'

Dickenson said nothing, just moved through to the hall and then out.

McQuade was lounging through Princes Street Gardens, ogling the foreign students, when his mobile rang.

'Get your chum and meet me in two hours.' It was Sandy Bell. 'You know that place where you goosed the waitress and she slapped you?'

Only too well, thought McQuade. 'Is it good news or bad?'

'It isn't wonderful,' Bell muttered before hanging up.

'Terrific,' said out loud and causing heads to turn. 'Naw, not you, hen.' He waved before heading for the Royal Mile and the hotel.

In the car, with all the gear loaded, Ricketts was ill at ease. 'I don't know what it means, he didn't say. However my major fear,' he said, nosing the car along Princes Street, 'is that the same bloody waitress'll still be at the Rogano.'

When they reached Glasgow McQuade decided not to make for the city centre but to follow the motorway to Charing Cross and branch off down Woodlands Road and dump the car near the underground. 'I'll leave it at the park-and-ride at Kelvin Bridge and we can travel in under the pavements, just in case.'

The car was fitted with an alarm, but as a double precaution McQuade pulled some clothes out of his bag and strewed them over the bits of technology on the back seat.

He felt like a fugitive as they hung on to the straps in the Clockwork Orange, one of the tiny underground trains in the bilious transport authority paint job, but as he gazed round his fellow hunched passengers there didn't seem to be anyone intent on apprehension or even covert surveillance.

They got off at Buchanan Street and walked down to the restaurant, ducking in through the door and down the stairs to its cheaper quarter. Bell was waiting for them at a table. The newcomers took the two seats to either side of him.

'Well?' almost in unison from both of them.

'No dice. They're putting out warrants on both of you, for theft and reset of police property. You, McQuade' – Bell took a nervous swig of a large glass of whisky – 'they're also talking about prosecuting for withholding evidence.'

'Wh-a-a-t?!' He slapped the table. 'What the fuck for? What have I done?'

'Eye-witness to a killing – I'm sorry.'

'You didn't tell them?' Ricketts came in while McQuade was still trying to formulate words and control his outrage.

'It came out somehow, I'm sorry.'

He shook his head and looked away. 'What now?' McQuade said at last.

'The lawyer says that you should talk to him and then you should turn yourselves in.'

'Fuck that.' He looked round the restaurant, feeling the walls pressing in. 'I need a drink,' he croaked and then he caught sight of the waitress. He put his hand over his eyes. 'Oh no.'

She was standing next to him now. 'If this was America I could have sued,' she said.

'Look, I'm sorry. I was drunk.'

'That's no excuse.'

'I know.'

'Anyway, what do you want?'

McQuade looked up. She was about twenty, hair cut in a bob, flaring nostrils and dark eyes. His head was almost level with her chest, her left hand picking nervously at a button on her cardigan. He noticed the sparkle of an engagement ring on her finger. 'Mmmhh? Oh, something in a corked bottle, so I know it hasn't already been poisoned.' He tried to smile at her but she ignored him.

'Two large brandies,' Ricketts added, 'and two Pils.'

She shook her head, glared at McQuade and went, left hand swinging at her side, the occasional bluish flash from it in the electric lighting. And then McQuade knew for certain who had killed Fat Boy. He remembered King Tut's and the diamond in the ring on Harris's hand, he could see once more the crackle of a cut light in the killer's hand just before Fat Boy scrambled and stumbled and died on the pavement.

'All I can do is write the story,' McQuade said after a while, almost talking to himself. 'There's nothing else. The whole thing from Blantyre to the night of the shooting, admit I was there, all the rest. Everything.'

'Then you won't just have the Old Bill on your tail, Stark'll be looking for you to find out what you know about the death of his boy. And whoever else it was' he paused 'who might have killed the Fat Boy.'

'What else can I do?'

356

'Turn yourself in, take the lumps and forget about it,' Bell said almost by rote.

McQuade leaned over and took Bell's drink from in front of him and took a swig. 'Thanks for all the sympathy and the sensible fuckin' suggestions. I can't do that.' He shook his head. 'I'm going to write it.'

After the lunch, which was several more drinks and a desultory poke around the plate at the food that had been ordered, they walked back to the office. McQuade looked at the people passing by, free people, and asked. 'The paper is going to support me, isn't it?'

'No question.' Bell wasn't even looking at him. Then: 'Oh, there's something I forgot to say back there. That shooting the other day of the drug dealer in Paisley? Well, we've had a rock solid source say the bullets were from the same gun as killed Stark. A light-calibre weapon. Point two-two. Mean anything?'

McQuade, looking down at the pavement now as if counting his footfalls, shook his head.

Burns got the coded call – four rings, the hang-up, then three – which told him there was a message downstairs. He walked down and retrieved the package then went back up to his flat. When he tore open the envelope and poured the contents on to the table and sifted them he saw an official-looking photograph with a name on the back, a torn scrap of newsprint with a fuzzy face staring out, a page from a map book of the city with a ring round a building and what looked like a symbol from the Highway Code. He stared at the different elements for several minutes before he fully appreciated what was required of him.

He had spent more than five hours making the calls and working up the story. He had spent a long time talking to Mike Berry in New York, who had sent him on a round of calls to contacts which had tripped lots of little switches, tiny facts, factoids, and pieces of colour about Blantyre, without dropping the main charge on her. He knew her middle names, Mary Elizabeth, where she had been brought up, Long Island, her parents' names, where she had gone to college (she had a master's degree in law) and the fact that she had two commendations for bravery, the second of which had involved her dropping, from fifteen yards, a shooter who had killed a colleague. But the mist swirled around her just at the point where she entered the special task force on organised crime.

He rang the NYPD and the commissioner's office and asked to speak to her. He was told she was 'out of town'. He put it to both offices that she had recently been in Britain as part of a joint Anglo-American operation and was blanked with the usual 'We cannot possibly comment on the operational duties of any serving officer.' He called Berry again and had him fax some cuts on Guiliano the mobster to weave into the story, and promised him in return a black of it – shite, he thought, Berry was probably black. 'Sorry, that's the vernacular here, I meant a copy.'

When he had done all that he switched on his machine, trawled the wires and the messages, and then began writing his intro. Ricketts was sitting opposite, drinking coffee, looking ill at ease. At least I've got something to get on with, McQuade thought. He looked back to his screen and wrote: 'The recent upsurge in drug-related murders in Glasgow was triggered by the setting up of a secret Anglo-American crime-busting operation to target drug barons and the secret arrival in the city of a senior member of that team.' He sat back and thought, That will set the cat among the pigeons, then bit his lip and started typing again, occasionally asking Ricketts questions as he went.

It took him less than an hour to complete the story and it detailed his part in it, beginning in the third paragraph about how he had seen the killing of Junior, but he left the description of the killers sufficiently opaque so that a reader might infer he knew more than he was saying. He posed questions about why the surveillance had suddenly been withdrawn from Stark and asked what Blantyre's part in this was. He pointed up her sudden disappearance and asked why no one would officially comment on whether she even existed, far less describe what she was doing in Britain. He left a hole for the ritual 'No comment' from the police, pressed the keys for a print-out and sent the story on its way. Then he shouted across the newsroom to Sandy Bell. 'It's there, Sandy. Can you get someone to do the "No comment" ritual with the polis and add it in? We'll be in the canteen.'

For some reason he felt ravenous, as if something had eaten a hole in his stomach. Probably nerves. 'C'mon, Ricketts, it's on me.

The condemned meal.' As they left the newsroom he ripped off the print-out of the story from the printer.

They were drinking coffee when McQuade spotted Bell making his way between the tables and he could tell from his expression that he was not happy. 'Oh, oh!' he said to Ricketts.

'The editor wants to see you. With the MD.' Bell was avoiding his eyes.

He looked at his watch. 'The MD, at this time of the evening. Who called him in?'

'McQuade, I don't know anything, just get in there.'

Canterbury, the editor, predictably known as the Archbishop behind his back, was sitting behind his desk; Warren Brackley, the managing director, was staring out of the window. There was not, McQuade could immediately sense, any aura of any pleasure in the air.

'Sit down, Dermot.' Canterbury motioned to the seat facing him across the desk.

McQuade glanced at Brackley then back. 'I'll stand, if it's all right with you, Tom.' He put his hands in his pockets and waited.

'This is a real mess, Dermot.'

'It is.'

'This business of the files, the stolen files, what have you got to say about those?'

'I haven't stolen any files, Tom. And where did you get that from anyway?'

'I've been talking to the police.'

'I see.'

'Well, you'll obviously see that we cannot possibly use any information from stolen property.' Canterbury glanced at Brackley, who was now leaning against the window ledge, arms folded.

'I haven't. But go on.'

'You know where this is leading. Do I have to spell it out?'

'Sorry, yes and yes. Please!'

'We're not running the story.'

McQuade took a deep breath. 'Have you checked it with the lawyers? No, you haven't, have you? Who you've checked it with is the police. That's it, isn't it? The police have nobbled you.'

'The story's all speculation anyway.' Brackley came in for the first time. 'It's not even our kind of thing.'

McQuade felt his anger rise. 'I've witnessed a murder and that isn't my kind of thing. And a mate of mine has been set up as a subsidiary in it, which, unfortunately, does make it my kind of thing. We've had more than a dozen drugs shootings in the last six weeks, junkies are going down like flies on the end of poison needles and who gives a shit, eh? I suppose they deserve it. They're only fuckin' low-lifes anyway, and they're not shooting up or shooting each other in Bearsden or Giffnock, so that's all right, isn't it? Who cares that we've got US cops and our own lads setting up the shooting gallery?'

'You don't know that,' Canterbury interrupted.

'Like fuck I don't. Setting it up or even executing it. And we're going to ignore all that, are we? As long as they keep killing each other – and the innocent remember to duck – we're simply going to regurgitate press releases and deep background from the cops and call it the pursuit of truth.' He looked at both men in turn. 'Sorry, it's not on.'

'Dermot' – Canterbury had stood up and was moving round the desk, presumably in an effort to reduce the tension and the formality – 'it's important to be calm and rational about this.' McQuade was clenching his fists in his trousers and rolling on the balls of his feet. 'You've caught the tail of something, or believe you have, something which may be vitally important. Look, I don't want to be pompous and talk about a greater good—'

'Hold on' – McQuade had his hands out of his pockets now – 'hold on a minute here. What greater good, who's defining a greater good for us here? The great and the good, is that it? It is, isn't it? You've talked to the chief constable or the fuckin' minister, or someone nameless and faceless, and you've read them the story, or as near as dammit, and we're getting the "It's not in the public interest, old boy," claptrap.'

'There's no point in continuing this.' Brackley had moved off the wall. 'The story doesn't run. It's over.'

'Not for me, it isn't.'

'It is, I'm afraid. Give him the envelope, Tom.'

Canterbury turned back to his desk and pulled a manila envelope across to him. 'There's a cheque for a year's pay, a glowing reference,

I'm sure you'll agree, and of course the company will pay any legal costs, QCs, whatever. It's as much as we can do.'

McQuade looked at the envelope in Canterbury's hand and slowly took it, shaking his head.

'We'll work out a freelance contract,' Canterbury said, 'so that you can continue to do regular pieces for us.'

'I don't think so,' he said, looking up from the envelope to Canterbury. 'I really hope you can feel shame, Tom. What's in it for you? A nod and a wink about a knighthood in due course? Or do you really just not give a damn?' He turned away, feeling wearied and emotional. 'I'll just clear my desk and do a few photocopies of my CV and be on my way.'

He shut the door with a click behind him, and without looking back.

Burns had taped the two likenesses, the photograph and the newspaper cutting, to the dashboard. He sat in the car in the darkness. He was wearing a pair of spectacles, a hooded training top and a baseball cap pulled down low on his forehead. The night-sight binoculars lay on the seat beside him and occasionally he pulled them up to squint through. There were very few people about – most of the city centre workers and the university staff had gone home – and fewer cars. There had been no trouble parking in the street. He was about seventy-five yards from the door of the building from which, every few minutes, two or three people would slowly emerge, usually moving to the pub next door. There was lots of time and even more opportunity.

He had brought a Thermos of hot black coffee with him and now he unscrewed the plastic top and the stopper and poured himself a cup, making sure that the steam did not condense on the windscreen.

If not here, he thought, somewhere else later. Plenty of time, he told himself again.

'We need to speak, but not here,' he told Ricketts, who was talking to another reporter, Colin Sugden, now that the first edition had gone. 'The ba's on the slates, I'm afraid. I'm not sure whether we need a plan, a confessor, or just to get drunk. If we start at the last one maybe we can work back to the devious plan. What d'you think? I have in my pocket a large cheque' – Ricketts stared at him – 'yes, it is what you think. That's two of us now. Maybe we should go into business? Anyway, at least I was right about one thing, it was the last meal.' Sugden was looking puzzled. 'Fancy a curry, Colin, and about seventeen pints of lager? I'll even pay.'

'There's something wrong, isn't there? You sure you want me along?' Sugden said. He had recently joined the paper from a regional evening in England and was having difficulty finding his feet. He was about the same age as McQuade, seemed to be a nice guy, trustworthy, eager to be helpful. In short, he probably wouldn't cut it.

'Of course. If Harry and me want to talk in private then we'll simply lapse into the argot, the Glasgow patois, and it'll be like code for you, you English bastard.' He smiled. Where that came from he did not know but it was clearly part-way convincing because Sugden returned it and grabbed his jacket. McQuade added: 'I've just got a few things to pack.'

He walked up the stairs to the canteen and blagged a handful of black binliners and then skipped back down and began emptying the contents of his drawers into them. 'This is what I think it is, isn't it?' Sugden said across at him.

'You're quick. That's right, spring cleaning.' He noticed, in passing, that Ricketts's brows would never unknit.

It only took him a few minutes to fill three plastic sacks; he handed one each to Sugden and Ricketts, slung the last one over his shoulder. 'Right, let's get the fuck off this floor. We can call a taxi from the time box downstairs.'

When they reached the first floor McQuade remembered that he had forgotten to run out a copy of his address files from the closed part of the computer system. 'Shite! You two go on down. I've forgotten something. I'll only be five minutes. Order the taxi, Colin, and I'll see you outside. Take this.' He handed Ricketts his bin-bag and began to run up the stairs.

There was another thought too, probably the most inappropriate possible. He wanted to phone Stick and persuade her to conjoin her body with his. Hell, maybe she even had a friend for Ricketts, or, if not, might be amenable to jointly or serially soothing a couple of bruised souls.

Burns put down the night glasses and turned on the engine, only the spurting lights in the dials in the dashboard the evidence that the engine had really caught. Christ, he loved this car, it was a pity he would have to get rid of it. He put it into gear and moved away slowly, the lights off, but he could see the two figures clearly in the light from the doorway. He pushed the cassette into the hi-fi – he had cued it up precisely beforehand and adjusted the volume controls – and the Ride of the Valkyries boomed into the enclosed space. He put the foot down hard and grinned to himself.

'Where about in England are you from?' Ricketts was saying to make polite conversation while they waited for McQuade. He did not really know what you said to other journalists, apart from 'Fuck off out of here,' and 'Take it up with a superior officer.' Vaguely he became aware of what sounded like the deep throaty roar of an accelerating car and, when he politely and casually looked away from Sugden, to his right, he caught only the distinctive metal grille of a Mercedes before it bore down on him.

McQuade was chuffed, Stick even seemed pleased to hear from him. He had been almost apologetic, giving her plenty of opportunity to back out by saying, 'I'm sure you've got something already fixed,' but she didn't, she hadn't and she wanted to see him. He told himself that as well as the sex there would be the possibility of finding out something about Harris. 'I almost believe that,' he said out loud before leaving the editorial floor for the last time. Again.

He heard shouting and the sounds of running footsteps as he jogged happily down the stairs. Two men, whose faces he couldn't see because their heads were down, ran past him, bumping him as they went. He felt a prickling feeling in the back of his neck and he knew something was badly wrong. He began to run down the stairs, jumping several as he went, feeling panic in his gorge and sickness.

When he slowed down at the bottom and walked out into the street he stopped. All became silent, despite the mouths of the group of people he could see on the pavement evidently shouting and screaming. He saw the one body lying at the base of the wall of the building, the other half on and half off the pavement. The sodium light from above the door gave the blood a curious shade, almost a bluey-purple. He recognised Ricketts's shoes first, Weejun loafers, one of which had been kicked several feet away from his leg. He noticed that there was a hole in the toe of his sock as he lay in the gutter. 'Aw, Harry,' he said, getting down on his knees in the blood which was leaking from his friend.

The hardest part, the grisly irony, was that apart from a little blood around the nose and dribbling from his mouth he looked fine, eyes open a bit quizzically, almost as if he was in a sun-bathing position on his back on the pavement. Only the thick wet patch behind his head gave it away.

He smells warm, McQuade thought on his knees beside him. 'Harry! Jesus, Harry!' he shouted at the body, then put his right hand inside the jacket to search for a heartbeat. He could hear everything now, roaring around him, and his fingers felt as if they were crackling, but there was no beat from the chest and as he leaned over his face, no breath from the mouth. With his hand still inside Ricketts's jacket he pulled out his wallet from his inside pocket and palmed it. 'I'm sorry, pal,' he said, and then stood up.

Someone put an arm round him, he heard a jabber of voices and then in a lull one say, 'It was a hit and run, right up on the pavement. God, the driver must have been drunk. Look at them, just look at them. The polis are on the way.'

McQuade looked at the two bodies on the ground, from one to the other, from his friend to the crumpled shape which should have been him, at the wind blowing at the papers and books which had spilled from his bin-bags, and then he disengaged the arm and began walking slowly, then quicker and finally, when he was round the corner, into a searing run which did not stop until he reached George Square, and the tears.

He was more than an hour late getting to Tennents in Byres Road. He didn't expect her to be there, but she was. From inside the door he could see her shaking her head and laughing and making dismissive gestures, like swatting away persistent flies, at the boys gathered round her. For a moment he wondered which part of the bar he was in, the gay or straight, then he took a deep breath and walked up to her. She smiled, her eyes sparkled and she leaned forward and kissed him, then put her arms round him. 'I missed you,' she said and he had to catch his breath so that he would not cry again.

'I'm sorry.' He looked at her. 'Can we go, d'you think? I have to get away, talk – I don't know.'

'Sure.' She stroked his cheek. 'Do you want to come back to my place?' He nodded and hugged her so that she felt he would never let go.

Back at her flat, which was just off Hyndland Road on a quiet street he did not even note the name of, she almost supported him up the two flights of stairs. She opened the door and took him into the living room which was huge and spare with polished wood and impressionist paintings and African sculptures – he was capable of taking in only one portion of the room at a time. She switched on the gas fire which crackled and fumed like real logs, then flicked on low lighting which cast mellow glowing pools around, and then she poured him a large brandy in a huge crystal glass.

As his teeth chattered on the glass as he sipped she said, 'What's wrong?' But he shook his head and then clung to her in front of the fire, as she smoothed his hair and occasionally urged him to drink the brandy, pushing it towards his mouth.

Eventually, when he had finished it and the shivering had stopped, she kissed him slowly on the tip of his nose and on the cheeks and then something broke in him, he pushed his face into hers so that their teeth ground, and he struggled with her clothing and tore as she pulled at his trousers. Then he found her and started pumping as if he would never stop, bouncing on top of her chest in the firelight as if he were vainly trying to bring something back to life.

When he had finished she kissed him and asked him to talk to her. It came out in a long anguished gush, not disjointed and pausing, but almost as if he had been rehearsing it all evening. Then she took him by the hand and led him to her bed, tucking him in as he wept quietly. She went to the kitchen, poured a glass of water and found the bottle of pills in the cabinet. Uncorking the plastic top, she shook out two and took them to him with the water, made him take them and drink the water and then slipped in beside him. He felt fiery and unquenchable to her.

She lay there in the dark, looking at the ceiling, and when his breathing became slow and regular she sighed, saddened by the impossibilities, and got up and slipped through to the hall where she picked up the telephone.

Stark heard the knocking on the door, looked in the video screen, saw the elongated face hold up something which looked like a warrant card, then the knock again. He cursed and opened the door. The warrant card flashed under his view. 'Can I come in, Mr Stark?'

Stark stood aside. 'What now?' he said. 'Haven't you got enough.'

'Can we talk privately?'

'Not at the station then?'

'No.'

Stark shook his head and led him into his room. He watched as the cop checked and looked at the wall of icons. 'Wonderful, stunning,' he said. 'Humbling.'

'You've already checked them and couldn't find anything wrong. They're no' nicked. So just get on – what did you say your name was?'

'I've got information for you, Mr Stark. I'm afraid I misled you, I'm not a cop, I'm a reporter but No! – hold on – I'm not looking for a story, nothing from you.' He put up both hands as Stark moved towards him. 'I want to give you a story. That warrant card belonged to a friend of mine. He was killed in a hit and run yesterday. Except, I know that's not what it was and I know that it was connected to the death of your son. There's a car outside, a Cavalier. In the boot you'll find a bunch of police files about you.' He fished in his pocket, retrieved the keys and lobbed them to Stark. 'They're yours. I don't know who killed your boy for sure, but I know who set it up. My friend was one of the two officers on surveillance on the night John died and he was called off, by the other cop, who was an American called Blantyre. Here' – he went into his inside pocket and pulled out a crumpled wad of paper – 'here's my story, the one I couldn't get published.'

He handed it over and then went back to the pocket again and pulled out his wallet and then a business card which he scrawled with his mobile number on the back. 'Read the story, Mr Stark, read the files, do what you want with them. And then, if you believe what

I've been saying, if you trust me enough to believe that I'm going to find out who's behind this, call me, give me a number or some numbers of people in the States who can help me. That's it.'

He looked at the icons on the wall and, for some reason, crossed himself. Then he fished in his jacket pocket and retrieved the warrant card with two fingers of his right hand. 'There,' he said, passing it over, 'that was him. That was me.' And he turned and left.

He was exhausted and it seemed necessary to put his life in as close to order as he could get it. He walked until he managed to pick up a taxi. He had only a few pounds in his pocket, but as well as a cheque for more than thirty thousand pounds he had all that he stood up in and a few divisions in his wallet of credit and charge cards. As the shops flashed past he tried not to look at the newspaper billboards. The taxi dropped him at Central station, he bought a ticket for Ayr and then a few newspapers which he took with him on the train, but did not open, leaving them folded on the seat when he got out. Then he took another taxi to the car park – he could not remember what it was called, only rough directions to it and a few nearby landmarks – and then he closed his eyes until he got there.

He had no idea why he was retrieving the car. It seemed incumbent on him to tidy up the mess he had made of his life, of others', and this was one of the few ways he could attempt to begin it. He paid with most of the money which was left in his pocket and then drove north, glad of the lull in happenings, and when he reached the south side of the city, rather than take the left turns towards the airport, he decided to drive on towards his flat, or what was left of it, to begin to sort that out too.

He was going slowly over the Kingston Bridge in a traffic jam when the phone rang. 'All right,' the gruff voice said. 'I'll give you some numbers. And a word—'

'Sorry,' he had to say, 'can you just hang on a couple of minutes while I find a spot to park and make notes.' He inched across the bridge and stopped outside Habitat, took out his notebook and began jotting down the numbers. 'I'll say you're coming,' the voice said in his ear. 'They'll know who you are if you give the name of the Rose. The Rose, tell them that, I'll make sure they know.' And then the line went dead and he was sitting behind the big steering wheel, unprepared for anything that was to come.

After a few minutes he left the car where it was, not bothering about the inevitable parking ticket, and walked down until he came to a bank, where he paid in the cheque. He considered shopping for clothes, realised that he was not up to it, stood looking at the traffic in Hope Street and across at the station he had left a couple of hours before, then went back to the Saab.

He did not know what to expect at the flat. Pulling out the padlock key he let himself in to the jumble of clothes and upended furniture and mouldering dishes and havoc. Somehow it made him feel better. Chaotic and in a guddle it might be, but it was still a locator, a point of permanence for him.

When he had thrown a few clothes into a bag and locked the padlock behind him, he felt strangely renewed, hopeful despite it all, and trotted down the stairs to the car.

The Saab's big engine sounded powerful and resilient. As he drove towards the Expressway he began to look forward, deciding that he would fly Club Class, drink himself into a stupor, then check himself into the Waldorf on the other side. He decided that he would probably fly to Ireland first, change planes in Dublin, to avoid having to show his passport at this side, just in case.

And then in New York, after getting rid of the hangover, he'd buy some clothes, classics without being tweedily pretentious, just relax for a couple of days – a hotel with a pool was mandatory – before he made contact. He thought about Stick, told himself that he would send her a ticket to come and join him, and smiled, looking forward to it, catching his grin in the windscreen reflection as the light changed going into the Clyde Tunnel.

Then put his hand up to adjust the driver's mirror. Sliding into a space two behind him in the line of traffic, he caught sight of a dark-coloured Mercedes, with what looked like a bashed wing. And he knew instantly what it was doing there and who had sent it.